Received 9-21-93
from The Science
Fiction Book Club.

SNOW
WHITE,
BLOOD
RED

EDITED BY

ELLEN DATLOW &
TERRI WINDLING

An AvoNova Book

William Morrow and Company, Inc.
New York

AVON BOOKS
A division of
The Hearst Corporation
1350 Avenue of the Americas
New York, New York 10019

Published by arrangement with the editors

ISBN: 0-688-10913-6

Printed in the U.S.A.

For Thomas Canty, my artistic partner, dear friend, and companion through the lands of fairy tales.

T.W.

For Doris Leibowitz Datlow, who read the fairy tales to me and along with me when I was growing up. Thanks mom.

E.D.

And in memoriam to Angela Carter, whose peerless adult fairy tales have inspired so many of us, and shall keep true wonder alive.

E.D. & T.W.

Acknowledgments

The editors would like to thank the collectors of fairy tales past and present. Also Wendy Froud, Robert Gould, David Hartwell, Merrilee Heifetz, Keith Ferrell, Don Keller, Tappan King and Beth Meacham, Valerie Smith, Ellen Steiber, Jane Yolen, John Douglas, Claire Wolf, and Robert Killheffer.

Contents

A true fairytale is, to my mind, very like the sonata. If two or three men sat down to write each what the sonata meant to him, what approximation to definite idea would be the result? A fairytale, a sonata, a gathering storm, a limitless night, seizes you and sweeps you away. The law of each is in the mind of its composer; that law makes one man feel this way, another man feel that way. To one the sonata is a world of odour and beauty, to another of soothing only and sweetness. To one the cloudy rendezvous is a wild dance, with terror at its heart; to another a majestic march of heavenly hosts, with Truth in their center pointing their course but as yet restraining her voice. Nature is mood-engendering, thought-provoking; such ought the sonata, the fairytale to be.

George McDonald, in *Fantasists on Fantasy*,
edited by Robert H. Boyer and
Kenneth J. Zahorski

Introduction

White as Snow: Fairy Tales and Fantasy

Terri Windling

IN ITALY IN ONE OF THE EARLIEST RECORDED VERSIONS of the story of "Sleeping Beauty," the princess is awakened not by a kiss but by the suckling of the twin children she has given birth to, impregnated by the prince while she lay in her enchanted sleep. In "The Juniper Tree," recorded from oral storytellers in Germany, a jealous stepmother cuts off the young hero's head and serves the boy up in a stew to his dear father, who unwittingly tells her, "The food tastes great! Give me some more! I must have more!" In an early French version of "Little Red Riding Hood," the wolf disguised as Grandmother tells the little girl to undress herself and come and lie beside him. Her clothes must be put in the fire because, he says, she will need them no more. The child discards her apron, her bodice, dress, skirt, and hose . . .

O Grandmother, how hairy you are.
It's to keep me warmer my child.
O Grandmother, those long nails you have.
It's to scratch me better my child.
O Grandmother, those big shoulders you have.
All the better to carry kindling from the woods, my child.
O Grandmother, what big ears you have.
All the better to hear with my child.
O Grandmother, the big mouth you have.
All the better to eat you with my child.
O Grandmother, I need to go outside to relieve myself.
Do it in the bed, my child . . .

If this is not the version of "Little Red Riding Hood" you learned as a child, it is no surprise, for this is not a nursery tale—as indeed most fairy tales were never initially intended for nursery duty. They have been put there, as J. R. R. Tolkien so evocatively expressed it, like old furniture fallen out of fashion that the grown-ups no longer want. And like furniture banished to the children's playroom, the tales that have been banished from the mainstream of modern adult literature have suffered misuse as well as neglect.

This banishment is a relatively recent thing, due largely to the swing of fashionable literary taste toward stories of social realism in the nineteenth and early twentieth century and to the growth at that time of the literate middle classes who came to associate these tales, with their roots in oral narrative, with the lower and unlettered segments of society. From this stems the Victorian belief (still prevalent today) that these tales are somehow the special province of children, for it was children who continued to have access to the stories, told to them by nannies and governesses and cooks, during the years when they fell out of fashion with the adults of the upper classes.

Although fairy stories have been written down since the art of literature began, it was during Victorian times that fairy tales began to be widely collected and published in editions aimed at children in the forms that we know them best today. Thus, when we examine the fairy tales current in modern society, we must keep in mind the source through which they came to us: Victorian white, male publishers combed through the thousands of tales gathered in the field by scholars and selected those which they deemed most suitable for their children—or they edited and changed the tales before publication to *make* them suitable. This bowdlerization of fairy tales continued in the twentieth century, reflecting the social prejudices of each successive generation.

And so we arrive, by the 1950s and 1960s, to the Walt Disney-influenced versions of fairy tales that most of us know today, filled with All American square-jawed Prince Charmings, wide-eyed passive princesses, hook-nosed witches, and adorable singing dwarfs. And so Sleeping Beauty is awakened with a chaste, respectful kiss. And so Little Red Riding Hood is rescued by a convenient woodman before the wolf can gobble her up. And so tales like "The Juniper Tree" are placed on a high and dusty shelf where they are soon forgotten.

Even the term fairy tale is misleading, as most of the stories from the folk tradition that fall under this category do not contain creatures known as "fairies" at all. Rather, they are tales of wonder or enchantment; they are *marchen* (to use the German term, for which there is no satisfactory English equivalent); they are, as Tolkien poetically pointed out in his essay "On Fairy Stories," "stories *about* Fairy, that is *Faerie*, the realm or state in which fairies have their being. *Faerie* contains many things besides elves and fays, and besides dwarfs, witches, trolls, giants, or dragons: it holds the seas, the sun, the moon, the sky; and the earth, and all things in it: tree and bird, water and stone, wine and bread, and ourselves, mortal men, when we are enchanted." One significant result of the bowdlerization of the old stories is that the term *fairy tale*, like the word *myth*, can be used, in modern parlance, to mean a lie or an untruth. A proper fairy tale is anything but an untruth; it goes to the very heart of truth. It goes to the very hearts of men and women and speaks of the things it finds there: fear, courage, greed, compassion, loyalty, betrayal, despair, and wonder. It speaks of these things in a symbolic language that slips into our dreams, our unconscious, steeped in rich archetypal images.[1] The deceptively simple language of fairy tales is a poetry distilled from the words of centuries of storytellers, timeworn, polished, honed by each successive generation discovering the tales anew.

In his many works on comparative mythology, Joseph Campbell reminds us that to turn our backs on the old

---

[1]As explored in the works of such psychologists as Carl Jung, Marie von Franz, James Hillman, Bruno Bettelheim, and Alice Miller.

stories, to dismiss them as primitive and irrelevant to our lives, is to turn our backs on a great human treasure and a precious heritage that is rightfully ours. In this century, myths and stories from the folk tradition have been pushed to the sidelines of education, and from the central place they have played in the literary, visual, and dramatic arts in centuries past, through the same cultural shortsightedness that causes fine old buildings to be razed instead of preserved and cherished for the beauty they can add to our lives today, connecting us to the men and women who lived before us.

To stretch the building metaphor a little further: there are two ways a lovely old house can be saved from the developer's wrecking ball. One is to declare it historic and inviolate, to set it carefully aside from life and preserve its rooms as a museum to the past. The other is to adapt it to modern use: to encourage new generations to live within its walls, look out its diamond windows, climb its crooked staircase, and light new fires in its hearth. In the case of fairy tales, scholarly folklorists serve the first function, collecting the stories, preserving them, often setting them in glass where they must not be touched or changed. This is a worthy job, for it helps us to see the tales in a historical context. But this is not the job of a storyteller.

The storyteller (or modern writer of fantasy fiction) is more like the carpenter who adapts the house for modern use. This is also a worthy job, and a dangerous one—one that must not be taken too lightly lest the storyteller be like the carpenter who would take a medieval thatched-roofed cottage and cover it with aluminum siding. A storyteller must be respectful of the work of the former builders—the twelfth-century hall built on Bronze Age foundations, the second floor added in the sixteenth-century, the kitchen wing built in the mid-nineteenth—but perhaps not too respectful, lest she too take on the folklorist's job and create a museum to the past where one dare not sit and touch instead of a new home filled with laughter, tears, and the tumult of life.[2]

Over the centuries the symbols and metaphors that give *marchen* their power have been worked and reworked by the storytellers of each generation and each culture around the globe. Tolkien envisioned this as a great soup of Story, always simmering, full of bits and pieces of myth, epic, and history, from which the storyteller as Cook serves up his or her particular broth. In addition to oral narrative, through which tales pass anonymously from culture to culture, when stories were written down and then widely disseminated (due to the invention of movable type), a new kind of fairy tale was created—the literary tale, attached to a specific author. Sometimes these in turn passed *back* into the oral tradition—and thus few people today recounting the tale of "Cinderella" for their children realize that

[2]I say "she" when I speak of this storyteller because in the field of fantasy literature women have, in greater number than in most other fields, surmounted the obstacles historically put in front of women in the arts to contribute works of enduring value—aided, perhaps, by the notion that fantasy is suitable only for children and thus for women as well. Fairy tales have also been called Mother Goose Tales, Household Tales or Old Wives' Tales; and Alison Lurie points out in *Once Upon a Time,* that "throughout Europe (except in Ireland), the storytellers from whom the Grimm brothers and their followers collected their material were most often women; in some areas they were all women. For hundreds of years, while written literature was almost exclusively the province of men, these tales were being invented and passed on orally by women."

only parts of the story come from the anonymous folk tradition (from the pan-cultural variants of the "Ash Girl" tales tracing back to ancient China). Some of "Cinderella's" most familiar elements (the fairy godmother, the midnight warning) were the invention of a single man, a seventeenth-century French civil servant by the name of Charles Perrault. His version of the tale (and others, such as "Donkey-Skin" or "Puss-In-Boots") so delighted its audience of French aristocrats, and so entranced successive generations of listeners, that it remains the best-known version of the Ash Girl tale in Western culture. Another seventeenth-century French writer, Madame Leprince de Beaumont, is the author of the well-known story "Beauty and the Beast." In the nineteenth-century the English writer Goldman wrote the story we know as "Goldilocks and the Three Bears," and Denmark's celebrated Hans Christian Andersen created "The Little Mermaid," "The Ugly Duckling," "The Nightingale," "The Snow Queen," and numerous other tales that have so thoroughly seeped into our culture that the average reader is likely to think these are anonymous folk tales, too. That is because these writers have taken the ingredients for their stories from Tolkien's great Soup; and into that soup the stories have returned.

Thus, when we asked the writers in this anthology to take the theme of a classic fairy tale and fashion a new, adult story from it, we were really asking them to work in an old and honorable tradition, adapting these "houses" built of folkloric material to modern use—just as Perrault did, and the Brothers Grimm when they edited and occasionally rewrote the stories they collected in the German countryside. Just as Mallory did when he fashioned Celtic legend into *Le Morte d'Arthur*. Just as Goethe did when he wrote "The Sorcerer's Apprentice" (never dreaming that one hundred years later we would come to associate his poem with Mickey Mouse and dancing brooms). Or as Antoine Gallard did when he translated the shockingly bawdy Arabian tales of *One Thousand and One Nights*.

It is a relatively newfangled notion to believe a story's worth (or that of any other art) must lie in its originality, in novelty, in a plot that cannot be anticipated from page to page or an idea that has never been uttered before. This has its place and its appeal, but our modern obsession with novelty has produced some of our most facile (and quickly dated) art. For many, many centuries the audiences for stories, drama, music, and visual art have better understood the particular fascination of an old, familiar story made fresh and new by an artist's skill—much as a piece of jazz improvisation is best appreciated if one has a familiarity with the music on which it is built. Fairy tales and folklore have provided rich, recurring themes throughout the history of English-language literature, cropping up in the plays of Shakespeare; the poems of Spenser, Keats, Tennyson, and Yeats; in Oscar Wilde's fairy stories and Christina Rossetti's *Goblin Market*; in G. K. Chesterton and James Thurber's wry and timeless tales; in the works of C. S. Lewis and Sylvia Townsend Warner and Mervyn Peake and Angela Carter—to name but a few of the many highly literate authors whose deft uses of fairy tales were never intended for Children's Ears Only . . . or indeed, in many cases, for children's ears at all.

In focusing on the history and the value of fairy tale literature for adult readers as we've explored it in this collection, I do not wish to imply a disdain for the efforts of authors whose books are published as children's literature. I believe fantasy should not be limited to the realm of children's fiction, but it should also not be taken away from that ground where it has been nurtured and has thrived throughout this century—in spite of sporadic attacks from those who believe that fairy tales are bad for children. Usually this is an argument against the sexism or classism of the tales (which assumes all fairy tales resemble the Walt Disney-fied versions). Or the staunch realists, made uncomfortable by the shifting, shadowy landscape of Faerie, warn us against the grave danger of "escapism" which they believe that fantasy encourages in children, teaching them to avoid real life.[3]

It is the blunt truth that a poorly written fantasy story—for either children or adults—may have little more to offer than its escapist or wish-fulfillment elements; but that is a function of the limit of the writer's skill, not the limits of the fantasy form. Simplistically executed works in most fields, from mainstream literature to popular music to television drama, offer little more to their audiences than a brief diversion from daily life; fantasy fiction has hardly cornered the market on escapism. In fantasy, as in most fields, the badly written examples can seem more numerous—and occasionally more popular—than the complex works that make writing fantasy fiction an art. But to dismiss the fantastic in modern literature because of some prevalent bad examples of the form is precisely the same as dismissing the

[3]Child psychologist Bruno Bettelheim, in his influential book *The Uses of Enchantment*, suggests that just the opposite may be the case; that many adolescents lost in drug-induced dreams or seeking magic in a religious guru were deprived of their sense of wonder in childhood, pressed prematurely into an adult view of reality.

whole of English letters because Harold Robbins' books reach the best-seller lists.

A good fairy tale, or fantastic novel, may indeed lead us through a door from daily life into the magic lands of Once Upon a Time, but it should then return us back again with a sharper vision of our own world. Instead of replacing real life, good fantasy whets our taste for it and opens our eyes to its wonders. The fairy tale journey may look like an outward trek across plains and mountains, through castles and forests, but the actual movement is inward, into the lands of the soul. The dark path of the fairy tale forest lies in the shadows of our imagination, the depths of our unconscious. To travel to the wood, to face its dangers, is to emerge transformed by this experience. Particularly for children whose world does not resemble the simplified world of television sit-coms (*there's* escapism for you), this ability to travel inward, to face fear and transform it, is a skill they will use all their lives. We do children—and ourselves—a grave disservice by censoring the old tales, glossing over the darker passages and ambiguities, smoothing the rough edges. In her essay "Once Upon a Time," Jane Yolen points to the case of "Cinderella":

> *Cinderella, until lately, has never been a passive dreamer waiting for rescue. The fore-runners of the Ash-girl have all been hardy, active heroines who take their lives into their own hands and work out their own salvations. . . . Cinderella speaks to all of us in whatever skin we inhabit: the child mistreated, a princess or highborn lady in disguise bearing her trials with patience, fortitude, and determination. Cinderella makes intelligent decisions, for she knows that wishing solves nothing*

without concomitant action. We have each been that child. (Even boys and men share that dream, as evidenced by the many Ash-boy variants.) It is the longing of any youngster sent supperless to bed or given less than a full share at Christmas. And of course it is the adolescent dream.

To make Cinderella less than she is, an ill-treated but passive princess awaiting her rescue, cheapens our most cherished dreams and makes a mockery of the magic inside us all—the ability to change our own lives, the ability to control our own destinies. [The Walt Disney film] set a new pattern for Cinderella: a helpless, hapless, pitiable, useless heroine who has to be saved time and time again by the talking mice and birds because she is "off in a world of dreams." It is a Cinderella who is not recognized by her prince until she is magically back in her ball gown, beribboned and bejewelled. Poor Cinderella. Poor us.

Jane Yolen is one of the writers whose modern fairy tales for children are subtle and complex, and provide evocative reading for adults as well. Nicholas Stuart Gray, Richard Kennedy, Patricia McKillip, Robin McKinley, Allison Uttley, and other contemporary writers of *marchen* whose works are found on the children's book shelves have followed in the footsteps of Hans Andersen and Charles Perrault, creating new tales that echo the clear poetry of the old—and some of their tales too may slip back into the great pot of soup to be served up by future cooks in some distant generation.

In this century that simmering broth has come to include not only the fairy tales themselves but the pictures that have illustrated them; for ever since the Victorians began widely publishing children's storybooks, fairy tales have been linked, more than any other kind of fiction, with lavish pictorial imagery. Thus when modern writers work with the symbols of fairy tales, they are drawing upon not only centuries of stories, but one hundred years of visual imagery as well, disseminated through a growing publishing industry. The turn-of-the-century works of the Golden Age Illustrators (the twisty trees and sly fairies of Arthur Rackham, the attenuated Art Deco princesses of Kay Nielson, the misty lands of Edmund Dulac) have in particular become such an integral part of the experience of reading fairy tales (or having them read to us as children) that these images too have surely found their way into the soup of Story. The best of this art, like the best of the tales, is not meant for children only, is not overly saccharine or cute, but acknowledges that the power of Faerie, and its beauty, lie in the interplay between the light and the shadowy dark.

It is this interplay of light and shadow that we have sought to explore in creating this collection of stories, combining the Snow White of "high" fantasy fiction with the Blood Red of horror fiction. Some of the stories contained herein fall easily into one or another of these camps; others choose instead to tread the mysterious, enchanted path between the two—both bright and dark, wondrous and disturbing, newly fashioned and old as Time.

Ursula Le Guin, in her essay "Dreams Must Explain Themselves," cautions us not to tread unwarily on this path through Faerie. Fantasy, she tells us,

> *is not antirational, but pararational; not realistic but surrealistic, a heightening of reality. In Freud's terminology, it employs primary, not secondary process think-*

> *ing. It employs archetypes which, as Jung warned us, are dangerous things. Fantasy is nearer to poetry, to mysticism, and to insanity than naturalistic fiction is. It is a wilderness, and those who go there should not feel too safe. . . . A fantasy is a journey. It is a journey into the subconscious mind, just as psychoanalysis is. Like psychoanalysis, it can be dangerous; and* it will change you.

Those of us who have carried a love of fairy tales out of the nursery and into our adult lives have felt that power, that danger, that transformative quality of the old stories. The German Romantic poet Johann Schiller once wrote: "Deeper meaning resides in the fairy tales told me in my childhood than in any truth that is taught in life." My own devotion to fairy tales began with a single book, an oversized Golden Book collection of dark, unbowdlerized tales illustrated by a Frenchwoman, Adrienne Segur. This book with its ornate, stilted, lovely pictures had a strange kind of power; over the years I have found a surprising number of others for whom that edition was a touchstone of their childhoods and who have subsequently chosen, like myself, to write or paint or edit fairy tale works as the profession of adulthood. The princes and princesses who lived in those pages, the elegant, capricious fairies, the talking animals, the haunted woods, were indeed for me a bright escape from the paler reality of the factory towns and trailer parks I grew up in—but to any child, the world outside the front door, or the familiar town, or beyond the state line, can seem as fantastical and unattainable as any Never-never Land; and a fairy tale quest is a metaphorical road map that can point the way out into the wider world.

Fairy tales were in the air in the 1960s and 1970s, even for those of us growing up in bookless environments and thus largely unaffected by the boost in popularity Tolkien's *Lord of the Rings* gave to fantastic fiction, for fantasy permeated the popular folk music of the time—the imagery in lyrics by musicians like Mark Bolan, Donovan, and Cat Stevens, and in old British ballads performed by new folk-rock bands like Fairport Convention, Pentangle, and Steel-eye Span. I suspect that I am not the only reader of fantastic fiction who came to it through this musical back door; and here is another example of the endurance of the old stories, adapting themselves to the radio airwaves and the bass line beat of rock-and-roll.

Finally, J. R. R. Tolkien reminds us that to leave fantasy in the nursery, or to believe that there is some particular connection between fairy tales and children, is to forget that children are not a separate race, a separate kind of creature from the human family at large. Some children naturally have a taste for magical tales, and plenty of others do not. Some adults never lose that taste; something still stirs deep inside us when we hear those old, evocative words: *Once Upon a Time* . . . .

To such adults this book is dedicated, this journey into the Wood.

Introduction

Red as Blood: Fairy Tales and Horror

Ellen Datlow

WHEN TERRI AND I BEGAN TO SOLICIT STORIES BASED on fairy tales for *Snow White, Blood Red,* the first question we were asked by many of the writers we approached was: "What counts as a fairy tale?" In a couple of specific cases, I wasn't sure and went to Terri as the expert/final arbiter. Fairy tales are stories that come to us through the folk tradition, stories of wonder and enchantment, as well as literary tales (like those of Hans Christian Andersen and Oscar Wilde) that have passed back into the folk tradition. They are kin to but separate from mythological stories about gods and the workings of the universe—for fairy tales are about ordinary men and women in extraordinary circumstances. Fairy tales are not fables like the animal tales of Aesop; they are not social satire like *Gulliver's Travels*; and they are not the nursery rhymes of Mother Goose. We found that the easiest way to say what a fairy tale is, rather than what it is not, is to direct people to the old tales themselves, the ones most familiar in our Western culture: the German tales collected by the Brothers Grimm; the French tales of Charles Perrault, Madame d'Aulnoy, and Madame Leprince de Beaumont; the Italian tales collected by Italo Calvino; the Irish tales collected by William Butler Yeats; the Scottish tales collected by J. P. Campbell and Robert Burns; the nineteenth-century tales of Andersen and Wilde; and the multivolume treasure trove of stories gathered from many cultures known as *The Colored Fairy Books* published by the Victorian editor Andrew Lang and his wife (and still in print from Dover Books).

Bruno Bettelheim, the Freudian analyst and author of *The Uses of Enchantment*, has very strict criteria as to which stories are actually fairy tales. In addressing their importance for children, Bettelheim makes much of a fairy tale's power to "direct the child to discover his identity and calling," or expects it "to suggest what experiences are needed to develop his character further." He also claims that to be considered a fairy tale a story must have a happy ending. Thus stories like "The Little Matchgirl" or "The Steadfast Tin Soldier" or my own favorite, "The Happy Prince," are not actually fairy tales at all. To him, "The Ugly Duckling" doesn't teach anything worthwhile to children because, after all, children cannot change their genetic inheritance. In my opinion he misses the point of the story, which is that looks might be deceiving and that even an ugly duckling may grow into a swan, that beauty is not always immediately apparent and often lies in the eye of the beholder. We ought not underrate the subtlety of fairy tales, for their power emerges from the lack of a single, unique "meaning" in each tale. Every listener finds within it something different and personal. Perhaps we must let fairy tales define themselves through the infinite variety of commonalities among them.

In my childhood I was an avid reader of the fantastic, and some of the more sorrowful or violent images in fairy tales are the ones that have stayed with me, haunting me still. In Oscar Wilde's story "The Nightingale and the Rose," the eponymous bird overhears a young man courting. The object of his affection asks for a red rose, even though it's the middle of winter. The bird uses its lifeblood to create such a rose for the lovers. The result is the death of the bird and the woman's eventual rejection of her ardent suitor and his dearly bought flower. My mother read this fairy tale to me one summer day under some trees in front of our Bronx apartment building (where I lived until I was eight years old, when the south Bronx was still predominately middle class). I was devastated and I cried and cried, moved by the bird's futile sacrifice, saddened and horrified by the young woman's carelessness. I think this little fairy tale brought home to me at a very young age how thoughtlessness can lead to unforeseen consequences.

I also remember reading through a large book of Grimm's fairy tales by myself. One of the images that stayed with me most strongly was, again, a dark one, from "The Goose Girl," in which Falada, the faithful horse, is killed by the bad folk and her head nailed to the castle gate, where it tells the king the truth as to who is the real heir to the throne. I felt horror at the murder of this faithful creature, who helped her mistress even in death. Another vivid memory is of Hans Christian Andersen's "Little Matchgirl" freezing to death selling matches on the street in the middle of the winter. I have no explanation as to why these horrific images remained with me all these years, but certainly my adult love of fiction and interest in the grotesque can be traced to my glee in reading those stories.

Many adults dismiss fairy tales as being too childish, too sweet and innocent, but fairy tales are far from that. The ones that touch us most deeply are often blunt about the darker side of human nature, filled with violence and atrocities: The evil stepmother in "Snow White," who had asked a huntsman to kill her daughter and bring back the bloody heart for her supper, is forced, at the end, to wear redhot iron slippers and dance at the wedding until she dies—a lovely wedding gift indeed. The usurping chambermaid who has taken advantage of the princess in "The Goose Girl" is asked by the king to describe what she would do to a usurper of the throne, and once she does is condemned to those punishments, which consist of "being stripped naked and put inside a barrel studded with sharp nails. Then two white horses should be harnessed to the barrel and made to drag her through the streets until she's dead." "The Six Swans" are all turned back into human boys, except the poor youngest, who is left with one swan wing in place of an arm. The sisters of Cinderella are persuaded by their mother to chop off their heels and toes in order to fit their too-large feet into a tiny glass slipper (evoking images of footbinding in ancient

China, from whence the earliest versions of the story come). And those sweet pigeons that sit on Cinderella's shoulder at the wedding pluck out the eyes of both stepsisters, blinding them for the rest of their lives in order to punish "their wickedness and malice."

The fairy tales that were most meaningful to me as a child, Bruno Bettelheim notwithstanding, were the ones that had a darker side. And so it seemed natural to put together an anthology of fairy tales retold for contemporary audiences that included both fantasy and horror.

There are precedents in print and film media, in both the fantasy and horror genres, for the retelling of fairy tales. For example, Peter Straub's magnificent and moving retelling of "The Juniper Tree," Ray Garton's Pied Piper motif in *Crucifax Autumn* and Jonathan Carroll's retelling of "Rumpelstiltskin" in *Sleeping in Flame*, and, of course, the many tales of Angela Carter and Tanith Lee. Films that immediately come to mind are Cocteau's *Beauty and the Beast* and Neal Jordan's *The Company of Wolves*, based on several Angela Carter stories. A friend has also suggested that *Pretty Woman* (a fantasy movie in which prostitution is treated as just another job) is based on "Cinderella."

Terri and I have tried to assemble an anthology with many varied voices and tones. Neil Gaiman, known for his graphic novels and as coauthor of *Good Omens*, has written a contemporary story about lost chances; Esther Friesner, often the writer of light, frothy books and stories, here presents a very dark interpretation of "Puss-in-Boots"; Jane Yolen and Patricia A. McKillip, most renowned as writers for young adults, provide a dark, adult poem and a highly sensual story; and Gahan Wilson, best known for his entertaining, macabre cartoons except, perhaps, by readers of his very fine stories, provides a tale of failed analysis; and Lisa Goldstein, an award-winning writer of speculative fiction, contributes a version of "Hansel and Gretel" that is not actually fantasy at all, but is rather *about* fantasy working deep in the human psyche. Together, all twenty-one writers have produced richly imaginative retellings of existing fairy tales, as individual as the authors themselves, penned for a contemporary, adult audience.

And so we begin our journey to the heart of *marchen* at a time not so long ago, in a land much like our own . . . with no guarantee of safe travel, timely rescues, or of ending Happily Ever After. Much like life itself.

Like a Red, Red Rose

Susan Wade

Susan Wade lives in Austin, Texas, and has sold fiction to New Pathways *and* Starshore. *She originally wanted to write a story about magic gardens and stealing roses—like "Rapunzel" or "Beauty and the Beast"—but she claims that when she started, things got away from her. She is convinced it came from having been steeped in fairy tales as a child, and says, "You tap into that strata of consciousness and all the archetypes start mutating. The result is like that of recombinant DNA; not really the offspring of any one fairy tale, but a splice of several that wound up as something else."*

Thus we begin the anthology with "Like a Red, Red Rose." This story contains several fairy tale motifs—a cottage in the woods, an innocent girl, a witch, and a prince. In her unusual weavings of these various motifs, Wade creates a new tale, effective as any of those of old.

Like a Red, Red Rose

AT A TIME NOT SO LONG AGO, IN A LAND MUCH LIKE our own, there was a cottage at the edge of a dark, haunted forest. In that cottage lived a woman and her daughter, and it was said by those in the villages and landholdings nearby that the woman was a witch.

Martine and her daughter lived in solitude, tending their animals and their garden, gathering herbs in the forest where none other dared go. The cottage was plain, perhaps a bit larger than most, but the only thing to set it apart was the magnificence of its garden. Luxuriant growths of every succulent fruit and vegetable known to that land (and some unknown) graced the garden: lush figs and grapes and pomegranates and perfect almonds and pears and beans and a myriad of other bounty. Even the stream that fed the garden was lined with watercress and mint. Among the villagers, it was whispered that the witch's magic was so powerful that, in her garden, a discarded rose would take root and flourish.

And if, of a dark night, people slipped away to visit the cottage by the wood—young girls in search of a love philter by which they might marry, or young men in search of a potion by which they might gain love without benefit of clergy—such things remained unspoken in the town.

So it was that little Blanche, for that was the name of the witch's daughter, lived with her mother, never knowing what it was to play with other children: no May games or ring-a-rosy or catch-as-can. Her games were fashioned for one: rose petals floated on the surface of the small garden stream, or pine cones stacked to form a castle in which tiny flowers bloomed, visited by princely bees. It may have been that Blanche was lonely, but having never known company other than her mother's, she did not notice it.

She was called Blanche (we must assume) because of her milky-fair skin, as pure and fine and fragrant as a petal from the great white rose tree which grew at the boundary between the cottage and the wood. Her hair was richly brown, as if carved from the polished wood of that same tree; her eyes as deep and true a green as its leaves. And each day, as soon as she had risen from her narrow bed, her mother would say to her, "It is morning, Blanche. Fetch me a rose from your tree, my child, that I may see how my daughter grows."

Blanche would scamper to the rose tree to pluck a newly-awakened blossom (and her mother must have been a witch indeed, for even in the depths of winter there would always be at least one glowing white bloom).

And bringing that blossom to her mother, Blanche would always hear, "Ah, I see my child is like a white rose, as pure and sweet as the morning." And her mother would catch Blanche up in her arms, and Blanche would place the rose in her mother's auburn hair where the flower would remain all that day.

As Blanche grew older, her life continued its solitary course; the only differences were in the nature of her games and the fact that her mother could no longer lift Blanche in her arms. But each morning, she still asked Blanche to bring her a rose from the tree, which she would wear in her hair for the day.

One day, as Blanche and her mother returned from gathering herbs and roots in the wood, Martine collapsed. Her face was pale and lined, her breathing labored. Blanche raised her mother's head and gave her a sip from the bottle they always carried with them, filled from the spring that fed their garden.

Martine's color became more its usual shade, rosier than Blanche's fair skin ever was. Even so, Blanche thought her mother looked ill and far older than she had that morning. Blanche quickly crushed the amaranth flowers they had collected for one of the potions, a healing salve, and fed them to Martine. The deep purple-red of the blossoms stained her fingers, and she scrubbed them on the grass.

Her mother's breathing became easier and she laughed a little. Blanche was reassured. "The peasants call it 'Purple-Heart' or 'Love-Lies-Bleeding.' " Her voice still sounded strained. "Shall we go now?"

Blanche decided that it was too soon for them to continue; they would wait until Martine seemed more herself. So she merely looked at the dark stain on her fingers and said, "You never told me that."

"I prefer its true name," her mother said. "Amaranth."

Martine sat up then, determined to go home. She needed help to reach the cottage, but once there seemed to revive.

"Mother?" Blanche asked, once Martine had recovered. "What is wrong? Are you ill?"

"It is nothing," said her mother. "Only that I am no longer young."

Blanche found this difficult to credit, seeing her mother's face, its lovely color restored. With her smooth skin and rich auburn curls, Martine seemed unchanged from Blanche's earliest memories of her. "You must tell me if you are unwell," she said. "You must rest."

Martine sighed. "Perhaps it would be better if you went alone to collect the herbs. You know as well as I what is needed."

And so Blanche became chief gatherer, while her mother remained at the cottage to prepare and blend her potions, and life flowed much as it always had for the two of them.

Until the son of the largest landholder in the area, arriving early of an evening, caught a glimpse of the witch's lovely daughter (for she was quite lovely, as you have no doubt surmised). He had come for a consultation during which he would purchase a certain potion he found useful; the witch kept such sundries in a cupboard near her front gate, as she was reluctant to allow local folk to enter the cottage.

He himself was a comely youth, with a lavish tangle of black curls and eyes like midnight. His name was Allain, and he was well known among the women of the village, a fact which pleased him.

Yet, clever as he was in the arts of love, his expertise deserted him when he first saw Blanche. He abandoned his conversation with an abruptness few would have dared, and demanded of the witch the name of the irresistable creature who had appeared beside the stream.

"She is my daughter," Blanche's mother said, speaking with an awful emphasis which even a smitten lover could not misapprehend. "Do not trouble your heart with her. She will never marry."

And so taken was Allain that he never considered that it was not ordinarily marriage which he sought from his *inamorata*. At least his experience of women did not desert him with Blanche's mother; at her angry words, he bowed swiftly and said, "Ah, it is clear then whence came her beauty." And concluding his business with great charm and greater dispatch, he spoke not again of the vision glimpsed beside the stream: of a girl with hair like polished wood and skin as fair as a pearl.

All his way home, that brief scene was reenacted in his imagination: the lovely apparition, as of a nymph from the forest, with gleaming hair and brilliant eyes that glanced toward him and swiftly away. He recalled she had carried a basket woven of peeled willow branches, overflowing with greenery. It was not difficult to deduce that she had come from gathering herbs in the forest.

And with that deduction, a simple solution to Allain's dilemma was found: he would seek the witch's daughter in the wood, which, whatever its reputation, was far less intimidating than the witch herself. He knew from personal experience how effective Martine's magic could be.

So it came about that on a day soon after (as soon

as he had learned the name of the witch's beautiful daughter, in fact), Allain entered the wood. He kept to its nearer boundaries, despite his reputation for daring. But the forest growth was of such density as to be nearly impenetrable, so he was well hid from the witch's view even as he passed by the cottage. And he was well rewarded for entering that dark place, for not much of the day had passed before he came upon Blanche, seated on a fallen pine in a small glade as she investigated a promising growth of bit-moss.

A more striking pose could not have been found had she studied for one: with a beam of sunlight touching her hair to reveal strands of gold hidden among rich brown, and her back a graceful curve which led the eye naturally to the even more graceful curve of her waist. And her skin! So pure and milky-fair was she that, for an instant, Allain wondered whether her mother had magicked the girl from a lily.

But then she turned, and saw him, and started; as shy as a dove. Any thoughts of her sorcerous nature faded from his mind.

"Blanche," he whispered.

Appearing even more startled, she looked up at him again, and he saw fully the glow of her eyes, so brilliant that they put the emerald shade of the forest to shame.

He came nearer, and when she would have gathered up her basket and fled, stayed her with a soft, "Ah, no, please!" And when she paused, he said, "I've come such a long way to speak with you, you couldn't be so cruel as to run away."

She turned to him at that, all her wondering curiosity in her eyes, and asked, "You've come to speak to me?"

"Why, yes," he answered. "Did you not know I would, after our souls met in the garden? I could not but come," he added, and possessed himself of her hand.

Blanche turned as if she would escape, and a hint of delicate color came into her cheeks.

The flesh of her hand, just of her hand! was so softly sweet and firm that Allain longed to test it with his teeth, trace it with his tongue; to consume that flesh with all the passion of which he was capable. But she was clearly innocent. Allain contented himself with a chaste kiss.

And saw, as his mouth caressed the tender curve of her palm, her lips part and her eyes become darker and lose their focus.

For Allain, these delicate signs of awakened passion were more inflaming than the intricate tricks of a seasoned courtesan.

His heart was lost from that moment.

For Blanche, the brief encounter in the forest filled a need she had never before recognized, never named. A need born of loneliness, perhaps, or simply a longing for companionship both more complex and less demanding than that of her mother. And with the satiation of that unspoken need, there came an awareness of an entire enchanted dimension beyond companionship.

Blanche turned in her narrow bed to see dawn light streaming through the high, small window. Had she slept at all? Or had it been simply a reliving of that waking dream of him? He had touched her, his mouth against her palm. She twisted her face against the bed linens to cool her skin.

She heard her mother stir in the single bedroom of the cottage, then footsteps as she came into the main room, where Blanche's small bed occupied a corner.

"It is morning, Blanche," her mother said, as she did each day. "Fetch me a rose from your tree, my dear, that I may see how my daughter does."

Blanche smiled at the familiar request. She rose and stretched, then pulled her gown over the simple shift that served her as nightwear.

In her bare feet, because it was summer (though, in truth, the garden was always in summer), she ran to pluck a rose from her tree. But when she reached it, she stopped, stunned.

In place of the snowy blossoms that had graced the tree all her life were creamy buds with a dusky golden-pink tinging the edge of each petal.

What could it mean? She reached a trembling hand to touch a blossom, then drew back. The roses were lovely, with a scent richer and more enticing than she remembered. And yet, and yet . . . they were not *her* roses, not the roses that were Blanche. Yet she knew she could not have mistaken the great rose tree, queen of all the garden, there on the verge of the wood.

"Blanche!" her mother called from the cottage. "Do not be dallying in the garden or your porridge will be done without you."

Blanche plucked a bloom then. It came to her hand no differently than the white rose had come the day before. Her mother would explain this to her; her mother's magic may have caused this to happen. Blanche turned and went to the cottage with hurried steps.

But the instant her mother saw the altered rose, her face grew terrible. She snatched the flower away and grasped Blanche's shoulder with a harsh hand. "Where did you see him?"

Shock tore the strength from Blanche's legs, and she

nearly fell. Her mother had never spoken to her so, never looked at her so.

Her mother dropped the rose and shook Blanche. "Where?" she cried.

"In the forest," Blanche said.

At that, her mother released her and turned to pace a few steps. Then Martine turned back. "You are no longer pure, no longer the white rose. But it may not yet be too late to prevent the thing I fear most." She came close again to Blanche, her dark gaze holding the girl prisoner. "You know nothing of your own nature, nothing of what the world holds for such as we are. But you are my daughter and I will see that you do not live with the grief that I have borne. I will see you to a new life, whatever it costs."

Blanche trembled. The things Martine was saying made no sense, and her intensity was frightening; the more so because it was unaccustomed.

"We must take the love potions and the amaranth salve I use to heal wounds. As large a quantity as we can manage. They will support us until we have the opportunity to establish ourselves elsewhere," her mother went on. "As for clothing and household goods, very little will be necessary. Some food and water is all. Perhaps we can sell the chickens and the goat in the village."

Blanche stared at her mother. "We are to leave? Where will we go?"

Martine said distractedly, "That is to be seen, but, yes, we will leave. Tomorrow."

"But why?" Blanche asked. "I was born here. Why must we leave?"

"It is the only escape, I tell you. I will not let you suffer as I have."

"My only escape from what? If my life is to be changed, I must know why."

Martine hesitated for only an instant. Then she looked down at the creamy rose petals scattered on the floor, each limned in dusky color. "We leave so you will not lose all that you love. Now gather your things. We must be gone by first light."

The next morning saw them on the road leading south to the nearest village. Blanche's heart was heavy at leaving her home, its garden never more lovely than it was at that dawn: a glittering array of nature's jewels, all scent and color and light. Blanche was curious as well as frightened; her only experience of the world outside her mother's garden had been to wander in the forest, which seemed more an extension of the garden than a separate place.

The road was of dun earth, dull and gritty. Blanche was footsore before they had traveled far; keeping the goat and chickens to the road was a worrisome task, and the barrow she helped her mother push was heavy.

It was yet early morning when they reached the village. Blanche looked to her mother for guidance, but Martine was pale and listless and merely stood with her head low.

Blanche glanced around, curious at what the town would hold. A group of men stood by the village well, watching the two women. One of them moved forward at a difficult pace. His few strands of white hair did not conceal the brown marks of age on his skull. When he came within a few steps of them, she noticed that the whites of his eyes had yellowed, a condition for which her mother often prescribed an infusion of vervain. He cleared his throat and spat at Martine's feet.

"Witch!" he said. His voice cracked. "There is nothing here for you. Go back to your devil's garden."

Martine raised her head for the first time when he spoke the word "garden." She did not answer the old man, but only gazed at him. The other villagers crowded around. Blanche waited, certain her mother would wither this rude man with only a look.

He spat again. "Go back," he repeated. "None here will have you." Then he swung around and glared at Blanche. She saw that his yellow eyes were crazed with red lines. They looked as if they might crack open and spill blood in the dust, he stared so hard at her. "Nor her neither," the old man said, pointing at Blanche, "for all she is so fair. There's those here old enough to remember what your kind is. Go back."

Martine spoke then, in a voice so faint it was as if only the wind answered. "We won't trouble you. We only wish to sell the stock before we go on." She paused, then added as if in afterthought, "I will not even drink from your well."

The old man cackled. "That you won't," he said. "Nor any here take your stock. Raised on the devil's flesh, they was, and we know it. There's nothing for you outside that plot sown with devil seed. Go back and reap what you have planted, witch." The other villagers crossed themselves and made signs against the evil eye.

Martine said quietly to Blanche, "Leave them, then, the animals. You must take the barrow now, for I cannot any longer." Blanche had never known her mother to betray weakness. What was wrong?

Then Martine tossed her head back in her imperious manner. Blanche, seeing the moisture bead on her mother's brow, wondered what even that small gesture had cost.

"Yes, Mother," she said.

Martine walked past the villagers, then paused. "Perhaps those with more sense will take these animals and care for them," she said to Blanche. Her voice was pitched to carry. "Not all the people here disdain the fruits of my garden."

Several of the townsfolk moved back at Martine's words, glancing aside when Blanche looked at them. Now she recognized a face or two, those who had come to her mother for remedies.

Blanche singled out a kindly-faced matron from among them, one whose youngest child had been healed of a fever by Martine's magic. "Will you see the animals are cared for?" Blanche asked her. "They are not accustomed to feeding themselves."

The woman turned away.

Martine had stopped a little beyond the town and now looked back to summon Blanche with a gesture. The chickens had scattered to peck at grit beside the well, and the goat was nibbling at a coil of rope that hung nearby. Blanche sighed and lifted the handles of the barrow to follow her mother.

The road seemed very long, stretching before them without any known destination at its end. Blanche was worried about her mother, whose skin now looked waxen and damp. Martine walked stiffly and seemed barely aware of moving.

It was quite still on the road; even the dust barely stirred under their feet. As their distance from the forest increased, the trees lining the road became more widely spaced. The rays of the mid-morning sun stung Blanche's skin. "Mother?" she said. "Could we stop for a moment and rest in the shade?" Since they had no particular place to go, there was no reason to hurry their arrival. And it was very hot.

Blanche released the barrow's handles and blew on her blistered palms. Martine continued as if unaware her daughter had spoken.

"Mother?" Blanche left the barrow and hurried to catch Martine.

She did not stop until Blanche touched her arm, and then the cessation of motion seemed to overwhelm her, so that she swayed on her feet.

Blanche put an arm around her and led her to a small grove of trees which offered some shade. "Sit here and rest," she said. She went back onto the road to get the barrow. After only a moment in the shade, the sun's heat seemed too fierce to be borne.

When Blanche returned, her mother was asleep. Deeply worried, Blanche searched for one of the jugs of spring water Martine had insisted they bring.

She splashed the water into a small cup and knelt to hold it to her mother's lips. With the water's kiss, Martine's eyes opened and a bit of color returned to her cheeks.

"Are you ill?" Blanche asked. "You seem very tired, Mother."

Martine lifted a trembling hand to take the cup from her daughter. Blanche had to steady it as her mother drank. "If I am, there is nothing to be done for it," Martine said. Her voice shook as much as her hand. "We must go on."

"But it is the heat of the day," Blanche protested, "and you seem so tired. Perhaps we could rest here until it grows cooler."

Martine's eyes closed again. "Very well. Just for a short time, then," she mumbled. Then she opened her eyes and looked at Blanche. "Promise me," she said sharply, "that you will not return to the garden. Promise me, Blanche."

"Yes, Mother, I promise," Blanche said. "We will go to make a new life for ourselves, as you said we should. We will go together." Yet, as she spoke, she thought of Allain, of love left behind.

Martine's lips curved in a faint smile and her eyelids dropped. "Perhaps," was all she said before she slept again.

Blanche watched over her mother. As the afternoon wore on, Martine's breathing grew shallower, her skin more colorless. She could barely be roused to drink and did not speak. By late afternoon, Blanche was certain her mother was gravely ill.

It was not long after that Martine spoke again. "Remember your promise," she said to Blanche. "You must not go back." Her wax-white skin had shrunk against the bones, so that her face looked as bleached and spare as a naked skull.

"No, Mother," Blanche assured her.

Martine sighed then, a long, deep exhalation that shook her entire body. It was not followed by another breath.

It was thus that Allain found Blanche, bowed weeping over the body of her mother.

So grateful was he to have found his love that even the looming prospect of nightfall in the company of a dead witch did not daunt him. He called Blanche's name as he dismounted from his horse.

Blanche looked up at him, her drowning eyes such a clear and powerful green that, for an instant, Allain felt himself engulfed in forest shade. Then she came to him, flinging herself into his embrace. And his world became defined by the sensation of her body pressed to his: the velvet plush of her skin, the satin flow of her hair against his hands, the gentle stir of her sobbing breaths against his throat.

"Blanche," he whispered, caught by a desire more intense than he had known physical desire could be.

He stroked her hair, and her sobs quietened. She sighed and asked, "What shall I do?" Allain felt the brush of her lips against his throat and he trembled.

"Why, you will marry me," he said. "For you are my own true love. And lovers wed, do they not?"

She drew away and looked up at him, trouble burnishing the fairness of her face to an aching beauty. "I am to go away. I promised my mother." She choked and turned her head a little, toward where the still body lay. "Her dying wish."

Seeing her tremor, her anguish, Allain could no more resist her than he could resist breathing the air. He kissed her.

And as he took her lips, tasting of honey and mint and the sweetest of green grasses, and felt her mouth tremble in response to his touch, he knew that he must soon have her or die of it.

"Marry me," he whispered, and kissed her again: her lips, the silken splendor of her neck, the delicate arch of her ear.

"Marry me," he cajoled, stroking her throat, kissing her lids, bringing her hands to his face for yet more kisses.

"Say yes," he murmured.

"Yes," she said.

Out of concern for Blanche's weariness, Allain decided they should rest until moonrise. Sitting in the deep shadows of the trees, Blanche might have been a shadow herself, so quiet and withdrawn was she. Allain supposed that her mother's death weighed heavily. Martine had been Blanche's only relation; more, her only friend.

When the moon rose to pour its light over the world like silver syrup, Allain set to work. Cautiously, his respect only partly that a man shows for the mother of his betrothed, Allain swathed the body in his cloak and placed it over the withers of his horse. The beast shied and snorted until its eyes showed white, but when Blanche came forward to lead it (at Allain's instruction), the animal calmed.

Allain took the handles of the barrow and started back toward the village.

Blanche hesitated.

"Come along, my love," he coaxed. "I know you are weary, but we must see your mother safe home."

"I—cannot," she said then. "I must not return home. It was my final promise to her."

"Very well," he responded gently. "We shall take her to my father's priest, then, so she may be buried properly. And you will come to my home, to meet my family, as is suitable for my betrothed."

Still she hesitated.

"Please, love," he said. "It is only right that my parents comfort and sustain you at such a sad time. You would not want them to believe you disdain their hospitality, I know."

Blanche said, "It—the villagers would not take our animals. They called us 'devil's spawn.' "

Allain met her gaze steadily. "And were you surprised, love? The villagers fear what they do not understand."

"Yes, but . . . Your father . . . will he not feel as the

villagers do? That I am of the devil? He may not wish such a wife for his son."

Allain came to her then, to lift her hand to his lips. "Ah, but my father is not a villager, sweet Blanche. He will be pleased that I have found such a beautiful bride."

She looked up at him then, her face as lovely as a budding rose. "Do you truly believe so?"

Allain pressed her palm to his chest, and said, "With all my heart."

It was nearing midnight when the two reached the village. Fearful of the townsfolk, Blanche was grateful to find it dark and still, the square deserted.

Allain was inclined to insist on lodgings at one of the cottages, so that Blanche might pass what remained of the night in comfort. But she was reluctant to face the villagers again, and preferred to continue. The road they must use wound past her home, and it may have been that Allain had hoped to spare her the painful reminder of her life there with Martine. But her tears persuaded him to complete their journey that night.

As they neared the witch's cottage, Blanche's steps grew more eager. It was not that she would ever disregard her mother's wish, she told herself, only that she longed to look once more on the place where her mother's memory dwelt. Mindful of her promise, she kept to the far verge of the road and did not slow her steps as they approached.

But when the garden came into sight, flooded with the silver moonlight, Blanche stopped in her tracks. Gone was the lush abundance, the boughs so burdened with fruit, they groaned, the profusion of flowers that had graced the plot of land for as long as Blanche could remember.

The garden was withered, sere. Dead branches carried only the dried husks of their former bounty. A few shriveled petals were all that remained of the thousand blossoms Blanche had left behind.

Except, at the far side of the garden, glimmering in the moonlight, she saw the great rose tree, still abloom. Only now the roses blushed, their petals a rich, true pink.

Blanche cried out and would have run to the garden, though she knew she could not restore it; but Allain caught her in his arms and held her back.

"Your promise," he said then. "Your mother must have known her magic was ended, and thought to spare you this. You must not let her last wish go unbidden, love."

She wept then, for her mother and for her mother's garden, both lost now forever. And perhaps, a bit, for herself, for she felt very lost, too. But Allain was there to comfort her and eventually, to lead her beyond the boundaries of the witch's property, so that she might reach safety and shelter that night.

It seemed an omen, like a promise of dawn, when at last they rounded a bend to see the portal of Allain's home aglow with torchlight.

"See?" he said to his betrothed. "Already my family welcomes you." And all his curiosity at the lighted torches dissolved with her answering sigh of pleasure.

Allain left the barrow then, and tied the horse behind it. "Come, my love," he said, and took her arm to lead her to his home. "Father?" he called out. "What's to do?"

The door opened then, and a great dark-haired bear of a man emerged, a-thunder with aggravation. "Allain! Is that you?" he shouted, his voice a growling rumble. Torchlight gleamed on the richly oiled curls of his black beard.

Several of the household came running at the sound of his shouting.

"Where have you been all the day and half the night? The villeins are nigh dead with exhaustion from searching for you," Allain's father said as he moved forward. He stopped abruptly when Allain stepped into the circle of the torchlight with Blanche on his arm. "We had word from the village," Allain's father said then, and his voice was lower, more ominous, "that you had gone after the witch and her spawn, but I knew they lied."

Allain stiffened and raised his head. "Did you, now? And why would you be so sure of that, Father?"

The older man descended from the doorway with a speed that belied his size. "Because you are my son and not a fool."

Allain drew Blanche closer to him. "And is it foolishness to give my heart to one so lovely as this? Am I a fool to take this fairest of flowers to wife?"

His father looked at Blanche, and his eyes were hard and cruel; like tiny black pebbles set in his head. "A fool, indeed, to marry a witch," he said. "Priest!" he yelled then. "Fetch my priest!"

Blanche shrank back, because his anger frightened her. The servants began to whisper among themselves.

Then the gossiping servants were jostled aside, making way for a slight man wearing vestments. "I am here, sir. I came as soon as I heard shouting, thinking I might be needed. Has there been an accident?"

"An accident of nature, perhaps," said the lord. "Look at her," he flung a hand toward Blanche, "and tell me if she is a demon."

Allain started forward in fury, his fist raised to his father. The big man captured and held his son's hand as easily as he might a butterfly. "Nay," he said. "You'll stay and hear what the priest says of her, before there's any talk of marriage."

Allain's eyes flashed, and he turned back to Blanche. She shook her head at him, knowing that nothing good would come of defying his father. But perhaps if the holy man reassured him . . .

The priest stepped toward Blanche, who stood shivering, half in moonlight, half in torchlight. "Mmmph," he muttered. "I see no obvious mark of magic on her, though she is extraordinarily fair. Are you baptized, girl?"

Blanche shook her head and struggled to speak well, for Allain's sake and for her own. "My mother said the visiting priest refused to do it, because we lived so close to the forest, which he believed was haunted."

The priest snorted and nodded knowingly. "Some of these village priests are woefully ignorant."

Heartened, Blanche went on, "I am called Blanche, and I would be baptized so, if you are willing, sir."

The priest ruffled himself up like a pigeon and said, "Good, good." He looked at Allain's father and added, "Her name is Blanche, in praise of Our White Lady. I am willing to baptize her."

Allain still stood beside his father, but when he looked at Blanche, his eyes shone. "Why that seems quite satisfactory, don't you agree, Father?" he said.

His father looked at Blanche, and she saw his black eyes narrow. She fancied she caught a glimpse of some secret malice there. But all he said was, "Perhaps. We shall see how she seems once she is sprinkled with holy water."

The priest cleared his throat, then said to Blanche, "You wish to be baptized, here and now?"

She nodded, then remembering what Allain had spoken of earlier, said, "We came also to ask you to see my mother buried." Her voice shook as she said, "She was taken ill and—and—"

"Ah!" said Allain's father, and his face lightened. "Dead, is she?"

Blanche looked down, unable to speak. It was Allain who answered, talking so softly to his father that Blanche could not hear his words.

Then Allain's father nodded at the priest, who fidgeted briefly before saying, "Very well, have the body brought—"

"Not in the chapel," Allain's father said. "Do it here."

"It is most irregular—" the priest began.

"Here," said Allain's father, and his voice held a note of finality.

"Yes, well, bring the body to the steps here," said the priest. "And you—boy," he indicated one of the servants, "run fetch my stole from the vestry."

The boy ran off as commanded, but none among the servants moved toward the dark bundle on Allain's horse.

After a moment, Allain laughed. "I will bring her to you, priest, as I have brought her this far." He walked to the horse, which waited patiently beside the barrow, and untied the reins to lead it forward. When he reached the torchlight again, he handed the beast's reins to Blanche with a smile.

"Soon over, my love," he whispered to her, before he lifted her mother's body from the horse.

He laid the body on the steps as the priest had instructed, then lifted away the shrouding cloak.

Blanche saw his face go pale and rushed to his side.

Her mother's body was gone.

All that lay within the folds of the cloak was a bundle of shriveled rose canes, dried and black. At its root clung a clump of dark earth. At its crown clustered a few faded rose petals, which had once been red.

A cry of horror rose from the servants, and Blanche clutched Allain's hand.

As they watched, a wind stirred, and the earth that clung to the roots was swept upward. It became a whirling dark cloud, which hovered near Blanche for a moment, then spun off into the night. For an instant all was still.

Then Allain's father screamed, "Kill the witch! Stone her!" Blanche gasped and turned to see him pointing at her. "Loose the dogs!"

Most of the servants crossed themselves and huddled together, but two men dressed in leathers raced off toward the mews.

"Stone her!" Allain's father commanded again. One of the servants stooped to grope for a stone.

Allain jerked the reins from Blanche's numb fingers. Before she knew what he did, she was astride the horse, with Allain swinging up behind her.

And then the two of them were fleeing into the moonlit night, as the baying of the hounds echoed behind them.

Allain meant to make it a desperate race, there under the waning moon. But his horse was already spent, and the hounds were fresh. The sound of their baying grew ever louder over the faltering hoofbeats of the weary horse.

They came to a place on the road Blanche recognized, and she reached for the reins and tried to pull them back. "Stop," she said.

Allain yanked them free and slapped the horse's withers, but the lathered beast stumbled to a stop anyway, too exhausted to run further. "We cannot stop, love," Allain said. "The hounds are too close."

She turned then, as much as she could, so that she might look at him. "You must go back alone," she said. "Your father will not blame you, he will say you were bewitched. I cannot bring you death as a betrothal gift."

"No," he said. "Though it may be that I am bewitched, because the thought of leaving you is more horrible than that of dying in your arms. We will go on together."

Blanche grasped his arm. "No!"

He laughed then, a bright and vibrant sound, there on the empty, moon-soaked road. "But yes," he said. "Although I confess I would prefer to lie in your arms and *not* die."

The hounds gave voice then, in a rising howl that made Blanche shiver.

Allain said, "Sadly, it seems unlikely, for they are very near. Give me a kiss, my love, before we run."

Their kiss was sweet, a fatal sweetness born of danger and sparking passion. After a breathless moment when it seemed to Blanche that the stars wheeled overhead, Allain wrenched away.

"We will give them a run they will long remember," he said.

But Blanche laid an urgent hand on his. "Wait—the forest. The hounds never hunt there. And I know it well. We could hide there."

Allain hesitated. "The dogs are running on our scent now. It may be they will follow anyway."

"This poor horse is too tired to run anymore, and," Blanche smiled at him, "I would prefer to live through the night, too."

He looked at her, and perhaps it was her smile which swayed him. Or perhaps it was the belling of the hounds, almost upon them. "Very well." He swung off the horse and lifted Blanche down. "Quickly then." He pulled the reins so they hung loosely around the pommel of the saddle, then slapped the horse's rump. The startled beast broke into a shambling trot, and Allain took Blanche's hand. "Now you must lead," he said.

They ran to the edge of the road, and Blanche drew him into a narrow space between two trees. The undergrowth was thick and seemed to grasp at them. Every muscle, every nerve demanded urgent speed. It was not possible.

And then the clamoring voices of the hounds were there, very close, and Allain pulled Blanche to him. When she would have spoken, he pressed a finger to her lips. "Stillness will serve us best," he breathed in her ear, and she nodded, knowing they were yet too close to the road for safety.

The dogs were near enough that Blanche could hear their panting breaths whistle over their fangs. They snarled, and the sound seemed to surround the two lovers. One of the dogs began to bark excitedly, and a rough male voice shouted. Blanche was certain they were discovered.

And then, farther up the road, several dogs howled in a distinctive note of discovery.

The pack swept on, past the section of wood where Blanche and Allain waited. Allain flinched when he heard his horse's screams.

They waited, hearts thundering, until it was clear the pack would not return, then worked their way deeper into the forest.

Blanche had said she knew the forest well, and she

did. But now, masked by the night's darkness and her own exhaustion, the trees did not assume their familiar shapes. It was not long before she knew they were lost.

"Never mind," Allain said. "In the morning we will find our way again. For now, I am grateful we are alive and together."

They came to a small stream and drank thirstily. The cold water was like a tonic to Blanche, seeming almost to sparkle as it touched her tongue. She splashed her face and throat and felt revived.

"It is almost dawn," Allain said. "Hear the stillness? You should rest."

They were sitting beside the stream. Blanche touched his face. "If you will hold me, so I know we are together, then I shall rest. Otherwise, I will not sleep for fear I should wake and find you gone."

And so they lay together, on the mossy bank of the running stream, and found that they were not as weary as might have been expected.

For to find themselves safe and in each other's arms was a restorative. They spoke softly of things that lovers speak of, and touched and kissed and touched again.

The feelings Allain's touch aroused in Blanche were frightening. And yet it was such a small fear compared to that she had just overcome. His hands were gentle, each caress an experience in texture and fire and sensation, until she no longer needed gentleness; her own urgent hands showed him that.

They became lovers in truth, there on a moss-covered bank in the dimness of false dawn. And there was a wildness to the act, perhaps emanating from the forest itself, or perhaps merely stirring in Blanche's blood that which had been part of her always. It was an elixir that made her passionate and fierce and stronger than she had ever been. And so, when the pain came, and with it her virgin's blood spilled to the forest floor, that too was part of the wildness, and so the joy.

And when the joy grew unbearable, and her mind dimmed with it, then there was sleep, safe in the circle of Allain's arms.

The sun was long risen when Blanche awoke, bathing the glade where they rested in green-filtered light.

Allain lay on his stomach beside her, having turned during the night to sleep with one arm beneath his head; the other still curved over her hip. She sat up, and gently lifted his arm away. To see him sleeping so soundly made her smile.

A bubbling, contented happiness filled her; a feeling she could not recall ever experiencing before. It was as though she had been filled with sunshine; she thought her body might radiate light.

She stretched and looked around. And was shocked to see that the stream they had slept beside was the very same that ran below her mother's garden. They lay in the forest at the very edge of her own home.

Or what had been her home, until her mother's magic faded. And yet, it seemed the fearful moonlight of the previous night had been deceptive.

The garden was not withered, not completely. No, not at all.

For she could see blossoms swelling from their stems, with not a single bloom a moment past its prime. And even as she watched, bare boughs began to put forth fruit and budding leaves. Her mother's magic was *not* ended. The garden was restoring itself.

Delightedly—for however uncertain their future, they would at least break their fast in a familiar place—Blanche turned to waken Allain.

"Love," she whispered in his ear, and shyly kissed him. But he slept on, so she gave him a playful shake.

Still he did not stir.

Blanche cupped a handful of spring water and sprinkled it over his bare back.

And then fear grasped her in icy claws, because he stirred not at all, not even to draw breath; and she took his shoulders and pulled him around to her, though he lay so heavily she could scarcely move him.

And saw the enormous thorn that pierced his heart, its jagged edge as wide as her thumb.

And saw, in the earth beneath him, the deep-soaking stain of his heart's blood.

And could not weep, nor cry out, nor even speak his name, as she gazed beyond the spilled rivulet of her true love's blood. That bitter stain ran straight to the root of the queenly rose tree that spread its tangled canes above them.

Every branch bore a pale pink rose.

But, before her eyes, the blushing petals suffused with darker color, until each perfect bloom was blood-red.

She cut the treacherous rose tree off at the root and burned its thorny branches. Then she buried Allain at the boundary between the forest and her garden, near where they had lain together. And for some time, it mattered not at all to her whether the villagers or the servants of Allain's father would soon come to kill her.

But then she found that she was with child, and knew that indeed it did matter whether she lived or died, for her child's sake. And before fear could cause her to leave that place, an impenetrable thicket of thornbushes grew to surround her garden. She knew none of the townsfolk would dare breach its sorcerous guard.

So she ate of the garden's fruits and drank of its spring, and though she often wept knowing Allain would never share these things with her, it was enough that his child soon would.

And when her time was upon her, she labored alone to bring their babe into the world.

It was a long and difficult labor, but as soon as she was physically able, she swaddled the newborn babe and took it to where Allain lay.

To find an enormous rose tree thriving there, its root buried deep in her dead lover's heart. Its every bloom was purest white.

She named her daughter Amaranth.

The Moon Is Drowning While I Sleep

Charles de Lint

Charles de Lint is the Canadian author of Moonheart, The Dreaming Place, The Little Country, *and numerous other books of fantasy, horror, and suspense. He is also the author of the fairy tale novel* Jack the Giant-Killer *which, like much of his work, mixes folklore and mythic motifs with modern urban settings.*

"The Moon Is Drowning While I Sleep" returns us to Newford, de Lint's imaginary Canadian city where the lines between the real and the fantastic are vague and often crossed. Much of de Lint's best contemporary work is set among the street punks of Newford, but previous acquaintance with the street artist Jilly Coppercorn, her painter friend Sophie Etoile, Geordie the fiddle player, or Christy Riddell, collector of urban folklore, is not required to enjoy the following story. It is based on the fairy tale "The Dead Moon."

The Moon Is Drowning While I Sleep

If you keep your mind sufficiently open, people will throw a lot of rubbish into it.
—WILLIAM A. ORTON

1

ONCE UPON A TIME THERE WAS WHAT THERE WAS, AND if nothing had happened there would be nothing to tell.

2

IT WAS MY FATHER WHO TOLD ME THAT DREAMS WANT to be real. When you start to wake up, he said, they hang on and try to slip out into the waking world when you don't notice. Very strong dreams, he added, can almost do it; they can last for almost half a day, but not much longer.

I asked him if any ever made it. If any of the people our subconscious minds toss up and make real while we're sleeping had ever actually stolen out into this world from the dream world.

He knew of at least one that had, he said.

He had that kind of lost look in his eyes that made me think of my mother. He always looked like that when he talked about her, which wasn't often.

Who was it? I asked, hoping he'd dole out another little tidbit about my mother. Is it someone I know?

But he only shook his head. Not really, he told me. It happened a long time ago—before you were born. But I often wondered, he added almost to himself, what did *she* dream of?

That was a long time ago and I don't know if he ever found out. If he did, he never told me. But lately I've been wondering about it. I think maybe they don't dream. I think that if they do, they get pulled back into the dream world.

And if we're not careful, I think they can pull us back with them.

3

"I'VE BEEN HAVING THE STRANGEST DREAMS," SOPHIE Etoile said, more as an observation than a conversational opener.

She and Jilly Coppercorn had been enjoying a companionable silence while they sat on the stone river wall in the old part of Lower Crowsea's Market. The wall is by a small public courtyard, surrounded on three sides by old three-story brick and stone town houses, peaked with mansard roofs, dormer windows thrusting from the walls like hooded eyes with heavy brows. The buildings date back over a hundred years, leaning against each other like old friends too tired to talk, just taking comfort from each other's presence.

The cobblestoned streets that web out from the courtyard are narrow, too tight a fit for a car, even the small imported makes. They twist and turn, winding in and around the buildings more like back alleys than thoroughfares. If you have any sort of familiarity with the area you can maze your way by those lanes to find still smaller courtyards, hidden and private, and, deeper still, secret gardens.

There are more cats in Old Market than anywhere else in Newford and the air smells different. Though it sits just a few blocks west of some of the city's principal thoroughfares, you can hardly hear the traffic, and you can't smell it at all. No exhaust, no refuse, no dead air. Old Market always seems to smell of fresh bread baking, cabbage soups, frying fish, roses and those tart, sharp-tasting apples that make the best strudels.

Sophie and Jilly were bookended by stairs going down to the Kickaha River on either side of them. The streetlamp behind them put a glow on their hair, haloing each with a nimbus of light. Jilly's hair was darker, all loose tangled curls; Sophie's was soft auburn, hanging in ringlets.

In the half-dark beyond the lamp's murky light, their small figures could almost be taken for each other, but when the light touched their features, Jilly could be seen to have the quick, clever features of a Rackham pixie, while Sophie's were softer, as though rendered by Rossetti or Burne-Jones. Though similarly dressed with paint-stained smocks over loose T-shirts and baggy cotton pants, Sophie still managed to look tidy, while Jilly could never seem to help a slight tendency toward scruffiness. She was the only one of the two with paint in her hair.

"What sort of dreams?" Jilly asked her friend.

It was almost four o'clock in the morning. The narrow streets of Old Market lay empty and still about them, except for the odd prowling cat, and cats can be like the hint of a whisper when they want, ghosting and silent, invisible presences. The two women had been working at Sophie's studio on a joint painting, a collaboration that was going to combine Jilly's precise, delicate work with Sophie's current penchant for bright flaring colors and loosely rendered figures. Neither was sure the experiment would work, but they'd been enjoying themselves immensely, so it really didn't matter.

"Well, they're sort of serial," Sophie said. "You know, where you keep dreaming about the same place, the same people, the same events, except each night you're a little further along in the story."

Jilly gave her an envious look. "I've always wanted to have that kind of dream. Christy's had them. I think he told me that it's called lucid dreaming."

"They're anything but lucid," Sophie said. "If you ask me, they're downright strange."

"No, no. It just means that you know you're dreaming, *when* you're dreaming, and have some kind of control over what happens in the dream."

Sophie laughed. "I wish."

4

I'M WEARING A LONG PLEATED SKIRT AND ONE OF THOSE white cotton peasant blouses that's cut way too low in the bodice. I don't know why. I hate that kind of bodice. I keep feeling like I'm going to fall out whenever I bend over. Definitely designed by a man. Wendy likes to wear that kind of thing from time to time, but it's not for me.

Nor is going barefoot. Especially not here. I'm standing on a path, but it's muddy underfoot, all squishy between my toes. It's sort of nice in some ways, but I keep getting the feeling that something's going to sidle up to me, under the mud, and brush against my foot, so I don't want to move, but I don't want to just stand here, either.

Everywhere I look it's all marsh. Low flat fens, with

just the odd crack willow or alder trailing raggedy vines the way you see Spanish moss in pictures of the Everglades, but this definitely isn't Florida. It feels more Englishy, if that makes sense.

I know if I step off the path I'll be in muck up to my knees.

I can see a dim kind of light off in the distance, way off the path. I'm attracted to it, the way any light in the darkness seems to call out, welcoming you, but I don't want to brave the deeper mud or the pools of still water that glimmer in the starlight.

It's all mud and reeds, cattails, bulrushes and swamp grass and I just want to be back home in bed, but I can't wake up. There's a funny smell in the air, a mix of things rotting and stagnant water. I feel like there's something horrible in the shadows under those strange, overhung trees—especially the willows, the tall sharp leaves of sedge and water plantain growing thick around their trunks. It's like there are eyes watching me from all sides, dark misshapen heads floating frog-like in the water, only the eyes showing, staring. Quicks and bogles and dark things.

I hear something move in the tangle bulrushes and bur reeds just a few feet away. My heart's in my throat, but I move a little closer to see that it's only a bird caught in some kind of net.

Hush, I tell it and move closer.

The bird gets frantic when I put my hand on the netting. It starts to peck at my fingers, but I keep talking softly to it until it finally settles down. The net's a mess of knots and tangles, and I can't work too quickly because I don't want to hurt the bird.

You should leave him be, a voice says, and I turn to find an old woman standing on the path beside me. I don't know where she came from. Every time I lift one of my feet it makes this creepy sucking sound, but I never even heard her approach.

She looks like the wizened old crone in that painting Jilly did for Geordie when he got onto this kick of learning fiddle tunes with the word "hag" in the title: "The Hag in the Kiln," "Old Hag You Have Killed Me," "The Hag With the Money" and god knows how many more.

Just like in the painting, she's wizened and small and bent over and . . . dry. Like kindling, like the pages of an old book. Like she's almost all used up. Hair thin, body thinner. But then you look into her eyes and they're so alive it makes you feel a little dizzy.

Helping such as he will only bring you grief, she says.

I tell her that I can't just leave it.

She looks at me for a long moment, then shrugs. So be it, she says.

I wait a moment, but she doesn't seem to have anything else to say, so I go back to freeing the bird. But now, where a moment ago the netting was a hopeless tangle, it just seems to unknot itself as soon as I lay my hand on it. I'm careful when I put my fingers around the bird and pull it free. I get it out of the tangle and then toss it up in the air. It circles above me, once, twice, three times, cawing. Then it flies away.

It's not safe here, the old lady says then.

I'd forgotten all about her. I get back onto the path, my legs smeared with smelly, dark mud.

What do you mean? I ask her.

When the Moon still walked the sky, she says, why it was safe then. The dark things didn't like her light and fair fell over themselves to get away when she shone. But they're bold now, tricked and trapped her, they have, and no one's safe. Not you, not me. Best we were away.

Trapped her? I repeat like an echo. The moon?

She nods.

Where?

She points to the light I saw earlier, far out in the fens.

They've drowned her under the Black Snag, she says. I will show you.

She takes my hand before I realize what she's doing and pulls me through the rushes and reeds, the mud squishing awfully under my bare feet, but it doesn't seem to bother her at all. She stops when we're at the edge of some open water.

Watch now, she says.

She takes something from the pocket of her apron and tosses it into the water. It's a small stone, a pebble or something, and it enters the water without a sound, without making a ripple. Then the water starts to glow and a picture forms in the dim flickering light.

It's as if we have a bird's-eye view of the fens for a moment, then the focus comes in sharp on the edge of a big still pool, sentried by a huge dead willow. I don't know how I know it, because the light's still poor, but the mud's black around its shore. It almost swallows the pale, wan glow coming up from out of the water.

Drowning, the old woman says. The moon is drowning.

I look down at the image that's formed on the surface and I see a woman floating there. Her hair's all spread out from her, drifting in the water like lily roots. There's a great big stone on top of her torso so she's only visible from the breasts up. Her shoulders are slightly sloped, neck slender, with a swan's curve, but not so long. Her face is in repose, as though she's sleeping, but she's under water, so I know she's dead.

She looks like me.

I turn to the old woman, but before I can say anything, there's movement all around us. Shadows pull away from trees, rise from the stagnant pools, change from vague blotches of darkness into moving shapes, limbed and headed, pale eyes glowing with menace. The old woman pulls me back onto the path.

Wake quick! she cries.

She pinches my arm—hard, sharp. It really hurts. And then I'm sitting up in my bed.

5

"AND DID YOU HAVE A BRUISE ON YOUR ARM FROM where she pinched you?" Jilly asked.

Sophie shook her head and smiled. Trust Jilly. Who else was always looking for the magic in a situation?

"Of course not," she said. "It was just a dream."

"But. . . ."

"Wait," Sophie said. "There's more."

Something suddenly hopped onto the wall between

them and they both started, until they realized it was only a cat.

"Silly puss," Sophie said as it walked toward her and began to butt its head against her arm. She gave it a pat.

6

THE NEXT NIGHT I'M STANDING BY MY WINDOW, LOOKing out at the street, when I hear movement behind me. I turn and it isn't my apartment any more. It looks like the inside of an old barn, heaped up with straw in a big, tidy pile against one wall. There's a lit lantern swinging from a low rafter beam, a dusty but pleasant smell in the air, a cow or maybe a horse making some kind of nickering sound in a stall at the far end.

And there's a guy standing there in the lantern light, a half dozen feet away from me, not doing anything, just looking at me. He's drop-down gorgeous. Not too thin, not too muscle-bound. A friendly, open face with a wide smile and eyes to kill for—long moody lashes, and the eyes are the color of violets. His hair's thick and dark, long in the back with a cowlick hanging down over his brow that I just want to reach out and brush back.

I'm sorry, he says. I didn't mean to startle you.

That's okay, I tell him.

And it is. I think maybe I'm already getting used to all the to-and-froing.

He smiles. My name's Jeck Crow, he says.

I don't know why, but all of a sudden I'm feeling a little weak in the knees. Ah, who am I kidding? I know why.

What are you doing here? he asks.

I tell him I was standing in my apartment, looking for the moon, but then I remembered that I'd just seen the last quarter a few nights ago and I wouldn't be able to see it tonight.

He nods. She's drowning, he says, and then I remember the old woman from last night.

I look out the window and see the fens are out there. It's dark and creepy and I can't see the distant glow of the woman drowned in the pool from here the way I could last night. I shiver and Jeck comes over all concerned. He's picked up a blanket that was hanging from one of the support beams and lays it across my shoulders. He leaves his arm there, to keep it in place, and I don't mind. I just sort of lean into him, like we've always been together. It's weird. I'm feeling drowsy and safe and incredibly aroused, all at the same time.

He looks out the window with me, his hip against mine, the press of his arm on my shoulder a comfortable weight, his body radiating heat.

It used to be, he says, that she would walk every night until she grew so weak that her light was almost failing. Then she would leave the world to go to another, into Faerie, it's said, or at least to a place where the darkness doesn't hide quicks and bogles, and there she would rejuvenate herself for her return. We would have three nights of darkness, when evil owned the night, but then we'd see the glow of her lantern approaching and the haunts would flee her light and we could visit with one another again when the day's work was done.

He leans his head against mine, his voice going dreamy.

I remember my mam saying once, how the Moon lived another life in those three days. How time moves differently in Faerie so that what was a day for us, might be a month for her in that place. He pauses, then adds, I wonder if they miss her in that other world.

I don't know what to say. But then I realize it's not the kind of conversation in which I have to say anything.

He turns to me, head lowering until we're looking straight into each other's eyes. I get lost in the violet, and suddenly I'm in his arms and we're kissing. He guides me, step by sweet step, backward toward that heap of straw. We've got the blanket under us and this time I'm glad I'm wearing the long skirt and peasant blouse again, because they come off so easily.

His hands and his mouth are so gentle and they're all over me like moth wings brushing my skin. I don't know how to describe what he's doing to me. It isn't anything that other lovers haven't done to me before, but the way Jeck does it has me glowing, my skin all warm and tingling with this deep, slow burn starting up between my legs and just firing up along every one of my nerve ends.

I can hear myself making moaning sounds and then he's inside me, his breathing heavy in my ear. All I can feel and smell is him. My hips are grinding against his and we're synced into perfect rhythm, and then I wake up in my own bed and I'm all tangled up in the sheets with my hand between my legs, fingertip right on the spot, moving back and forth and back and forth. . . .

7

SOPHIE FELL SILENT.

"Steamy," Jilly said after a moment.

Sophie gave a little bit of an embarrassed laugh. "You're telling me. I get a little squirmy just thinking about it. And that night—I was still so fired up when I woke that I couldn't think straight. I just went ahead and finished and then lay there afterward, completely spent. I couldn't even move."

"You know a guy named Jack Crow, don't you?" Jilly asked.

"Yeah, he's the one who's got that tattoo parlor down on Palm Street. I went out with him a couple of times, but—" Sophie shrugged, "—you know. Things just didn't work out."

"That's right. You told me that all he ever wanted to do was to give you tattoos."

Sophie shook her head, remembering. "In private places so only he and I would know they were there. Boy."

The cat had fallen asleep, body sprawled out on

Sophie's lap, head pressed tight against her stomach. A deep resonant purr rose up from him. Sophie hoped he didn't have fleas.

"But the guy in my dream was nothing like Jack," she said. "And besides, his name was Jeck."

"What kind of a name *is* that?"

"A dream name."

"So did you see him again—the next night?"

Sophie shook her head. "Though not from lack of interest on my part."

8

THE THIRD NIGHT I FIND MYSELF IN THIS ONE-ROOM cottage out of a fairy tale. You know, there's dried herbs hanging everywhere, a big hearth considering the size of the place, with black iron pots and a kettle sitting on the hearthstones, thick hand-woven rugs underfoot, a small tidy little bed in one corner, a cloak hanging by the door, a rough set of a table and two chairs by a shuttered window.

The old lady is sitting on one of the chairs.

There you are, she says. I looked for you to come last night, but I couldn't find you.

I was with Jeck, I say and then she frowns, but she doesn't say anything.

Do you know him? I ask.

Too well.

Is there something wrong with him?

I'm feeling a little flushed, just talking about him. So far as I'm concerned, there's nothing wrong with him at all.

He's not trustworthy, the old lady finally says.

I shake my head. He seems to be just as upset about the drowned lady as you are. He told me all about her—how she used to go into Faerie.

She never went into Faerie.

Well then, where did she go?

The old lady shakes her head. Crows talk too much, she says, and I can't tell if she means the birds or a whole bunch of Jecks. Thinking about the latter gives me goosebumps. I can barely stay clearheaded around Jeck; a whole crowd of him would probably overload my circuits and leave me lying on the floor like a little pool of jelly.

I don't tell the old lady any of this. Jeck inspired confidences, as much as sensuality; she does neither.

Will you help us? she says instead.

I sit down at the table with her and ask, Help with what?

The Moon, she says.

I shake my head. I don't understand. You mean the drowned lady in the pool?

Drowned, the old lady says, but not dead. Not yet.

I start to argue the point, but then realize where I am. It's a dream and anything can happen, right?

It needs you to break the bogles' spell, the old lady goes on.

Me? But—

Tomorrow night, go to sleep with a stone in your mouth and a hazel twig in your hands. Now mayhap, you'll find yourself back here, mayhap with your crow, but guard you don't say a word, not one word. Go out into the fen until you find a coffin, and on that coffin a candle, and then look sideways and you'll see that you're in the place I showed you yesternight.

She falls silent.

And then what am I supposed to do? I ask.

What needs to be done.

But—

I'm tired, she says.

She waves her hand at me and I'm back in my own bed again.

9

"AND SO?" JILLY ASKED. "DID YOU DO IT?"

"Would you have?"

"In a moment," Jilly said. She sidled closer along the wall until she was right beside Sophie and peered into her friend's face. "Oh, don't tell me you didn't do it. Don't tell me that's the whole story."

"The whole thing just seemed silly," Sophie said.

"Oh, please!"

"Well, it did. It was all too oblique and riddlish. I know it was just a dream, so that it didn't have to make sense, but there was so much of a coherence to a lot of it that when it did get incomprehensible, it just didn't seem . . . oh, I don't know. Didn't seem fair, I suppose."

"But you *did* do it?"

Sophie finally relented.

"Yes," she said.

10

I GO TO BED WITH A SMALL, SMOOTH STONE IN MY MOUTH and have the hardest time getting to sleep because I'm sure I'm going to swallow it during the night and choke. And I have the hazel twig as well, though I don't know what help either of them is going to be.

Hazel twig to ward you from quicks and bogles, I hear Jeck say. And the stone to remind you of your own world, of the difference between waking and dream, else you might find yourself sharing the Moon's fate.

We're standing on a sort of grassy knoll, an island of semisolid ground, but the footing's still spongy. I start to say hello, but he puts his finger to his lips.

She's old, is Granny Weather, he says, and cranky, too, but there's more magic in one of her toenails than most of us will find in a lifetime.

I never really thought about his voice before. It's like velvet, soft and smooth, but not effeminate. It's too resonant for that.

He puts his hands on my shoulders and I feel like

melting. I close my eyes, lift my face to his, but he turns me around until I'm facing away from him. He cups his hands around my breasts and kisses me on the nape of my neck. I lean back against him, but he lifts his mouth to my ear.

You must go, he says softly, his breath tickling the inside of my ear. Into the fens.

I pull free from his embrace and face him. I start to say, Why me? Why do I have to go alone? But before I can get a word out he has his hand across my mouth.

Trust Granny Weather, he says. And trust me. This is something only you can do. Whether you do it or not is your choice. But if you mean to try tonight, you mustn't speak. You must go out into the fens and find her. They will tempt you and torment you, but you must ignore them, else they'll have you drowning too, under the Black Snag.

I look at him and I know he can see the need I have for him, because in his eyes I can see the same need for me reflected in their violet depths.

I will wait for you, he says. If I can.

I don't like the sound of that. I don't like the sound of any of it, but I tell myself again, it's just a dream, so I finally nod. I start to turn away, but he catches hold of me for a last moment and kisses me. There's a hot rush of tongues touching, arms tight around each other, before he finally steps back.

I love the strength of you, he says.

I don't want to go, I want to change the rules of the dream. But I get this feeling that if I do, if I change one thing, everything'll change, and maybe he won't even exist in whatever comes along to replace it. So I lift my hand and run it along the side of his face. I take a long last drink of those deep violet eyes that just want to swallow me, then I get brave and turn away again.

And this time I go into the fens.

I'm nervous, but I guess that goes without saying. I look back but I can't see Jeck anymore. I can just feel I'm being watched, and it's not by him. I clutch my little hazel twig tighter, roll the stone around from one side of my mouth to the other, and keep going.

It's not easy. I have to test each step to make sure I'm not just going to sink away forever into the muck. I start thinking of what you hear about dreams, how if you die in a dream, you die for real, that's why you always wake up just in time. Except for those people who die in their sleep, I guess.

I don't know how long I'm slogging through the muck. My arms and legs have dozens of little nicks and cuts—you never think of how sharp the edge of a reed can be until your skin slides across one. It's like a paper cut, sharp and quick, and it stings like hell. I don't suppose all the muck's doing the cuts much good either. The only thing I can be happy about is that there aren't any bugs.

Actually, there doesn't seem to be the sense of anything living at all in the fens, just me, on my own. But I know I'm not alone. It's like a word sitting on the tip of your tongue. I can't see or hear or sense anything, but I'm being watched.

I think of Jeck and Granny Weather, of what they say the darkness hides. Quicks and bogles and haunts.

After a while I almost forget what I'm doing out here. I'm just stumbling along with a feeling of dread hanging over me that won't go away. Bogbean and water mint leaves feel like cold, wet fingers sliding along my legs. I hear the occasional flutter of wings, and sometimes a deep kind of sighing moan, but I never see anything.

I'm just about played out when suddenly I come upon this tall rock under the biggest crack willow I've seen so far. The tree's dead, drooping leafless branches into the still water at a slant, the mud's all black underfoot, the marsh is, if anything, even quieter here, expectant almost, and I get the feeling like something—some*things* are closing in all around me.

I start to walk across the dark mud to the other side of the rock until I hit a certain vantage point. I stop when I can see that it's shaped like a big strange coffin, and I remember what Granny Weather told me. I look for the candle a see a tiny light flickering at the very top of the black stone, right where it's pushed up and snagged among the dangling branches of the dead willow. It's no brighter than a firefly's glow, but it burns steady.

I do what Granny Weather told me and look around myself using my peripheral vision. I don't see anything at first, but as I slowly turn toward the water, I catch just a hint of a glow. I stop and then I wonder what to do. Is it still going to be there if I turn to face it?

Eventually, I move sideways toward it, always keeping it in the corner of my eye. The closer I get, the brighter it starts to glow, until I'm standing hip deep in the cold water, the mud sucking at my feet, and it's all around me, this dim eerie glowing. I look down into the water and I see my own face reflected back at me, but then I realize that it's not me I'm seeing, it's the drowned woman, the moon, trapped under the stone.

I stick my hazel twig down the bodice of my blouse and reach into the water. I have to bend down, the dark water licking at my shoulders and chin and smelling something awful, but I finally touch the woman's shoulder. Her skin's warm against my fingers, and for some reason that makes me feel braver. I get a grip with one hand on her shoulder, then the other, and give a pull.

Nothing budges.

I try some more, moving a little deeper into the water. Finally I plunge my head under and get a really good hold, but she simply won't move. The rock's got her pressed down tight, and the willow's got the rock snagged, and dream or no dream, I'm not some kind of superwoman. I'm only so strong and I have to breathe.

I come up spluttering and choking on the foul water.

And then I hear the laughter.

I look up and there's these things all around the edge of the pool. Quicks and bogles and small monsters. All eyes and teeth and spindly black limbs and crooked hands with too many joints to the fingers. The tree is full of crows and their cawing adds to the mocking hubbub of sound.

First got one, now got two, a pair of voices chant. Boil her up in a tiddy stew.

I'm starting to shiver—not just because I'm scared, which I am, but because the water's so damn cold. The haunts just keep on laughing and making up these creepy little rhymes that mostly have to do with little stews and barbecues. And then suddenly, they all fall silent and these three figures come swinging down from the willow's boughs.

I don't know where they came from, they're just there all of a sudden. These aren't haunts, nor quicks nor bogles. They're men and they look all too familiar.

Ask for anything, one of them says, and it will be yours.

It's Jeck, I realize. Jeck talking to me, except the voice

doesn't sound right. But it looks just like him. All three look like him.

I remember Granny Weather telling me that Jeck was untrustworthy, but then Jeck told me to trust her. And to trust him. Looking at these three Jecks, I don't know what to think anymore. My head starts to hurt and I just wish I could wake up.

You need only tell us what it is you want, one of the Jecks says, and we will give it to you. There should be no enmity between us. The woman is drowned. She is dead. You have come too late. There is nothing you can do for her now. But you can do something for yourself. Let us gift you with your heart's desire.

My heart's desire, I think.

I tell myself, again, it's just a dream, but I can't help the way I start thinking about what I'd ask for if I could really have anything I wanted, anything at all.

I look down into the water at the drowned woman and I think about my dad. He never liked to talk about my mother. It's like she was just a dream, he said once.

And maybe she was, I find myself thinking as my gaze goes down into the water and I study the features of the drowned woman who looks so much like me. Maybe she was the Moon in this world and she came to ours to rejuvenate, but when it was time for her to go back, she didn't want to leave because she loved me and dad too much. Except she didn't have a choice.

So when she returned, she was weaker, instead of stronger like she was supposed to be, because she was so sad. And that's how the quicks and the bogles trapped her.

I laugh then. What I'm making up, as I stand here

waist deep in smelly dream water, is the classic abandoned child's scenario. They always figure that there was just a mix-up, that one day their real parents are going to show up and take them away to some place where everything's magical and loving and perfect.

I used to feel real guilty about my mother leaving us—that's something else that happens when you're just a kid in that kind of a situation. You just automatically feel guilty when something bad happens, like it's got to be your fault. But I got older. I learned to deal with it. I learned that I was a good person, that it hadn't been my fault, that my dad was a good person, too, and it wasn't his fault either.

I'd still like to know why my mother left us, but I came to understand that whatever the reasons were for her going, they had to do with her, not with us. Just like I know this is only a dream and the drowned woman might look like me, but that's just something I'm projecting onto her. I *want* her to be my mother. I want her having abandoned me and dad not to have been her fault either. I want to come to her rescue and bring us all back together again.

Except it isn't going to happen. Pretend and real just don't mix.

But it's tempting all the same. It's tempting to let it all play out. I know the haunts just want me to talk so that they can trap me as well, that they wouldn't follow through on any promise they made, but this is *my* dream. I can *make* them keep to their promise. All I have to do is say what I want.

And then I understand that it's all real after all. Not real in the sense that I can be physically harmed in this place, but real in that if I make a selfish choice, even if it's just in a dream, I'll still have to live with the fact of it when I wake up. It doesn't matter that I'm dreaming, I'll *still* have done it.

What the bogles are offering is my heart's desire, if I just leave the Moon to drown. But if I do that, I'm responsible for her death. She might not be real, but it doesn't change anything at all. It'll still mean that I'm willing to let someone die, just so I can have my own way.

I suck on the stone and move it back and forth from one cheek to the other. I reach down into my wet bodice and pluck out the hazel twig from where it got pushed down between my breasts. I lift a hand to my hair and brush it back from my face and then I look at those sham copies of my Jeck Crow and I smile at them.

My dream, I think. What I say goes.

I don't know if it's going to work, but I'm fed up with having everyone else decide what happens in my dream. I turn to the stone and I put my hands on it, the hazel twig sticking out between the fingers of my right hand, and I give the stone a shove. There's this great big outcry among the quicks and bogles and haunts as the stone starts to topple over. I look down at the drowned woman and I see her eyes open, I see her smile, but then there's too much light and I'm blinded.

When my vision finally clears, I'm alone by the pool. There's a big, fat, full moon hanging in the sky, making the fens almost as bright as day. They've all fled, the monsters, the quicks and bogles and things. The dead willow's still full of crows, but as soon as I look up, they lift from the tree in an explosion of dark wings, a circling murder, cawing and crying, until they finally go away. The stone's lying on its side, half in the water, half out.

And I'm still dreaming.

I'm standing here, up to my waist in the smelly water, with a hazel twig in my hand and a stone in my mouth, and I stare up at that big full moon until it seems I can feel her light just singing through my veins. For a moment it's like being back in the barn with Jeck, I'm just on fire, but its a different kind of fire, it burns away the darknesses that have gotten lodged in me over the years, just like they get lodged in everybody, and just for that moment, I'm solid light, innocent and newborn, a burning Midsummer fire in the shape of a woman.

And then I wake up, back home again.

I lie there in my bed and look out the window, but it's still the dark of the moon in our world. The streets are quiet outside, there's a hush over the whole city, and I'm lying here with a hazel twig in my hand, a stone in my mouth, pushed up into one cheek, and a warm, burning glow deep inside.

I sit up and spit the stone out into my hand. I walk over to the window. I'm not in some magical dream now; I'm in the real world. I know the lighted moon glows with light borrowed from the sun. That she's still out there in the dark of the moon, we just can't see her tonight because the earth is between her and the sun.

Or maybe she's gone into some other world, to replenish her lantern before she begins her nightly trek across the sky once more.

I feel like I've learned something, but I'm not sure what. I'm not sure what any of it means.

11

"HOW CAN YOU SAY THAT?" JILLY SAID. "GOD, SOPHIE, it's so obvious. She really *was* your mother and you really *did* save her. As for Jeck, he was the bird you rescued in your first dream. Jeck *Crow*—don't you get it? One of the bad guys, only you won him over with an act of kindness. It all makes perfect sense."

Sophie slowly shook her head. "I suppose I'd like to believe that, too," she said, "but what we want and what really is aren't always the same thing."

"But what about Jeck? He'll be waiting for you. And Granny Weather? They both knew you were the Moon's daughter all along. It all means something."

Sophie sighed. She stroked the sleeping cat on her lap, imagining for a moment that it was the soft dark curls of a crow that could be a man, in a land that only existed in her dreams.

"I guess," she said, "it means I need a new boyfriend."

12

JILLY'S A REAL SWEETHEART, AND I LOVE HER DEARLY, but she's naive in some ways. Or maybe it's just that she wants to play the ingenue. She's always so ready to believe anything that anyone tells her, so long as it's magical.

Well, I believe in magic, too, but it's the magic that can turn a caterpillar into a butterfly, the natural wonder and beauty of the world that's all around me. I can't believe in some dreamland being real. I can't believe what Jilly now insists is true: that I've got faerie blood, because I'm the daughter of the Moon.

Though I have to admit that I'd like to.

I never do get to sleep that night. I prowl around the apartment, drinking coffee to keep me awake. I'm afraid to go to sleep, afraid I'll dream and that it'll all be real.

Or maybe that it won't.

When it starts to get light, I take a long cold shower, because I've been thinking about Jeck again. I guess if my making the wrong decision in a dream would've had ramifications in the waking world, then there's no reason that a rampaging libido shouldn't carry over as well.

I get dressed in some old clothes I haven't worn in years, just to try to recapture a more innocent time. White blouse, faded jeans, and hightops with this smoking jacket overtop that used to belong to my dad. It's made of burgundy velvet with black satin lapels. A black hat, with a flat top and a bit of a curl to its brim, completes the picture.

I look in the mirror, and I feel like I'm auditioning to be a stage magician's assistant, but I don't much care.

As soon as the hour gets civilized, I head over to Christy Riddell's house. I'm knocking on his door at nine o'clock, but when he comes to let me in, he's all sleepy-eyed and disheveled and I realize that I should've given him another couple of hours. Too late for that now.

I just come right out with it. I tell him that Jilly said he knew all about lucid dreaming and what I want to know is, is any of it real—the place you dream of, the people you meet there?

He stands there in the doorway, blinking like an owl, but I guess he's used to stranger things, because after a moment he leans against the door jamb and asks me what I know about consensual reality.

It's where everything that we see around us only exists because we all agree it does, I say.

Well, maybe it's the same in a dream, he replies. If everyone in the dream agrees that what's around them is real, then why shouldn't it be?

I want to ask him about what my dad had to say about dreams trying to escape into the waking world, but I decide I've already pushed my luck.

Thanks, I say.

He gives me a funny look. That's it? he asks.

I'll explain it some other time, I tell him.

Please do, he says without a whole lot of enthusiasm, then goes back inside.

When I get home, I go and lie down on the old sofa that's out on my balcony. I close my eyes. I'm still not so sure about any of this, but I figure it can't hurt to see if Jeck and I can't find ourselves one of those happily-ever-afters with which fairy tales usually end.

Who knows? Maybe I really am the daughter of the Moon. If not here, then someplace.

The Frog Prince

Gahan Wilson

In addition to being a fine cartoonist of the macabre, Gahan Wilson has written some memorable stories. One of my favorites is his take-off of Lewis Carroll's "The Walrus and the Carpenter"—"The Sea Was Wet as Wet Can Be." Here he presents a perfectly appropriate version of "The Frog Prince," inspired perhaps by Bruno Bettelheim's use of Freudian psychoanalysis of fairy tales.

The Frog Prince

"AH, SO, AGAIN THE SAME DREAM," SIGHED DOCTOR Neiman, without any trace of accusation, of course, making a note among many other notes in his notebook. "Always the same dream."

Frog rolled the tiniest bit to the right on the couch, selecting another part of the ceiling to look at, the part with the crack which ran out of the edging of plaster flowers like a questing tendril, perhaps his favorite part.

He was aware that the continuing emanation of sweat from his armpits was once again soaking itself into the twin bunching of his shirt underneath the tweed jacket, making the material into two hard, swelling, highly uncomfortable lumps.

There was so much moisture in him! Saliva, as always, had nearly filled his mouth and he would soon have to swallow, silently, as silently as possible, since Doctor Neiman often incorporated Frog's frequent gulpings into his little analytical summations near the ends of their sessions. Frog always felt particularly vulnerable when it came to gulpings. With reason, of course, with reason.

And then there was the constant wetness in his eyes which would increase and brim and finally spill over the edges of his heavy, puffy lids and roll down his round, pale cheeks each and every time he spoke or thought of sad or moving things, which was often. Not to mention the constant moisture on his palms which turned them into little, pale suction cups and made them cling alarmingly to the soft leather of the couch, or the ever renewing dampness of his socks so that the unending process of evaporation taking place continued to bring uncomfortable and unnerving coolness to the wide bottoms of his feet.

Sometimes, lying there, he wondered if he was making visible rivulets and pools beneath himself on the surface of the couch. Sometimes he wondered if it had got so bad it was running off the couch's sides and darkening the thick Oriental carpet, and that only Doctor Neiman's professional politeness was preventing him from making some totally understandable comment about the potential damage this flood of sweat and tears and drool—yes, even drool!—represented to his property.

Again and again he would turn on the couch—always just the tiniest little bit—and think these thoughts, and each time he moved he would anticipate and listen, with repressed winces, for the squishings and squelchings which he never heard, thank God!

But when he finally rose to leave at the end of his

session and was not able to resist the impulse to look back down at the couch and see if the damage done by the flood of moisture from his round body was anywhere near as bad as his imagination conjured, he would observe, with perhaps the smallest wisp of disappointment, that the couch had not been reduced to a sodden, dripping mass, that it seemed startlingly dry, and that the only visible trace of all that steady gushing seemed to be a faint dampness on the disposable paper cover on the pillow—a dim round spot representing his head with a short, wide, vertical tail below it representing his neck, the whole thing vaguely suggesting a sun or moon reflected in water more or less as it would be done if painted by Edward Munch.

"The king in your dream," Doctor Neiman said, frowning and making another note, perhaps underlining it. "You say you feel he is your father?"

His father, yes! his father. Holding him high in his heavy, hard metal gauntlets, holding him over the battlements of the topmost tower so they could look down upon their kingdom together and see the glinting of gold, the long banners flapping, the dust rising from the wide earth road and settling on the gaudy wrappings of the horses; holding him high so he could clearly hear the trumpets, the loving cheers from the crowd, the drumbeats! The king had been, indeed, his father.

But then had come the spell, and the separation, and the desperate, unsuccessful hunting which had once come so close, so terribly close that he had felt the water shaking, the whole pool trembling, as the hooves pounded the soft earth of its round shore, could even see the ripples caused by nearness of the trumpets' high, brassy notes.

Worst of all had been the horribly brief glimpse of a rider larger than all the others, bound in golden armor, wearing a long, billowing, red cape, and calling out his name over and over in a cracked, frantic lion's roar.

Not that he hadn't loved the pool, loved the modulations of its greenness as he swam this way and that underwater; loved digging into the cool, soft, receiving blackness of its bottom mud; loved to squat waiting on the smooth warmth of its lily pads, letting the hunger lazily grow and watching the buzzing bugs circle overhead, their wings sparkling in the sunlight, until they came too close.

It was a warm July day and he had fed particularly well and was swimming just below the surface with wide, easy strokes when he saw a great, bright pinkness shimmering ahead of him through the water, a blur of color so dazzling that his limbs stopped moving where they were and only his momentum pushed him through the water, closer to that vast glowing, in a dreamy, hypnotized, forward drifting.

The wide, round, golden bulging of his eyes with their long black slits strained past aching to absorb the sight of this gorgeousness as it came nearer and nearer, and he sank into a trance far, far deeper than his tiny pond.

Then the pinkness moved, faceted by the water into an enormous, glittering wall of multitudinous shades of rose and pale reds, and he realized how huge, how tremendous the thing that made it must be, and backed away speedily, sculling to the security of the far end of the pond and a cluster of willow roots where he cowered behind the slimy stems a moment, gathering himself and letting his heart slow so its pounding didn't frighten him quite so much.

But the pinkness continued to fascinate him absolutely, and he found himself slowly and carefully raising his head, keeping his eyes the highest part of him until they gently and very quietly broke the surface of the water and stared directly at a beautiful woman kneeling by the side of the pond and smiling intently into its mysteries.

The pinkness had been her face and neck and shoulders and arms leaning over the surface of his pond. The rest of her was clad in a long, green dress flecked with gold and had blended with the water. Her hair was a piled mass of gold and Frog knew he must have taken it for the sun.

He realized, then and there, that he would love her always and forever, hopelessly and beyond redemption. Clinging to the smooth curving of a willow root with his tiny, emerald forefeet, he gazed at her with a helpless wonder for long, uncounted minutes. His ordinarily unnoticed blood stirred strangely within and seemed to warm him and he almost half believed that he could sense it taking on a redness in his veins.

It began to dawn on him, watching her make one precious, unforgettable, irreplaceable move of her body after another, that he had been alone in his quiet little pond for a long, long while. He observed her slim, pale, perfect fingers trail along the surface of the water and was astonished to realize how far ago that day of hoof poundings and harsh trumpet blasts and hoarse shoutings of his name must have been. He watched her darling arm straighten as she stretched forward to gently nudge a floating leaf and was amazed to see how faint and dim and blurred with time the recollections of his castle and his father's face had grown in his mind.

With an incredible effort, he tore his eyes from his

beloved and let himself slide noiselessly down the willow root to the soft, yielding mud at the bottom of the pond, and then he walked on the tips of his toes over the vagueness of the mud's dim, uncertain surface until he came to a little heap of algae-covered rocks. He moved the stones gently to one side and then carefully dug into the bit of mud which they had marked. At first his gropings only found deeper mud, and a terrible anxiety swept through him, but then he clawed just a little further and felt a flood of enormous relief when the pale little pads on the ends of his front feet made contact with a smooth, hard, curving surface.

He reached down, and when all his green digits were curled around the object hidden under the mud, he pulled mightily with every bit of strength in his stout little body and at last, with a wet sucking and a dark, swirling cloud of mud, he pulled out his treasure.

It was a lovely, great ruby carved beautifully into the sharp of a heart, and as he gently stroked the mud from its surface, it glowed brightly, even here, in the deepest, darkest corner of the pond. It had stayed with him, he had no idea why or how, through his losses and transformations, and through all the endless aeons which had passed over him since.

He had always suspected there was something wonderful and magical about it, it had always been a great source of hope, and now, holding it with a clear plan forming easily and effortlessly in his mind, he was sure of it. He knew, in the deepest part of his speckled green body, that he and it had been waiting together in this lonely pool all along, through all these stretching years, for just this moment.

He fondled it, clutched it to his breast, hugged it fiercely, and then, gripping it as firmly as he could with all his might in both his tiny front feet, he kicked his way up through the whole height of the pond to the underside of a large lily pad.

He peered carefully and cautiously out from under the pad, and when he was sure his beloved's gaze was thoroughly absorbed elsewhere, he climbed over the pad's edge and sat on its exact center. He arranged his small body carefully, folding the roundness of his legs neatly along his sides, and spreading the toes in order to show off their webbing to its best advantage. Then, lifting his head just so in order that the curve of the bulge of flesh under his chin might echo exactly the swelling of his belly in the classic frog mode, he held the heart-shaped ruby toward her, and waited patiently, breathing tiny, anxious breaths and gazing at her with his wide, adoring eyes.

She turned and saw him and at first she only smiled affectionately with a slow parting of her lovely red lips at the sight of the little fat, green creature, but then a look of curiosity grew in her eyes as she noticed the heart-shaped ruby and the oddly human way he held it, and then her curiosity in turn changed to wonder when she saw the tiny, golden crown which rested on the flat, green-speckled top of Frog's head.

Very carefully, doing all as gracefully as he possibly could, Frog bent and placed the ruby on the pad before him. Then he made a formal little bow, stepped back, and waited again.

The ruby glistened on the lily pad, looking more like a drop of liquid than a solid thing. The beloved reached out in its direction, moving gently, keeping her eyes on Frog to make sure she was not startling him, and touched the ruby cautiously with the tip of the softly curving, delicately pink nail of her forefinger. Only after she saw Frog solemnly blink his bulging, golden eyes and nod approvingly did she take hold of the ruby between her finger and thumb and lift it from the leaf's waxy surface.

She held it up before her face, turning it as she did so, and her lovely eyes widened as she watched the sun shine through its heart-shaped redness in endlessly wonderful ways. Frog watched from his lily pad, confident that the magic would work on its own, that his salvation was approaching, that this endless time of solitude was coming to its end, and that all of it had served a purpose.

Eventually her gaze traveled slowly from the ruby to the little frog, and a look of understanding crossed her face. She took the heart-shaped jewel between her fingertips and pressed it to the center of her chest, just above the parting of her breasts, and as she and Frog watched together, it sank gently into her flesh.

She sat a moment longer, her fingers resting quietly over her beating heart, and then she leaned forward and gathered Frog's small body up in her sweet hands, and lifted him closer and closer to the full, round, swelling of the softness of her lips.

"And this is where you wake up," sighed Doctor Neiman, making yet another note in his little book. "Always, this is where you wake up."

Frog turned his head to the wall and felt the burning tears cascading from his bulging eyes, felt them scald his puffy cheeks, sear the whole wide gape of his lips, and tumble from him onto the disposable paper cover of the pillow on the couch.

"Yes," he croaked. "Always."

Stalking Beans

Nancy Kress

Nancy Kress has authored six novels, including a fantasy called The Prince of Morning Bells *(her first) and, most recently, the science fictional* Brain Rose. *She has also written numerous short stories, winning the 1985 Nebula Award for "Out of All Them Bright Stars," and the 1991 Nebula Award for her novella "Beggars in Spain."*

It has always seemed unfair that in the original tale of Jack and the Beanstalk, Jack—thief and betrayer—got away scot-free. So Kress's version, with an older, bitter "Jack," is a more satisfying story on several levels.

Stalking Beans

SOMETIMES I TRY TO MAKE MY WIFE ANGRY. I CLUMP in from the dairy in boots fouled by cow dung; I let the hearth fire die; I spill greasy mutton on the fresh cloth Annie insists on laying each night as if we were still gentry and not the peasants we have become. I wipe my nose with the back of my hand, in imitation of our neighbors. I get drunk at the alehouse. I stay away all night.

It's like fighting a pillow. All give, and feathers everywhere. Annie's pretty face flutters into wispy dismay, followed by wispy forgiveness. "Oh, Jack, I understand!" she cries and falls on my neck, her curls—that but for me would be bound in a fashionable coif—filling my mouth. "I know how hard our fall in the world is for you!" Never a word about how hard it is for her. Never a word of anger. Never the accusation,

You are to blame. Always, she invites me to sink into her understanding, to lie muffled in it as in the soft beds we once owned, to be soundlessly absorbed.

Sometimes it takes every fiber of my muscles not to hit her.

Only when, drunk, I traded our best cow to a dwarf for a sack of beans did Annie show a flash of the anger she should feel by right. "You . . . did . . . what?" she said, very deliberately. Her pale eyes sparkled and her thin, tense body relaxed for one glorious moment into anger. I took a step toward her and Annie, misunderstanding, cried, "Keep away from me!" She looked wildly around, and her eye fell on the shelf with our one remaining book, bound in red leather and edged with gold. She seized it and threw it at me. She missed. It fell into the fire, and the dry pages blazed with energy.

But she couldn't make it last. A second later her shoulders drooped and she stared at the fire with stricken eyes. "Oh, Jack—I'm sorry! The book was worth more than the cow!" Then she was on my neck, sobbing. "Oh, Jack, I understand, I *do,* I know your pride has been so badly injured by all this, I want to be a good wife to you and understand . . ." Her hair settled into my mouth, over my nose.

Desperate, I said, "I cast away the beans in the forest, and vomited over them!"

"Oh, Jack, I understand! It's not your fault! You couldn't help what happened!"

What kind of man can never help what happens to him?

I can't bring myself to touch her body, even by chance. When one of us rolls toward the center of the sagging mattress, I jerk away, as if touched by rot. In the darkest part of the night, when the fire has gone out, I hear her sobbing, muffled by the thin pillow that is the best, thanks to my stupidity, we can now afford.

I get out of bed and stumble, torchless, into the woods. There is no moon, no stars. The trees loom around me like unseen giants, breathing in the blackness. It doesn't matter. My feet don't fail me. I know exactly where I'm going.

She is taller than I am by perhaps a foot, and outweighs me by thirty pounds. Her shoes are held together with gummy string, not because she doesn't have better—the closet is filled with gold slippers, fine calfskin boots, red-heeled shoes with silver bows—but because this pair is comfortable, and damn how they look. There is a food stain on her robe, which is knotted loosely around her waist. Her thick blond hair is a snarl. She yawns in my face.

"Damn, Jack, I didn't expect you tonight."

"Is he here?"

She makes a mocking face and laughs. "No. And now that *you're* here, you may as well come in as not. What did you do, tumble down the beanstalk? You look like a dirty urchin." She gazes at me, amused. I always amuse her. Her amusement wakes her a little more, and then her gaze sharpens. She slides one hand inside her robe. "Since he's not here . . ." She reaches for me.

It's always like this. She is greedy in bed, frank, and direct. I am an instrument of her pleasure, as she is of mine, and beyond that she asks nothing. Her huge breasts move beneath my hands, and she moans in that open pleasure that never loses its edge of mockery. I ease into her and, to prolong the moment, say, "What would you do if I never climbed the beanstalk again?"

She says promptly, "Hire another wretched dwarf to

stalk another drunken bull." She laughs. "Do you think you're irreplaceable, Jack?"

"No," I say, smiling, and thrust into her hard enough to please us both. She laughs again, her attention completely on her own sensations. Afterwards, she'll fall asleep, not knowing or caring when I leave. I'll wrestle open the enormous bolted door, bang it shut, clump across the terrace to the clouds. It won't matter how much noise I make; she never wakes.

The morning air this high up is cool and delicious. The bean leaves rustle against my face. A bird wheels by, its wings outstretched in a lazy glide, its black eyes bright with successful hunting, free of the pull of the earth.

Annie is crying in the bedroom of our cottage. I'm not supposed to know this, since she thinks I'm still at market with this week's eggs and honey. I poke at the fire, adding up weeks in my head. They make the right sum. Annie must have her monthly flow again, our hopes for a child once more bleeding out between her legs.

I creep quietly out of the cottage to the dairy and sit heavily on a churning cask. I should go to her. I should take her in my arms and reassure her, tell her that maybe next month . . . But I can't go to her like this. The edge of my own disappointment is too sharp; it would cut us both. I sit on the churning cask until the two remaining cows low plaintively outside their byre.

Inside the cottage Annie has lit the candles. She flies around the dingy room, smiling brightly. "Stew tonight, Jack! Your favorite!" She starts to sing, her voice straining on the high notes, her eyes shining determinedly, her thin shoulders rigid as glass.

* * *

The tax collector stands in my dairy, cleaning his fingernails with a jeweled dagger. I recognize the dagger. It once belonged to my father. Lord Randall must have given it to this bloated cock's comb for a gift, in return for his useful services. The tax collector looks around my cottage.

"Where is that book you used to have on that wooden shelf, Jack?"

Once he would never have dared address me so. Once he would have said "Master John." Once. "Gone," I say shortly. "One less thing for you to tax."

He laughs. "You've still luxury enough here, compared to your neighbors. The land tax has gone up again, Jack. You owe three gold pieces instead of two. Such is the burden of the yeomanry."

I don't answer. He finishes with his nails and sheathes the dagger. In his fat face his eyes are as shiny as a bird of prey. "By Thursday next, Jack. Just bring it to the castle." He smiles. "You know where it is."

Annie has appeared in the doorway behind us. If he says to her, as he did last time, "Farewell, pretty Nan," I will strike him. But he bustles out silently, and Annie pulls aside her faded skirts to let him pass. The skirts wouldn't soil his stolen finery; Annie has washed and turned and mended the coarse material until her arms ache with exhaustion and her skin bleeds with needle pricks. She turns to watch the tax collector go, and for one heart-stopping moment her body dips and I think she's going to drop him a mocking, insolent curtsy. But instead she straightens and turns to me.

"It's all right, Jack! It wasn't your fault! I understand!"

Her arms are around my neck, her hair muffling my breath.

* * *

Her name is Maria. Seven times I have climbed the beanstalk, and I've only just learned it. "Why did you need to know it before?" Maria said lazily. "You're not exactly carrying my favor into battle." She laughs her mocking laugh, the low chuckle that says, *This is not important, but it's amusing nonetheless.*

I love her laugh.

"If I know your name is Maria," I argue lightheartedly, "I can call you that when I demand something. I could say, to give an instance, 'Maria, rub my back.' 'Maria, take off your shift.' "

"And do you wish me to take off my shift?"

"It's already off," I say, and she laughs and rolls over on her stomach, her enormous breasts falling forward onto the rumpled sheets. For once she hasn't fallen asleep. On the bedside table is a half-eaten orange, the skin dried and wrinkled as if it had been there several days. Maria yawns mockingly.

"Shall I put my shift back on so you can take it off again?"

"Do you want to?"

"I don't mind," she says, which is her answer to almost anything. She puts a hand on me, and a shudder of pleasure pierces from groin to brain. Maria laughs.

"What an amorous poppet you are."

"And how good you are to be amorous with, *lux vitae,* Maria," I tell her. But even then she doesn't ask me my other name, just as she has never asked my circumstances. Does it strike her as odd that a man dressed like a peasant can flatter her in Latin?

She reaches for her shift, puts it on, and then proceeds to take it off so slowly, so teasingly, lifting a corner over one thigh and lowering a strap off one shoulder, bunching the cloth between her legs, mocking me from under lowered lashes, that I can barely keep my hands off her until she's ready. Not even when I was who I was, before, not even then had I ever known a woman so skilled in those arts of the body that are really the arts of the mind. When at long last we are sated again, and she is drifting off to sleep, I impulsively say to her, "You are extraordinary in bed. I wish I could take you back down with me."

Immediately a cold paralysis runs over my spine. Now I've done it. Now will come the start of feminine hope, the fumblingly hidden gleam of possession, the earnest, whispered half-promise designed to elicit promises from me: *Oh, do you think someday we actually might be together . . .*

I should know better. Instead, Maria gives me her mocking smile, rich with satisfaction. "Ah, but that would spoil everything. One always does most stylishly the things one cares nothing about. Don't you even know that, you ignorant boy?"

In another moment she's asleep.

I get out of her bed and start for the door. But in the corridor I stop.

I have never explored the rest of the castle. What I wanted—the careless mocking smile, the voluptuous body, the instant dismissive sleep—were in this room, the room I stumbled into on my first journey. But now I walk down the stone passageway and open a second door.

And am staggered.

He must be gargantuan, different from Maria not just in degree but in kind, as she is not from me. The bed stretches the length of my father's tiltyard. An oaken chest could serve for my cow byre. How can Maria, lying in that enormous bed, be large enough to . . . I don't want to know. Whatever they do, it certainly hasn't soured her for bedding.

I have already turned to leave when I catch the glint of gold beneath the bed.

There is a pile of coins—not on his scale, but on mine. Human coins. They look small there, unimportant, and maybe that is why I only take three. Or maybe it's from shame, having already taken from him so much else that he doesn't know about. Or maybe it's neither of these things, but only my sense of justice: I only need three to pay the tax collector. Justice is one of those things that separate me from such as Lord Randall. I am still an honorable man.

As I leave the room, I hear a harp begin to play, light and mocking as Maria's laugh.

Annie is in the yard beside her washpot, stirring hard. Steam rises in smelly clouds. All over the bushes and lines and the rough-hewn wooden bench I made for her are clothes I don't recognize: tunics and leggings and shifts too fine for our neighbors but not fine enough for Lord Randall and his thieving sons. Annie looks up, pushes her damp hair off her forehead, and smiles through exhaustion.

"What are you doing? Who do these things belong to?" I thunder at her.

Her smile disappears. "To the servants at the castle. I took them to wash. If I can do eight pots every day I can earn—"

"You'll earn nothing!" I shout. "Do you think I want my wife to be a washerwoman! *You,* who should have been Lady Anne? How much do you think you can make me bear?"

Annie starts to cry. I hurl the three gold coins at her feet, and my arm remembers casting away the beans in the forest, which only increases my rage. "Here's the tax money! Why did you once again—*once again,* Annie—assume that I'm not man enough to get it? That only *you* possess will enough to save us?"

I don't think she hears me; she's crying too loud. But then Annie stoops and picks up the coins. She bites down on one, and her tears stop. She looks at me, smiles tremulously, and takes a step forward. "Oh, Jack, you earned the money for us—you're so *good*!"

Her face glows with light. She understands with her whole tense, determined body how good a man I am.

Annie returns the clothing to its owners. Before she does, I rub the unwashed ones with dirt. I don't want anybody paying her anything, she who should be issuing orders to them. Annie watches me ferociously scrubbing dirt over a pair of breeches and says nothing. I don't look at her face.

The next time I go up the beanstalk, Maria is asleep when I arrive. It's hard to wake her. The smell of sex lies heavy on her ripe body. I pause a moment, but then the very fragrance makes me try even harder to wake her; I have no right to be repulsed by being second with her. In fact, it seems to me that I owe him that. To leave now would be to insult him further by refusing to accept second place.

I finally wake her by sucking on the wide, sweet aureoles of her breasts, first one and then the other, alternating until she stirs drowsily and reaches for me. Afterward, she falls asleep again, and I creep down the stone passageway.

The pile of gold coins under the bed is gone. Instead, the room is full of giant chickens.

I stand in the doorway, astonished. All the chickens turn their heads to look at me, and they start such a cheeping and squawking that I might be a puny fox. I back out and slam shut the door, but not before one of the watch-chickens—what else could they be?—has darted past me into the passageway. The stupid creature is shrieking to wake the dead. I punch it; it's like punching a mattress. Even Maria, sated with sex, must hear it squawking.

I grab the chicken and run from the castle. Halfway down the beanstalk it gets its claws loose from against my jacket and rips open my left forearm. I scream and drop it. The chicken plunges to the ground, far below.

When I reach the forest floor, the dead chicken is staring at me with reproachful eyes. Its rump, on which it landed, has been reduced to pulp. Among the oozing meat and dingy, scattered feathers is a golden egg, slimed with blood.

I stay in bed for two days, waiting, but nothing happens. Annie brings me hot ale and broth and a porridge she says is nourishing. She says very little else, but she smiles brightly, and hums with so much determination that it is painful to hear.

Maria's voice mocks me: *One always does most stylishly the things one cares nothing about.*

By evening of the second day I decide that nothing is going to happen after all. The room was full of chickens; probably he didn't even know how many he had. Probably one was not even missed.

I get out of bed, wash, dress in what is left of my

finery, and kiss Annie good-bye. I tell her I'll be gone for many days. She smiles brightly and clings to me too long. For many miles I feel her arms clenched on my neck.

In the city I put up at the Swan and Rose, pose as a traveling merchant set upon by robbers, and set about selling my one remaining piece of stock, a golden egg fashioned for a foreign princess who died before it could be completed. I get a good price. I pay my inn reckoning, buy a good horse, and travel home with dress material for Annie, a new leather Bible to replace the one she cast into the fire, and sixteen gold pieces.

Halfway home, sleeping in the best room of yet another inn, I have a dream of Maria's body. The dream is so powerful that my body shakes and shudders in ecstasy. In the dream, Maria and I were not in her bed but in *his*, while birds swoop around us unfettered as the wind.

At home, Annie fingers the dress goods. For once she doesn't hum, or smile, or sing. She looks at me quietly, her pretty face pale. "Don't go out again tonight, Jack. You just arrived home. Please . . ."

But it seems that somewhere I can hear a harp play.

"You took a hen," Maria says, later, in bed.

I freeze. She had said nothing, hinted at nothing, seemed the same as always . . . I'd thought nothing had been noticed.

At the sight of my face, Maria laughs. "Do you think I care, little one? What's one hen more or less?" She reaches for her shift, a single lazy motion of bare arms, and leans back against her pillows.

"The hen . . . did *he* notice . . ."

"Of course he noticed," she says, amused. "He always

knows what is his." She follows this chilling remark with a malicious smile. "But not always what is not."

"I don't understand you," I say stiffly, the stiffness because instead of falling asleep she has become more bright eyed, more alert. This is not the pattern.

"I have a harp," Maria says. "Small—you would like it, little one—and very pretty. He had it ensorcelled. You see, he very much wants a child, and very much wants to keep accounts on everything he owns or does not own. From the moment he owns it. So the harp sings when I am with child. Listen."

I heard it then, a high sweet tune, very faint.

"I shut it in a cupboard," she says. Her eyes are as shiny as a bird's. "After all, one can't listen to a damn harp all the time, can one? Even if it knows the exact moment one is to double its keeper's chattels?"

The exact moment. I remember the smell of sex on her that day, and it seems I can feel all over again the sharp claws of the hen ripping my skin.

"It could . . . he and I both . . . it could . . ."

"Oh, it could indeed," Maria says, and laughs. "He won't know which of you it is for months yet. Not even the cursed harp will know for months yet." Her face changes, the first time I have ever seen on it anything but amused pleasure. She says in a low, quick rush, "And he thinks he can *own* me. *Me.*"

I climb, naked, off her bed. My legs buckle at the knees. Before I can speak, a door slams and the whole room rumbles.

"Oh!" Maria cries, and stuffs her hand in her mouth.

Looking at her, I know that her amused indifference, which pulled me like a lodestone, has finally run out. She did not expect him home so soon. Her eyes dart around the room; the skin on her neck pulls taut; her mouth rakes down in fear. She looks ugly. There is no stylishness to her now.

She cares about being caught.

I turn my back on her.

The door opens. A huge voice shouts, "Where is he? I smell blood . . . I smell *human* blood!"

I dive under the bed. The floor shakes, and a boot as tall as my cow byre looms into view. On hands and knees, I scuttle backward under the bed, until I can slip out the far side and run toward the door. I cross the open floor, but to my surprise, the giant doesn't follow. He doesn't seem to see me. I realize that he is blind.

"I smell him!" he bellows, and the great head turns and peers, contorted with anger. But smell is not sight. He cannot tell from which direction it comes. I run out the open door, my bare feet soundless on the stone.

In the passageway, I hear the sound of a cupboard door yanked open. A harp sings a melody I don't recognize.

A bellow rips the air, followed by Maria's scream. Then there are footsteps behind me, shaking the world. I scramble down the beanstalk, expecting at any moment to be yanked back upward into the murderous sky. Birds circle me, crying with excitement, and one of them flies so close its talon creases my neck.

On the ground, I cut down the beanstalk, working feverishly. It crumples to the earth not like a tree but like a rope, falling in stringy loops, its leaves whispering softly. It falls a long time, unnerving in its breathy quiet. But at the end there is a sudden noise: wood splintering and the sharp discordant sound of strings snapping, as the harp knotted into the top tendrils hits a pile of curling vines and shatters.

* * *

Naked, I stumble home through the forest—where else should I go? Annie is not there. She has not even taken her new dress goods.

Once more it is deep summer. The hay is thick and yellow in the fields of the manor house. Summer flowers, looseweed and bouncing bet and wild roses, scent the warm nights. I sit outside my cottage and play the harp, which I have mended. The music is not very good; the harp was badly damaged in its fall, and I am no musician. Or maybe it's not that at all. The best music, the kind made by careless laughing musicians at the yearly Harvest Fair, is made by a light hand. One touch on each string, barely there. And the next day the musician moves jauntily on to another town, another fair, whistling down the road he may never see again.

I know where Annie is. But she will not see me, not talk to me. I have tried.

I know, too, that my child has been born. I heard it in the heavy music of the harp, lugubrious with exile. There are many things to hear in mended music of such as my harp.

Last night I went to the inn. A dwarf in the taproom had beans he was trying to peddle. Magic, he said. The start of an adventure. He winked, one dirty eyelid sliding lewdly up and down, the other eye still. But even without him and his greasy beans, I would have known that Maria was alive, and stalking again, and unchanged. Except to me.

Or maybe it's I that have changed.

I work my one field in all weathers. I milk, and plant, and mend, and weed. The sweat runs down my neck and under my collar, and birds follow me quietly in the furrows, nibbling on grubs overturned by my hoe. As I work, I try to plan, but all my plans have the rhythms, the tinkling inadequacy, of mended music.

I could buy the beans from the dwarf. I could grow the beanstalk, mount it until I found Maria asleep and *him* away. But what then? An infant is not a coin, nor a hen, nor even a harp. It might wake and cry. If it squalled too loud, I would have to drop it and run, or put my hands around its neck until it was quiet again, or let it fall down the beanstalk to make good my own escape. And I couldn't do that. Even though only a child will bring Annie back, I couldn't do that. Even though I have spent every spare moment carving a cradle with swooping birds on the wooden hood, I couldn't do that. I would botch the job, strain too hard and so ensure that the situation itself cracked.

I would, finally, care too much.

I don't know what to do. By the firelight within my cottage the empty cradle swings, and the one book sits upon its shelf, and the stolen harp sings.

Snow-Drop

Tanith Lee

Tanith Lee is a prolific British writer of works of fantasy, horror, and science fiction—including several dark adult stories with fairy tale themes. Her collection of these, Red as Blood: Tales from the Sisters Grimmer, *is particularly recommended, along with her most recent collection,* Forests of the Night.

The story of Snow White and the Seven Dwarfs is one of the most disturbing in the fairy tale canon. In spite of Walt Disney's best attempts to turn the earthy dwarfs into benignly comic, almost genderless creatures, and the amoral stepmother into a one-dimensional caricature of evil, the story remains chilling in its evocation of a mother's hatred toward her child and an aging beauty's obsession with a younger rival in a world where beauty is the basis of power. In "Snow-Drop," Lee has taken some of the familiar elements of the story and created a new tale that is equally chilling.

Snow-Drop

CRISTENA'S HUSBAND LEFT HER AFTER A MONTH OF marriage, and went away on business to a distant country. She had known, when she married him, that this would be the arrangement, that she would frequently be alone. Her function was to live in the handsome house above the lake, like the blue center of a clockwork eye. The house cleaned and scented itself, cooked meals to order from the groceries which were delivered twice a week, did the laundry, even kept the sweep of garden, pruning the trees, digging the earth and planting, and offering up cut irises and denim roses to match Cristena's bright blue clothes. Cristena, her blond hair wound about her head, was a physically lazy, mentally active woman. She liked to read, watch television, listen to music, and sometimes she would write a slim wild novel without any effort, which would sell well for a year or two, and then slip from view. The house suited her ideally. She had always wanted such a house, and such a life. Even the long absences of her husband were actually perfect. They left her time for herself, and would give every homecoming excitement, every leave-taking the drama of high romance.

However.

Before he had married Cristena, her husband had lived in the house with another woman. This woman, some years his senior, had been dark, passionate, and energetically creative, an artist. She had died alone in the house, under rather dubious circumstances of wine and pills. She left behind no trace of her being, for the house had fastidiously washed and redecorated itself after the funeral and given her clothes and treasures to charities. All that remained were some small watercolor paintings, very graceful and fine, and in fact worth quite an amount of money, for the artist had been highly esteemed. These paintings were to be found in every room, along every corridor. The subject was virtually the same in each: a young girl, about fourteen years of age. She was slender and eloquent, sometimes depicted sitting and sometimes standing, often in an expanse of pure snow. Her skin was white as that snow, and her long smooth hair was black as wood. She had a pale red mouth.

At first Cristena barely noticed the paintings. They did not interest her very much—she preferred landscapes—and besides were all so alike that it seemed if you had looked at one you need never look at any of the others.

As the summer days passed, though, the lake darkened and the birches in the garden turned mellow; the coldness of the pictures, like little oblongs of winter brought indoors, began to annoy Cristena. They ached at the edge of her eyes, distracting her from her books and her Shostakovich. In the roomy passageways, they waited like white sentinels. They reflected in mirrors, duplicating themselves. They were even in the bedroom. Cristena removed them from there and hung instead two warm violet prints of hills.

The initial homecoming of Cristena's husband was not so astonishing as she had thought it would be.

He brought her a sapphire ring, which was very nice, although it did not quite fit. But rather than ardent, he was tired and irascible. He spoke of business throughout their candlelit dinner. In bed, he kissed her, turned away and fell unconscious. He snored. Cristena found she could not sleep. Near morning, when she had managed to doze, her husband woke her with insistent lasciviousness. He made love to her in a sort of drunken somnambulism, and while he did not hurt or distress her, he gave her no pleasure either. He fell asleep again on her breast, and she almost smothered until eventually she had prised herself out from under him. She achieved an hour's slumber on the brink of the mattress, where his bulk had gradually pushed her, for he too, apparently, was more used to sleeping alone.

At breakfast, a very ornate and sparkling one she had arranged for the house to prepare, Cristena's husband read papers and documents and made verbal notes on his pocket recorder.

Finally he looked up.

"Where are her paintings from the bedroom?"

"Oh, I didn't think you'd seen . . . I took them down.

The prints are much more in keeping with the colors of the room."

"Maybe, but not a hundredth the value. She was famous, you know."

It was only in this way that he ever referred to his previous liaison, her fame. He did not like to discuss her as a person.

"Well, if you want," said Cristena, "I can put them back. Personally—"

"Yes, I'd prefer that."

Irritated, Cristena said, to irk him in turn, "They're all the same, aren't they. That girl. Self-portraits?"

Her husband grunted. "She wanted children," he said.

"You mean it's the fantasy portrait of a daughter she couldn't have?"

He frowned and did not reply.

He was quite ugly in the morning, Cristena thought, and he had put on weight which did not suit him.

She took the two pictures of the artist's unborn daughter out of the house storage and set them back on the bedroom wall. Now she stared at them a long time. They had assumed a macabre importance, expressions of barren desire. No wonder they were capable of projecting such a horrid animation of their own.

That night Cristena wore her hair loose and a low-necked dress of midnight blue. Her husband seemed bemused, but nevertheless he made love to her on the rug before the fire, knocking over a brandy glass in the process, which the following day the house would have to clean with an odorless acid preparation. Cristena found after all that she was not going to enjoy this sexual union any more than the first. In contempt, she pretended, and her husband floundered into a relieved climax. In bed they both swallowed sleeping capsules. Cristena woke at dawn with the white pictures shining above her head like two slices of ice, and all the covers pulled off her, leaving her peculiarly vulnerable in the draftless room.

Cristena's husband spent only ten days at the house before he had to leave the country again. On the afternoon of his departure Cristena did indeed weep. They were tears of nervous thankfulness. But he was enraged by the scene, shouting that he did not want a clinging vine. He would be gone five months.

In the weeks which followed, winter came. The garden and the landscape, the road which led to the city, and up which the delivery vehicle still beat its way on heated runners, turned snow white. The lake froze to a silver tray. The daylight shrank, and by night the sky flickered with luminescent coils of phantom hair.

The house was of a faultless temperature, airy and bright, all its mechanisms performing helpfully. But Cristena began to feel threatened. She was anxious, and found it difficult, for the first time in her life, to concentrate on her books and music. A novel she had begun grew sluggish and contrived, and she left it.

She tried not to look at the pictures of the artist's unborn child, but they glowed on the walls and in the mirrors. A snow girl, nivea skin and ebony tresses and red water-ice mouth. As Cristena sat in the rooms of the house, she felt the pictures watching her, and when she walked through the corridors, the pictures blinked past like eyes.

Cristena removed the two pictures from the bedroom again, and the larger picture from her bathroom, and all the pictures from the living room. She put them into the house storage and ordered other pictures from a catalogue, and hung up those.

But now it seemed to be too late. The artist's paintings had left an imprint on the atmosphere of the rooms where they had hung, and in the places where they hung still they seemed to have amassed a greater strength.

The winter light, too, which shone in penetratingly through all the clear windows, left drops of whiteness as if fresh watercolors hung there.

There was nobody to talk to. This had never before mattered.

Cristena took down all the paintings, every one, and put them into the storage. The blank marks on the walls where they had been glimmered like candles.

Cristena kept the blinds lowered and the curtains drawn, and the lights burned day and night, and the television fluttered and sang in every space. She had to be stern with herself as she went along the passageways.

On the morning that it happened, Cristena was making up in her dressing room.

She had decided to travel to the city in an automatic hire car, to shop, eat her lunch in a restaurant, visit the theater. The idea of going among people nearly frightened her, she had been alone so long, but she was also exhilarated, and she had poured a little vodka into her tea.

The dressing room was very attractive to Cristena. It was hyacinth with accents of gold. In the tall cupboards hung elegant dresses her husband had bought her, and in the drawers, folded among perfumes, lay undergarments of bone and lace, stockings embroidered with flowers, erotic items that once she had put on eagerly to please him when he had been her lover. Cristena ignored these articles, as she ignored the jewels her husband had given her, especially the sapphire ring which was too small and so almost insulting.

She dressed her face carefully, and it was as she was applying her dark blue mascara that she glimpsed behind her—something. Something white and slim and girl-shaped, standing between the mirror and the wall, there, on the carpet, visible.

Cristena lowered the mascara with a painful slowness. She glared into the mirror through a blue hedge.

The snow girl was about three meters away, over Cristena's shoulder. She was quite distinct. She wore the same white, seamless, vaguely formfitting garment as in the paintings, matched by her snowy skin. The long glissade of hair was wood-black; her lips were red.

Cristena screamed. She jumped up and spun around.

The room was empty of the artist's unborn child. Only a white gown gleamed from a half-open door, with a mass of dark shadow above and a transparent scarlet rose sewn on its sleeve.

Swinging sharply back, Cristena took up a steel ornament and smashed the mirror. Fragments of glass tore off and flew about the room. The house would clear it all up.

Cristena pulled the white dress off its peg and crumpled it into the disposal chute. It was carried away with a disapproving hiss.

She was trembling but angry. She realized the anger had lain dormant in her and now sought release. She ran out of the dressing room, through the bedroom, along the passage and down the stairs. All the way, flashing razor glimpses, like a migraine attack, assailed her eyes—the spots where the pictures of the artist's daughter had hung.

When she reached the living room, Cristena pressed the button and the blinds flew up with the noise of furious wings.

Outside was the unearthly snow, and there in the garden under the birches stood the snow child, the dark of a pine her hair, a single red berry her mouth.

At that moment the door called tunefully.

Confused, Cristena flung up her head. There was no delivery expected today.

"What is it?"

"A man is at the door. He carries no weapons."

Cristena drifted in a trance into the hall and signaled the door to open. Beyond the security bar stood a large and powerful young man, who beamed at her. He was incredibly ordinary, and real. Cristena had no notion who he was or what he was doing there, but her awareness fixed on him voraciously. He was here for a purpose: hers.

"Lady," he said directly, "I'm a photo-hunter. Look at this."

And into the hallway over the bar leapt a wolf, which stood looking at her with its beautiful eyes. It was a holostet the young man had constructed from photographs taken in the woods on the far side of the lake, so he explained. It could be hers for a reasonable sum. For a fraction extra, it could be fixed to run about the house and howl.

"I can't buy the wolf," said Cristena. The young man looked sorry. "But come in. There's something you can do."

After she had plied him with alcohol and resisted his

amorous advances (which plainly were what he supposed she wanted), Cristena, lit by vodka and hot tea, had him pile up on the lawn the many watercolors of the artist's daughter. The house was programmed not to harm its own possessions, but he, with a large gardening implement, smashed these pictures and mashed them. After which, together, they burned them all, and the yellow flames rose glamorously into the winter sky. When it was done, not a crumb remained of the snow child, not a flake or shard. The young photo-hunter dug the snow over the black wound of the fire. Cristena gave him some money, and he went whistling away along the road with his holostetic wolf leaping about him.

And that was the end of it. The end.

And that night, Cristena's husband called from a sky-scraping mansion countless miles off, having clinched some deal. He was a little drunk, too.

"I've destroyed them," said Cristena. "All of them."

"Good. All of what?"

"The icons of her bloody child that she never had."

"What icons?"

Cristena shrieked into the phone: "The ice maiden. *Her pictures*. I burnt them."

Cristena's husband was in the wrong place to make a noisy fuss. He told her she had lost him thousands of international dollars. Cristena laughed. He should have, she said, all the royalties of her next novel.

When he had rung off, she put on a disc of Shostakovich and filled the house with it. She let the windows blaze toward the lake. She sat late working out a scenario for the house to redecorate itself again, in saffron and blue. All the furniture should be moved around, and she would buy new drapes in the city. When her husband returned, he would wonder where he was.

* * *

In two weeks the house was changed to a gas flame, azure and yellow. There were new pictures and prints in all the corridors and rooms. Cristena had spent two or three days in the city, choosing blueberry and primrose curtains. The contact with people, of whom the photo-hunter had been the herald, hardened and revived her. At length she was ready to withdraw again into her mental vase of music, books and television.

Outside, the world stayed obdurately white, the lake shiny black beneath its ice. Cristena had had the berries stripped off all the bushes.

Cristena had almost finished her novel, the first part of which she had limpidly and easily rewritten. She sat working on the re-upholstered couch, her back supported by flaxen cushions. The television fluted faintly in the corner of the room. Something about the picture summoned Cristena's attention, and she looked up. Snow had filled the screen. It was utterly white. Cristena frowned. She was about to press the adjustment control when the whiteness opened out into a petal, and so into a single flower, and then the camera sprang back to reveal a girl dressed in white and holding the white flower. She bowed low, and her long black hair, smooth as poured ink, fell forward to the ground. Cristena sat bolt upright, and her writing smacked on the carpet. Without knowing what she did, she turned up the volume.

"And here is Snow-Drop," said the voice of the television, "one of the stars of the circus."

The girl wore a short white costume and white tights that covered her from neck to toe to wrist, but described every inch of her young pliancy. The whiteness was corruscated by spangles. When she sprang suddenly over in a somersault, she glittered like a firework and her hair sprayed out in fantastic smoke.

Seven small figures ran across the space, which seemed to be that of a large arena. They wore red and black. Cristena thought they were children, but their thick dark hair, muscular faces and forearms enlightened her. They were dwarfs. They formed a pyramid and tumbled down, rolling expertly to the white satin feet of the girl called Snow-Drop. She then arched over backward, making a hoop, and they trotted in a train under her. Next they lifted her up high and raced along carrying her, in the way ants carry a leaf.

There was a familial resemblance. Cristena wondered if Snow-Drop was related to the dwarfs. Although perfectly proportioned, she was very slight and petite. She looked about fourteen years old.

The dwarfs set Snow-Drop down. She coiled herself up into a cross-legged snake, while her seven companions bounced into position about her. In tableau, the dwarfs grinned. They had poised, good-looking faces and seemed quite composed and happy with their lot. The girl also smiled.

This image was replaced by a garish sign, the fiery neon of the circus, which was performing in the city. Snow-Drop and the dwarfs were to be seen every night.

The television reverted to a rather sedentary play.

Cristena switched it off.

She walked uneasily about the room, feeling a strange, excited dread. It was as if she herself had conjured up Snow-Drop in the mirror of the television. As if, by breaking and burning Snow-Drop's image, she, Cristena, who had never wanted children, had given

Snow-Drop life. For Snow-Drop was the artist's unborn daughter, correct in each detail, even to her pale red mouth.

Every evening, for several nights, the same advertisement came on the television, and Cristena watched it. Sometimes other circus acts were shown as well, a man who swallowed clocks, a woman who danced extravagantly on the head of a pole. But Snow-Drop was always there, bowing, somersaulting, making herself into an arch, being carried by the ant-like dwarfs, sitting in their midst. Beyond her name, which was probably false anyway, no information was given.

It seemed to Cristena that a net had been cast for her and that slowly she was being pulled in to a snowy shore. It was useless to dissemble. She knew she would eventually go to the city, to the circus. There was even a vague fear that if she delayed too long, the circus might have moved on and she would have missed it. At last this fear got the better of her.

An automatic hire car drove her along the frozen road, back into the icicled city, and delivered her at the entrance of the theater where the circus was resident.

Cristena took a gilded seat at the front of the auditorium. She was nervous, and as the spangled performers swung or pirouetted or leapt past, she imagined they stared recognizingly into her face with eyes as cruel as knives.

When the moment came for Snow-Drop's act with the seven dwarfs, Cristena was trembling, and she took some large gulps from a golden flask.

The dwarfs came springing out like seven sable cats. Snow-Drop appeared ethereally, wafted down on wires from the ceiling. She was dressed like a princess, in a long alabaster gown and diamanté tiara. But she peeled off the dress and wires to reveal her sequined second skin, and turned a series of cartwheels. At each revolution she went by one of the dwarfs, who in turn began to cartwheel. The eight forms twirled about each other until Cristena was giddy and shut her eyes.

When she opened them again the dwarfs were busy raising a body mountain up which Snow-Drop walked, and next they became a body sea on which she swam.

The dwarfs made Snow-Drop the axis of every pattern. They were landscapes over which she traveled and buildings into which she went and from whose windows she looked out. By prancing off each other's shoulders, they made her seem to juggle them—the audience laughed and clapped—and at one point they became an animal, a dwarf for each leg and three dwarfs composing a body, head and waving tail. Snow-Drop sat on its back as it cantered to and fro, at last rearing up and catapulting her away into a scintillant triple spin.

Unlike all the other acts, neither the dwarfs nor Snow-Drop seemed ever to glance into Cristena's face. As they went through their plasticene antics, their eyes were fixed wide and brilliant and far away.

Cristena's nervousness gradually left her. She observed the acrobats with condescending interest. She began to want them to notice her. She wanted beautiful Snow-Drop, white and black and red, to look at her, to *know* her. It was not possible realization should be only on one side. It occurred to Cristena they were actually ignoring her, cutting her, but that of course was absurd.

Finally there was a *danse macabre,* during which three of the dwarfs stood on each other to fashion a tall man, with whom Snow-Drop waltzed. But Snow-Drop grew dizzy and fell down and died. The dwarfs bore her to the center of the stage, where they described a funeral, and buried her in their dark bodies. Then a spotlight sun shone on the mound, and a white shoot pierced up through the earth of dwarfs. Snow-Drop dived in graceful slow motion up into the air and was reborn like her name flower, to great applause.

As they bowed, Cristena stared at them, the seven handsome dwarfs and Snow-Drop. But their faces were like enamel masks. When they darted off the stage, anger flushed through Cristena, hotter than the vodka in her flask.

Soon after, she was outside the theater, standing back among some bare trees below the Stage Door, while across the street the hire car waited like an obedient ghost.

A group of other people had also gathered here, and a number of children with autograph books. Artists emerged and were beaming and gracious. Presently the dwarfs came out all together in wonderful fake fur coats. They were jolly, and teased the patrons and scared the children. In the streetlamps their eyes were now wicked and wise. Long after they had gone, when the autograph hunters had become impatient and many drifted away, Snow-Drop emerged. Unlike the dwarfs, she wore a skimpy black jacket and ankle boots. Her hair was done in a long plait. She spoke to her admirers solemnly and signed their books quickly, like a thief. Cristena watched, and wondered what she would do. But when Snow-Drop's fans had melted away, she walked directly down toward the trees. Cristena stepped out as if on cue.

"Hallo, how are you? Perhaps you remember me?"

Snow-Drop did not seem startled although she had halted at once. In fact, an immediate slyness was apparent, a vixenish glaze of evaluation passing over her eyes. Then she smiled without opening her mouth and shook her head.

"Your mother . . ." said Cristena. She added patronizingly, "You would have been too young to recall."

"I'm older than I look," said Snow-Drop primly. Her voice was flat and unpolished, and the statement offered its own obscure meaning, redolent of something murky.

"Well, would you like to see the house?" said Cristena boldly. She had planned nothing, but the words came as simply as in one of her novels.

"The house? Your house?"

"Yes, naturally mine. And we can have some wine, and perhaps dinner. The kitchen's fully automated."

"That would be nice," said Snow-Drop, in her cheap little voice. Only the under-pavement heating must have kept her slim legs from the cold in that short skirt and those unsuitable boots.

Cristena walked across the road, and Snow-Drop followed her neatly, docilely. Under the lamps her face was exactly the face of the paintings, and her mouth had been lipsticked an even redder red.

There was no one left by the Stage Door, the street was empty, and Cristena did not think anyone had seen Snow-Drop come with her to the car. She was glad, for after all Snow-Drop was a little embarrassing. Yet, as the car drove them away into the countryside, Snow-Drop's awful loveliness filled the atmosphere like a low buzzing. Cristena felt the need to talk. She lied sumptuously.

"Your mother was very fond of you. I haven't seen her for so long."

Without protest or overt cunning, Snow-Drop announced, "I never knew my mother. I was brought up by the troupe."

"Are you close to them, the seven—"

"Oh, they don't like me," said Snow-Drop, reasonably.

The house glowed at them from across the lake, and when the car brought them to the door, extra lights flamed on in welcome. Cristena could see Snow-Drop was impressed. A nasty complacency had thinned her lips.

They went into the living room. Here, where the watercolors had hung in such abundance, Snow-Drop made a living sculpture. Cristena tensed for the house to respond in some way. But, when it did not, when no poltergeist activity of any sort took place, she decided that she had already exorcised the architecture.

They drank a fresh yellow wine.

Cristena asked Snow-Drop questions about her life, and rather to her surprise Snow-Drop responded without either reticence or verbosity. She laid out events in bleak rows before Cristena. It was a sordid, unjoyful existence which Snow-Drop led, out of all keeping with her looks. And it had made her mean and ordinary in spite of herself. She had not ascended to tragedy or grotesqueness, but plummeted to the mealymouthed and the dull. Only glints of acquisitiveness distinguished her, and it was obvious she reckoned she would get—was getting—something out of Cristena. Otherwise she dwelt in the shadow of the circus and especially of the dwarfs. She was their slave, seeing to their laundry by hand, shopping for and cooking their meals on those occasions they demanded it. Cristena suspected that Snow-Drop was also their sexual toy. For that matter, almost anyone's, maybe. There was a metallic fragrance of willingness, which grew stronger as the wine left the decanter and filled their bodies.

"Off-stage, do you always plait your hair?" asked Cristena.

"Shall I undo it?" asked Snow-Drop.

"Yes, why not? I've got a marvelous comb that perfumes the hair. We can go upstairs. I'll show you my dresses. You might like to choose some. They'd be too big for you, but we can always have them re-tailored."

They went up the stair and along a passage where the artist's paintings had hung, and into Cristena's dressing room.

Cristena threw open doors.

"Look, that crimson silk would suit you. My husband bought it. I never wear red. And this black one with sparkles."

With a studied unself-consciousness, Snow-Drop slipped off her tawdry skirt and top and stood in faded under-things, dim pants and tights, and since she did not wear a brassiere, only a thin little cotton bodice to conceal her bosom. Her acrobat's body was perfect, firm slim muscle lightly padded by white satin, and the symmetrical rounded young breasts bobbing in their vest. She tried on the dresses greedily. Cristena pinched in material to show how well they would suit Snow-Drop once they had been altered.

From its case she brought the magic comb and switched it on. When it had heated up, she combed Snow-Drop's amazingly long, tendrilly hair. A scent of warm roses, jasmine and cinnamon throbbed in the room. They drank more wine.

"There are some gorgeous underclothes, too," said Cristena. "I never use them."

She opened the drawers, and let fall a shower of black and white silk corsets, black stockings sewn with orchids, garters of crow lace with silver buckles.

With no apparent modesty or reluctance, Snow-Drop pulled off her drab tights and pants, and up over her delicate head in a whirlwind of hair went the inadequate bosom-bodice. She sat on a chair and drew the embroidered stockings along her dainty legs, and fixed on the garters. She flexed her thighs and her firm, curved stomach moved; her breasts quivered like smooth white birds. Cristena assisted her into the black corset shot with ivory silk. She fitted it around the swaying stem of body and tilted into the bone cups the birds of the breasts, so the candy pink tip of a nipple rose just above each frill. Cristena laced up the corset severely. "You must wear it tight."

Snow-Drop posed before the mirror. She raised her arms artlessly, and the pink sweets rose further from their black froth containers. Between the silky limbs, under the corset's ribboned border, Snow-Drop's private hair, dark and thick like the fur of a cat, seemed the blackest thing in the room.

"That's very pretty," said Cristena.

She felt heavy, languid, tingling, mad. She put her hands around Snow-Drop's body and made a small adjustment to the corset top. Her fingers brushed an icing-sugar nipple. Snow-Drop giggled.

"Now, you mustn't be ticklish," said Cristena. She tried the nipple again.

Snow-Drop squirmed, pressing back against her.

In the mirror Cristena saw the beautiful doll with its bosom popping from the frills, its hands-span waist, and its naked lower limbs, wriggling. Snow-Drop's eyes were shut and her red lips parted.

Cristena pulled the girl backward against her body. She caressed her breasts, sought the V of coal-black fur. She watched in the mirror. Snow-Drop writhed. She parted her legs and thrust her buttocks into Cristena's belly. She uttered tiny, shrill squeaks.

Fire engulfed Cristena. She pinioned Snow-Drop, rubbing, tickling, squeezing, choked by the perfume of roses and cinnamon, hair and skin, drunken and furious, and the girl was screaming, in the glass a demon of black and white and red.

Cristena felt the climax roll up between her thighs, turning her inner life, her soul, over and over in blind ecstasy, as Snow-Drop wailed in her grip and the room exploded.

When Cristena came to herself, Snow-Drop was sitting cross-legged on the floor. She sucked her thumb and played with the ribbons of the corset, like a spoiled child who knows it has been naughty, but that this will not matter.

Cristena told herself it would *not* matter, over and over again, as she assisted the kitchen in the preparation of a lavish supper. Never in her life had she experienced such alarm. It was not shame, more terror. For Snow-Drop came of a dangerous, scurrilous race. Who knew now what she might do? For the moment she sat on the couch, still in the corset and still half nude, drinking wine and looking at the television, in whose speculative lens she had first appeared. Later it was possible she might be persuaded to go back to the city. But then again she might want to spend the night here. And after tonight, how many other nights? What payment would she exact, in emotion or hard cash? How luminous her eyes as she glanced about her at the furnishings of Cristena's husband's house.

Cristena put the last touches to the food and drink. Her hands were shaking, but she pulled herself together and made herself survey what she had done. It was a meal of red, white and black, although she doubted Snow-Drop would take this in, let alone appreciate it. White soft rolls and creamy cheeses, slices of palest chicken in an almond sauce, caviar, fat grapes as black as agate, pomegranate seeds, burgundy apples whose crisp hearts were the shade of virgin ice. In the decanter, a rich ruby wine.

As she followed the service trolley into the living room, Cristena wished there had been someone to pray to. But there was not, she must deal with this herself.

"I hope you're hungry."

"Oh yes. I like my food," said Snow-Drop, who had looked as if she lived on honey-dew.

She began to eat at once; alcohol and orgasm had evidently stimulated her appetite.

Cristena observed. She was prepared to say, if pressed, "No, I had dinner earlier. You have it all." But Snow-Drop, gobbling up everything in a prissy yet vulture-like way, did not bother with Cristena, did not seem to notice that her hostess ate nothing.

As more and more of the food and wine were consumed, Cristena's shaking increased. When Snow-Drop plucked up one of the gleaming red apples, Cristena flinched. Of all of the feast, she was afraid she had taken a chance with the apples.

Snow-Drop put the apple to her mouth and bit into it. Then, quite slowly, her jaw dropped. Cristena saw inside her mouth, to the piece of white and red apple lying on Snow-Drop's tongue. Snow-Drop looked at Cristena, mildly inquiring. "Mmr," she said. Then her eyes turned up in their sockets and she slid from the couch to the carpet.

She lay there half an hour, motionless. Then there was a small spasm, which did not wake her. Crystal urine flowed out and wet the rug. A thread of scarlet slipped between Snow-Drop's lips. That was all. She was dead. She could not be anything else. Cristena had crushed twenty tasteless, soluble sleeping capsules in the wine, and in the sauces, meat, fish, cheese and fruit had gone the odorless soft corrosive cleaning acids of the house, the unsmelling garden pesticides. She had burnished the apples with a vitriolic substance employed to polish the mirrors.

The house buried Snow-Drop's body without any difficulty in the garden. After the job had been done, the digger took up deep snow from the lawn and packed it in above the grave. But in any case that night new snow came down and covered everything.

If there were reports on the television of Snow-Drop's disappearance, Cristena, who studied the screen closely, did not see them.

Presumably no one knew where Snow-Drop had gone on the night of her vanishment, and perhaps ultimately nobody cared. The seven dwarfs had not liked her and would probably find it challenging to locate and train another beautiful lost child as their helpmeet and victim.

Cristena felt no compunction. She had had to protect herself. She settled down and completed her novel, then put it into the machine to be typed. By the time her husband returned to the house, the book would be in the hands of her publishers, and she could present him with the advance, which would humiliate him.

He came home some weeks early, when the snow was still down across the landscape. Calling her from the airport, he told her that he was bringing two of his business associates, and in the background she heard their hearty, stupid and inebriated voices. Cristena was not pleased, but she made believe she did not mind, sure he would bring the men to upset her and she could ruin his trick by seeming unconcerned.

She went about the house behind the automatic dusters. For months she had thought of it mostly as hers. She did not suppose he would like the new color scheme, and he was capable of having it changed. Cristena braced herself to be merry and careless.

The men arrived in the afternoon and came swaggering up to the house. Her husband was in the lead. He had put on yet more weight, and she had never seen him look so ugly, as if he had done it on purpose.

For an hour or so the male colleagues sprawled in the living room, eating things the kitchen prepared and drinking beer. Cristena's husband had greeted her with affectionate disinterest and now largely ignored her, but he had not remarked adversely on the redecoration. Indeed, he abruptly praised it. "The house is looking good. But wait until you see what I've brought for the garden." And somehow he made it obvious he had deliberately not brought a present for Cristena, who did not deserve one, but for the house.

They went outside, into the freezing, twilit day.

With the help of the house porter, Cristena's husband trundled a large lamp-like structure into the garden and set it up among the birch trees. He threw a switch and the lamp began softly to hum. From its bowl a yellow light streamed out and bathed the slope. It became warm. Strange scents shot from the ground, the trees. They were the smells of spring.

"The snow will be gone in minutes," said Cristena's husband. "The plants start coming up in half an hour. You can have a spring and summer garden in the middle of winter. Expensive, I'll admit, this sunlamp, but wait till you see."

They waited, and they saw. And presently, after they had been splashed with snow and mud from the broiling, roiling earth, they retreated into the living room and looked on from there.

The garden was in flux, in tumult. Snow rushed in avalanches from the trees and along the ground. A kind of seismic activity thrust up huge tumuli, which seemed to boil. And on these peculiar black mounds, the porcelain flowers of spring bubbled through.

"You see?" asked Cristena's husband excitedly.

Cristena did. It was only a matter of time, and already she was leaden and self-possessed.

Finally, after only twenty minutes, sabotaged by the sunlamp, the lid of dense snow had melted off and the sides of the grave gave way. The upheaval in the earth pushed from below, and Snow-Drop came out once more from the dark.

The cryogenic cold had preserved her flawlessly. The pressure on her spine made her sit slowly up in the grave to the astonished wonder of the three gaping men. And she was as ever white as snow, black as wood, and her pale red mouth opened and the bit of apple, also exactly preserved, fell out. And so she sat there exquisitely, with her lips parted and her eyes closed, dead as a doornail, until the men turned to Cristena with their questions.

Little Red

Wendy Wheeler

Wendy Wheeler began writing science fiction, fantasy, and horror for publication in 1987, and has since sold short fiction to Analog, Critical Mass, Pandora, *and* Gorezone. *She is working on her first novel. Wheeler, like Susan Wade, comes from Austin, Texas (where they are in the same writer's group).*

Little Red Riding Hood is a fairy tale that has been embraced by pop culture—from Sam the Sham's rendition in song to the brilliant Neil Jordan film The Company of Wolves, *which combined several Angela Carter stories from* The Bloody Chamber. *Generally, the wolf is seen as predator, and Little Red Riding Hood and Grannie are viewed as helpless victims dependant on the woodcutter for rescue—or justice, depending on which version you read. In this version, Grannie is present only in memory. The tale takes place in twentieth-century Chicago, and the wolf is quite urbane, a very dapper and knowing wolf. Chilling.*

Little Red

I THINK IT BEGAN WITH THE HAT.

Helen had seen it in a shop on the way to our third rendezvous. Back then, we were still meeting in hotel rooms. She unbuttoned her shirtwaist dress as she told me about the hat and how it would look on her daughter, becoming all tittering and giddy, her pale face colored with something more than just anticipation of our lovemaking.

At this stage in my adventures, I enjoy making the grand gesture. "We'll go back together and buy it for your little girl," I'd said. "Afterward." I remember how dark my hand looked on her white shoulder. My swarthiness usually pains me; I have even plucked the black hair from the backs of my hand. But during these moments of passion, I find contrast only whets my appetite.

Helen had nodded, fingers to her lips, shivering from gratitude—or anticipation. The fresh smell of her was like an intoxicant. She didn't smoke or marcel her hair like some of the other women of my acquaintance. The planes of neck and collarbone above the bodice of her white slip had seemed achingly fragile. White slips have always excited me.

Later, after we drove in my new black Studebaker over to the store in one of the older sections of Chicago, I could understand her enthusiasm for the hat. When the shopgirl lifted it out of the window, I took it from her myself before Helen could even reach out a hand. I caught my breath at the texture and plushness of the yarn.

"And such a darling color, too," breathed Helen. "That crimson will look just stunning on Regina."

It was a beret sort of style, hand-knit in Italy according to the tag. The wool had a clean, animal scent. I turned it around in my hand and saw the thing that was to fire my imagination.

On the side, a tiny red bud, so cunningly crocheted it almost looked alive. A flower as red as the hat itself, but with a slim green stem and two diminutive green leaves. Those tightly curled petals held an almost unbearable promise.

"How old did you say your daughter was?" I asked.

"She'll be fourteen in two weeks," said Helen, taking off one of her white cotton gloves to stroke the beret. Her nails were plain and unvarnished. She usually didn't even wear lipstick unless I asked her to. "This will make a wonderful gift."

I handed it to her. "With my compliments, then."

Helen blushed and shot a look at the shopgirl. "Oh, I can't let her know it comes from you. But thank you,

Josef. I will accept it on her behalf. You—you're very generous."

As the shopgirl wrapped it up, I saw her unobtrusively stroke the tiny red bud. That caught my attention and made me look more closely at her, at the olive complexion free of makeup, the plain black dress, the dark hair pinned severely back. But there was a hint of fullness to her bottom lip, a certain set to her eyes. I fought the appetite that flared in me, tried to become totally the cultured man I truly am.

Still, I found a way to let my hand linger in hers as she returned my change.

Soon after, Helen and I began to meet at her mother's two-story brownstone on Bois d'Arc Street. Helen had inherited it upon her mother's death almost half a year earlier, but was unwilling or unable to do anything more with it than air it out every few weeks. Every piece of wax fruit, every antimacassar, every ceramic cat was left just as it had been when her mother died. I hated the dusty, old-woman smell, but stifled my discomfort to save the cost of hotel rooms.

It was here I saw my first photograph of Regina.

The picture sat with two others arranged on an ecru doily atop the Victrola. The pristine condition of the ornate frame told me this was one thing in the house that still received regular attention.

The girl in the photograph wore an antebellum costume with yards of lace and ruffles around a sweetheart neckline. Her back was arched and one hand toyed with her dark ringlets. And the face, the face was so . . . knowing. Dark eyes and brows (painted for the photograph in some middle-America version of stage makeup), a full lipsticked mouth, even a dimple in one cheek. This girl was born to wear the red hat.

"She's lovely," I had murmured. That tiny bud so tightly closed.

Helen was flitting around the room like a bird frantically beating its wings against a glass pane. It is the gentleness in women that speaks to me most. I missed that quality when Helen got so agitated.

What had attracted me to Helen that morning half a year ago was her hands. She'd come into my jewelry shop to resize her wedding ring, but the sight of her hands on the glass countertop, small and white and gentle, pious palms together and fingers laced as if in supplication, caused me to look again. When we began meeting at her mother's house, to calm her a little, I took to bringing a bottle of wine each time we met—that and cake. Helen loved *Gateau Robert*.

Now she paused in front of the photograph. "Yes, yes, she is. Boys just look at her and fall in love." Her smile was one of victory. "That was taken last year at the All-City Pageant. She won second place in that dress. I made it myself."

I knew about Helen's husband, The Right Reverend Henry Hunter of the Malletown Diocese, a pillar of the Episcopal church. I had even seen them together, he in his clerical garb and she kneeling on the benches before him. How had they managed to engender such a charmer? "You only have the one child?" I asked.

"Just Regina." The words were said with pride. "I was the oldest of four." Helen began her flitting again. "The only daughter. I had responsibilities at an early age. My mother kept me at one task after another. None of that for Regina. I'm raising her differently; she's a perfect beauty."

The records in the Victrola cabinet, I noticed, were all

ballroom tunes and German *lieder*. My own taste runs to Verdi and Puccini, the Great Masters.

When I moved my fedora from the overstuffed couch and sat down, eddies of dust puffed up from the thick green carpet. I had to clean my shoes with my silk handkerchief. Helen's words irritated me a little. She should complain, I thought. Precious little my mother had done for me. "Yet your mother left you this house."

"Yes, the house." Helen almost spit the words. "My brothers would have friends over, lots of boys, and not all younger than me. They'd laugh and play their music, then they'd go off, leaving me on the front porch with my chores. I was invisible to them. *Invisible.*" She tugged at a brown damask drapery as if she wanted to tear it down. "I *hate* this house."

I knew my cue. "You invisible, *ma chère?* You're much too beautiful." I stood behind her and put my hands on her shoulders. Her agitation had warmed her, making her perspire with a scent that excited me. In her dark gray dress, no jewelry, no lipstick on her mouth, she was like a shadow in my hands. Another man would have passed her by, would have considered her too plain, too timid. I knew better. I can see the fire even when it's banked deep within.

I pulled the pin from her hat and tugged at the coil of pale brown hair beneath. "Show me the bed we'll use," I breathed in her ear. Though it was only two in the afternoon, my beard was already heavy enough to scratch her. It gave me a moment of chagrin to see the red abrasions on her skin, then I decided I liked leaving my mark on her, and nuzzled her again.

Helen's pulse leapt in her neck. Later, later I would

kiss her there, open my mouth and feel her heartbeat against my teeth.

After I saw the photograph, I turned conversations with Helen more and more toward Regina. Helen had had her schooled in dance. She enrolled her in theater classes. Regina had taken charm courses since the age of five. They were considering voice lessons. Her mother was insisting Regina wear lipstick now that she had turned fourteen.

And Regina had loved the hat I bought her.

"The little minx almost never takes it off," said Helen. "Why she'd wear nothing but that hat if I let her!"

I think it was this mental picture that set events on their course.

We were lying side by side on her mother's cherry-wood four-poster bed. Helen was stroking the hair on my chest—my pelt, she called it. After some weeks, her distress at trysting in her mother's house had turned into something else. Now she seemed to relish having a lover in her mother's very bedroom. I was counting myself lucky to have found a woman like Helen, so proper outside this room and so wanton inside it.

I was still smarting from a discussion I'd had earlier that day with Madeline, the manager of my jewelry store. She'd raised her penciled eyebrows, blown cigarette smoke from the corner of her mouth and asked in a loud tone, "Where are you off to now, Josef?"

Madeline is a hard woman; some would call her a harpy, although she does have excellent business sense. But her hands! Large, veined and muscled, with blood-red nails. I almost shudder when she touches my sleeve. "An appointment with a special customer, Madeline. Shouldn't be more than a few hours." I always smile when I talk to her; it's the best way to deal with strong women.

Madeline had all but thrown some diamond brooches back into their case. "You have too many 'special customers,' Josef. I suggest you pay more attention to the clientele that comes into your store." She took another drag on her cigarette and watched me through narrowed eyes. I wouldn't know, but I'm sure Madeline is the type of woman to take many lovers. She has that brittle quality.

I'd shrugged, at a loss for propitiating words, but then the salesboy Peter had called out from the back of the store with a question, and I was able to slip away. During the whole drive to Bois d'Arc Street, however, I remained outraged.

I do take pride in my store. It is a small place, but in a very good location, and I carry only the highest quality merchandise. My business is the confirmation that I can deal successfully with the wealthy, the cultured. I've spent most of my life perfecting that knowledge. Yes, I have *petites amours*, but they are the prerogative of a sophisticated man. As long as you don't allow your appetites to rule you, these small adventures add piquancy to life.

Helen's pliant nature I found delicious. I could lead her in whatever direction I pleased. "What does your husband think of Regina?" I asked her now. "Does he know what a lucky man he is? Doubly lucky."

She sighed. "Henry listens to the Words of the Lord, Josef. With such competition, neither Regina nor I can much attract his notice." She put both arms around my neck. "But then, I'm a wicked, wicked woman."

To her thinking, she probably was, though I had courted her almost half a year before I'd won her.

How these quiet ones love being pursued! I bent to kiss her. "You're not wicked," I said. "Just not appreciated. Neither you nor Regina."

When I asked her later to meet me Wednesdays and Saturdays as well as Tuesdays and Fridays, she hesitated only a moment before agreeing. I would have to cut back time with my other women, perhaps drop one or two. I was not too concerned about their reactions. Part of the adventure, after all, is that grand dramatic scene at the end.

And I'd already decided that Helen and her little family deserved my special attention.

Helen was surprised when I met them on the street in front of Regina's school; in her eyes I was still her illicit lover. She stopped dead in the sticky Chicago air. But I had decided it was time to see Regina for myself. Enough of just imagining those knowing eyes beneath the red hat.

I knew the school, I knew the street, as I knew most things about Regina. I stood leaning on my Studebaker as they stood at the top of the steps, Regina and her mother, hand in hand.

Regina was indeed a tender young thing. Her black hair, unlike the ringlets in the photograph, was naturally wavy. She wore a green cardigan over an embroidered blouse, green plaid skirt and saddle oxfords. Perched at a captivating angle atop her head was the red hat. With only lipstick for makeup, her face seemed younger, but that didn't fool me. I knew utterly what type of creature she was.

I doffed my black fedora. Helen's cheeks were blazing. She moved forward again, but Regina had already noticed something amiss. Her dark eyes looked around until she saw me. As her glance swept over me, over my black pinstriped suit and red tie, my white silk shirt, my polished shoes, I felt an unarguable crackle of electricity.

"Come along, Regina," said Helen, as they descended the steps. "Head up." She tucked the girl's arm closer to her. "And walk decently."

"But, Mama, this is the man you meet at Grandma's," said Regina in a charming clear voice. "Aren't you even going to stop and say hello?"

Helen was speechless at that, but I recovered the situation for her. "Hello, Regina. May I call you Regina? I'm Mr. Volker. Yes, I've been consulting with your mother on her property, boring grown-up stuff. How was school today?"

Regina stopped. She put her head to the side and gave me a practiced smile, her dimple winking in and out. Yes, this was one knowing little female. "Just fine, thank you for asking."

Helen had finally recovered. "I—I'm surprised you know about our meetings, Regina. They're really nothing, nothing at all."

Regina patted her mother's hand. "I got curious when you brought me cake every day. And wondered why you always had sherry on your breath. Do you like horses, Mr. Volker?"

"Regina!" said her mother.

I ignored her. "Why, yes. Yes I do, very much. Do you like horses, Regina?"

"Oh, yes! I would much rather take horse-riding lessons than go to silly old ballet class. Mama says we can't consider it, though. It makes me so sad." Regina rolled her dark eyes and sighed.

"Regina is a very gifted dancer," said her mother

through clenched teeth. "In her lovely costumes, all the boys adore her. Please stop this nonsense, Regina."

Regina thrust out her bottom lip. "Those costumes are silly, Mother. I wish you would buy me riding boots and dungarees. I could get those all muddy and no one would say anything."

I opened my car door. "Well, I have no horse for you to mount, but I do have this black steed. Helen, may I offer you two a ride home?"

Helen shook her head, but Regina was already stepping inside. "What a lovely car! Thank you, Mr. Volker." I caught a flash of calf and thigh in the swirl of green plaid skirt. Pale skin, like her mother. Tender, young, untouched skin.

"We'll drive the long way," I said to Helen, ushering her to the car door. "Through the park to see the beautiful flowers."

Before she climbed in, Helen looked in my face as though something in my smile disturbed her. "I've never noticed before what white teeth you have, Josef," she murmured. "So large and white."

The flower beds at Littleton Park were so lush we decided to park the car and walk around. I was as charming to Helen as I could be, which mollified her quite a bit. As we strolled across the grass, Regina ran ahead of us, her sweater flying behind her.

"Regina, stop that!" called her mother. "Act like a young lady or we're getting back in the car." She rolled her eyes at me. "She has five young men calling her every day. She's a real heartbreaker, but then that's not her fault. I've told her be polite but don't let them get fresh."

"Gonna pick some flowers, Mama," called Regina, already tripping from bed to bed.

"Where's her lipstick?" said Helen, hand shading her eyes. "Is she wearing her lipstick?" She finally shrugged and sighed. "You gave me a terrible shock, Josef."

I took Helen's arm and led her to a bench. "I just had to show you how cozy we could all be together," I said. "I didn't mean to distress you. I would never hurt you and Little Red."

Regina had returned with an armful of gladiolus and daylilies. Her cheeks were pink and her hair wild as a hoyden's. It was difficult accepting this girl as the alluring creature in the photograph. But I see beneath the surface. "These are for you and Mr. Volker, Mother," she said. "Because you are so special. Who's Little Red?"

I brushed my fingers against the crocheted bud on her hat. "You," I said.

"I worship you and Little Red," I said to Helen. "You don't belong with him, that desiccated old crow. You deserve passion in your life. You didn't even know what passion was until you met me, did you?"

Helen lay spent across me. In my nose was the acrid scent of our cooling sweat. Her naked shoulders were pink with love bites. I could tell she was weakening. I'd been at her for almost a month to leave Reverend Hunter. She was in love with me, I could tell.

"But Regina . . ." she said, avoiding my eyes.

Regina was at the forefront of my mind. Regina and I spent several afternoons a week together, always in her mother's company, of course. Regina never took off the hat, and I would find myself sometimes almost hypnotized staring at that bud.

"I couldn't separate a child from her mother," I said, encouraged that it wasn't a flat no. "Little Red must live with us. She adores me, too, Helen, surely you can see that. I'll take care of you both, I promise."

Helen smiled. "She likes your name for her." She rolled away. "Oh, I don't know, I don't know. I was such a good wife, such a good mother. I took pride in my home, I was a tireless worker for the church. What am I now?"

"A woman," I whispered in her ear. "A passionate, beautiful woman. Your mother tried to keep you from it, your husband wouldn't acknowledge it. But that's what you are. I know that. I see that. Say yes, Helen. Say yes."

She curled on her side, for all the world like a kitten or a dressed hare. How delicious she seemed. "Maybe," she said.

Taking a wife was something I'd planned for someday further in the future. I'd achieved most of my other goals: my own business with a select clientele, handmade suits, an apartment (true, a tiny one) in the most exclusive high rise in Chicago. Having a wife would limit my adventures, but surely it would make it easier to keep my passions at a more cultured level.

My breeding, or lack of it, is something I've overcome. It's more than just shaving my beard twice a day or having the stray hairs in my eyebrows tweezed. I've read the complete works of Shakespeare, I'm a self-taught student of philosophy, I attend the opera and know all the words to "La Donna e Mobile." Some might call my predilection for adventures a weakness, but to that I say what better pastime for a man of taste?

And Helen would never be the kind of wife my mother was, though my mother had been a devout woman, too, in her own way. Her only halfway sober times had been Sunday mornings and confession. I could still see her sitting at our kitchen table wearing one of the white slips that had been her daily costume for most of my childhood. With each year, with each bottle, her pale skin had grown puffier, her red hair frowsier. She was always shrieking, always reaching out those big Irish hands of hers to grab at you, turn your head so you had to kiss her or, worse, pull you into her lap so she could pinch and maul you. All you could do was smile and duck away as fast as you could.

Six babies she'd had; me last. One right after the other, like some dog with a litter of pups. Disgusting. I could picture her lying on her side, six flat dugs on her chest to suckle us all at the same time.

I'd spent my life putting that all behind me.

Helen didn't say yes, however, until I asked her in Regina's presence. We were discussing whether or not to have lunch at a certain cafe where French dancers in berets and striped pullovers performed those semi-violent taxi dances. Helen was curious I could tell, but worried about Regina.

Regina was all anticipation. "I want to see them. I've heard about those men and women, Mother; it's not so terrible. Maybe they're in love and that's why they dance like that."

"I'm in love," I said quickly, my hand on Helen's back. I felt her stiffen.

"With who?" asked Regina. Again, she was wearing the red hat.

"Helen, please," I whispered in her ear. "I love you and want you to marry me. I can't go on like this."

"Oh," she moaned. Her eyes were closed.

"You love my mother?" said Regina. She moved close to us; I could smell her floral perfume. "This is so romantic, isn't it, Mother? My father almost never spends time with us. Would you be like that, Josef? Would I live with you too?"

I drew Regina closer to us. "I want you both. What do you say, Helen?"

She opened her eyes and looked at my hand, so darkly hirsute against Regina's skin. I barely heard her breathe a "yes."

I know I can offer Helen and Regina a life of richness and culture. And they will start me on a new road of respectability and propriety. I will conquer my appetites and be the man I've always known I could be. Unfortunately, my apartment is a tiny place, too small for three people. We've had to begin our life together by moving into Helen's mother's house.

Regina seems to have taken all the changes with grace. I know she loves her father, all girls do, but I have faith that I can replace him in her heart. My optimism is fed by how at ease she seems to feel with me. Her curiosity today, for example.

After a few hours of moving various boxes and bags, I bathed and came out of the bath dressed in my black silk robe, and sat down to read the paper. Helen was out, buying supplies of whatever one runs out of in a closed-up house. I put the paper down to find Regina sitting on the ottoman at my feet. She was staring at my legs.

"You have much more hair than my father does," she said. "But I notice you have more muscles, too."

"Thank you," I said. Then daringly added, "and what do you have under *your* dress?"

She stroked her bodice, but said with an innocent look, "Just my chemise. Your face looks so dark this morning."

Embarrassment flamed, then I leaned forward and took her hand. "You're right; I still need to shave. Feel." I put her small hand on my jaw, then laughed as she shivered at the roughness of it.

"Do you love my mother very much, Josef? Do you kiss her a lot?"

I nodded, and kissed Regina's palm.

"You will take care of me, won't you?" she said, looking into my eyes. "Now that I'm your little girl, you will take care of me?"

Oh, yes, I thought. Oh, yes, my darling little bud. I know what you want of me. I will take care of you.

Helen came through the door then, arms loaded with packages. She saw us sitting close, Regina's hand on my cheek, then turned back to shut the door. "Lots of yummies for my family," she said. "Come help me put these up, please, Regina."

Tonight I left the bedroom door open. Helen didn't notice; the change in her circumstances has distracted her beyond belief, but she'll be fine once we start her divorce proceedings. She crept into our bed fairly shaking with tension. I cooed to her, and held her, convincing her to drink another glass of sherry from the carafe we now kept on the nightstand. It was important we make love on this, our first night as a family.

I calmed Helen, then, with stroking, began to excite her. Helen cried out, as did I. The sounds created curiosity down the hall, as I knew they would. I was certain I heard footsteps outside the door. First lesson, I thought. Big eyes watched us from the doorway; big ears listened to everything.

It made me even more ardent. I kissed and nibbled, plunged and reared. I could almost smell the blood beneath Helen's skin. Delicious, so delicious.

When we finally lay quiescent, a patter of feet retreated back down the hall. Helen started awake. "What's that? Mother?"

"No, no, nothing." I calmed her. "Just the settling of this old house. Go to sleep now. Go to sleep." She dropped off in no time, thank God.

I can finally slip out of bed, my hunger only whetted. This is the reward for my role soon to come, husband and father. It's what I deserve.

I've been reading the looks. I know when she talks what the words really mean. I can see the fires banked deep within.

The black silk robe drops around my shoulders like a caress. The door swings open without a creak. Beneath my feet, the old hall carpet feels like the grass of some deep wood. I touch her bedroom door; I see the white hand in the moonlight beckoning me so gently. I hear her breath.

I'm all appetite.

I Shall Do Thee Mischief in the Wood

Kathe Koja

Kathe Koja's short fiction appears in A Whisper of Blood, Still Dead, The Ultimate Werewolf, The Best of Pulphouse, *and other anthologies. Her first novel,* The Cipher, *received much critical acclaim at its publication in early 1991, including the Horror Writers of America award for achievement for a first novel.* Bad Brains *appeared in March 1992, and she is currently working on her third novel,* Skin. *Koja lives in Detroit with her husband, artist Rick Lieder, and her son.*

Most of Koja's fiction takes place in contemporary times, so this historical piece—a world-and-time-away from the Wheeler tale—is an interesting surprise, as much for its detailed mise-en-scène *as for the twist and turns of its plot. Another variation on "Little Red Riding Hood," this story, like that by Wheeler, portrays the wolf's point of view. In both renditions the wolf (male) takes his sexual prerogatives for granted. A master of juxtaposed images, Koja rarely makes things easy, expecting the reader to participate in the experience of reading her work. So take your time, trust her, and join her in exploring the human psyche.*

I Shall Do Thee Mischief in the Wood

HER FACE WAS AS A BIRD'S: THAT AVIAN ARCH TO nose and startled eyes, round eyes and black as a sparrow's, as a crying guinea hen's. Her teeth showed slim and broken when she smiled, they said it was from eating nothing but the roots she dug from the forest floor where she lived, all alone save for her granddam. Who used to be, she said, in her vague sweet voice, a healer. And an herbalist. And a seer, and diviner of water (as if more water was needed in this sullen land, where rivers flowed relentless even in winter's cruelest clench), and, in the days when her fingers were more than mere knotted bone, a seamstress. See, she said, bright pitiful boast, her voice as high as the birds she resembled, granddam had even made her this fine cape: flushed velvet, the dark sticky red of menstrual blood, dirt-starched hem barely past her grubby knees; anyone could see it had been made for a child much smaller than she. Beneath it she wore rags less clothing than ties about her body, cerement twists as colorless as the dirt between her fingers, shadowed up to her bare ankles above the coarse and heeless shoes. In her hair was half a bow, inextricably snarled in the matted black braids.

Very young, and very poor, and the goods she brought for barter to the afternoon stalls not valueless but worse, quality without value. Miniature birds' skulls, tied with herbs that smelled of cumin and caper spurge. Black flowers pressed to dusty perfection and caught to bouquets with sleek ribbons of human hair. The skeletons of jointed lizards, dressed in the curious best of an age and yet another age before, when the women wore false feathers and piqué lace and men the wired doublets that made even the foppish seem dire; her granddam's age, she said, with another of her foolish smiles. Pieces of leaves on which curious rhymes were made, the ink no ink at all but the heavy juice of broken stems. Tiny dogs constructed of twigs and clinging moss, whose tails wagged slow back and forth when their sloping backs were pressed just so. A handful of treasures worth nothing at all, as around her women sold turnips heavy as boils, big slattern sacks of grain, the endless mills of butternut cloth made to be made into everything: aprons as well as sheaths as well as shrouds. Men convinced one another of the merits of spavined colts and trueless iron, children cheated over trinkets and she, there, with her ragged clothes and broken basket, unable to trade for even the poorest wares, weevily flour and reeking meat, not even a ladle's-worth of the heavy ale she said her granddam craved. Circling through the crowd, proffering her goods and silly smile, no one noticed either, they were used to her here.

"Twice a fortnight she comes," said the ale-seller to the man drinking slow from the heavy cup, its rusting chain rattling curiously sweet. "Round and round with t'damned basket, and no one ever to buy."

"A shame," said the man, with the heatless concern of the stranger. "She seems pleasant enough. Pretty girl."

"Can't you see? She's simple. Mad as rabbits," as he swabbed at the other cup, chained as the first; his was a poor stall and cups were dear. "Comes of living out in t'wood like an animal, eating t'dirt and stones."

The girl passed to the stall opposite the ale-seller's, bent to show the stallkeeper her basket. From where he stood the man could see the length and strength of her bare limbs, the occluded shine of all that hair. "She lives alone?"

"Nay, nay. With her granddam," and the practiced glance inside his cup, dry with all the talking, sir? The man smiled to himself as he passed across the counter a heavy copper, another, until there were four brown and dull against the duller planks. "Another cup for me," he said. "And one for yourself, if you please."

"My thanks to you, sir," said the ale-seller, smiling to show both teeth. "A good year for business, sir?"

"Good enough," said the man. Dirty beautiful hair and telltale cape, gone from the crowd but—there: head down, swinging the basket the way a child would, weaving walk down the hock-path that led to the forest, the wood they called it here: branches black and tangled as her hair, their shadows upon her like the hands of false friends and she still swinging the basket, head tilted now to catch the remnants of the trailing light as the path took her irrevocable and gone from his sight.

His name was Jude. He was a man of business and affairs; both were tolerably well but could have been better, and that was his reason to linger in this squat, benighted slum that called itself a town, there on the lip of a forest the magistrate of which was due to visit any day, bringing with him needs, perhaps, that a businessman might fill, needs unsatisfied by other, local channels. Any day, and in the meantime nothing to do but wait, spend his heavy purse on drink and the two available whores, one a beldam as stolid and fierce as a warhorse and the other a giggling slut with hair that came out in his hands when he stroked it; it was a sorry place. No tavern save the one he slept in, no amusements save the whores, no excitements save the marketplace and its stalls full of nothing worth buying—twice a fortnight this charade; it was a wonder anyone made money enough to eat.

The girl came twice a fortnight, too.

He did not even bother to chide himself, it was too ridiculous for that, but there he was, nodding to the ale-seller who now seemed to presume him a valued customer; well he might. "Good day, sir," and the cup no cleaner, the ale no less foul. A drier day than before, dust abominable, everywhere, the ale like soup in his dusty mouth.

"Come to buy?" the ale-seller inquired, pouring out a stingy half-cup for a heavy-breasted hag with two sour children twisting and snapping in her skirts, two bad-bred puppies and their ill-favored bitch. "Or only to look?"

He shrugged, forced barely half a smile past the scouring feel of dust in his eyes. "Perhaps. Perhaps the wares are sweeter today than on my last visit."

The ale-seller nodded without agreement, took the woman's empty cup and copper with one practiced hand. "Farrier has some new poultice he says will cure t'rickets in colts." The cup clattered a widening slow circle, arrested by its chain. "And Lanny over to Briermount is in, with cabbage and heavy-head potatoes."

Rickets and cabbage, and whores that smelled of sour milk and ale that smelled of drunkards' piss; he would certainly wait no longer for the magistrate, this very night would see him gone. Nodding a bare farewell, he left the ale-seller to make his own curt circuit of the booths and jiggering tents, sidestepping piles of dog shit and children who breathed through their crusty mouths, the yammering sellers who waved their worthless goods in his very face as he passed. Dust everywhere, and bodies in his way, he had to use his elbows in spots and in exasperation pushed a brat sprawling, the child risen up with a curse on his lips and beyond that child a rush of dark dirty hair, folds of reddish velvet far too hot for this stifling day.

Up close she was more lovely still, her foolish smile made with lips soft and heavy as a faint-corrupting flower, her fingers deft as a princess' as she sorted her fripperies on the counter of a gross goodwife selling spindly sausage that attracted only flies and the dirty hands of filching brats. When she spoke, in that high chirping voice, it was not with a lady's diction but a lady's unconscious air.

"Pretty toys, nay?" as with two of those slim fingers she made the twig-dogs wag their tails. "Prettier, too, if you like," and hurrying, before she could be stopped, from the battered basket a pair of court-dressed lizards, a stitched ball of withering aromatics, a long strip of bark worked to look like leather, reaching for yet other wares when the hag stopped her with a fat hand flat on hers.

"Take away your damned toys," and the same fat hand swept them down to the ground, rising with their impact a dirty cloud and as the girl dropped to her knees, peering and frantic, the trinkets disappeared with the settling of the dust; two of the children gone, one trailing the belt behind like a captured standard, and the girl knelt where she was for just a moment, eyes closed, dust settling pale upon the darker landscape of her cape.

Evil old bitch, he thought, and, still behind the girl, reached to raise her up; the flesh of her arm was warm and strong, more muscle than he would have guessed by looks alone. Touching her still though she was safe on her feet. "Hurt, are you, miss?"

No, no, a child's shy negation, smiling sideways at the ground. Her breath had a gingery smell; her teeth were indeed broken, snapped nearly flat in spots. Fastidious brush at her disordered cape and in the movement he saw the slope of a breast, faint toadstool knob of nipple; her clothing torn more grievously, perhaps, in the fall. Perhaps. She bent again, one last hopeful retrieval and he saw for half an instant both breasts bare beneath the cape; no wonder she wore it so closely even in this monstrous heat.

Did she wear it at all, in the wood?

"Would you like a cup of ale?" and then at her headshake, still smiling, still not meeting his eyes, "An ice then?" Did they even have ices here, in this miserable pisspot? What did girls like to drink? "An orange-cup?" Finally she gazed straight up, nothing coy behind the wide brown eyes, the drooping smile.

"Yes," in that sweet peculiar voice. "Please. Yes."

He offered to carry the basket but she shook her head again, no, granddam was very particular, granddam had entrusted the basket to her alone. But granddam apparently had said nothing of accepting favors from strangers; they took the drinks beneath a tree, half escaping the screech and dust of the stalls, the late sun's heavy pall. The orange-cup was sticky and smelled more closely of peel than pulp, but to her it was an obvious treat: slow and serious, those lips moving warm upon the sour juice, slow too the muscular motion of her throat as she swallowed. Faint glyphs traced by dust and sweat on that long throat, he remembered the sight of her breasts, those tiny nipples. Did they brush against the velvet? were they hard?

"Is your cloak hot?" and then the inner frown, it was embarrassing and absurd; all he need do was show her money, a girl this poor would do much for a handful of coin. Or less. Is your cloak hot, like a giggly boy afraid to speak the words.

"My granddam made it," she said proudly. "For me."

"It's lovely," taking a fold between his fingers. "She must be an excellent seamstress."

"Oh, yes. For years. But now, her hands," and she made them stiff before her, frozen into a spastic grasp. "She can barely work. So I make these," touching the basket's rim, slow unconscious sigh at the depleted wares. "She shows me how."

No, she did not sell much; yes, it was hard to live in the wood on nothing but what they found there.

Roots and flowers and clumsy snares, and she with her bare breasts and bird-voice and dirty glorious hair, gathering for granddam. He was touching her hair. He had not realized it.

"You're very beautiful," he said. Like the pelt of some exotic animal, like nothing he had ever felt before. His orange-cup fell over, juice against his thigh like piss; like semen. "You are."

Again, no coquetry; she merely shook her head, shook her hair gently free of his touch. Fingers damp with orange and sweat, her answering touch was very brief and no real answer at all. She finished her drink and carefully set the cup and skins aside. Basket in hand, "I have to go."

He had an urge as strong as pain to pull that cape aside, look at her again, touch her. Touch her hair. "I can take you. My horse is at the inn, I can—"

"This wood is wrong for horses," gravely, as if he must have known that. Sunset at her back, blurred triangled shape of cape and tilted head atop, gazing at him with a look he could not read, did not know.

"I, we'll walk, then, we'll—" but again that maddening sideways headshake, already turning away, and with a jerk he freed his coin purse, held it out in mute enticement but that was worst of all, now her smile was gone and she was hurrying, not back toward the stalls but toward the wood, the wood where she could lose him in instants, the wood her home and he an interloper with nothing but lust and money to recommend him; still he ran. And as expected she outpaced him, easily, he watched her do it and when she had utterly gone stopped still and hot, panting, arms loose and in one grasp still the Judas purse; Judas, yes, but he would not force her; he would not hurt her. Hair and breasts and little bird-like sounds, was it so hard, then, to understand?

In his rooms again, the whore built for the legions; better that than the balding one; today he had to have hair.

The rumor placed him there within the week, but the magistrate appeared, he and his retinue, instead within the day, half a dozen brigands astride nags unfit for the knackers and the magistrate himself like some great worn-out beast, filthy and hunched into leathers and bristling brass, shaggy head moving in the motions of harness. Still he was quite the personage: from the tavernkeeper with his hoarded wine to the two whores, rapt with bitter sniping, he was a bees' honeypot; oh he had money to spend indeed. And did, for himself and his men, drinking like a rock as they caroused, drinking and listening, or seeming to, as Jude spoke to him, man of business to his equal, over heavy mugs of wine.

The inn-tavern was hot, hot almost as the departed day, crowded with those with something to sell, vice or service, proffering to the retinue what did not first interest their lord. Business gainfully concluded, Jude left his spot at the magistrate's table, bound for his room; it was time to go. Too hot to sleep, what of it? He would ride under moonlight and cheat the sun.

He was halfway up the stairs when he saw her, still in that damnable cloak but her hair loose now, longer than he had supposed, ragged tumult to her waist. Basket in hand, she approached the tavernkeeper, who shrugged, nodded her toward the tables: try your luck. Hand on the jiggering bannister, staring down: had she waited in the wood, hidden like a sprite to watch him gone? Had she opened her cape to fan herself, watching with narrow eyes? Did it have to matter? No. What had the ale-seller said; mad as rabbits? Yes.

Resolute to his room, very little to gather and back down again to see her fail, again, this time more spectacularly, half the town saw the magistrate reach inside her cape for a casual squeeze, then spin her like a toy to put a foot to her backside, to her knees and gone. While the others laughed, or feigned to, her slow gleaning from the floor, trinket by trinket, and he thought he saw her tears. Out, again, to the wood; to the dark; she knew her way, did she not? He would not play the fool again to offer escort. Let her walk.

He paused to settle up with the tavernkeeper, who thanked him more than was necessary for his patronage, offered him a stirrup-cup, fuel for a pungent farewell piss somewhere along the road; he drank it fast, impatient to be gone and then the door: her voice, bird voice so loud that he nearly dropped his cup:

"A beast!" mouth crooked and wet with the tears she did not seem to notice through her obvious terror. "He waits for me, beyond me on the path!"

The magistrate blinked heavy eyes, a man of his began to rise before a local checked him back, explaining the girl with two words and a brief cruel smile. She cried out again, the same words. The tavernkeeper, half-angry, called, "Then take another," but this seemed to mean nothing to her, as if there were no other paths possible, as if this one was the only safe walking between the clutching fingers of the devil himself. Weeping harder now, round bird's-eyes staring, staring, she had lost half her worthless wares somewhere between the wood and the door; she did not seem to notice that, either, the dangling basket, the space within. She seemed as if she must take root there where she stood, and Jude felt a slow rage, with himself, with her, and then a strange paradoxical humor: he grabbed her arm, hard, at the elbow, and said loud enough for the tavern to hear, "I'll chart you home, girl."

And then out, into the dark, where he pushed her rough against the tavern wall and kissed her, eyes open, staring at that slack avian face. She seemed almost as if she did not feel his kisses, did not know she was being kissed, or stroked, or pressed up and down like a heifer at a fair. Finally when he paused, relief enough for this moment, she opened her eyes again and said, anxious and at once, "You will take me home? You have a weapon, a stave? Or a gutter's knife?"

Baring the pistol at his waist; there was no animal could stop a handful of ballshot and he told her so; still, "You are not a woodsman," but she spoke as if she wanted only to be reassured; he kissed her again, less painfully, and told her to wait, he would fetch his horse.

"It is not a wood for horses," anxious again and he laughed; very well, they would walk. "Lead me," and with one hand gripping his she did, away from the tavern, past the dirty booths now empty in the darkness, shuttered or struck to timbers and tent-rags, past the tree where they had drunk their orange-cups, into the woods where she had run from him; she was not running now. He halted them there, to kiss her again; vindication; but she was agitated, she kept looking round and round. "Can you see in the dark, like a cat?" but she did not catch his banter, she kept staring, insisting the beast was nearby, had to be. Had to be.

"And what sort of beast is it?"

That grave stare again. "There is only one beast in the woods," she said, and dragged him on.

Trees like iron with bars for branches, and moss as thin and sere as molding ribbons, as strips of beggars' skin; her wood was a dire place and he told her so, it was no wonder she and her granny were so poor. She shrugged as if she had heard imperfectly and did not care for the correction; her hand in his had begun to sweat, her grip still so very tight. Shadows had ceased to travel with them, but here and there the faintest lunar shiver, showing a dark more thorough than the mere absence of light.

"Where is your beast?" but again she did not seem to hear. Tension in the muscles of her face, in her crouching way of walking as if the slightest sound could mean some fierce betrayal. "Where is your home?"

"Not far," and then, in a rushing whisper, "Oh, granddam," as if she feared for granny too; never worry, he told her. If madame can bolt a door, she must be safe, and smiling to himself, he had begun to think that this beast perhaps was less real than she had let him guess; and the rest an amateur's overplay; why not? She had had time to rethink her modesty. He reached his free hand to slip beneath her cape, graze those breasts, but she called out, "There!" and pointed in the smothering darkness with the arrow of their linked hands.

It might have been heaven itself from her voice, but instead it was worse than a crofter's, half cave, half cottage, of a curious stone bent and interspersed with stalks of wood and the gnarled cusp of roots, lacing the structure as the girl's clothing barely laced her body. There were no lights inside that he could see, but presumably this was normal, granny no doubt an early sleeper, death's nightly rehearsal.

"You see?" and he stroked at her face, now, tried to catch more than the shape of her expression. "Your fear was for naught—there was no beast at all."

She shrugged a little, smiling finally in her relief; surely she understood what she owed for this squirage? Certainly she made no move to go inside. Kissing her, again, so deeply as to feel those small strange broken teeth, parting the cape to cup her breasts and he felt himself stiffen, pressing her against the door, thighs imprisoned between his own. Kissing her harder and harder, tasting blood, a thready gash in her lower lip as she pulled a trifling space away and her eyes were wide, looking not at him but at some point as far to her left as vision could reach and as he sought again for her lips the door behind them opened, just a little, just a space and as one they stumbled backward, into the sudden deep miasma of the airless cottage, and he saw her granddam, there to the left of the door.

There is only one beast in the woods.

And its eyes are a woman's; are hers, that same round glossy darkness though informed by some tremendous age. Naked in the dimness, hair like her granddaughter's, matted-thick but longer still, waving like the grey moss on the trees as she advanced. He meant to take his pistol, but young hands held his, two pairs of eyes stared black as blood on open lips, on teeth not broken but immensely worn and "Oh, granddam," again but happy now, the chore complete as she stepped from his side, the barest distance: hands before her, thoughtful, gaze bird-startled still but deeply unsurprised.

The Root of the Matter

Gregory Frost

Gregory Frost lives in Philadelphia, Pennsylvania. He is the author of Tain *and* Remscela, *novels based on Irish legendry, and other fantasy works that often have a wryly humorous flavor, albeit a humor that bites. Here he takes a very different approach to his retelling of "Rapunzel," a darkly sexual story reminiscent of Anne Sexton's version of the same tale (a disturbing poem published in her brilliant collection* Transformations*).*

"Rapunzel" is a story that has always had a dark touch: the witch craving possession of a child; the child growing to womanhood locked away in a desolate tower; the lover-prince blinded by his impetuous adventure. In "The Root of the Matter" Frost walks the line between fantasy and horror and emerges with a memorable tale.

The Root of the Matter

1. Obloquy & Sortilege

I WANTED A CHILD, YOU SEE. YOU.

The rest I'd sacrificed long ago and, really, I didn't miss it much, except maybe on holidays. I'd grown up on holidays, to be with my family and smell the old smells, relive my childhood a little bit. For most children, I suppose it was something to look forward to. That being at the core of the wretched life I'd abandoned, it didn't make much sense that I'd ever go back again. Nice, liver-spotted daddy seated on the far side of the cranberry sauce that's lumped in its bowl like somebody's heart, is the same daddy who hoisted my slick pink bottom out of the bathtub bubbles and spread me with his thumbs and tore out the childhood in me.

Childhood couldn't fit in beside his blunted cock, so childhood packed its bag and fled the same night; I had to wait another two years for a chance to follow it.

Now when I reflect back, I start to tell myself, "Gothel, there were plenty of alternatives to running away," but it isn't true. He was The Daddy. The God, the Almighty to whom the family were obedient. The "Don't Cry, Baby, Daddy's Here" savior. The Fucker. Besides, I didn't have any powers then, so I couldn't have dealt with him.

Some women, they just go find some other daddy, an adoptive daddy, a sweet sugar daddy. Not me, and not you—I've seen to us both.

I tried to remain in the city at first, but found I couldn't endure seeing the men. In the city, they were everywhere, with their little girls holding their hands. I'd see their eyes glittering like the cold eyes of birds, like his had done, and I'd know there was a stiffness in their pants and an ugliness like a tumor in their thoughts. I couldn't just sit by and watch the conspiracy take shape around some other poor wretch. That's what finally drove me from the city, into the wilderness—the conspiracy whereby fathers rape their daughters.

I was younger than you—I hadn't even been faced with my first . . . with the curse of bleeding. I'd no idea then what I would find in dark, redolent forests.

By the time I arrived at the place the Others called "The Rift," I hadn't eaten in days, I smelled dirty, and everything I had on itched. Little girls, running away from home, pack stuffed animals and jammies. They don't understand the first thing about what they'll need in order to survive in the soulless world.

I stopped where I stopped because there was a stream. I dangled a hand in it, found it uncommonly warm. I waded in and lay down in the middle. And it was like a big, downy bed with bedding of water. I'd never felt anything so soothing and safe in my life. I must have—I did—fall asleep there. I dreamt of sailing along, down to a river, past a quay and out into the sea.

The next I knew, people had come to the banks of the stream on both sides of me. The Others. Firefly people, I thought of them, because they burned, incandescent. I remember that I wasn't afraid but thought I should be. When I sat up, they reached and helped me out of the stream. Where they stepped, white light swirled in the water. They led me into the woods somewhere near, although I'm none too clear if it was the same woods as when I'd arrived. In any case, by morning, when they flitted away, I'd discovered my power. It had been there in me all along, dormant, needing cause or awareness for its release. I believe it sleeps in you, too, my love, and in all women. The Others taught me that, you see.

You're always asking for tricks, as if this is some kind of parlor game, this power, but there's a conservation of energy to sorcery, which means you don't produce it for free. It costs. To make magic is to burn off some of your own life. Like hurtful words, you can't take it back once it's done. If I performed right now every simple trick you've wanted in your fifteen sweet years, I'd turn five hundred years old myself in a blink and look twice that much. Silly girl.

Yes, I suppose they were fairies, the Others. A race, a people both strange and familiar, as though they lurked inside a forgotten dream somewhere. They were hermaphroditic, have I said? That means they had what you have as well as a tiny, useless, deflated cock. I know it's bewildering that I didn't react violently at seeing their maleness. Maybe because the display was so innocent, sexless—hairless bodies, and with little breasts, oh, much smaller than yours, my darling. More like castrated little children than men.

I worked to learn from them how to express my newfound sorceries. Afterward, I snuck back into the city.

There was a house there—my daddy had spoken of it a few times to my mother—that took me in. Only women lived in it. I made a bargain with she who owned it, once I'd demonstrated for her how I could manipulate her clientele. I had to use one of the other girls. Only a single other time have I ever directed my power upon a woman. But we'll come to that event soon enough.

I preyed upon men. Only upon men. I made them do humiliating things, ugly things, you'd think; they cowered, and crawled like insects, like worms, but they obeyed every foul request. And when they'd had their fill of debasement, they offered me more power. Money, property, jewels. I decided that I wanted the piece of wilderness where the Others dwelled, and I lured the man who held title and got it deeded to me. By then I had a reputation in certain circles, and he arrived at the house thinking to conquer me with his maleness. They all tried in their way to best me. I was a challenge no male ego could resist: the little girl who drains men dry without so much as letting them touch her. Each one had his sweaty fantasy of turning the tables on me; none of them ever did. You remember the story I told you about the witch named Circe? She lived on an island alone, but men wandered there all the time, pretending to be blown off course. She turned every one of them into pigs, but they kept coming. Just to nibble at her painted toes a while before the slaughter. Well, turning men into pigs is no particular feat. The real exercise is getting pigs to write checks.

Once I had the land, I made other men clear it and build me a house with a big wall around it, so that the stream would run through the property. Then I sent them away with no memory of where they'd been, and I was finally freed and wealthy and alone at the age of seventeen. I never needed to see another of them again.

What happened next was, I began dreaming about you, my love. I didn't anticipate you. For years I lived contentedly with only the Others for company. Maybe my dreams of you were an expression of the power they'd unleashed in me. The ache grew in me like a child itself. Like a hot wind, it would sweep over me as I lay in bed, and those nights I drove myself to pleasure, hoping to find peace in the aftermath of orgasm, but all I could think of still was the child who is you. I probably would have gone frustrated to my grave if civilization hadn't caught up with me.

I had never considered that if I could set down on a parcel of wilderness land so could anyone else. One morning, I woke up and there, right outside my wall, were men hammering together a frame, two stories, much higher than my wall. Men. Naked to the waist and covered with hair, bellowing and rude, exposing themselves and pissing into the wind—I thought I'd done with them and here they were like maggots crawling over the bones of a giant. I was so startled, so appalled, that I could only look on in horror as the roof was tarred and shingled, and leaded glass fitted in the windows, and the bricks mortared in place. In no time, as if the materials leaped into place with every blink of my eye, it was done. The house, casting my house in its shadow, filled the eastern sky.

I crept down to the stream and peered over the wall, only to find that other tracts had been cleared behind me as well. Machines had destroyed it all. My forest had gone and I could see, through the distant haze, the gleam of a city skyline. The water emerging under my wall was already befouled. The Others had seen it coming much sooner. They'd departed, closing the Rift forever. I would have gone with them—they'd taught me so much. I suppose they thought of me as part of this world, whatever else I meant to them. And I wouldn't have known you.

The first indication I had of the new occupants was the laughter of their children. You can imagine how that tore at me, ravenous as I was for you by then. Before long, there were lights at night. Bodies moved about, silhouettes in the windows—the man, a skinny little puppet thing; the woman, though, was titanic. An ungoverned earth-mother ripe as can be. I counted three children and here she was, pregnant with a fourth. As I hid in my shadowy hut, I heard her raise her squawking voice in anger, I heard a slap against the face of a disobedient babe. My cheek burned as if she'd slapped me. My resolve hardened into stone.

I used my power the same night, twice. First, I looked inside the ill-tempered cow and saw you, my tiny girl, the object of my dreams. I knew in an instant I'd found my destiny. Second, I set into motion an obsession. It was simple, because pregnant women are already poised on the brink of obsession; I had but to point a direction, give desire its goal, give the fat woman a push.

I had a garden that she could see from her high window. In it grew three rows of harebell—lovely big blue flowers that would catch her eye. She didn't call it harebell; where she came from the plant had a different name, which is your sweet name. You see, the magic was with the plant. I named you after it because you are part of that magic.

I made her crave the harebell root the way I craved the contents of her belly. She could not sleep because of it. She lost the energy to slap her children, though she raised her voice and railed when they dislocated her desire with their presence. Her mouth watered and she smacked her lips all the time, trying to find the missing flavor in every memory of food.

That was the second time I used magic on a woman, but she was so unkempt and irascible, I had no misgivings. Rejoice that you never knew her and never felt her hand across your cheek.

Bloated as she was, the woman couldn't possibly climb the wall to steal the plant. Naturally, she sent *him*. The husband.

I let him steal the roots the first time. That was part of the magic. He slithered back over the wall, and their house fell silent for the first time in a long while. I could imagine her devouring a sweet salad of root, her eyes rolling back in her head at the luscious pleasure squeezed out of each bite. No doubt for a while she squatted with oily fingers and drool upon her chin. Then the shouting, the wailing began. If I hadn't known he was in my garden before, I'd have known all about it from the cow screaming at the top of her lungs for him to "go get more rapunzel."

It was when he attempted to return that I barred his way. Caught him red-handed, with a half dozen slender, fleshy roots dangling from his fist. He began to cry. He fell to his knees, begging my forgiveness. He accounted for himself by describing how his wife had become mad for the roots because of her pregnancy. He offered to pay for them. I laughed at him, poor, pathetic creature that he was. As if I needed his few coins.

Finally, I pretended sympathy and agreed to let him go. I told him that I understood his wife's ailment better than he. Of course, he assumed I meant I'd borne children of my own. My offer of recompense took him utterly by surprise.

I demanded you. I would keep the woman subdued, sated, absolutely sodden with rapunzel throughout the remaining five months of her pregnancy, at the end of which he would give me the baby.

Oh, no, he cried. Anything but that. It was all sham, his struggle with ethics.

He probably would have fought longer, except that the obese shrew began bellowing like a foghorn for him to get back there with her rapunzel. He positively squirmed, which was worth the years I was using up in working my magic on her. It was my offer of a holiday from that monster which ultimately turned him around. "All right," said he, "I have three already, don't I?" He wasn't really asking, he was justifying it, setting it right in his mind the way men do easily when they need to accept a break with decency. I'm sure my daddy had cleared my rapes with himself by calling them something morally proper that I deserved.

I let the man pass, brushing the roots as he did with a soporific dust. He went home and the bellow of the beast ceased that night. His children came to laugh freely again, and I even heard him joining in now and again. The sound of children laughing made my blood race as I bided my time.

When the night of delivery came, I waited at the window, listening for your first cries. No sweeter music have I ever heard, except your singing nowadays.

I saw him at the window—he made the agreed sign. I flew over the wall and sailed through his house like a ghost, past his sleeping children, right into the room where the exhausted woman slept. He was pacing the floor there, wringing his hands, the nails still black with my dirt.

The imminent act had driven him half mad. I could see that he might recant at any second. I told him not to worry, that you would be well looked after. I promised to raise you right. Whatever he considered "right" to be, he didn't pursue it. After all, he hadn't carried you, kicking inside his belly; he hadn't been tied to you, feeding you all the time you were growing; he didn't know any bond so close. You were a thing outside him, as all women are to all men. Now you see how that is true for you right from birth. And now you see how a man can steal anything from a woman, even a part of her own flesh; but you, my dearest, were fortunate, in that you were passed to me. Finally, he handed you over, then turned his back and told me to get out.

I never saw either of them again. What he told her, or if he told her anything, I have neither idea nor care. They didn't want you enough to fight for you even a little bit, to protect you as I have done for so many years.

The rest you've been party to as you've grown. The forest where we lived, until you began your monthly cycle—and I've explained already that I removed you here to protect you from those men who began to come around, inevitably sniffing out your woman-scent. I knew they were there in the forest, watching, creeping closer every day. They would have had us both if we'd lingered longer.

No man will ever lay a hand upon you. Only I, because I know how to touch your heart, as you touch mine, my beautiful girl. I know what pleases you best because it pleases me the same. Never to strike you, to harm you, as that horrid creature that bore you would have done. As men would have done. If I spoil you silly with everything you want or need, well, who do I harm? And I always shall. I adore you, don't you see, my Rapunzel, my little blue-eyed bellflower. I adore you so very much.

2. Penetration

Dear Diary,

Mother Gothel had her sherry again and told me the story of how I got here, which I've heard maybe a hundred times already. It gets bigger every time she tells it, and the facts get changed. I mean, *I* never saw men creeping in the forest. Mother Gothel goes on about them constantly—how she rescued me from terrors I can't even imagine, about all these other things she'd saved me from. The filth of the city; my cruel family. And the men. Touching me, sticking me with their weird pricking things; the way she describes cocks, it's like big pronged knives grow out of their bodies. When I was little, I used to cry when she described them. I had nightmares and everything. Now, I'm not so sure. The story looks threadbare to me. How did my mother have me, if she had to get cored by this thorny potato peeler of a cock first? She'd be dead, I'm sure.

When we came to the lighthouse from the forest, I was twelve. That was only three years ago, but when she's in her cups, Mother Gothel behaves as if I don't remember the order of events, or recall that I never saw any men, or that she used her power to keep me unconscious the whole way here. In truth, I've no idea where "here" is. Near an ocean is all.

Her transformation and mine definitely began the night of my first period. I woke up with something warm between my legs. I'd been feeling cranky and bloated for a week, and all of a sudden there I was, bleeding to death. I started screaming for my life. God, I was *dying*, I was just certain of it.

She cursed me and cursed me when she saw the blood; she stomped around the bed, slapped the mattress, called me a bitch, a slut, a cunt—I don't even know what that means. It's the nearest she's ever come to hitting me. I thought it was *my fault* what had happened. I kept crying, "I'm sorry, I'm sorry," even though I didn't know what for. Then, after she'd exhausted us both, she finally announced that she'd been expecting this. "It's a curse all women share but I'd prayed God it would skip over you." That moment I began to doubt everything she'd ever told me. It was *my* fault, was it? She was blaming *me*, but at the same time she'd known it would happen because it happens to all women? I couldn't wrestle sense from that, and I hated her for twisting me up in her perjury.

No more than two days after that, she began asking had I noticed anyone lurking about. Anyone like naked men hiding behind the trees. There was no one, of course, I hadn't seen a soul; I mean *ever*.

In my whole insular life I'd never met anyone on a path, in the stream, climbing a tree. We might have been the only two people in the whole world if she hadn't rattled on about these "men" who pursued us. And thereafter it was me—they smelled *me*, they hunted *me*. I'd like to see one, just to know that they're really down there somewhere.

Next she came in agitated and told me she'd spotted these men lurking near the garden, waiting to pounce on her if she went to gather her vegetables. For days she wouldn't let me go out, or even get close to a window. Finally, she locked me in and disappeared for a week herself. When she returned, she worked an enchantment on me. I slept there and awoke here.

We live on three floors at the top of the lighthouse; the rest is bricked up. For companionship now I have screeching gulls and a wide plain of ocean that glistens day and night. Sometimes objects float by, far away. They never come close. Never.

I'm the only means available for coming or going in this tower. I have a feeling she planned it that way all along. We were going to move to this tower from the day I was born.

She has never cut my hair. I think she thinks it would be the equivalent of beating me. My earliest memory is of being brushed at bedtime. Every night she takes out her brushes and unravels my braids. They lie near the glass door, coiled up like big ropes fastened to my head. Sometimes I imagine I'm a machine that runs on steam, and the braids are the hoses that connect me to the engine so I don't run down.

Whenever she wants to go out, Mother Gothel touches me and says into my ear, "Rapunzel, let down your hair now." Together, we carry the coils out onto the walkway girdling the turret. The railing has big hooks attached to it that I can wrap each braid around for support before dropping it over the side. My hair nearly touches the ground.

There's a small ladder of five rungs, an opening in the rail. Mother Gothel climbs onto it, takes hold of both braids and slides down the side of the tower as though she were a girl no older than me. I've never seen her do any sorcery, not really *real* sorcery—she complains that it wears her out—but I know she has secret powers, otherwise how could she move on the strands of my hair so easily? I hardly even feel her weight.

I can never leave. I am the ladder, how can I climb me?

Dear Diary,

Today is the strangest of all days ever.

It began simply enough. I was lying on my bed, with my earphones on, listening to something Baroque. Mother Gothel only brings me Baroque music. I've asked for something else, a variety, but she claims the other tapes are too expensive.

The morning had heated up early and was humid from yesterday's rain. I had chores to do but could not make myself stir. Mother Gothel came up beside me and gently stroked my braid where it joins my head. I dragged one phone from my ear. "Rapunzel, you lazy girl," she cooed, "get up. I have to go shopping."

I raised my head and looked at her. I was pretending to be a turtle. I blinked at her and tried to draw back into my shell.

She didn't like that. "The morning's half gone," she said sharply. "You haven't even dressed." That was true. I was lying naked on the bed. But just thinking about the effort of putting on petticoats and skirts in that heat exhausted me. I thought, the sooner I get rid of her the better.

I got up and wrapped the sheet around me and marched out to the balcony. If she saw that I was mad at having to get up, I didn't care. She ignored me, the way she always does when she's preparing to leave. She's always counting things in her mind, rummaging.

I don't even exist for her, not really. She keeps this image of me in her head, of what I am. When she speaks to me the way she does when she reminisces, she's talking to the illusion. Whenever I do something awful—like setting her birds free from their cages, making her capture them again—she sighs and says, "The child will be willful from time to time." What is that supposed to mean? The false-me can't get into trouble, no matter what I do. But then I'll have my monthly flow and she'll start screeching at me as if I did it to vex her. The image again—the image doesn't bleed. It's always twelve years old. I wish it would pop out from inside her head so I could grab it and throw it over the balcony. Then she would have to deal with *me*.

Before she climbed down, she gave me a peck on the cheek. "I'll be back at dusk," she said. "Have dinner ready, won't you?" I nodded, to let her know I'd heard, to avoid an argument. So many of them lately. I surprise myself these days with how readily I pursue arguments. I'm not certain I understand this any more than Mother Gothel does.

I watched her walk away from the tower as I hoisted the braids back up. She entered the hawthorn maze ringing the hilltop. Her magic grew that dark barrier. She claims the way through it is treacherous—between the thorns and all the dead ends—an added layer of protection against whatever's out there. *She* threads it easily enough.

When I'd piled the hair up, I slumped down beside it. The boards were warm beneath my face and smelled of brine. There came into my head the notion of swimming out to one of the ships on the horizon. I needed a miracle right then, although I couldn't say what shape it should take. I think it was a premonition of the change about to occur.

I hadn't yet unlooped the braids from the hooks when I heard the soft call, "Rapunzel, Rapunzel, let down your hair." What, I wondered, was she doing back already? What had she forgotten? I didn't care, but I did hesitate to respond right away. When I thought she'd been frustrated enough, I pushed the hair off the side. A sea gull had landed on the rail, and he flapped up, shrieking, at my movement. I watched him sail out in a great arc, catching an updraft and soaring higher than the lighthouse roof. I was dreaming about flying beside him, and the next thing I knew, there were footsteps on the ladder, and I turned my head and found a stranger staring at me.

I jumped up. The sheet caught in the board. I had to undo it and pull it, and of course it tore. I rewrapped myself, backed into the doorway—or tried to, anyway. But I remained hooked to the railing and couldn't retreat. I stopped, unable to decide what I should do.

The stranger stood motionless at the rail, holding the two strands of my hair together in front of him. His wide, dark eyes had the power to touch. Each glance brushed over me like fingers, almost like the caress of Mother Gothel's hands in the bath. All the while my heart was beating as wildly as in the bath. It was practically in my throat. The sun wheeled in the sky, and still we didn't move, either of us. I can't imagine what my own expression must have been. After all, he'd seen a girl before. But he was my first man.

He wore odd, torn clothing. I couldn't help darting fearful glances at the spot where his legs met, but there was no treacherous blade visible.

All of a sudden, and the more shocking because I wasn't prepared for it, he spoke my name. His voice was soft, but deeper than Gothel's or mine, as his hair and skin were darker. The sound of my name plucked a string inside me, set me all to vibrating.

Without my asking, he undid the braids and drew them up, coiling them as if he had been doing it his whole life. I hadn't yet said a word, and I was free then to run, but I stayed. I waited. I wanted to know.

He came and sat down beside my hair. He began talking to me. "I spent the night inside your hawthorn trap. It's very clever. Looks like normal growth from without. You'd never know until you're in it how tricky it is to navigate." He had come upon Mother Gothel in her garden and followed her. Our tower, he said, hadn't been used since his grandfather's time, when great ships with huge sails as tall as the tower itself came rounding the point of land. He gestured out at the blue sea as he spoke. His words produced a warmth inside me, and all at once I blushed, thinking I'd begun my flow; but a quick look at the sheet told me I was wrong. Still, I was wet there.

He said, "I had to spend the night inside the maze. Last night I heard singing. A lullaby. It was the most wonderful voice I've ever heard. I lay back in there, a rabbit trapped in a snare, and just listened to the song. By the time it ended, I couldn't live without its sound. If it was a drink, I wanted to be intoxicated. It was water for my thirst, food for my hunger. And I know that the singer was you."

"Yes," I admitted. I could feel myself blushing, because of course I *had* been singing last night. He had heard me. He said he'd fallen in love with *me*. An emotional upheaval nearly drowned me. The realization came all at once, like lightning: I was no longer by myself. There was someone else. As he spoke, as he described how he'd set off from home and wandered through the country to seek the unknown of his future, I came to sense that he was in many ways more like me than Mother Gothel was.

Initially, I tried to deny this, falling back behind the security of her warnings about men's treacherous lies. But his were no lies. He was simply telling me his story, not trying to beguile me, flatter or cajole me. Mother Gothel warned me about the shape of the words of men, but she'd neglected to tell me how I would feel in the presence of one. Did all of them have hypnotic charms? If I entered a room full of them, would I become butter, melting away?

He spoke of faraway places, of markets and trains, of his family—he had both brothers and sisters. I tried to imagine what such a family must be like.

All at once I started. The sun was setting behind him. I'd sat down to listen but I jumped up now and told him he had to leave. He looked on dumbly. He didn't understand.

"Mother Gothel will be returning," I told him. "She has powers, fierce powers. She'll destroy you. You have to go before she returns."

He considered. "All right," he said. "But I must come back, now I know the way." He looked down over the rail, studying the maze, its pattern open to him. "What a jewel she guards."

I lowered my eyes when he said that. This was the sort of talk Mother Gothel had warned me about—calling us "jewels" or "goddesses." I'd enjoyed his company so much that I didn't want to think he was capable of it.

"Go," I urged. He looked forlorn, as if he'd been hoping for something else. He grabbed at me playfully, to make me come and kiss him, but I slapped his hand aside. "Don't be stupid," I said. "Go." He sullenly climbed back over the edge, took hold of the braids and disappeared over the side.

He had barely let go when I saw Mother Gothel approaching from outside the ring of thorns. He must have hidden somewhere around the other side of the tower, because she did not see him. But when she climbed up, she began right away to shout at me. "Never let down your hair until I call to you! Ever."

I protested that I had done it as a courtesy. This seemed to work pretty well. At least, she stopped squawking about that and began complaining instead that I'd spent the whole day on nothing at all. I hadn't gotten dressed. I hadn't fixed a meal. And look how I'd torn a perfectly good bedsheet.

I had to turn away then, because I almost started to laugh, and if I'd done that, then she would have known. I couldn't have hidden the pleasure overtaking me.

Before I came in here tonight, I sat on the balcony and sang again. This time I knew he could hear, and I sang for him alone, wherever he hides in the woods. My heart races when I picture him listening.

He will come back. I will see him again. I wonder if I'll dream about him tonight, if in my dream I'll give him a name.

Dear Diary,

It has happened. I think now it was inevitable from the moment he arrived; or maybe it was when he confessed his love for my song.

Jon (for that's his name) climbed up again as soon as she was gone. He had new clothes this time, not torn by the maze. He didn't press for a kiss this time either, so I invited him into the tower, gave him a tour of all three floors.

He was most curious about the disused apparatus that had once signaled the ships. It's a lamp of some kind, with two large rods in the center. Even though he had never seen it before, he understood its workings, and showed me where the rods had melted in the middle. That was where the light was produced. "An arc," he said, when the two rods were brought close together. The light had reflected off large mirrors, but the remaining one lay now disassembled on the floor. It was curved like a shallow bowl, and distorted our faces as we peered into it. He prattled on about its power to cast light far out to sea in a great sweeping beam that ships even over the horizon would see. He was showing off, but I didn't pay much attention. I couldn't help looking at the two of us in the mirror. What I did next surprised us both.

Jon didn't notice, so caught up was he in the fantasy of sailors and lights that guided them through their darkness. He wasn't watching me, I know, because I'd taken off everything and settled into the mirror before he turned and saw me, and whatever he was about to say was lost forever. His mouth hung open, shaping a word.

"This mirror is cold," I said.

He replied, "It's glass." He swallowed.

I leaned forward and stared at myself upside down looking up at me over my breasts. "I'm divided in two," I said. I was teasing him now, beginning to explore my power over him, which was proving substantial. Is this how Mother Gothel feels toward me?

"What should I do?" he asked, barely able to look my way.

I had but to open my arms for him to understand me. He turned his back to undress. Unlike him, I watched boldly as more and more of him was unveiled. His body had a hardness to it that neither I nor Mother Gothel shared. His muscles seemed chiseled in his sides, his legs. His stomach, when he turned, had ridges over it.

His cock was nothing like I'd expected. It bore no resemblance to the razor-edged and barbed weapons Mother Gothel had described. It seemed both rigid and flexible, and the tip sparkled with a drop of liquid. I could see how we were supposed to close together. She'd never discussed this except in ways to make me dread it, and jittery things did flutter in my stomach, but it wasn't dread, it was something else.

For all of his posturing the day before, he came to me shyly, clearly at a loss as to what we must do. I lay back and drew him up beside me. His cock slid along my thigh. We became arms and legs for a moment, an uncoordinated heap of limbs trying to establish mutual comfort and support. He propped himself on one elbow. His touch arrived light as a feather, and I twitched with pleasure. Each of us wanted to explore the same regions of the other, and it took us no time at all to excite ourselves. The knowledge must have been inside me all the time. If my monthly flow is woman's ancient curse, then maybe this comprehension of union is the ancient blessing accompanying it to balance the equation. I couldn't wait for him to decide. I took hold of him and urged him to fit himself between my wetted thighs.

In one respect Mother Gothel had foretold honestly—there was pain. It lasted an instant, a flash of fire, a brief scorch. But, then . . . then followed a consuming warmth like hot water poured through me. The tip of his cock touched somewhere deep inside, and stars seemed to burst round my eyes. I arched my back. I think I cried out. All that warmth filling me blasted down and out of me. Jon had his head up, the muscles rigid in his neck. He looked wild, feral as a demon, but almost as if he were in agony, as if he were dying. Abruptly, he collapsed on top of me. He twitched a few times, then let out a deep sigh and kissed me once more. It was that last, lingering kiss which told me he hadn't lied. Mother Gothel had so many times described how, the instant men were finished with you, they got up and left you to your pain and emptiness. "You mean nothing to them, the pretty words are all lies. They discard you." Jon did not behave like that. He clung to me as I to him. In the bowl of the mirror, with the voices of the sea gulls like a chorus in the sky, we might have been at sea ourselves, rocking gently to and fro, a thought that prompted me to begin singing softly the lullaby he'd heard the first night. A great, drowsy smile spread over his face. His eyes so black gave me back my own face. "I love you, Rapunzel," he murmured. He closed his eyes and I sang him to sleep. I don't know if he knew I was crying.

I was reluctant to send him away again after that, but I had to. I had to. If she found him, who knows what she would do?

Diary,

I find her touch almost unbearable. Last evening, as we do regularly, we went down to the bath on the lower level. Mother Gothel lathered me as she has done since I was a child. She spends a great deal of time washing between my legs, and I've always let her. It felt so rapturous. Now, though the sensation's the same, I've no desire to let her enjoy me—that is what she does, why pretend otherwise? *She* is the one who takes her pleasure from me and walks away. She's the one for whom I'm a possession, an object. Why else am I kept here? If there are men, then let me deal with them. They're not half so fearsome as she believes. Jon says yes, there exist extraordinarily cruel men, evil men. But he admits the possibility (and proves it by existing) that there are good and fair men as well. Mother Gothel allows for no such thing. All are one color, one way. I cannot accept that. As Jon says, if it were all as she claimed, there'd be no people left.

Diary,

I've decided to run away.

It will be simple if I'm careful. Each time he comes now, he brings me a silk scarf to match the blue one I have already. I have eight of them, and I've begun knotting them together to create a ladder down which I can climb. Gothel will come after us I know, but Jon swears his family has power enough to bar her access once we've reached his home.

Today she never left, which was just as well, because I was sick the better part of the day. I don't want to be sick for him. When he arrives, he immediately wants to make love, and I want to make him happy. We've so little time together.

Diary,

My sickness returns almost daily. I can't even look at an onion now without my stomach twisting. Worse, even though I'm keeping less food in, I'm bloating up. When I wake up in the morning sometimes, my fingers are swollen. Sometimes my feet. Whatever this is, I'm scared. I've tried to hide the worst of it from both of them. Jon, I think, remains unaware, he's so much in love. I hide my discomfort and let him mount me, and afterward he's too drowsy to notice anything. But Mother Gothel has begun eyeing me suspiciously. She makes excuses not to leave on her usual rounds. I can't imagine how Jon endures day after day of living in the forest, waiting for her descent. My hair is all that binds us, binds us all.

Gods and saints, help me. She knows!

She ran my bath and I got in under the suds before she came in. But then she lathered my breasts and I could not help crying out. Her rough hands chafed my nipples. She asked what was wrong, her voice so sly.

"I'm not well," I said. "My breasts are tender, like it's my time of the month."

"What is it?" she asked.

"Flu," I told her. "It doesn't go away. And my clothes all feel uncomfortable. Mother Gothel, my dress is so tight now in the waist."

She withdrew her hands then, and stood up, staring in horror at my belly. I tried to be brave, but what could I do, knowing nothing of my own condition or what I had revealed?

"You monster," she snarled, "right under my nose. After all my warnings, all my declarations."

"I don't understand," I tried to say, but she interrupted me.

"Don't you dare try to pretend this is some immaculate miracle. No god climbed in here and fucked you, filthy whore." Then she cut loose with all of her sharp names for me. The litany of syllables that I don't have to define to understand. "Where is he? Are you hiding him here?" She pulled open a cabinet, tore out the shelves, threw linens every which way until the space inside lay empty. She stamped her foot on the sealed trap to the floor below.

"No," I said, but she dismissed me. She was clinging to that image of me again. The sweet girl hadn't done this. A beast had come in, a thing built of a dozen dirty names. She stormed out. I climbed from the bath and dried off quickly.

By the time I reached the top, she'd destroyed most of my room. The tapes she'd bought like candies for me lay strewn about, stepped on, crushed and unreeled. I thought of all the music lost to me forever, and my heart became stone. I struck out the only way I knew how. "He isn't here, he's gone," I said.

"Gone, I see." She looked right through me. I'd made the final blunder by admitting what she suspected. There could be no retreat from confession.

"He won't come while *you're* here," I told her.

"Of course he won't. He can't steal your soul with me around."

"He's not like that."

"They're *all* like that. Hasn't he promised to run away with you? To give you a life of luxury?" She began to shout. "Didn't you listen to me? I've told you time and again what they'll do to you."

"No," I replied, but her portrayal had gone to ice in my heart. Jon had made all the promises she said. Still I defended him. "*You* lied to me, Mother Gothel. A million times."

That brought her up. "I never lied. Who is it, hiding men's swollen pricks inside her? Who is it that's got a baby growing in her belly?"

The next I knew, I'd dropped down on the bed. I didn't know what to say to that revelation. This, too, she had kept from me all along. I would have a baby now. My baby. Not hers. I stared and saw her at last without the rosy glass of kindness between us. I saw a sour old woman with her watery eyes shining a hateful madness; she who'd already stolen one woman's child. She'd done nothing but set limits for me, telling me only what she wanted me to know, maintaining my ignorance as the ultimate power over me.

She went out and returned. "He's never going to have you," she swore. She drew a carving knife from behind her.

So, I thought, she means to kill me. She's going to cut the child from me. I had nowhere to run in that tiny room. I sat on the bed and watched her approach, ready to die. She yanked one of my braids and slashed down with the knife. Hair tore out of my head. She sawed through the braid and threw it aside. Then she cut away the other. The braids belonged to the daughter Mother Gothel kept inside her mind, and I was no longer attached in any way to that image. She'd released me, a fairy princess from an evil queen's spell.

She kicked the braids out of the room and slammed the door. "You'll not climb down to him, either. No, my corrupt beauty, you're leaving us, but not like that." Again I thought she meant to kill me, but she went out. I heard the key scrape in the lock. I ran and tried to tear the door open, too late.

Now, as I sit here on the bed, there's a rising wind outside. The sky splits open with flashes of lightning but without thunder. The light is barely an arm's length beyond my window. Her voice rattles the door with chants in a foreign tongue. This is her sorcery that she would never let me see. How can I combat this? Jon, do you know? Can you see what's happening? Fly, my love, run far from here, go home to your protective family. Be the liar she says you are, and abandon me while you can. Find another singer whose song offers you pleasure. Maybe in her voice you'll find enough of me to satisfy you.

I do sense something like an electricity on the air, constricting in a band around me, enclosing me tighter with each blink of the eye. The tower's swaying like it's alive. I think I'm falling, falling. Mother Got

3. Rates of Exchange

From where I sat in the wood at dawn, I couldn't see a thing. A fog had moved in after that storm.

Because of Rapunzel's condition, the old woman went out less and less, and I didn't want to miss her because of the fog. I would like to say I was worried for Rapunzel, that my desire to get into the tower again was in order to look after her. The shameful truth is that I only wanted to fuck again. My body wanted her, and its desire completely overrode what ought to have been my real concern. Fortunately, as the sun rose, the fog thinned until I could clearly see the tower.

Soon enough, the golden hair came unfurling down the side, followed by the bulky spider-shape of Gothel. She descended out of sight behind the hawthorns, but I held my place until she'd emerged and vanished over the hill before I got up and raced into the ring. The treacherous path led me all round and round the tower. Running, I kept trying for a glimpse of her on the balcony.

I climbed the lighthouse faster than I ever had, leaped over the rail like a gymnast. In my eagerness I was already tugging my shirt loose.

The balcony lay empty, washed in a sense of doom. Some of the planks had been ripped up. One of the large panes of glass had shattered inward. For a minute, taking in the obvious destruction, I didn't see what had happened. It was too enormous, too impossible. The severed braids hung right beside me, dangling from their hooks like bloody stumps. All at once I understood. I turned to escape—and there stood Gothel, the ogress, at the rail.

You've never seen anyone mad the way she was, and I hope you never will. Her face had twisted up till every fold and crease etched her with malice. Her eyes contained so much hatred of me, they couldn't blink.

"You interloper," she called me. "Invader. You freely bathed in my poor girl's innocence till it was all used up, poisoned by your pricking as if you were a thorn from the maze." She lifted a braid to her breasts. "You taught her how to cheat on me. All my precautions, all my barriers, and one of your kind still got through. Damn you, boy."

"I want—" I hesitated, choosing words more carefully in the face of her madness. "Madame Gothel, I *wish* to marry Rapunzel." In truth I hadn't considered it with anything but the lightest heart, but I was seeking to represent myself with more fairness than she gave me. But she knew me better than that.

"Fine enough to say," she answered, "yet we both of us know it's a lie of convenience to extricate yourself from a situation you'd rather not be in. Don't we? You lie and you lay her, it's all so casual." I could not meet her gaze. "The same as she—soiled in a way that no scrubbing can ever clean."

"All right," I said petulantly, "then I guess you won't mind if we two base creatures take our leave of you. Where is she?"

She became sly. "Oh, you'd like to know that, I'll bet. Transgressor, thief, plunderer. You'd like to, all right, but you won't."

"Rapunzel!" I called.

"Go on, look. In every cupboard and corner. Better check the bath to be sure I didn't drown her in it." She fingered the braid.

I believed she'd murdered her in the bath and was daring me to look. I ran down the spiral stairs, finding the room empty and in chaos. I went from room to shattered room. Each time I failed to find anything, the fear grew inside my head, till I nearly tore out my own hair from the pressure. I begged God forgive me. I confessed how I *had* taken Rapunzel for granted, and myself, and what we were doing. Let the punishment be mine, I asked, not hers.

Gothel waited at the rail. I had to come back to her, what else could I do? Where else could I go? She looked up at my approach as if I'd startled her, as if she'd forgotten I was there.

"Where?" I cried. "Where is she?"

"Far. I've sent her to a place made from all the hells in the world. You'll never reach her. You'll never slide on top of her again. You'll never ever see her." Her triumph dwindled, her expression weakened. "Neither of us will." She had done something irreversible and, admitting it, she began to wail. Black tears ran from her eyes. "Gone!" she shrieked.

I screamed, too, at least I think so. Maybe it was hers hammering at me. None of us knows what we're capable of in moments like that. I could've killed Gothel, that might have been my response, but I chose instead to kill me.

Shoving her aside, I launched myself in despair over the rail. I've a vague recollection of Gothel reaching out, but everything is jumbled from that moment. I know that I'd inadvertently looped a braid around my ankle, that as the ground shot toward my face, the braid snapped taut and dropped me. I spun dizzily, not to my death, but into the dry hawthorns. The interwoven branches broke my fall while a thousand thorns as long as my finger tore the skin off me. Two of them pierced my eyes like spikes. A flash of red paint burst inside my head. I struck the ground an instant later.

I lay in amongst the branches I've no idea how long. When I tried to crawl out, I screamed at the first movement. I thought I'd broken all my bones; thorns snagged me or stabbed into my palms. I thought it was night but of course it wasn't. I was blind. But so complete was my agony that the lack of sight seemed trivial. By instinct alone, I made my way out of the maze and crawled off toward where my camp must be. Before each pull forward, I patted the ground, certain that I was actually crawling toward an unseen cliff.

Eventually, I found myself on a carpet of leaves. Then my hand touched cloth. It was a shirt of mine. I could smell my own smell upon it. With a little effort, I located my canteen and drank deeply. Farther back, where it would be hidden, I had pitched a tent. Taking the canteen, I dragged myself there, where I collapsed.

I knew I'd been punished for playing with her affections. Gothel's accusations, like the thorns I pulled out with my swollen fingers, had pinned my guilt to me. All I'd ever thought about was the pleasure of thrusting into the old woman's daughter. I'd let obligation to my family hang—I was long overdue to write them and now they might never hear from me again. I had no hope for forgiveness because the one I'd wronged was gone forever. The old woman had banished her.

I deserved to die. Yet, I didn't die.

I healed up well enough to walk—the soles of my feet were about the only place the thorns hadn't penetrated. My sight was gone for good, though, and I couldn't wait there in the woods any longer: Gothel might come after me and finish the job I'd failed to do, but more than that, I couldn't stop hoping I might still find some trace of Rapunzel, some trail that I could follow. I packed as well as I was able, and set off using my walking stick as a cane on what I thought was the path that had brought me there. Instead, I wandered far afield. For days on end I stumbled about. No doubt I crossed the real path a hundred times and never knew it.

When I came across streams, I would wash and drink and refill my canteen. I had food enough for a few weeks, but I came to a town before that.

It was a small town, but I had to be guided through it. I might easily have been run down, or robbed—certainly I was easy picking—but I had the good fortune to befriend an honest man. He led me to a tavern, what's called an alehouse, where most of what you get is a variety of beer. I asked if they'd seen Rapunzel. They in turn asked me who she might be, and I told them. The whole story from my first step setting out from home. To them, to strangers I couldn't even see, I admitted my guilt. As if I were standing before a jury in a courtroom, I confessed to them, seeking their condemnation.

By the time I finished, the room had gone still.

Someone cleared his throat. A coin dropped on the table, then another and another. No condemnation—to my incomprehension I was being rewarded. My guide said, "You've a talent in you, storyteller. You can do well round here with tales of that sort." *Moral fables,* he called them.

That's how I survived, telling my tale till I also began to see the moral center of it. My guide stayed with me for a time. He may have been skimming money from our take, but I don't begrudge him. May it make him rich. Wherever we went, I asked for Rapunzel and, when no one knew of her, told my story. They all thought it a fiction, although my guide admitted, before he left, that he had come to believe most of it on account of I never changed or added anything.

Alone, I ventured out into new territory. Soon I could smell the tang of the ocean but did not reach it for another two days. There was a town there, a port with a seawall and a quay at the mouth of a river. By now, I'd come to believe that Rapunzel was nowhere in the lands I knew. I intended to search elsewhere.

I set out for the docks, smelling a storm in the air, being slapped by cold winds. But as I reached the quay, the storm collapsed, and I felt the warmth of sunlight on my face. For whatever reason, the sailors greeted me as I shuffled along the riverside. They'd decided I had driven off the storm, and therefore I was hailed as good luck. Booking passage on one of their ships was made easier as a result. I found a tramp freighter going where I wanted. If Rapunzel was in a land knitted from all the hells, then I would go to the most hellish lands on Earth.

Somewhere out at sea, one of the crew came and whispered to me that he knew I was under the protection of an angel but that he would keep my secret safe if I blessed him. I heard him dumbly, barely half aware of what he was suggesting, I'd become so preoccupied with Rapunzel. So many times had I relived the events, so often had I placed her face, her body, her sweet voice in my mind's eye, that she now rose up every few moments like a ghost inside me, blinding me finally even to my own thoughts.

In this state of mind I cast about for four years, first upon the sea. At port after port I asked about her, and told my story till it seemed to have happened to someone else separate from me. I felt as if I were sitting there, listening with them. Finally, the ship was to return home. I disembarked into the unknown again.

The land where I went had been scorched daily for millennia. The winters hardly existed, and far more people endured them without homes or possessions. I became one among an endless sea of beggars. Their language took me months to learn. It might have taken me years, but my survival depended upon it.

I began thinking about my family. By now they would be certain I'd died. What other explanation would suffice? My guilt increased as I thought of the anguish I'd inadvertently caused them all in undertaking my fruitless quest. I asked myself, why hadn't I died? Why, when I was ever more certain that *she* was dead, didn't I join her? Compulsion is my only explanation—I would sift every inch of the Earth before I conceded defeat.

Leaving the cities and most of the hapless nomads behind, I entered more arid regions. The store of food I'd saved dwindled to nothing. Nothing seemed to grow wherever I cast about for food—even lizards were faster than the skinny, sun-baked blind man I'd become. No one met me on the road.

When the last of the food and water ran out, I quickly became delirious. A horrible vision of Rapunzel burned alive confronted me, and I defeated it only by remembering that I had no eyes and therefore couldn't be seeing anything real at all.

By then, however, I didn't know where I was. I'd fallen into a patch of shade beneath some rocks, where I passed in and out of consciousness. I awoke at some point to the sound of flapping great wings—vultures settling down nearby. I swung my stick and shouted, and the birds angrily flew off.

On trembling legs, I got up and started walking again. You'll say I was guided, maybe by the angel that I never saw.

After a while a distant refrain came to me. A lilting music. I thought I must be hallucinating again. The song refused to go away. It continued to grow. Like a beacon, it brought me across the cracked desert until I was running to embrace it.

All of a sudden, the song stopped. I stopped. Wheezing, I stumbled in a circle, straining to hear it again above my own ragged breaths.

I licked my cracked lips. Then, hoarsely, I called out that name I'd kept inside me too long. "Rapunzel!"

I heard footsteps. Quick and light. They came right up to me. A hand touched my brow. Her voice said, "Jon?"

"It is you, isn't it?" I asked. "I'm not mad, you're there?" I pressed my fingers to her face, her shoulders. She was unknown to me. Her body had become lean and hard. The voice, the song, belonged to no one else. She replied brokenly, "Yes, it's me." She hugged me close. So weak was I that I collapsed at her feet. She sank down beside me, drew me to her and placed my head in her lap. We said nothing. What could we say, who'd believed each other dead for so long?

Her tears dripped onto my face, ran down my cheeks. They splashed into my ruined eyes. I blinked, and made to rub the tears away, but stopped. With each blink, there seemed to come a flash of light. A flash of pain. I sat up. "Wait," I said, turning to her. "Wait." A milky image swam before me. I blinked again and it came clearer.

The face was lined and weathered, the hair a golden tangle around it. The years had worn her, weathered her, but not destroyed her. "I can see you," I said. "Rapunzel."

I kissed her then, softly against my pain. She had magic in her the same as Gothel; what one had taken away, the other had the power to restore. She was the angel.

Behind her lay a hut and a pathetic field of weedy crops. Two naked, bony children stood there, big-eyed and uncertain of this ragged stranger in their mother's arms. Do you remember? The girl was gypsy-dark, the boy as golden as his mother.

I remember that you led me inside the hut together, that your small hands took hold of mine. I can't recall the meal at all.

She and I had become very different people. I think the people we became were far better ones than who we'd been; I know I am. I think no longer of me, of my pleasure, but of her and of you. In that miserable desert, when your mother and I vowed our love finally, we knew its range, its depths, its endurance.

I love her past the point encompassed by words. And I love both of you, my children.

Oddest of all is finding myself indebted to Gothel, your grandmother, whom you can't expect to meet in this life. Her tower, when we finally returned to it, had collapsed into a heap of broken stone and glass and dust.

The Princess in the Tower

Elizabeth A. Lynn

Elizabeth Lynn is a Bay Area writer of fantasy best known for her novels The Northern Girl, Watchtower, *and* The Dancers of Arun, *all volumes in* The Chronicles of Tornor *trilogy.*

She is also the author of a handful of excellent short stories and of fantasy for children.

"The Princess in the Tower" is the second of our "Rapunzel" retellings, each very different from the other. Here, Lynn takes the humorous high road, while Gregory Frost, in "The Root of the Matter," travelled a darker path. The following version of the fairy tale of the girl locked in a remote tower is a clever and unusual one, and thoroughly delightful.

The Princess in the Tower

TRAVELLERS RARELY GO TO I______. FEW OUTSIDE THE O______Valley even know of its existence. Among those who do it is a closely guarded secret.

To get to I______ one must travel on the steamer up the coast to a location just north of Venice. At a certain lagoon (the name of which I will not divulge) one disembarks, hires a car (commonly an ancient Ford pickup, more recently a Bronco or a Jeep) and driver, and continues northeast. Barely passable roads traverse hideous tracts of marshland populated largely by mosquitoes, gnats, and other biting insects. After V______, the land wrinkles into scabrous rocky hillsides. The scenery, for those who care about such things, consists mostly of goats and scraggly trees. At C______, one's driver becomes a negotiator, haggling with the folk who live along the tributaries of the river, who would rather rob you than work. (Experienced travelers usually arm themselves with extra pairs of boots and a box filled with bone-handled hunting knives, especially those from Finland, which are much prized here.) However, once through the pass at O______ such inconveniences vanish. The harsh chill of the mountains seems to fall away, replaced by warmth and softness and the delicious smells of *salcsicce* and bacon and prosciutto, of onions sautéing in oils, of garlic sauce without compare, faintly undercut by the pungent, rich, salty scent of the sausage factories. Here one may dismiss one's guide and move confidently across the valley to I______.

Once (so our story goes) in I______ there lived a beautiful and wealthy widow named Favorita Z______. She was a woman of substance, as they say, being possessed of land, a large villa, and a fine herd of pigs. Her husband, whose name is not germane to this story, had survived the war (and indeed had prospered through it) but then, unfairly, had died young, leaving his widow grieving but with a home, an excellent stud boar, a well-endowed wine cellar, and with his legacy, their only issue, a daughter.

She was christened Margheritina, after the pasta, which, everyone knows, looks like *funghini* only larger. This is common practice in I______; children are named Perciatello or Millefiora or Anellina. Even the priest has no objection, though I was told of one priest who refused to baptize a child Ditalino, saying it was sacrilegious.

Favorita, herself the youngest of six girls, had feared she was barren, and doted on the child, and was determined that Margheritina would grow up to be worthy of her heritage and to make a great marriage. As an infant, Margheritina was distinguished by the rich buttery color of her hair (but then, her great-grandmother Mafalda's hair had been so blond as to have been nearly white) and by the fact that she was, compared to the other babes of I______, oddly thin. At the time, no one thought much of it, though Favorita observed that she would turn from the breast quite early, well before one would think she had been sated.

As Margheritina grew older, those about her remarked with some concern that she did not seem to eat very much. She would push away from the plate while others were only into their second portions, and upon being questioned she would merely say, "I'm full." She also had a strange aversion to sweets. The cook would prepare a creamy zabaglione, a sweet peach ice cream, a fresh fig tart, or even a chocolate soufflé with the finest bittersweet Swiss chocolate stirred into the unbleached flour, only to have the child say, "That's too sweet for me." Her mother cajoled, her aunts frowned, her cousins teased, but Margheritina remained adamant. At seven, which is when the girl-children of I______ begin to blossom toward the rosy lushness that informs their adult beauty, she was skinny and pale, "Thin as a dinner plate," as they say in the valley.

"Favorita, something's not normal about that girl," Regina, her mother's oldest sister, said bluntly.

But Favorita would not hear it, insisting that the child was simply developing late, and that she would soon be as buxom and beauteous as all the women of her family were, for not one, she pointed out, was under one hundred kilos (or, if you prefer American measure, two hundred twenty pounds), and hadn't their mother told them stories of their great-grandmother Mafalda, who was nearly twenty-four before she reached her full girth? And she ordered Teresa, the cook, to feed

Margheritina six times a day, small portions, and only the most delicate of dishes, *capellini, foratini fini, semi di mela, perline microscopici,* prepared with the freshest of vegetables or fish, sauced with cheese or cream or butter, and spiced to make the angels weep.

But it made no difference: the girl continued to pick at her food. Her nickname in the village school was Carrotshanks, not because of her coloring but because of her leanness. At twelve, the age the girls of I______ begin to develop that heft and softness of flesh, that billowy, cushiony bulk which their men so prize, Margheritina was narrow hipped and flat breasted, bony as a Tuscan cat.

One blithe April day, midway through Margheritina's thirteenth year, her uncle, the widow's brother-in-law Luciano, came to the villa, sent by Regina to discuss their niece's troubling condition. Luciano had not wanted to come. He disliked exertion, and interference (he felt) into so private a matter would only make his sister-in-law annoyed with him. Moreover, he did not believe the situation could be that bad.

But Regina had insisted. "Go. You have not seen the girl since Christmas," she said. "When you do, you will understand."

So Luciano climbed into his Ford pickup and drove to his sister-in-law's villa. As fate would have it, he arrived just as Margheritina, seated on the terrace under the awning, was finishing the second of her six daily meals. The cook had prepared a tasty plate of vermicelli all'alba: sliced truffles, butter and cheese over a mound of thin pasta.

Seeing her uncle, Margheritina rose politely to greet him. Luciano barely managed to suppress his shudder. She had a pleasant enough face (all the woman of her family were fine-featured) and excellent height, and her eyes, which were dark blue, and her hair, which was golden and lustrous and fell nearly to her knees, were really quite lovely. But she was thin as a skeleton; one could see her wristbones through her skin! (He himself had never seen his wife's wristbones. She was plump and luscious as a Piacenzian squab.)

He was quite shocked. Nevertheless, he spoke kindly to the girl, inquiring about her health and her appetite.

"Thank you, Uncle, I am very well," she said, pushing the half-filled plate away. "Would you like some pasta? I am sure there is plenty."

Normally Luciano would not have refused such an offer. But he was so upset by this niece's appearance that he had lost his appetite, a rare occurrence indeed.

"No, thank you, my dear child," he said. "I came to speak with your mother." And he entered the house, where he encountered his sister-in-law, dressed, as was proper, in black, drowsing on the sofa.

"Luciano, what a surprise," the widow said, blinking. "How lovely to see you. What brings you to my home? Would you like bread, cheese, some wine?" Then, becoming sensitive to Luciano's agitation, the widow woke more fully and struggled to her feet. "There is nothing wrong, is there? Is all well with Regina and the children?"

"Regina and the children are fine," Luciano said. "But there is indeed something wrong. My God, Favorita, you must take that girl to the doctor. She is most assuredly not normal. My daughter Anella, at ten, is twice her size. This condition could be serious!"

It took some argument before poor Favorita could be persuaded to follow her brother-in-law's advice. But at last, convinced and unhappy, she enlisted the aid of another brother-in-law, Vittorio, who owned a Ford sedan. In it she brought her daughter to be examined by the village doctor.

Doctor V______ had heard about the child, mostly from his wife Angela, whose sister Lumachina was married to Mario the Trout (so called because his favorite meal, beyond question, was that soup called *occhi di trota*, trout's-eye soup). Gravely he accepted the gift which Favorita brought him (a bottle of Barbera and three pounds of sausage) and gravely he examined the girl, without demanding that she do more than remove her stiff, high-necked cotton shift, while her mother watched tensely. His gentle questions elicited from the girl the information that she felt perfectly well, that she rarely ate more than one portion of any meal, and that yes, she had begun her menses.

After the examination, he told Margheritina to go outside, where she was instantly encircled by a small crowd of delighted urchins, who speculated aloud about the fatal, wasting disease she had obviously contracted.

"She is small for her age, I know," the widow said, defensively, "but she will grow. Her great-grandmother Mafalda was twenty-four before she reached her full girth."

Doctor V______ shook his head. "No," he said, with sad conviction, "she will not. I know the signs. Favorita, you must be brave."

The widow gasped. "Is she dying, then?"

"We are all dying," Doctor V______ said in his most profound tones.

The widow snorted. "You sound like a priest, Bruno V______. Tell me what is wrong with my daughter."

"It is a very rare condition, mostly seen in cities, and most common among the daughters of the rich," said Doctor V______. Really he had no idea what was wrong with the girl. He was perfectly at ease sewing up the gashes the men suffered when some fool came hungover to the sausage factory, or setting the occasional broken bone, but the ills of women he left to the midwives and the specialists at the hospital in O______. But a dim memory of something he had once heard, that the daughters of rich Americans sometimes starved themselves in order to be thought beautiful, came to his mind. "It is called anorexia nervosa, and there is no cure."

"Is it contagious?" the widow asked.

"No. But"—Doctor V______ lowered his voice portenteously—"it affects the brain."

This was truly awful. Favorita actually trembled, which the doctor found most attractive. He went on to explain that women afflicted with this disease often fell into melancholy and did inexplicable, destructive things. "It would be safer for her to be at home, of course."

"Why, where else would she be?" said the widow, who did not approve of this modern idea of women working in factories or as teachers, to say nothing of those poor women whose husbands allowed them to work as government clerks. They spent all day in public places and could be seen by anybody! "Except for school, and church."

"No school," said the doctor. "How old is she? Thirteen? They" (he meant those despised representatives of authority, the social workers) "won't care if she drops out now."

So Favorita informed the school that her daughter was ill and would have to leave. The school received this news with disinterest; the teachers were tired of chiding the other children for their malice toward the skinny, ugly one who was, indeed, quite bright—she could read and write, and had spirit and some imagination. "It's a pity," said Cettina, who had taught Margheritina from her fifth to her tenth year. "She would have made a good wife for some ambitious man." But she knew very well that would never happen.

Margheritina herself, though her mother did not ask how she felt, was not sorry to leave the schoolyard. Though she was not, by nature, either mean or melancholic, the torments and taunts of the other children had begun to rub on her nerves. She observed their appetites (and those of her relatives) with awe and the increasing majesty of the other girls in the village with wonder tinged with envy. At home she prayed to the Virgin to forgive her. She knew envy was a sin, but still, comparing her own meager arms and legs to Peppina or Tortellina's robust limbs, and her scrawny chest with its two bumps to Ninetta's, she felt that the Virgin would understand. After all, hadn't She sometimes wished wistfully for a more normal household, a lusty husband instead of a dried-up old man, and a son who chose to stay at home, instead of preaching in the markets and disturbing the proper order of things?

So she went home. There she stayed, mostly alone, though her mother was there, and old Teresa who cleaned and cooked. The aunts visited, of course, and with them the cousins, under strict orders to refrain from teasing, which made them walk about Margheritina softly and speak in hushed tones, as if visiting some national monument. There were a few books in the house besides the New Testament, for her father had had some pretensions to scholarship and once had a letter published in a newspaper in Padua. So she read them: Cipolla's *History*, Pieri's *Venetian Tales*, and an illustrated book of fairy stories, translated from the German. There were also cookbooks. Margheritina read them, too, not for the recipes, but in the hope that one of them might contain some simple explanation of her puzzling malady. She took long walks across her mother's acreage, and held whimsical conversations with the pigs.

In July she celebrated her fourteenth birthday. Her uncle Luciano, feeling obscurely guilty over his part in her isolation, brought her a gift, a radio. It was ivory white, with a dial and two knobs, and said *Emerson Radio and Phone Corp. N. Y. U. S. A.* on the face. With it Margheritina could pick up three stations, all relayed through the transmitter tower in O______. One of them played the most wonderful music, not at all like the syrupy sweet stuff her mother loved; it was cheerful and bouncy and made her want to spin, alone in her room, spin about in crazy, dizzying circles.

Her aunt Regina, out of the same feelings, presented her with an old Singer sewing machine. Margheritina, after a few false starts, discovered that she could sew. She mended all Favorita's clothes. She made new curtains for the kitchen. She made herself a pair of blousy trousers (we would call them harem pants) out of dark green velvet. Favorita would not let her wear them.

One morning, she appeared at breakfast in a green floor-length satin gown, clearly resewn to fit her.

Favorita, looking up from her panettone, was astonished. "What are you doing with that? It's ridiculous. Where did you find it?"

"In a chest in the attic," Margheritina said. "I think it's beautiful. Do you know whose it was?"

"Your great-grandmother wore it," Favorita said. "Take it off. It's not suitable. You look like you belong in a bordello!"

Margheritina smiled. There was a bottle of Sangiovese on the table. She poured herself a larger-than-usual glass. "To bordellos!" she said.

She is mad, Favorita thought.

In alarm and despair, Favorita forbade the girl to leave the house. Margheritina ignored her. If they want me to be mad, she thought, I will *be* mad. Being mad was easily more interesting than being sane and sober. She turned the radio on at all hours. Her favorite station played songs by a new English group; they were raucous, rhythmic, with growled lyrics which were doubtless obscene. She turned the volume as high as it would go and danced about the house in her green gown, singing the words to "She Loves You" in fractured English. She drank: Barbera, Albana, Lambrusco, whatever lay in the cellars, and when the amber bottles were empty and dry she inserted into them bits of paper on which she had written, in her round schoolgirl's script, *I am the princess in the tower*. Then she would walk across the fields and hide the bottles. Sometimes, when tipsy, she would throw them from the terrace, to watch them tumble end over end and fall to the rocks. She imagined the bottles breaking, freeing her scraps of paper to fly with the wind.

"What should I do?" Favorita asked of Regina. The telephone had come to I——— that spring, and the two women spoke frequently. "She will hurt herself, I'm sure."

"Lock her in," counseled Regina.

So in September, when the harvest moon blazed dangerously down upon the house, Favorita locked the doors. She kept the keys to them all on a string around her neck. Naturally, since the telephone was a party line, the entire village knew within twenty-four hours that poor Margheritina had gone quite mad, and was wandering about the house stark naked, singing obscene songs. The only thing that seemed to quiet her was wine. How sad for Favorita, the titillated villagers told each other as through the autumn and the long winter they absorbed bits and pieces let fall by Luciano, by old Teresa, and by Favorita as she spoke with her sisters, with Margheritina's teachers, with Doctor V——, and once with a neurological specialist in Venice. The good doctor would have been pleased to help, but the static and Favorita's distress made the call mostly unintelligible. He concluded that his caller was deranged and that the unhappy daughter was probably compensating for her mother's pathology as best she could.

Into this situation arrived the young man from T——.

His name was Federico Dominico Tommaso L——. Under the circumstances I believe it would be best for me to refer to him as Fred. At the time of this story, he was nineteen. Why he came to I—— is a matter for conjecture. Hints have been dropped of a quarrel with a domineering father, or a romantic interlude gone astray. As the eldest son of a prominent landowner, Fred was destined for inheritance, authority, possibly the town mayoralty. It made him twitch. He had had some vague notion of going south, to Venice or Ravenna or even Bologna when he left home. It may have been that I—— was simply on the way. I prefer to think (and Fred has never disputed this) that in the warm spring night, the wind from the south blew across the valley, carrying to his nostrils the scents of garlic and pepper and anise, of red wine, of buttery pasta, and principally, marvelously, of sausage. Enchanted, unconscious of this powerful stimulus, innards rumbling gently, he followed his taste buds to I_____.

He had spent two nights in the chill damp of the foothills, and it was therefore understandable that at his first sight of the valley and the town therein he thought that perhaps he had died in the night and gone to, if not Heaven, then one of its anterooms. I_____ lay sleeping under a honey-colored sky. Smoke from the rendery streamed upward like a prayer. Pigs moved across the hillsides, snuffling and chewing, and the smell of bacon frying on the griddle rose from three hundred smoke-blackened chimneys. Just a short walk from him, a large house loomed on a hillside. Someone in it was sautéing onions. Wishing he had a mirror, and conscious that he had not shaved for three days, Fred ran his hands through his thick dark hair. Then, brushing the dirt off his clothes and with his knapsack on his back (it contained cheese, and bread, and a clean shirt) Fred took the path toward the villa.

As he neared the terrace, someone thrust a window open, and a rock-and-roll beat challenged the serenity of the dawn. A woman's voice sang along with John, George, and Paul as they crooned, "I Want to Hold Your Hand." Astounded, Fred stopped. The singer stepped out onto the terrace. She wore a long green gown. It looked like something out of the previous century. Fred, transfixed, watched her twirl in graceful circles. He had never seen anyone so beautiful. The scrawny American models who graced the covers of his sisters' magazines had never appealed to Fred, and Margheritina was not, by his standards, scrawny: she weighed sixty-eight kilos, one hundred fifty pounds. Her long, golden hair swung like a skein of silk. He thought her eyes were blue. She was Venus under the morning star, Juno in her majesty, a goddess.

Margheritina looked down and saw a handsome, if unshaven, young man with dark curly hair staring at her with a look of absolute adoration. She stood still.

"What are you doing here?" she said.

Fred cleared his throat. He did not think he could talk. "Falling in love with you, I think," he answered.

It was the right thing, possibly the only thing, to say. Margheritina had never seen a movie, or read a romance novel. But she was fifteen and a half, and her sense of drama was instinctive and acute.

"Who are you?"

He told her.

"Where are you from?"

He told her that, too. She had never heard of it; the teachers at the school had not been strong on local geography. He asked her name, and did not smile when she told him.

They had both forgotten the radio. The music stopped, and a man's voice came on, cajoling his listeners to buy meat from such and such a butcher and to vote for the Christian Democrats. Margheritina turned it off. Into the sudden silence a woman's voice called.

"My mother," Margheritina said. "I have to go." She thought quickly. As it so happened, all the sisters except Gemella, who was pregnant, were going to the market that morning: Vittorio would be coming by after breakfast to take Favorita away in the big, dusty Ford. "Wait. Are you hungry?"

"Starving," said Fred.

"I'll be back. Stay out of sight!" And she went in. Fred looked about for some hidey-hole from which he could watch the house, and found a niche between two boulders. He settled into it, spine against his knapsack, and closed his eyes. He saw her face, her hair, the glow of her bare flesh, the white line of her breasts against the green fabric of her dress. . . .

When she reappeared an eternity later, she was wearing ordinary clothes and carrying a plate. Her long fall of hair was prosaically confined in two long, thick braids. She knelt. "Can you get up here?"

He had no doubt that he could. A brisk scramble brought him to the terrace. Crouched in a corner, he devoured a huge breakfast of eggplant, sausage, bacon, a frittata, breadsticks, all washed down with red wine. As he ate, Margheritina sat near, watching him gravely, wondering what it would be like to cook for him, and if he was really who he said he was, and what he would look like without a shirt on. His shoulders were attractively broad, and his arms muscular and shapely, with dark curly hair along them. He might even have hair on his chest.

The noise of the Ford made them both start. "That's Vittorio," Margheritina said. "Get down and hide. I'll let you know when it's safe to come up again." Fred descended to his boulders. Margheritina went inside. After the black car appeared and then drove away again, Margheritina returned to the terrace, Fred reascended, and the two entered into conversation. Fred confided that he was going to Venice (or Ravenna, or Bologna) to seek his fortune. Margheritina explained that her cruel mother had locked her away forever because she was so ugly. I need not further describe what ensued, save to mention that the green harem pants and the clean shirt in Fred's knapsack were both exceedingly useful. Four hours later, Favorita went into her daughter's bedroom to find an incoherent farewell note pinned to the pillow, signed, *Your loving daughter.* Coiled about it lay two long, lustrous, butter-colored braids.

Favorita screamed and raged, and managed to use the telephone to confuse the entire town. Luciano, summoned from the sausage factory, received the impression that Margheritina had been kidnapped by a band of ruffians from the river, the ones everyone knew would rather rob than work. A stout group of men from the factory drove to the river, where they made much noise hunting along its eastern bank and shouting threats to the indifferent herons. Much later, Alberto N_____ remembered the dark youth with the knapsack and his blond, delicately featured companion, who had passed his wheat field, singing one of those indecent songs to which his fourteen-year-old son listened all the time. But by then it was too late. Fred hired a car in O_____ and by the next day he and his beloved were sixty kilometers away.

They were married two weeks later, in R_____, by a sympathetic mayor, a staunch Communist, to whom they lied about Margheritina's age, something he very well knew but, as he pointed out to his wife, someone had to marry them, or the baby when it came would be illegitimate, and that would be a great pity.

From R_____ they took the train to B_____, where Fred found work mending stoves. Margheritina stayed home, and within the first four months of their marriage Fred gained twenty pounds.

One afternoon he offered a taste of Margheritina's sausage to the chef at a restaurant whose stove he had just repaired.

After two bites, the chef's eyes widened. "This is your wife's cooking?"

Fred nodded proudly. "Good, isn't it."

"I have never tasted better."

Fred blinked. Then, not being a fool, he said, "Perhaps some arrangement could be made . . ."

The restaurant sits in the same place, on a little alley off the Piazza, six blocks from the new movie theater. Outside, it looks the same as it did twenty-five years ago, with blue tile around the shuttered windows and pink geraniums in planters facing the cobbled street. Inside it is larger; Fred bought out the laundry next door fifteen years ago, and the two grime-encrusted stoves are long gone, replaced by huge, white German ones with big, natural gas ovens. Margheritina presides over the kitchen, assisted by Paolo and Giorgio, her two younger sons, and Anellina, her cousin Anella's daughter. She will not go back to I——, but she calls her mother monthly, and sends photographs of the family. Favorita proudly displays them to all her friends. Margheritina has gained weight over the years, and though she has never developed the taste for sweets which a woman of substance should have, she looks very much like her great-grandmother Mafalda. To Fred, of course, she is a goddess. Fred is stouter than he used to be, and doesn't see as well as he once did (the doctor says he has cataracts), so Giovanni, the eldest son, manages the restaurant and keeps the books. If you go to R——, you can find it by the smell. There is only one other place in the world that gives forth quite that odor of oil and garlic and onions, of *salcsicce* and prosciutto and bacon, of anise and pepper and cream and buttery pasta, and rough red wine, and it is far away, and even harder to find.

Persimmon (After *Thumbelina* by Hans Christian Andersen)

Harvey Jacobs

Harvey Jacobs began his career with The Village Voice, *then published* East, *a weekly newspaper on New York's Lower East Side. He joined ABC-TV where he became active in the early development of the global satellite system as an executive with ABC's Worldvision Network. Since 1973, he has lived the freelance life based in New York City, publishing the novels* The Juror *and* Summer on a Mountain of Spices *and the short story collection* The Egg of the Glak. *His short stories have appeared in a wide variety of magazines including* Omni *and* The Magazine of Fantasy and Science Fiction, *and in some forty anthologies. He has also written widely for TV.*

Jacobs writes peculiar novels and stories imbued with a wicked sense of humor: from The Juror *about an ordinary citizen who once every ten years, while on jury duty, commits mayhem, to "Stardust," in which a woman literally eats stars. "Persimmon," based on Hans Christian Andersen's sweet "Thumbelina," is no exception.*

Persimmon
(After *Thumbelina* by Hans Christian Andersen)

ON HER FIFTIETH BIRTHDAY, ESSIE FLICK PAINTED A picture of a Jack-in-the-Box. The box was a coffin disguised as a tail-finned Cadillac. Jack's head was poised at the end of a thick, rusty spring. Jack's crescent moon face, contorted into an expression of utter puzzlement, loomed over an abstract sea. From a canyon mouth, Jack puked miracles: flight, the atom, the microchip, television, space travel, genetic engineering. Along with the miracles came a gush of blood in which victims of war, disease, prejudice, famine splashed like children in foamy surf. She titled her picture *My Century, Sic Transit*.

Contemplating the work, Essie concluded that this

was an excellent century in which to be some sort of artist. Even a maker of advertisements or greeting cards. Essie herself had tried many disciplines. Alas, she had no real talent beyond a wonderful capacity for accepting rejection. So, long since, she had left a boiling New York for a simmering life in the Berkshires. There, teetering on her dotage, Essie prepared for death. She hoped she would be good at dying and prayed for a long, lingering illness that would allow her a last chance at success.

Leaving as little as possible to random chance, Essie had selected her burial plot (a vista view), composed her epitaph (MY Way), and made friends with the local undertaker. From her rickety porch, Essie watched the days dawn, wrinkle and perish. Her social contacts were mostly with strange neighbors, an inbred crowd. They lived in truncated school buses or ancient trailers circled like Conestoga wagons on shoddy lots. They spoke of winds, floods and tornadoes—things that help control the trailer population. Like them, Essie agreed that Mother Nature was a sly bitch.

Still, on certain mornings—lovely Spring mornings, crisp Winter mornings, lush Summer mornings, delicious Autumn apple mornings—the dregs of puddled hormones stirred what Essie recognized as splinters of hope. These she dealt with quickly. Essie had no tolerance for that seditious emotion, however transient. But one such morning in April, weakened by a persistent cold and made vulnerable by sneezing and antihistamines, Essie yielded briefly to a spasm of optimism.

She went walking down by the abandoned textile factory that once fueled the town's economy. There had been a huge statue to The Spirit Of Yarn hewn from granite by WPA artists during the depression of the 1930s. It stood just outside what had been the main gate, an androgynous worker holding spools and bobbins, anchored in a nest of thread. Somehow the statue had collapsed, probably helped by cretin teenagers with mallets.

The fractured statue reminded Essie of herself, so she went closer to explore its parts. Still buoyed by the evanescent flame of good feeling, she peered deep into what must have been an armpit and there she found a seed which had been blown over the continent by a powerful wind. It was an ugly, hairy, malevolent-looking seed. Essie wondered what kind of life it held inside its fibrous skin. Moved by a maternal urging, she wrapped it up in a used kleenex and carried it home.

There she placed the seed in a bed of cracked, dry earth lumped inside a clay pot that came with the house. Instead of simply watering the miserable foundling, Essie poured sputtering bacon fat over the unlikely womb. It was all very spontaneous and peculiar and she felt sudden guilt, so she added a dollop of sour cream and a splash of warm red wine. "This is all the chance you're going to get," she said. "Take it or leave it."

The next day, Essie woke and weighed herself to test the strain she put on the planet. Then she tested her blood pressure to measure her own level of stress. Next she ate a meager breakfast of oats. To complete the ritual, she went out to the porch to test the weather. She had placed the clay pot out there to enjoy what there was of sun and breeze. She saw that it had been transformed. A single stalk of camouflage green protruded from mucky mulch. At the stalk's tip was a carbuncle bud. It challenged assault with the irresistable demand of a ripe boil. So Essie plucked a hairpin from her head and, even as a portion of her gray mane tumbled down over her neck, she stabbed into the hideous growth.

She heard a shriek. The damaged casing trickled molasses. The bud burst open. Lying inside speckled yellow petals was a tiny girl wrapped neatly in a caul. From somewhere, a stray kitten leapt onto the pot. It licked away the caul, burped, made a circle with its tail, then ran off into a clump of woods.

Essie harvested the child, placed it in her palm and saw that it was more adolescent than infant. It was delicately formed, beautifully made, entirely enchanting. It blinked up at her and then, like the agile kitten, jumped from Essie's open hand and fell facedown into a patch of grass. A dragonfly dipped from the air to help the sweet creature upright. The child darted among the blooms of Essie's skimpy garden, kissing flowers, stroking bees, singing in a splendid contralto to a group of Japanese beetles who seemed to applaud with their legs.

This delightful creature immediately reminded Essie of two discrepant items. First, a singer/actress named Pia Zadora who was granted slim media fame largely because she was a kind of sensual thimble, a wee thing, a doll that dripped honey. Pia was a miniaturized mistress who could be carried in a pocket like a travel alarm—a perfect sex goddess for a transistorized age, a Venus designed to dangle from the sun shield of a compact car. The second thing Essie was reminded of was the penis of her first lover, who had told Essie that he had been the victim of a demented Rabbi who believed in excessive circumcision and was later confined to a mental hospital in Jerusalem. *Pia, penis* and *pious* evolved in Essie's mind into Persimmon. This became the name for her unexpected offspring.

Essie quickly confirmed that she had little interest in nurturing. But she did enjoy watching Persimmon thrive in a world Essie had learned largely to ignore. Persimmon was not only at home with things of nature, but even adored reading the daily paper. The child quickly broke the code of language by watching endless hours of *Sesame Street*. The day's disasters filled her with wonder and appreciation both for the scope of tragedy and the triumph of survival. There was nothing Persimmon did not love. She held hands with the sun and moon. Life was her sustenance and energy. The very movement of atoms were her vitamins.

As the years passed, Persimmon achieved detente with her "mother." A natural athlete, she could easily dodge Essie's foot when it attempted to stomp her after some disagreement. She could always tolerate Essie's envy and resentment through a reasoned analysis of motive. Persimmon was moist, wise and forgiving. She cleaned the house, cooked the meals, did sundry repairs, even drained the septic tank without complaint or desire for reward. If Essie did not know she was blessed with a treasure, everyone in town knew.

Persimmon's local fame was especially interesting to the undertaker, Bertram Dritz, who knew Essie's desire for a splendid burial. He had been prepaid for final rites and services, and spent many hours browsing casket catalogs with his eventual client. He probed for information about Persimmon and liked what he heard.

Dritz lived and worked in the mansion that had once belonged to the scion who built the doomed textile plant. He was a widower who was burdened with one son, Lance, who shared the magnificent house and assisted his father in his work. Decades before, when Lance vanished from kindergarten, a willing conspiracy of silence prevented any inquiry by authorities. He was not a well-behaved boy. Now a man, Lance never came out into daylight. He was content to remain inside the stucco shell of his dark, damp, dank home. Except for his nightmares, he hardly made trouble.

But of late, Lance had become more cantankerous and romped through the halls on all fours. Bertram Dritz understood that this behavior could be traced to a surfeit of sap flowing from gonads to brain (if brain there was). In an effort to contain Lance's male eruptions, Bertram enticed Leticia Dor, the community slut, to spend a night with his son. That resulted in a costly settlement involving the loss of a part Leticia insisted was essential for symmetry.

Bertram realized that Lance needed a loving wife who could not testify against him. Persimmon seemed an obvious candidate. The girl had a giving manner, was certainly economical of input and generous of output. She could help the Dritz cause both domestically and professionally, being the proper size to deal with difficult orifices and indentations.

So, on a dour February evening, Bertram came to plead his case to Essie Flick. At first, Essie was reluctant to agree to the match. She did not want to lose her daughter's company. Lance was a man of darkness and despair, not the ideal husband for an outgoing girl like Persimmon. The more Essie resisted, the more Bertram offered. When his offer expanded to include an aboveground mausoleum, a reasonable cash payment and certain fringe benefits, Essie was forced to yield. Persimmon was informed of the betrothal and immediately began to prepare her trousseau and weave the cloth from which she would fashion her wedding gown.

Outwardly cheerful, Persimmon knew sadness for the first time. The prospect of tending to corpses in a large, silent house, of being wife to an unevolved churl, did not please her. Her doubts and qualms, albeit invisible, began to affect flora and fauna alike. Butterflies allowed their rainbow wings to droop, trees hung their branches, birds dived beak-first into mudflats, caterpillars lost their fuzz and curled into foetal commas. Being a dutiful child, Persimmon never openly complained, and Essie was content to ignore the crystallized fog of despair that draped over her cabin like a shroud.

The awful wedding date was set. It was decided that it would help both Lance and Persimmon if the bride-to-be could move into the Dritz mansion a few days before the nuptials. The idea was for the couple to have some courting time, if only for the sake of future memory. There was no honeymoon planned, no celebration. And, in those carefree limbo days of sweet acquaintance, Persimmon could train in the fundamentals of human taxidermy.

Thus, with one suitcase in hand, Persimmon said farewell to Essie Flick, who almost shed a tear. Essie knew her sprite was totally innocent. More than once she had attempted to introduce Persimmon to the mysteries of penetration and its consequences, but Essie's own inhibitions prevented any clear communication. Essie assumed that Persimmon would take to conjugation the way she took to everything else. With grace, charm and diligence.

Lance, meanwhile, gorged on oysters. He worked himself into a seminal frenzy. Polaroids of Persimmon flamed his passion. She seemed small but beautifully turned, and he lusted to hang her from a picture hook and just stare for a while. Or watch her swim in his aquarium like a mermaid among the flaking goldfish. Impatient for his wedding night, Lance's scrotum had gone musical. Whole orchestras of sperm played symphonies.

The moment she crossed the Dritz threshold, Persimmon felt like an extinguished candle. She went pale as a mushroom. She shivered and twitched. Bertram took this for girlish glee and was pleased. It was planned that she would meet her intended over dinner.

Dinner was a fiasco. At his first sight of Persimmon, Lance heard his scrotal symphony become atonal. He ate like a jackel, told off-color jokes and made sexist remarks about the role of women in necrology. Even his father was appalled and ordered him upstairs. Bertram apologized to the microcosmic guest and offered to show her around what he called "the establishment."

As fate would have it, a single body lay on a slab awaiting ministration. Persimmon had known only the death of animals, flowers and vegetables. She had never seen a dead person or even considered that people did anything but age. The encounter with a lifeless form, a rotund, florid gentleman with a hedge of gray hair and a copious beard, naked and rigid with rigor mortis, came as something of a surprise.

Persimmon was so moved that after Bertram sedated Lance, chained him to his bed then went to bed himself, the elfish maiden went back to the embalming chamber. Alone with the deceased, Persimmon wept hot tears that fell on the massive chest and belly. Since all the flowers were of polyethylene, Persimmon was forced to make do. She fashioned a bouquet of roses, then spread plastic petals on the dead man's face. She knelt from his icy forehead and kissed his sleeping lips.

The sound of a thunderous kettledrum made her

start. The body revived. Heat flushed through clogged veins and arteries. The result was an unexpected resurrection.

"Who is it that has returned the gift of life to me?" the man said, sitting up on his slab. "Are you some angel?"

"Just a young bride-to-be," Persimmon said modestly.

"Then you shall be rewarded. I am very well fixed, quite comfortable as they say, and with friends in high places. Your wedding will be the best money can buy. After that, seven days and six nights in some paradise of your choice. Unless there is something else your infinitesimal heart desires."

Persimmon took time to explain that her act was gratuitous and that she expected no thanks beyond a smile. But the comfortable man insisted that she accept some more palpable token. "As you may have noticed, or shortly will, this world can be a hard place. A few dollars can make the difference between grotesque misadventure and bearable madness. There must be something I can do for you."

"Well then, yes, there is," Persimmon said coyly. "I don't think I want to be married just yet. And in those soft hours when I dreamt of my future, I admit that the image of Lance Dritz did not come to mind."

"Lance Dritz? What demented matchmaker coupled such a radiant creature with such an unromantic infection of a spouse? I refuse to hear of such nonsense. Let's be gone quickly."

While the newly awakened capitalist dressed in the suit he was destined to wear to heaven, Persimmon said, "Sir, can I just go? Without so much as a word?"

"Momentum is salvation. Worry later, at leisure."

Moments later, Persimmon and her newfound friend, who was named Sebastian Plunkett, left the Dritz mansion. After a brief stop at his former residence to pick up some personals, Sebastian took her to the nearest airport. There he purchased full-fare tickets to an island he owned in the blue Caribbean.

Persimmon loved flying. She even enjoyed the airplane food, which delighted Sebastian, who, like most men his age, was as jaded as his prostate. She made him feel truly renewed and reborn.

During the flight, Persimmon told him of her mysterious arrival and of the seed that bore her. Essie had kept the thing in a mustard jar for sentimental reasons. "It was not very attractive to see," Persimmon said. "It made me question my roots. My heritage. My DNA. It left me with some kind of complex."

"Pishtush," Sebastian said in his vibrant voice. "Consider the origins of beauty and you soon realize that it is a triumph of accident. Be it human or art, the chances are its parents were toxic waste."

When the plane landed smoothly on Sebastian's island, called New Eden, the companions went immediately to the grandest home on the highest hill. It became clear that Sebastian had not exaggerated his importance. His first act was to telephone the President of the United States of America and inform him of his return to the land of the living.

On New Eden, Persimmon spent her days at pleasure, which included writing snide postcards to Essie and the Dritzes. Sebastian indulged her like a loving father. And like a loving father, he recognized the first vague symptoms of loneliness in the waif.

One day, without warning, Sebastian called Persimmon to his beefy side. He cradled her in his lap and told her to pack her things. Even as he said it, he sighed the sigh of loss. But there was bittersweet satisfaction in his tone. Persimmon was alarmed, but did as she was commanded.

When she came downstairs holding her ancient suitcase, she found Sebastian seated on a cart, holding the reins to several mules wearing pink and lavender hats. Persimmon took her place beside him, and the mules clopped off through lavish vegetation on a path that carried them beyond even the sound of the eternal sea.

"I hate to lose you, my dear," Sebastian said. "But it would not be fair to keep you with me. All I ask is that you think kindly of me from time to time."

"Where am I going? To what fate?" Persimmon inquired.

The mules turned a corner, and there Persimmon saw an entire battalion of uniformed soldiers guarding a metal door cut into a cliff.

"I feel agitated," Persimmon said.

"Just act like you have maximum security clearance," Sebastian said. "That, in a nutshell, is the secret of success and the best advice I can give you. Just let me tell you again that I love you with paternal intensity, and even past that. Who can say what might have been if you were older and more substantial? Or, for that matter, if I was younger and less significant."

Here Sebastian snapped his stubby fingers. The door immediately sprang open. The soldiers came to attention. A single gesture told Persimmon what she must do.

She left the cart and carried her suitcase to the door. There she paused, blew a kiss to Sebastian who pretended to catch it, then crossed the unknown threshold. The door slammed shut behind her.

Inside, Persimmon saw that she had entered a wide corridor lit with sconces in the Art Deco style. She walked over black marble tile to a curving staircase. Without hesitation, Persimmon descended with whatever aplomb she could muster. It was like walking into dawn. The light grew brighter and brighter.

At the base of the staircase, Persimmon saw a tremendous atrium, pulsating under waves of golden lumens. And she saw a sight that tingled her most secret memories.

She was standing in a great garden. A forest of single stalks grew from repulsive seeds and produced depressing pods. Yet Persimmon felt what she had never felt before, a sense of life's gravity, the comforting inertia of belonging.

Some of the pods popped open. Each contained a tiny person, some more lovely and charming than others. Persimmon experienced a surge of satisfaction though she also felt competitive for she had owned a rather exclusive domain of littleness until that moment.

It was then that she noticed a very well-built, excellent-looking young man with all kinds of possibilities climbing down a stalk just beside her.

"Without knowing anything about you I see that you are a terrific person," he said. "I feel as if we've known each other through gestation. Will you be my wife?"

Assessing his qualities of leadership, spirituality, sincerity and endurance, Persimmon accepted him for her groom. If he lacked Lance's enthusiasm, something she thought of with nostalgia on balmy evenings, he did have massive credentials in his favor.

"But what is this place?"

"Ah, that. Your friend and benefactor, Sebastian Plunkett, cultivates this garden. As I understand it, the planet upstairs has become very crowded, its resources strained to the breaking. This will certainly lead to violence, destruction, extinction of the present inhabitants. We are their replacements, the new rulers of the globe. Vital, vigorous veggies who do not pollute but rather revivify. Of course, Sebastian holds patents not only on our pods but also on the products that please us. His company is called *A Gift to Be Simple.* The man has foresight."

"Then how am I explained?"

"Your disappearance was a major concern. Somehow your seed was separated from the cluster. It caused quite a stir. But you are back where you belong, and together we will pollinate as many tomorrows as there are stars in the sky. Have you ever seen a star?"

"Billions," Permission said.

"Tell me about each one."

His eloquence and boyish enthusiasm won Persimmon's heart. She even felt tenderness toward the new pods growing from their mounds of muck. And she felt compelled to tell her fiance that she was both a meat eater and an occasional smoker, but that could wait. Rapture is as rare as it is precious, and more fragile than any web.

The couple embraced. They kissed.

At that very moment Essie Flick quivered, quaked and died. Her soul, smaller even than Persimmon, headed toward an unknown place, wondering if it was properly dressed for the occasion.

Little Poucet

Steve Rasnic Tem

Steve Rasnic Tem has sold over 170 short stories to publications of the mystery, horror, science fiction, and western genres. Most recently, his short fiction has appeared in Best New Horror 2, New Mystery, Stalkers #3, Dark At Heart, Cold Shocks, Dead End: City Limits, Tales of the Wandering Jew, *and* The Years Best Fantasy and Horror: Fifth Annual Collection. *He has been nominated for the Bram Stoker Award, the British Fantasy Award, and the World Fantasy Award for his short fiction, winning the British Fantasy Award in 1988 for his short story "Leaks." A collection of his short fiction,* Dark Shapes in the Road, *has recently been published by the French publisher Denoel.*

"Little Poucet" is one of the less familiar fairy tales. Tem stays close to the original, adding a touch of eroticism by concentrating on the more sexual aspects of the story. The original comes to us from Perrault, and was the last of the tales Perrault included in Histoires du contes du temps passe *in 1697, under the name "Le petit Poucet."*

Little Poucet

LITTLE POUCET WAS BORN SMALL AS HIS FATHER'S MIDdle finger, smaller than a mouse, smaller by far than his six brothers who had all come out normal sized. Although he would eventually grow a bit larger, inside he would always feel that same size. His parents ignored him, expecting him to die, because he was so small, and because he was mute.

Because he was mute he had never found much use in words. Words were walls and boxes enormous adults built: the caves and castles and impassable mountains that made lies and broken promises out of each new day. Words could not be trusted. The adults in his life used words with an emphatic pounding of fist against table and a broad, fleshy palm across the face as they told you who you were, what was to become of you, and what you must believe. Little Poucet vowed that when he eventually used words, as he knew he would someday, they would be practical words. They would *mean* something.

But in the beginning Little Poucet relied on dream, and memory, and for as long as he might remain a child, he knew these would be very much the same.

Little Poucet's most important dream was the lush memory of his mother's bedroom, where he would spend every minute of his life until departing on the journeys which would make him so famous later on. He supposed it was his father's bedroom as well, although this faceless mountain of flesh (except for the whale's eye of him which would stare at Little Poucet even in sleep) visited the bedroom rarely. When his father did visit, the children were kept asleep with warm, oily drinks before bedtime. This was so that the mountain that was his mother and the mountain that was his father could crash into each other with a great moaning and quaking of the bed, without the children disturbing them. But Little Poucet never drank the drink. Little Poucet never slept, waiting up all night to hear the words his parents used with each other.

He had no experience of other bedrooms, so he could not know whether the world of his mother's bed was grand: for someone of his small size it was preeminent. He had entered the world into the pale, soft folds and dark-haired shadows of this bedroom, as had all his six brothers, and if his parents had so decided he would have left the world by way of this same room. He remembered lying on his mother's immense white breast, her billowy flesh extending in all directions across the bed and toward the dark walls of night beyond.

Always a small lamp glowed in this room, but it

served only to intensify the darkness of those distant walls until Little Poucet was compelled to give them the name Terror. The lamp spotlighted his mother's oily flesh, the pink nipple, the heavy wet smell of her as she breathed in and out like waves pushing the raft of him to another side of his contained world.

His mother was always the central event of this world, her size at times making her indistinguishable from the bed, her creams and perfumes and powders and foods ranked on the tables beside her head and the forest spread of her thick black hair, her sighs and moans and gaseous eruptions providing a background music to his day, her silvery flickering black box a gate to one side of the darkness beyond the world of the bed, a gate full of noise and words and dancing dreams which Little Poucet would not gaze at for long for fear he'd be struck blind as well as mute.

And beyond this, the cracked rectangle of yellow-brown shade that covered the window, made to glow half the day with loud noises from other giants and hard smells close to, but not as pleasant as, the smells his mother created.

So central in fact to this world was his mother that on those rare occasions she gathered her heaving flesh and left to Get Something from the Kitchen or to Go Potty, Little Poucet would huddle to himself with his eyes closed, desperate to find in his dreams some comforting memory of her.

When time came for Little Poucet to Go Potty it was small and insignificant (later he would understand this to be from the rarity of food) and collected into a can his mother kept in the nighttime beyond the bed. Sometimes he would see her smelling the can before she put it away, smiling and nodding so that her great black tresses fell all over flesh and bed, covering his own scarce flesh like a web that caught and thrilled him.

Sometimes she'd pull him up to her huge blue eyes (the whites slightly yellow, the entire eye long and fish-shaped) and watch his nose. A smell sour enough or sharp enough would make his nose wiggle, and she would know to put more powder on, or more perfume, or she would rub herself with a wet cloth, moving him like a divining rod over every bit and crack of her. What he did not think she understood was that his nose wiggled out of pleasure, because as much as he enjoyed the perfumes and powders which hung in a cloud over the great bed, it was the slightly corrupt fragrances underneath that really thrilled him.

Sometimes she would pull from behind her tables a large book smelling of insects and dirty linen, and she would read to Little Poucet alone written-down dreams of giants and trolls and nightmare castles and missing princesses and ravenous wolves and even solitary elves such as himself who lived out their lives in lands no bigger than this, his mother's bed.

Besides his mother and the smells and the murmuring gate and his own small presence and the occasional mounds of his six larger brothers (although usually they slept on the Rug in the dark outside the bed), there were always the pillows, of various sizes—each one bigger than he, and ranging from four to eight in number. The pillows were marvelous because, although not as soft as her skin, they always smelled of his mother and remained accessible to him when she was out of the room or quaking with the powerful presence of his father. Sometimes they surrounded him like her own breasts and legs, and sometimes he mounted them where they carried him off to dream. In his head he made up songs about the pillows, about their softness and firmness, about their sizes and shapes, about how they sometimes resembled his sleeping brothers, and about his occasional fear that they might be used by his mother to smother him.

Then into this world of his mother's bed his father might loom, a towering cliff as dark as the walls. He was more a voice than anything else, and sometimes a pair of huge, rough hands. His father always picked up Little Poucet and moved him to some distant valley of pillow when the giant came and entered her bed, there to roll and rumble and laugh, and to backhand Little Poucet off into unkempt shadows if the baby ventured too close to the adults' play. But they were never very careful about what they had to say to each other, thinking Little Poucet's mind to be small as well as his size, and no threat to the slap and tickle that went on each night.

Sometimes his father smelled of distant rooms and other giants, however, and at those times Little Poucet's presence was welcome in the family bed, as was that of his brothers, and they all played naked in the family caverns and on the mountain ranges the adult bodies made and remade throughout the evening, their motion so constant, fluid, and restless that Little Poucet could not tell where his own self ended and these ancient forms of creation began.

As grand as these reunions were, Little Poucet most loved the secret times when he was shoved to a corner of the bed and wrapped in pillows. His father the giant uncovered the thing Little Poucet understood to be Brother Eight, who seemed every bit Little Poucet's size when he stretched his muscle, who had dark hair gathered about his feet leaving his glistening head bald, and who had been born with no face at all, which explained why his father kept him hidden.

During these frightening, exciting, secret times, his father would plunge Brother Eight back into the dark original folds of his mother as if desperate to allow the distant ancient seas of her to effect a change, and at last to provide Brother Eight with a face. These attempts never worked the necessary magic, however, and so Little Poucet vowed never to tell the other six brothers of the secret of Brother Eight. Instead Little Poucet contented himself to lie beside the still, soft form of the only brother who was even more an embarrassment than he himself. Sometimes his mother's hand came down during these times to stroke Little Poucet, in a way to suggest that she might be confusing Little Poucet with the almost identical Brother Eight. In his dreams they were two damp, slim little pixies, secretly smarter than their brothers, and by far the favorites of their monstrous parents.

"Can't feed them no more. Nothing left, Sadie."

Little Poucet almost missed the significance of his father's statement in his wonder at the sound of his mother's name, which he was sure he had never heard before. But having heard something once, of course Little Poucet never lost it, and going back over his father's words he felt a growing alarm.

"Enough food for me and you. Even as little as they eat, still too much."

His father spoke softly, deeply, as he did when he was trying to make Brother Eight a face. His mother's face had grown soft and blurry, as if her flesh were melting.

"Hush now. You'll wake the others," his father said, looking at him with that great whale eye the way he might look at Brother Eight, something without sense and with only one purpose, and in Little Poucet's case, a purpose his father obviously valued very little.

"Tonight, couple hours after dark. You dress 'em, I'll take 'em out into the city. Stop your blubberin' now. Here, I'll give you somethin' for the pain of it." Adult words, all of them.

And the rolling and heaving of the bed put Little Poucet back to sleep.

He woke some time later from dreams of a giant troll beneath the bridge of his bed. The whale eye was closed, and his mother smelled of night. Carefully Little Poucet crawled over the dark coverlet of her hair and reached for the bag of black cookies with the dazzling white fillings, brighter than the bed sheets, that were his mother's favorites. He hid the bag beneath one of the pillows, thinking of whose clothes might hide them best tonight when his mother dressed him and his brothers for their journey outside the world. He closed his eyes and pretended to sleep, searching his head for the words he might use for the first time to persuade his brothers of the value of his plan.

When he opened his eyes again it seemed as if he had indeed slept, and were still in the midst of a dream. Six of his brothers (Brother Eight, as expected, was off with his father somewhere) stood groggily upon the expanse of bed, his mother slipping over their heads rags she referred to as Their Clothes. Little Poucet had never seen these clothes before. As his brothers gradually awoke they smiled and winked at each other, as if on the verge of a great adventure.

"Pierre, Maurice, Charles . . ." She counted and recounted, stroking their sweaty heads. Then when she turned, Little Poucet slipped the bag of cookies into the back of Pierre's trousers, which were much too big for him anyway.

Pierre turned in surprise as Little Poucet whispered behind him, "Be still until I relate my plan to the others," keeping his mouth shut in obvious shock at his mute brother's use of words.

Their father came in then, Brother Eight hidden behind heavy coat and pants (*He's to stay behind because he's mother's favorite,* Little Poucet thought). "Come along," his father boomed. "It's time you boys helped your father earn his living."

And so Little Poucet was forced to leave the world of his mother's bed for the first time in his life.

Little Poucet was surprised to find that the world of the city was not unfamiliar. It was the world of the dark night walls in his dreams. The city was all buildings (this Little Poucet knew from the flickering gate) and what were buildings but walls that went on forever, filled with night and the stink of garbage and sour flesh and sheets? His father pushed the seven of them in front of him, prodding them along with a thick stick as if they were dirty, ill-fed geese. Now and then he would stop to retrieve a wallet from some drunk or addict sleeping it off in an alley, or he would gaze at the unbarred windows of stores and warehouses with a look of intense concentration on his great face, as if he were considering matters of stress, strength, approach. It was only then that Little Poucet understood how it was their father made his living.

Every few yards, hiding them with care and a small, swift prayer, Little Poucet scattered the dark cookies with their creamy fillings. He was careful not to let the others see him, for he knew they were so hungry they would have gobbled them up instantly. It was hard enough for Little Poucet to handle them himself without risking a surreptitious lick.

Once they were deep within the tallest walls of the cool, smelly city, Little Poucet realized he had not felt his father's sharp prod or heard his heavy footsteps for some time. He turned around and looked behind him. His father was nowhere to be seen.

"So, the old man's taken off and left us little fools here all by ourselves," Little Poucet said.

His brothers turned and stared at him in amazement. "He talks!" Maurice exclaimed.

Jean Paul stepped forward and examined Little Poucet's mouth. "Maybe it was someone else," he said. "A ventriloquist." Little Poucet bit down sharply on his brother's finger. Jean Paul did not cry out, but examined his bloody finger in the streetlight's dim gray. "He bites as well," he said.

"I will try to control my hunger," Little Poucet said, but found himself gazing at his brother's finger as if it were his mother's huge and wonderful tit. He forced himself to look away. "I've left a trail. We must hurry and find the bits of it before someone eats it."

They found each and every one of the cookies, passing them back and forth between them for nibbles, Pierre licking the fillings and Little Poucet taking the smallest bite for himself each time.

By dawn they had arrived back at the dark and greasy brick wall beyond which lay the apartment of their mother and father. Upstairs and outside the door, they could barely hear their mother's sobbing above the chatter of the flickering gate. "With that score you made on the way home we might have kept them!" she cried.

"We can always make more where those came from," the father shouted, and again the great bed began to rock and their mother's cries to subside.

Little Poucet had neglected to plan what they all should do when they arrived back at their parents' apartment, and before he could make a suggestion his brothers had beaten down the door and poured into the grand bedroom shouting, "Here we are! Here we are!"

Little Poucet ran in behind his brothers, and was not surprised to see that Brother Eight had taken his place in their mother's bed and now nestled his quivering form at his mother's pale breasts. The giant father stared at Little Poucet then left the bed. His mother opened her arms, and he and his brothers stripped off their traveling clothes and disappeared into her embrace.

Only two nights passed before Little Poucet's father had exhausted his recent earnings and there was no food again. During those two nights their father and Brother Eight were gone from the apartment, returning fatter on the third. As his mother and father crashed together with even greater clamor than before, Little Poucet again overheard their conversation:

"No food no room no peace no food no good good good . . ." his father chanted in a low growl. After his parents were asleep, Little Poucet again slipped up to his mother's bed table and stole more of the black cookies with the dazzling white centers.

On the next night their mother dressed them again, kissing each good-bye with tears on her fat cheeks as their father took them out exploring. Little Poucet planted a bag of cookies each on Jean Paul and Maurice, but this time letting those two—the oldest of his brothers—in on the details of his plan.

This night their father took them even deeper into the dark valley that was at the city's center, where there was no air for the stench and no lights other than the shining whites of their small eyes. Half the time they couldn't see their father at all—so dull and oily was his outfit, his skin—so it came as no surprise to suddenly find him gone.

They stared at each other: at the whites of their eyes, at the bright fillings of the two remaining cookies Little Poucet held in his hands. "Don't worry, my brothers. I've been making a trail as I did last time."

But then Pierre opened his mouth to laugh, and his tongue and teeth were dazzingly white with the thick, gooey fillings from the cookies Little Poucet had planted all along the way.

"Hmmm . . ." Pierre sighed.

Little Poucet shook his head. "You've killed us, my brother."

Little Poucet led his brothers on a snaky trip through the cold night of stone and damp asphalt, but nothing was familiar. Everywhere the walls towered above them, stinking of garbage and the press of generations of sweating, dying bodies, so dark that they blended and became indistinguishable from the night sky around and above. Now and then they would stumble over some form or other, sleeping or dead on the greasy pavement. Hands with long, slick fingers clutched at their ankles and trousers, slipped inside their cuffs to creep toward their thighs and groins. Maurice tittered, and Little Poucet told him to hush. Some of the bodies in the dark leaked fluids, and they gave these a wide berth.

When the others complained of hunger Little Poucet warned them not to stray from the path he was reimagining for them, so they kissed Pierre's sticky teeth and lips with their open mouths and tongues, sharing in the last bits of the sweet white goo, filling their bellies with the dazzling light that permitted them to continue through such darkness.

Muffled cries and howls floated just as slowly down from the dim windows high above, fixed there like distant, complaining stars. When they shuffled past the darker mouths of night, they could hear teeth rubbing, tongues lapping at the gritty stones.

At some point in the night it rained, but the night air had grown so thick they barely felt the drops.

"Where are you taking us?" Pierre whined.

"Home," Little Poucet replied, less and less sure of himself. "Wait here." He climbed a scarred and deadened lamp post and twisted his body round and round its head, searching for distant signs of life. Once upon a time he would have been able to fit his entire body on the head of such a lamp. He was surprised at how much larger he had grown. And how much his skin now smelled of adult garbage.

Down a corridor walled by two different shades of black, he saw a distant glimmer of light low to the horizon like a ground-floor window. Thinking of warm kitchens and broad beds and small boxes flickering, he slid down and led his brothers toward it. They complained that they could see nothing in that direction, but they had become used to following him so they did.

Often he lost all navigational sense and led them down into holes and wet places where invisible, spongy flesh rubbed against them. But eventually they came to the glowing window set beside a rough gray door in the back recesses of an alley stacked high with soggy cardboard cases of rotting meat.

Little Poucet reached as high as he could and pounded his fist against the door. After a few minutes a frail, worried-looking woman with stringy yellow hair answered.

"What do you children want at this time of night?" she demanded. "If it's stealing you're thinking about, I warn you my husband is not a forgiving man."

"Food, ma'am," Pierre spoke up. "We're *so* hungry!"

She jittered her eyes from one face to the next, finally resting on Little Poucet's diminutive form. "Looks like someone has already eaten the best part of this one." She paused, considering. "Very well. Come in then and I'll toss you an old fruit or two before sending you back to your parents, if you should have any."

Inside the dusty building Little Poucet tugged on her skirt. "We're lost, ma'am. Perhaps you could call the authorities?"

"Authorities?"

"The police? Social services?"

The withered little woman began laughing. "The *police*? Oh, my husband would dearly love that!" Then she laughed some more and Little Poucet could see that when she laughed she looked even thinner, her skinny arms flapping and beating her narrow torso, the loose material of her dress lifting away from her tight skin and pressing against it again, so that he found himself thinking of his mother, because this woman was the complete reverse of his enormous mother and in that was a kind of a negative twin, a sister to her.

"Perhaps just a bit of food, then," Little Poucet said softly, and the woman started laughing even louder than before. Little Poucet was embarrassed, and gazed down at his feet.

Just then the scrawny woman's head shot up, her neck stretching like a startled chicken's. "You hear? It's *him*, my man come home! You hear? Oh, you poor children—he'll be murdering you for sure! Here . . . here . . ." She stretched out her arms and legs and gathered the seven brothers to her, and despite her resemblence to a gigantic praying mantis, Little Poucet allowed himself to be gathered with the others. "Here, here . . . let Auntie hide you. Auntie won't let bad old Otto get to you!"

With desperate pattings and shooings of her long-fingered hands, she rushed them into the back of the building, pushing them past greasy piles of old clothing, dusty collections of children's shoes, children's toys, through passageways littered with dirt and what appeared to be yellowed animal bones, dried chicken skin, and a scattering of tiny teeth—Little Poucet figured dog, cat, badger. Pierre was sniveling, but there was no time to comfort him as she practically lifted them up to the first landing of the back stairs, whispering hoarsely: "First room on the left. Get under the bed there. But *don't* wake my daughters if you know what's good for you! Get under the bed there. I can't think of a better place to hide you."

Little Poucet waited until his brothers were all safely tucked away under the bed before joining them. As he rolled under the bed he looked at its twin on the opposite side of the room, and one great bloodshot eye peering over.

His brothers huddled together silently, staring at him. He could hear the sound of a bear-like voice downstairs, much like his father's. He heard a slap, then crying. His eyes now adjusted to the dim light, he looked around: several small skulls, a rib cage that might have housed the tiniest of birds, leg bones and arm bones, a tiny skeletal hand with a small child's ring on one of the fingers. Tiny teeth marks on all the bones, aimlessly crisscrossing the tops of the skulls, like the tracks of some small animal, like a tattoo. Downstairs more bellowing, and a breaking of furniture.

"But I can *smell* them, dammit!" And suddenly Little Poucet heard the thunder move to the stairs. Another eye joined the first atop the bed across the way, equally bloodshot, then the long dirty blond hair, the high cheeks, the sharp nose and thin lips and teeth filed to points like knitting needles. The chin stained dark.

The thunder was right outside the door now. Little Poucet could hear the lightning strike, the torrents of rain as Auntie wailed for the seven brothers to flee, but Little Poucet knew of nowhere to run. Six more identical heads joined the first on the other bed. The heads leaned over the edge and smiled down at him, their long tongues slipping over their chins. They leaned forward some more, and he could see that they had no clothes on. They rubbed their tiny breasts (in two or three only one had begun its development) and made a sound like swarming moths.

Otto burst through the door, and at first Little Poucet thought that indeed it was their father who had followed them here. He had the size (*like a wall, a dark and heavy wall*), and the voice, and the way of wrinkling his nose as if he were always smelling a bad smell. And the large, broken teeth.

Otto strode over to the bed and lifted it to uncover the seven frightened brothers. "Such pretty boys . . ." he cooed. He turned to his wife. "Get them ready for bed! I'll want them rested in the morning. No challenge otherwise." Otto looked back down at Little Poucet. "Sweet little thing," he said, and patted Little Poucet's head, stroked his shoulders, felt for muscles in his arms and legs. Then Otto gently spread his great hand until it covered the whole of Little Poucet's chest. He leaned over him, his breath sour with beer. "I can feel your heart beating," he whispered. "I can almost taste it, too. Wait until the morning." He massaged the boy's rear, circled the boy's groin with a huge, blunt forefinger. "You'll see."

After Otto left (Little Poucet could hear him drinking and singing downstairs), Auntie gave them a quick dinner of cold noodles and helped the seven brothers strip off their clothes. She shook her head at each naked little boy. "Oh, you're all much too soft and tender. He likes them soft and tender." She handed each of them a ragged, dark-stained nightshirt, then turned to leave. Her daughters began to giggle. "Hush up now!" she told them. "There'll be time enough tomorrow for what you're wanting. Go to sleep now!" And she left the room.

The seven little girls looked over at the seven naked little boys and whispered excitedly among themselves. Then they all laughed one last time and pulled the covers over their heads.

Pierre started putting on his nightshirt. "Stop that!" Little Poucet cried. "Can't you see the stains, the torn places? It's like butcher's wrap!" He looked back over at the other bed, the seven sisters starting to snore and snarl beneath their covers. He pulled his brothers close to him. They snickered at his cold touch on their bare skin. "Hush up now . . . once he's got enough drink in him to bring out the beast he'll be back up here quickly, I think. I have an idea. Do you remember how our father trained us not to wet the bed?"

The other six nodded solemnly, their eyes pale and tight in their tiny faces.

First he gathered seven leftover noodles from the cracked plastic bowls Auntie had provided them (Pierre's bowl, of course, had been wiped clean). A bit of thick, flour-based sauce had settled into the bottom of each one. He dipped each noodle until it was heavy in the sauce, then with great stealth crept over to the girls' bed, pulled back the covers, and gently stuck a noodle to the sex of each one. They snarled and snapped in their sleep, but did not move off their backs. Soon, he knew, the sauce would become a paste, the paste would dry, and their disguise would be perfected. His brothers' hair was just long enough that in the dark Otto might not suspect.

After a quiet search of the room Little Poucet found enough string to take care of all seven of them. Each brother tied one end to the tip of his penis, passed the remaining string back between his legs, and gave the other end to Little Poucet (who also held the end of his own string). Little Poucet became the puppeteer: all he had to do to turn him and his seven brothers into instant females was to pull on the string and thereby tuck each of their penises back under their asses. With their soft bodies and bad teeth, and by pressing their arms close to their sides to accentuate their breasts, they became wonderful, matchless little girls. Lying there together on the bed Little Poucet found them quite irresistible.

To no one's surprise Otto did come up later that night, stumbling drunk, and went straight to the boys' bed. Little Poucet jerked hard on the string causing Jean Paul and Maurice to gasp, but they drew their gasps out quickly into yawns.

Otto reached under the covers and felt for their groins. "What's this? My daughters? I could have made a terrible mistake." He paused for a time, smiling, gazing off into space. Finally stirring himself he said, "But no time for this," stood up suddenly, and walked to the other bed.

He reached under the covers there and laughed. "Tiny they are, but unmistakable! Here's one seems a little stale." He pulled out a sharp knife and rapidly cut off the heads of his seven daughters and dropped them into a large bucket by the bed. He then proceeded to flay the bodies, making miniature vests and tiny leggings. He pulled out one of the heads and removed the skin of the face, turning it into a small mask. "This'll be a good mask for the dog to wear when he watches TV with me," he said, holding it up to the light coming through the window. He stared at it a time. Then dropping it as if it were something truly disgusting he cried out, "Imogene!" and spun around to the other bed.

But the seven brothers were already out the door and on the staircase, their strings trailing along behind them. Otto leapt up and ran after them, bellowing. He stepped on one, then another of the trailing strings. Pierre and Maurice screamed and tumbled down the stairs. Otto lost his balance and followed hard upon them. Auntie suddenly appeared at the bottom of the stairs, and, startled by the naked, bleeding children tumbling down her staircase, she went up after them, only to watch helplessly as they wheeled past her and her husband Otto, Otto the Butcher, Otto the Cannibal, crashed into her.

The seven brothers gathered what they could find in the litter and rot of the house: mostly jewelry and clothing from Otto's past victims, and all manner of cutting instruments and devices of torture. They dressed in the cleanest rags they could find, and when daylight finally came, Little Poucet led them home with their loot.

Their parents were of course overjoyed to see them, especially with all the items they had taken from Otto and Auntie's house. They were puzzled by the fact that both Pierre and Maurice had become girls while away on the journey, but this fact was of very little importance to them. "After all," their father would say, "children are children."

But the world of his mother's bed was never the same for Little Poucet again. He stayed awake nights. He listened for voices in the distant, dark walls. And sometimes when his parents were unusually noisy, when their cursings and crashings and complaints about how many mouths they had to feed became almost too much to bear, he would reach into his pillow and take comfort in the knife and the hook, the club and the razor, and dream of their readiness.

The Changelings

Melanie Tem

Melanie Tem's short fiction has appeared in anthologies including Women of Darkness, Skin of the Soul, Cold Shocks, *and* Final Shadows *and in magazines such as* Isaac Asimov's Science Fiction Magazine *and* Cemetary Dance. *Her first novel,* Prodigal, *published in Dell's Abyss line in June 1991, won the Horror Writers of America award for achievement in the first novel category (an award shared with Kathe Koja). Her second,* Blood Moon, *was published by the Women's Press of London in the spring of 1992.*

Melanie Tem often writes about parent/child relationships and the strong emotions—positive and negative—that bind families. In "The Changeling," her protagonist tiptoes that fine line between loving and hating a difficult child. It is based on a Scandinavian tale of changelings and forest trolls. (See Doris Lessing's novel The Fifth Child *for a different treatment of the same theme.)*

The Changelings

BRIDGET SAT QUIETLY IN THE HOUSE OF THE CREATURE who had stolen her child.

In her hand was a mug of the best coffee she'd ever tasted: strong and aromatic, and still hot even though she'd been mostly ignoring it for some time. On the table at her elbow was a bowl of dry-roasted peanuts, which even under the circumstances she had a hard time resisting; they nearly filled a dark, thick wooden bowl of an odd shape, whose polished planes made her want to keep running her fingertips over it. An old Waylon-and-Willie tape of love songs was playing, one of her favorites. The creature *knew*.

Crystal and Cynthia were practicing jump rope chants and cheers on the front porch. Bridget could see them through the window, although there were odd distortions in the pane; the heavy bone-colored shade was rolled at the top now, and she guessed that when it was down no one would be able to see inside this house at all. Sometimes she just glimpsed movement on the porch; sometimes she caught a little face or body in stylized animation. She kept a watchful ear and eye on them, terrified that, now that she had finally found her real daughter, she would somehow lose her again.

She'd recognized the child called Cynthia (not a bad name; not one she would have chosen, but not bad; she wondered if she'd have to change it) the moment she saw her on the school playground. She'd known for sure when Crystal started bringing her home to play, to have dinner, to spend the night.

The girls were so different from each other that Bridget knew they wouldn't have been friends if it hadn't been meant for her to right the wrong. Cynthia was like her: shy, not good with words, unable to stand up for long to Crystal's willfulness. Cynthia wasn't good in school, as Bridget had not been; Crystal was a star student, though she seldom paid much attention. Cynthia never got in trouble, was, like Bridget, skilled at discerning rules and following them; Bridget was forever getting notes or having to attend conferences about Crystal's behavior—stealing, fighting, talking back to the teachers—which she was powerless to affect, though she tried everything she could think of. Cynthia, like Bridget, never called attention to herself by achievement or by misdeed; Crystal was in the spotlight all the time.

Cynthia looked like Bridget, of course: the same wide-set pale blue eyes, flawless skin like white tissue paper, pink lips, hair somebody had once called flaxen. Crystal was dark, darker every year, and the palm-shaped birthmark on her right cheek more distinct; her skin was coarse, her hair thick and wild with a terrible cowlick on the crown of her head that no comb or brush or pick would go through, her mouth so naturally red that Bridget would have suspected her of sneaking makeup and would have punished her if it hadn't been that color since the first day of her life. Sometimes, because it had been, Bridget punished her anyway. Crystal's eyes changed color with her mood and with what she was wearing, but they were not the subtle, suggestive color called hazel; they were brilliant green, violet, vivid brown, translucent gray, utter black. Crystal's eyes made Bridget shudder; she had always avoided looking directly into them.

Through the screen door, Bridget could hear Crystal and Cynthia whispering together now like any other eleven-year-olds in the half-welcome company of their mothers. Cynthia was giggling; Crystal never laughed.

Dressed in yella
Went upstairs to
Kiss a fella
Made a mistake
Kissed a snake
How many doctors
Will it take?

Cynthia stumbled over the rope at the count of seventeen. They started the chant again, and Crystal was still going at fifty-three. Bridget wasn't surprised. Crystal had always been unnaturally strong and well coordinated. She herself wasn't the least bit athletic, and she didn't go to Crystal's games and exhibitions anymore because she couldn't bear to see how accomplished the child was, how alien.

"Can I get you anything?" asked the creature, who went by the name of Kathy. It was an ordinary name. It was an ordinary, hospitable question.

All this normalcy and friendliness only gave away her true nature, and so did her hands, which hovered with obvious intent over every object she touched, whether she ended up using it or not. And her eyes, which looked directly and audaciously at you, changing color even as you struggled to avoid meeting their variegated gaze. Her eyes, like Crystal's, were ringed with lashes so thick and dark that they made Bridget think of moustaches, or, disturbingly, of pubic hair.

"Do you need anything?" Kathy asked again, looking at her.

"No," Bridget lied. "No, thanks."

The girls' chanting had become more brazen, their delivery more sultry, and Bridget saw Crystal strike a sexy pose that looked much less like childish parody than it should have. Cynthia copied, but she was just an embarrassed little girl mimicking her elders. Crystal had a full bustline already, enhanced, over Bridget's objections, by a padded bra. Through the little-girl shirts Cynthia always wore, Bridget had noted that her breasts were just developing, and that one of them was larger than the other.

Cinder-ella
Dressed in red
Got a snake to
Take to bed
He's too skinny
Said her mother
Go back out and
Get another

How many babies
Will they make?

Before Bridget could avert her eyes to protect herself, she and the creature had exchanged maternal glances. Kathy sighed and said indulgently, "They grow up awfully fast, don't they?"

Bridget took another tiny swallow of coffee and one peanut. She was afraid to say much for fear of inadvertently providing Kathy with weapons to use against her. Of course, she might be able to use silence, too. Bridget coughed loudly.

"Although sometimes," Kathy said, "I worry that Cynthia isn't growing up fast enough. I mean, she doesn't know things now that I knew when I was seven or eight."

Feeling that she should keep up the pretext of making social chitchat even though the creature probably could see through it, Bridget cleared her throat. "Some of the girls in their class actually wear makeup to school. Can you imagine? In fifth grade? I fight with Crystal all the time to get her to wait."

There was a pause, and then Kathy said, "I *try* to get Cynthia to wear a little lipstick and blush, a little light eye shadow. She's so pale, washed out. But she won't. A couple of times I've insisted, put some of my makeup on her, told her how pretty she looks, and the minute she gets to school I know she washes it off."

"They're too young!" was all Bridget could think to say.

Kathy didn't say anything for a while. The tape ended and the machine clicked off; she made no move to get up and put on another. There was silence from the porch as well; nervously Bridget leaned forward until she could see the girls crouched together in a corner. She didn't like the look of it but, like so many things about Crystal, there was nothing so specifically objectionable that she could protest or punish or forbid.

Crystal gestured animatedly, long painted nails glittering, and she was talking a lot, while Cynthia sat with her knees up to her chin and made designs with her fingertips in the dust, then erased them gently with the flat of her hand. Bridget's heart went out to the sweet, self-effacing little girl, but she forced her body to remain in the chair, her face to stay composed.

"And she's always so *good,*" Kathy said, frowning. "She doesn't have much will of her own. She never says 'no' to anybody about anything. It's always 'yes' this and 'yes' that. I suppose I should be grateful that she's such an easy child, but to tell you the truth it worries me and it drives me crazy. When I was her age I was quite a little rebel."

Bridget sighed. Crystal said "no" to everything, even if she wanted to do what she was being told to do. She delighted in pouring soup on her new dresses, looking at Bridget out of the corner of her eye to see how angry she would get. She drove babysitters away by sprinkling sand in their hair, throwing their shoes in the garbage, hiding herself behind one bush after another for hours while the babysitter and Bridget searched frantically. Sometimes she'd spend the whole day in bed just because she wanted to, with the blankets pulled up to her ears, and if Bridget dared tiptoe into her room to see if she was all right, she'd shout, "Get out of here and leave me alone!" Sometimes she'd rise before dawn, while mist was still on the streets and the morning star was still in the dim sky, and would race around the neighborhood, gallop on an imaginary horse or spread her arms as if she would fly, hallooing and singing at the top of her lungs. Bridget couldn't do anything with her, no matter how severe her punishments were, how creative.

Carefully now, she said, "Crystal definitely has a mind of her own."

"You're lucky," Kathy said wistfully.

Bridget thought, *Serves you right* and *Take her back, then*, and for a moment entertained the ridiculous notion that the two of them might simply swap children again and go on with their lives.

But Kathy said, "My daughter is an awfully sweet little thing, though," and Bridget's heart sank.

Kathy had gold-red hair that touched her shoulders and stood out in a fan shape around her head. She was very tanned. In the dimness of the room—dark wood, spongy forest-green carpet and walls, the window and door distinct rectangles of light—she seemed to glow.

Bridget knew that was no illusion. The creature did have a certain incandescence about her that went beyond her beauty and warmth. If Bridget hadn't known who she was and what she'd done, she'd have liked her. For a moment that made her sad, but then the loss turned to relief, a sense of having avoided great risk.

"It's hard, isn't it?" Kathy said. "Being a single mother."

Bridget disliked conversations about men, tried to avoid such talk under any circumstances and certainly under these. Eleven years ago, not long after she'd realized that the infant in her care was not the one she'd borne, her daughter's father Dale had called once from California to say he almost had enough money for her and Crystal to join him. She'd told him not to bother. He'd said all right, he'd never bother either one of them again, and he hadn't. Bridget had seldom thought about him since, except sometimes to fantasize about sending Crystal to him once and for all. Not that she was his child, either.

Recklessly, Bridget said, "I kind of like it, myself."

"But it's so *hard*!" Kathy wailed. She ran a hand through her hair so that it fairly sparked. "Every decision is mine and nobody else's. Everything I want to do, there's just Cynthia and me. And there's so much I want to do, you know?"

"I don't want to have to share my daughter," Bridget said, and then, having gone this far, added deliberately, "with anybody."

"Do you date?"

Bridget frowned and shook her head.

"Not at all?

"No."

"God, how do you stand it?" Kathy's voice carried an exact replica of the sultry tone the girls had used for their chant about Cinderella and the snakes. When she got to her feet, crossed the room to the stereo, bent to change the tape, her suggestive movements were the original of Crystal's. "I haven't been *in love* lately," she went on, her back and round hips to Bridget, "but I *need* a man now and then, if you know what I mean."

Desire swept over Bridget and made her shudder so that she almost dropped her coffee. Shakily she set the mug down. Nausea swelled, and she closed her eyes. Waylon and Willie sang again, lyrics about things you could do something about, a melody whose passion was within limits.

Cinder-ella
Dressed in black

Spent all night
Upon her back
Snakes went in
And snakes came out
And Cinderella wondered
What it was about.
How many snakes
Did Cinderella take?

Abruptly, Bridget had had enough. "Crystal!" she called. "It's time for me to go home."

The chanting paused, and Crystal appeared at the door, her face distorted as she pressed it against the screen. "I want to come, too."

"I—I thought you were going to spend the night," Bridget objected clumsily.

"I don't want to! I want to go with you!"

Bridget tried to open the door. Crystal pushed against it from the other side. The girl's face was twisted into one of her horrible grimaces; she was rapidly escalating toward a fierce tantrum, and Bridget was glad Kathy would see it.

Very reasonably, she said, "Crystal, honey, I have plans tonight. Why don't you spend the night with your friend, like we planned, and I'll come tomorrow to pick you up."

Behind her, Kathy started to say, "Maybe another time—"

Crystal threw herself onto the concrete floor of the porch, howling, her strong lithe body twisted into impossible angles. "No! No!" She was saying more, but—as often happened when she was really upset—the words were impossible to understand. "No, no, no!"

Bridget went outside, let the door swing quietly shut behind her, straddled the child who was not hers, and slapped her hard across the face. Kathy gasped. The birthmark flared. The strong little body rose up between her knees. She lay forward, pressed her breasts against the child's too-large breasts, covered the wet mouth hard with the heel of her hand but could not shut her up. She slapped her again.

Cynthia was standing in the yard, entirely off the porch, with both hands pressed over her mouth; Bridget longed to comfort this passive, withdrawn child instead of trying to control the willful one. She knew instinctively how to be a mother to Cynthia.

Bridget said in a low voice, "Stop it," and slapped the writhing Crystal again.

Kathy grabbed her wrist. She was strong. "*You* stop it!" she cried.

Crystal's inhuman howls had dissolved into sobs now, and she looked and sounded so much like a normal little girl that Bridget felt sorry for her, even loved her. Dangerous emotions. She bent and kissed Crystal's hot, rough forehead, pulled back before the child's arms could work themselves around her neck. Once Crystal had you in her grasp, it could be a terrible battle to get free.

She got to her feet. "I think she'll be all right now," she said, panting a little, not looking at Kathy. Her palm and her wrist hurt, and she'd probably have marks from the pressure of Kathy's fingers, as over the years she'd often had scratches and bruises from Crystal's fingers, fists, feet. "I'll be back for her in the morning," she said, and left.

Cynthia took a step or two after her as she went out the gate. Kathy said her name softly, and the little girl stopped at once. Bridget thought: *Not yet, sweetheart. But soon.*

Crystal was a changeling.

Once she'd found the name for it—found it in an unlikely book as though it had been put there for her to see—Bridget's dreams had all but stopped. But she'd never been able to exorcise the waking memories of the morning Crystal had come to her and been taken away, and the other Crystal left in her place.

She sat on the couch, surrounded by mending, with the radio turned to a country western station. Once she'd sat down she'd realized she'd have preferred a tape, but by then her lap was full of Crystal's jeans with holes in the knees, Crystal's shirts with buttons missing, Crystal's Girl Scout uniform and sash and half a dozen new badges needing to be sewn on, Crystal's brand new spring coat with a huge rip in the seam whose cause Crystal hadn't been able or willing to tell her no matter how long Bridget tried to keep her in her room till she did. Bridget resented the work, the way it trapped her on the couch, the music on the radio that she didn't want to hear, all of it because of this impossible child.

A spring storm was building up. The radio had predicted snow, and the air through the open window at her back was much too cold. Crystal wanted windows open no matter what the weather, and Bridget was always cold in her own house. It was an old house with old windows; closing the window would have entailed getting up on her knees and forcing the stubborn sash down. Instead, Bridget shivered angrily, bent her head over the rip in the coat—which, she discovered, extended well past the seam and was not going to be easy to fix—and was chilled and warmed by memories so familiar they had the power of ritual.

Bridget had been barely sixteen years old when she'd had her baby, and alone. She hadn't seen Dale since she'd told him she was pregnant. Of her own father she had only one snippet of a memory: him coming into her room when she was in her crib, her wanting him to hold her, expecting him to hold her and he didn't. She didn't think her mother could see her much, through the haze of booze and dope and men in which she moved. When Bridget told her she was pregnant, her mother had laughed and cried and hugged her, reactions which didn't seem to have much to do with Bridget or the baby, and it was never mentioned again.

It was mid-morning when the pains started. At first Bridget didn't know what they were, and she was afraid. Then, finally, she began the process of rousing her mother, shaking her, calling out every time a contraction hit. Sullen from unnatural sleep, her mother drove her to the hospital and dropped her off, saying something about having to get to work. As far as Bridget knew, she didn't have a job right then. But maybe she had found one. It was possible.

It was all right with Bridget to be alone. She was, in fact, glad to be alone with her pain, her blood, her beautiful baby girl. She knew how beautiful the baby was even before she was born; she said so whenever the contractions allowed her to speak. "My baby is so beautiful! My baby is *mine* and she'll love me forever! My baby is so beautiful!"

When the baby was finally born, there was only a tiny ephemeral sound, a cry so sweet and shy that Bridget, in and out of consciousness, wasn't sure she'd heard it. For a long time after she woke up they wouldn't let her see her baby. "She's sick, honey," one or another of the kind nurses kept saying; their kindness scared her, made her want to beg them to leave her and her baby alone. But she was sick, too, and very tired, so she turned her head on the pillow and went back to sleep, crying a little for her beautiful baby daughter whom she couldn't see and could hardly hear.

Crystal. The name came to her in dreams, making her think of bright colors in the midst of gray, of ordinary light turned into something extraordinary. That morning, as if they'd been waiting for the baby to have a name, a kind nurse brought Crystal to her and laid her in her arms. Tiny, pink-faced, eyes squeezed shut. Very pale, very quiet. And beautiful. "Oh, she's so beautiful!" Bridget breathed.

"She's sick, honey," the nurse said again. "She's getting better, but she's still not very strong."

"Hi, Crystal," Bridget whispered, her lips just brushing the lips of the baby as if she could breathe the name into her. Crystal opened her blue eyes, moved her tiny mouth just a little. "Hi there, Crystal. My beautiful little Crystal." The nurse took her away after a short while and Bridget cried, but the nurse promised to bring her back and, anyway, there was nothing Bridget could do.

Crystal grew stronger, and Bridget grew stronger, and the kind nurses taught the child-mother as much as they could about how to take care of the child. But motherhood never did come naturally for Bridget; she always had to work hard, concentrate hard in order to do things right. She wondered then how her mother had learned to take care of her, and whether her mother had ever thought she was beautiful.

The nurses taught her how to hold the baby, how to change her and bathe her, how to nurse her, and then they sent them home. She couldn't reach her mother anywhere, so she took Crystal home on the bus. That was all right. Bridget enjoyed traveling alone with her daughter, who was still so new but who, somehow, had always been part of her life. People on the bus smiled and cooed and asked how old the baby was and what was her name, and Bridget was proud. None of them touched; none of them tried to take her baby away. They all said Crystal was beautiful. "She's really a beautiful baby." One lady said, "She looks a lot like you."

When she got home, the house was dark and empty. It smelled of booze and dope and, she thought, sex. She didn't like bringing her beautiful new daughter home to a place that smelled like that, but Crystal didn't seem to mind; Crystal lay quietly in her arms. There was no nursery, no crib even, so Bridget made a nest out of frayed blankets on the floor beside her own mattress and carefully laid Crystal there. The long trip home had exhausted her, and she was afraid of being alone in this house with a brand new baby. So she lay down on the sheets that hadn't been changed or smoothed since she'd left to go to the hospital and, with her hand close beside the baby's head, made herself fall asleep.

Crystal fussed once in the night, and Bridget fed her. The baby's mouth at her nipple shamed her, but there was no one to see. The next time Bridget woke up, cold gray light was coming like footsteps in through the window, voices from the street were shrilling sinister things like "beautiful baby" and "perfect little girl"—and Crystal was gone.

Bridget searched everywhere. At first in her terror she got confused and thought maybe Crystal had just wandered off somewhere, and she was all ready to be mad at her, maybe even spank her. Then she remembered that tiny babies couldn't wander off, that you didn't hit tiny babies no matter what they did. Trying to stifle her panic for the sake of her child, she crawled over every inch of the dirty floor, patting and slapping at the blankets, peering under chairs, running her fingers along the grimy baseboards as if somehow the baby could have slipped down there. "Crystal!" she called, at first in a whisper, at last shrieking the name until it lost all meaning in her own ears except to say how scared she was, how lonely. *"Crystal!"*

She stumbled out the door. The morning was quiet and gray and cold, with no color in it. She thought she could still hear somebody somewhere talking in high-pitched voices about her perfect and beautiful daughter, but that was all. It was as if Bridget had made it all up, as if she'd never had a baby. She stood in the doorway for a long time, shivering violently, waiting for something to happen to her next. Waiting for her mother to come home and tell her what to do. Waiting for Crystal to come back and explain why she'd left. Waiting for the eerie voices to speak again and tell her what they'd done with her child.

Finally, not knowing what else to do, Bridget went back into the house and curled herself into the nest of blankets she'd made for her baby. Music had started up, loud from the apartment next door. Traffic was heavy and the people across the street were already listening yelling at each other. Because these were not the sounds Bridget was listening for, she tried to put them out of her mind. Desperately she filled her mind with the words of an old prayer and the tune of a lullaby, and, though she had to sing the same few notes and recite the same few words over and over because they were all she knew, the spell worked and she did at last fall asleep.

And woke to the squirming and hiccoughing of a baby in her arms. Bridget stifled a scream and sat bolt upright, dropping the warm little thing into the tangled covers. This was not her baby. This baby was ugly. It had coarse dark curls all over its elongated skull; her daughter's round head had been downy. Its face was mottled red and it had a lusty yell; her baby had been pale and silent. Across the cheek of this baby was a faint brown birthmark, as if it had been slapped hard by a small hand; her baby's skin had been flawless, like white tissue paper when you first take it out of the package.

The baby bellowed and reached for her. Instinctively Bridget picked it up and put it to her breast. The baby sucked hard and couldn't seem to get enough; it hurt a lot. Horrified, but grateful that she had a baby at all and hadn't made it up, Bridget looked around for the mother of this child who had stolen hers. She couldn't see anybody, but gray light ringed her, and the air was cold, like wings.

Hating and loving this baby who was not her own, Bridget said, "Hi, Crystal." It was the only name she knew.

"I'm not going."

"You are going. We've had this planned for weeks. Kathy and Cynthia will be disappointed if you don't go. They're already on their way over here to pick you up. You can't change your mind now. Besides, Kathy already has your lift ticket and your ski train ticket. Those things are expensive. Besides, I have plans. I won't be here." Frustration was making her prattle.

Bridget forced herself to stop, adding only, "You are going."

"It's snowing out. They said on the radio it's dangerous to drive in the mountains."

"You're not driving. You're going on a ski train."

"You just want to get rid of me."

Crystal pushed past her out of the kitchen, where the windows were steamy from the kettle of vegetable soup simmering cosily on the stove. Bridget refused to be deprived of the satisfaction of making homemade soup, bread, cookies—the image of good motherhood that her own mother had never even tried to fulfill—even though Crystal wouldn't eat anything that didn't come out of a can or plastic wrap. Kathy didn't cook, probably didn't know how, and it made Bridget angry to think of what Cynthia was missing. A tin of homemade chocolate chip cookies was waiting on the counter to be sent along on the ski trip; she knew Cynthia would appreciate them.

Feeling a little guilty—she did, after all, care for this difficult child even though she was not her own—Bridget took a few steps after Crystal, reached for her, managed barely to brush her tangled hair. Crystal jerked away as if Bridget had tried to hit her. She'd always been stiff and suspicious of affection. The child never missed an opportunity to make it clear by her very existence that Bridget was a bad mother.

At the foot of the stairs, in the dim entryway, Crystal hesitated and stared back over her shoulder. Her eyes were bright black in the murky light, and for an instant Bridget thought she might attack, or fling herself out into the snow. Her features, distorted so often by fury or petulance and patterned by the birthmark that showed distinctly no matter how much makeup she wore, had a perverse beauty that made Bridget gasp.

"Crystal—"

"Leave me alone!" the child shrieked. "You don't understand *anything*!" She turned and ran up to her room. Her footsteps were heavy, as though she weighed much more than she actually did; the staircase shook, and plants teetered on the ledge. Bridget heard the bedroom door slam and felt the throbbing of music from Crystal's radio turned up as loud as it would go; then there was the familiar noise of Crystal throwing things, slamming things into the wall, breaking things. Fury seized Bridget again, strengthening her resolve. The child was destroying the house. The older she got, the worse it was; Bridget had to do something soon.

She looked outside. No sign of Kathy and Cynthia yet, but the blizzard that had gone on all night had stopped now. Surely that was a good sign; surely Kathy would be able to make it now. Wet, heavy snow lay like corpses on the eaves, weighed down the branches of the plum trees and lilac bushes that had been just starting to bud. Mourning the delicate, fragrant blossoms ruined for another season, Bridget allowed her anger with Crystal to grow. Of course the snow was not the child's fault—but it was, somehow. The sky was thinning gray, with outlines of individual clouds starting to emerge.

She should check on Crystal, make sure she was all right, make sure she was getting ready, find out what she was doing. Once in the aftermath of an argument Crystal had urinated all over her bed; Bridget had found her squatting on the stinking sheets and blankets, long arms around her knees, rocking and howling, and, even though she'd rubbed her face in the acrid wetness and spanked her like the animal she resembled, Bridget knew Crystal was quite capable of doing something like that again.

Familiar resentment made the climb up the stairs torturous, and Bridget was exhausted. When she reached the upstairs hallway she noticed that Crystal's door was open a little, as though the child wanted to be approached, and with trepidation Bridget pushed the door open and looked inside. Crystal wasn't there, but the room was filled with smoke.

Bridget shrieked the child's name—stolen, like everything else, from her own daughter. Of course there was no answer. She turned on the light, turned off the radio, frantically searched for the source of the fire, found it in the closet, crumpled newspaper blackened and Crystal's new and newly mended spring coat smoldering.

Bridget wrenched open the window, gasping at the rush of cold air, and bundled the whole burning mess out into the snow. She burned her hands; there was a searing pain across both palms. Then she raged into the bathroom, where Crystal crouched in the tub, hairy knees drawn up between breasts too long for an eleven-year-old, too long and pendulous to be human at all, hairy slimy with shampoo and dripping down her face, silently waiting.

She had filled the tub so full that the overflow drain couldn't handle it, and water was pouring onto the floor. Most of her body was distorted by the bluish water, and the drain gurgled whenever she shifted her weight, growled and snarled when Bridget plunged her stinging hands, her arms, her upper body into the water and dragged the child out.

This was not her child. This child was not human. She was not the mother.

Bridget fought with the hysterical child, clutching her in her arms. Crystal's hoarse, rattling sobs shook them both. The steel-blue snowlight through the high, steamed-over little window and the agitated bathwater reflected off Crystal's skin, which was greenish and coarse. She smelled bad; she had always smelled bad, as though she'd urinated on her clothes and Bridget hadn't changed her, as though Bridget couldn't keep her clean, but now her odor was rancid and nearly overpowering.

Bridget warded off the child's strong blows and answered her otherworldly shrieks with shrieks of her own. "Get out! Get out of my house!" Soaked by now with bathwater and sweat and whatever fluids were spilling from the pores and orifices of this mad creature, Bridget managed to drag her out of the bathroom and down into the much cooler living room. She tangled both hands in the thick hair and pulled the contorted face close to hers. "Get out!"

Crystal stared at her with eyes gone luminous, colorless, all colors. Then, in a cracked high voice that Bridget hadn't heard since the morning the child had come into her life, she began to chant:

Cinder-ella
Dressed in gold
Always does what
She is told
Don't be silly
Said her mother
Go away and
Fetch another
How many babies

Will it take?
One, two, three . . .

And then she laughed. Bridget had, of course, never heard her laugh before, and she wouldn't have recognized the shrilling as laughter if she hadn't seen the wide grin, the head thrown back, the long hands over the shaking belly. The counting was wild and rapid, a spell.

The child was on her, attacking or embracing, shrieking the syllables of "Mo-ther!" as if they'd been put into some magic new order, and then there was a rush of cold air and voices in the room and Kathy's high-pitched commands and Cynthia's sweet wailing and Bridget's own shout: "Get her out of here before I kill her! Take her back! And leave me my own child!"

Her vision cleared somewhat, and Crystal had let her go. She sat up. Kathy stood with her back to the window, her red hair lit purple by the bluish snowlight, a long-nailed hand on each of the girls.

The creature had grown very tall. Looking up at her, Bridget thought that the creature's hair brushed the ceiling and left glittering trails.

Now the creature was tiny. Bridget hadn't seen her change, but she was no bigger than a human hand, and she was cradling something in her too-long hairy arms.

Bridget held out her arms to the girls. Crystal, still laughing, took a step toward her, but it was Cynthia she wanted, and she said the girl's name although it wasn't the one she'd given her. "Cynthia. Cynthia. Stay here with me."

Cynthia's eyes were very wide; her pale, almost invisible lashes made them seem to bulge. Both her fists were at her mouth. She pressed herself against Kathy, who was human-size again, and mutely shook her head.

Bridget was incredulous. She tried to stand and couldn't, crawled across the floor until she could lay her hands on the girl's shoes. "Please," she whispered. "You belong to me. I'm your real mother."

Cynthia threw her arms around Kathy's waist and sobbed, "Mama, make her leave me alone!"

Although Bridget didn't see her move, didn't will her own body to move in response, she was suddenly not touching the child anymore, Kathy was between them, and the thing Kathy had been carrying was now in Bridget's arms, hard and lifeless against her aching breasts.

"Here's your child," the creature hissed. "Here's your child to suckle and raise. Here's your child to love."

Bridget looked down. In the crook of her arm was a stick of wood the shape and size of an infant, carved with features like those of the infant she'd lost long ago and imagined ever since—sweet silent rosebud mouth, placid eyes, gentle little hands and feet. It had no life, she knew, but it had been endowed by glamour with the suggestion of life, and that was good enough, that was even better.

Kathy and the two girls were gone—both of them changelings, neither of them hers. Bridget was alone with the image of the baby, seductively carved and painted and polished. She opened her shirt and eased her erect nipple into the baby's mouth, which was open just enough to receive it; the mouth made no sucking motion and she had no milk, but the baby was easily satisfied. She lowered her own lips to the perfect forehead, which was warm and smooth and pleasing even though it had no life of its own.

"Hi there, Crystal," she murmured. It was the only name she knew.

The Springfield Swans

ALL RIGHT, YOU'VE TOLD ABOUT YOUR GATOR GUIDRYS and your Mudcat Grants. I been sitting on this bus, hearing your stories for a coupla hundred miles. Might believe some of them too. But give your tongues a rest now and listen to me. 'Cause I can tell you about a pitcher and boy, he *really* had an arm.

There was a family once named Swenson, lived in a small town called Springfield. Mr. Swenson, he was a good man, hard-working and smart, and he loved baseball. Always said he wanted enough kids to field a team, all of them boys. Well, Mrs. Swenson maybe didn't get the idea right off the bat, 'cause their first was a girl, Annie. But then she got down to work and had one boy a year, regular as clockwork. I guess giving birth to a whole baseball team wore her down some,

The Springfield Swans

Caroline Stevermer
and Ryan Edmonds

And now, for something completely different, comes a charming tale with a dry, Midwestern twang. It is a retelling of "The Wild Swans," set on a baseball diamond.

Caroline Stevermer, author of The Serpent's Egg, *has become something of a cult writer among fantasy aficionados for her elegant prose and laconic wit. Ryan Edmonds is a talented new writer who hails, like Stevermer, from Minneapolis.*

'cause once the ninth boy was born, little Tommy, Mrs. Swenson just threw in the towel and died.

Annie did the best she could after her mother was gone, but nine healthy boys do take some looking after. So Mr. Swenson finally got himself married again, to a widow lady. But unlike the Swensons, man and child, she did not care for baseball. No, she did not care for it at all.

Well, spite of that, things went pretty well there in Springfield for some years. But then Mr. Swenson passed away. Died the day after Tommy's birthday, when the kid turned fourteen and was finally eligible for the Springfield township team, along with his brothers. That was the first year the Swensons could of fielded their own team and gave their dad his wish. It was a shame he never got to see it. And one of the boys, Edward, I think it was, he said so, right there next to the casket at the visitation.

Of course, it was only the truth. But the second Mrs. Swenson didn't like that kind of talk and to be perfectly honest, she didn't much like Edward either. When she heard what he said, she went stiff like a poker and turned 'round to look at him with her eyes all wide and kind of hard looking. "I am surprised at you, Edward," she said, very soft and gentle. "Surprised and disappointed. This is a solemn occasion and you're talking about *baseball*. You make me ashamed."

Well, Edward got red and shuffled his feet. But Annie stepped up to speak for him, which was kind of a habit she'd got into over the years.

"You can't say that to Edward," she said just as soft but not so gentle. "Daddy loved baseball and Edward loves Daddy. We always wanted a team of Swensons but now even if we get one, it's too late for Daddy.

Edward was just saying what we all think." She might of gone on, 'cause, to tell the truth, though she was a pretty girl, Annie was a real good talker and when she had something to say it generally got said.

But before she could say any more, Mrs. Swenson was drawing herself a big lungful of air like she meant to blow the funeral parlor down. She didn't say anything then, but somehow Annie went quiet too. For almost a minute Mrs. Swenson stared hard at Annie like she was a pitcher glaring in at a pesky batter on a three-and-oh count with first base open, and you know he's gonna let go of his meanest, hardest fastball, and if it goes wild and beans the guy, well maybe he doesn't much care.

I guess Mrs. Swenson was sorry later but you know how it is with stepmothers. They never know their own strength. There was no way she could get the words back once she said them and she said them before she had time to think.

"If I *ever* hear another word about baseball from any of you ever again," she said, very soft but not gentle at all, "I hope you all grow wings and fly away to hell."

And in the next second, before anyone could stop her, Annie snapped back, "You ought to go fly away yourself. You wouldn't know a bunt from a balk anyway."

That did it. In the time it takes to throw from second to first, all the boys were gone and where they had been were nine white swans, honking and hissing and trying to break through the windows and get away.

Well, that was a mess. The visitation was just shot to hell. There was no family at the funeral except Annie and Mrs. Swenson and they weren't speaking. No one could do anything with the swans, not the doctor, not the pastor, not even the vet. Finally Annie called the

University Extension and talked to some of the professors there. First they wanted to send someone out to band the swans. Then they suggested it was all a case of mass hysteria. But Annie was not about to let any professors talk her down. Finally she got ahold of the right department and they told her that her brothers had been transformed into swans by magic. And according to the rules of magic, they had just one chance of getting their real shapes back. If someone were to sew a shirt for each swan, without either smiling or speaking till they were done, then as soon as they put on those shirts, the boys would be human again.

That didn't sound too hard to Annie. After all, a good talker never really thinks she says a word too many, and Annie knew it was her job, for talking about baseball at such a time. She was going to dig in and make those shirts.

She got fabric at the dry goods store, and she used one of Edward's old baseball jerseys for a pattern. But that was the easy part. You see, Bo Jackson probably knows more about sewing than Annie ever did. When she took domestic sciences back in high school, the apron she made for the sewing project turned out about eight inches longer on one side than the other and it was so stained from the times she stabbed herself with the needle that it looked like a butcher was using it. But the teacher was kind and passed Annie anyway.

So Annie got down to work. The fabric frayed every time she cut into it, or else the scissors got some idea of its own and sliced a sleeve in half just as she was making the final cut. Her threads tangled into impossible knots or snapped after only three stitches, and the pins just leaped from her fingers and disappeared forever. Still, Annie persevered and she never uttered a word of complaint, not even when she realized that she had put in most of the sleeves upside down and had to unstitch them all and start over.

It was hard, slow work. The weeks went by and it was already time for spring training, but Annie only had six shirts ready. When the weather was nice, she'd take her sewing down to the municipal baseball field and sit there with her swan-brothers outside the left field fence—Mrs. Swenson wouldn't allow them in the yard 'cause of the mess they made. The swans would honk all forlorn-sounding while they watched tryouts for the Springfield team, and sometimes Annie looked up from her sewing to check the action on the field, too. But it was hard for her, what with the outfielders dropping easy fly balls or missing the cutoff man with their throws. Annie felt like she had to say *something* when that sort of thing happened, but every time she felt the words ready to rush out she'd bite her tongue hard and go back to her sewing instead.

Now, the Springfield team had a pretty fair reputation around its league. They'd hired a new coach that year, all the way from Winona, and he was mighty puzzled why he couldn't find enough players who even knew which direction to run the bases. He'd heard about the Swenson brothers, and he asked just about everybody where they had got to. Nobody wanted to tell him that his star players had all been turned into swans though, so they recommended he ask Annie. Well, Coach did ask Annie. He asked her every day out there behind the left field fence, but she didn't say a word—just kept her eyes on her needle and went on sewing. After a while, Coach stopped asking, but he'd still come out there where she was sitting 'cause he liked watching her work the needle so quiet, with the sun shining down on her hair.

Well, it looked pretty bad for Springfield on opening day that year. There was still no sign of the Swenson boys and out behind left field the nine swans were making such a racket that it was truly something horrible to hear. Somehow Coach'd found enough guys to fill the uniforms at least, but I guess they finally figured they were just embarrassing themselves, 'cause at the last minute they announced they had to study for a quiz bowl or something and slunk away.

The Albert Lea team had already showed up in their brand new uniforms and the bleachers were packed. A Springfield-Albert Lea game is always a big event and pickups full of the Albert Lea folks had been rolling into town all morning. The Springfield fans showed up too, even though they knew there was no team, 'cause they wanted to see what Coach was going to do.

The umpires said Springfield would have to forefeit if they couldn't put nine players in the field. But there was just the three of us sitting there on the Springfield bench: Coach, me—a scrubbini bat boy, and Annie, her arms full of new baseball jerseys, still trying to set one last sleeve that refused to go in right.

The situation was even more awkward than it sounds 'cause, the day before, Coach proposed to Annie while she was trying to sew a buttonhole. And even though Coach was not a bad looking man, Annie never said a word, never even smiled at him. "All right," Coach said, real slow. "I know how it is. You need time to think it over. Well, think all you want, Annie. You know how I feel. But I won't pester you to death. And if you don't give me your answer by game time tomorrow, I'll know what to think." Annie's needle went still and she stared down at the uneven stitching in her lap like she had never seen anything so peculiar in her life. Then somebody hit a pop fly and the sound of the bat on the ball started her needle going again.

So here it was, Annie still hadn't said a word to him and it was time to either turn in a line-up card or concede the game. Coach looked at her one last time. "Nothing to say, Annie?" he asked sadly. "Not even a smile?" For a second she looked up and he thought he saw tears in her eyes. But then she just turned her back on him and ran out to center field. So Coach shook his head and spat on the ground and began the long walk over to where the umpires were ready for him to forfeit the game. He had the words all ready and was just waiting till he could trust his voice to speak when a shadow went over the sun.

The crowd murmured like wind in the corn and then they gasped and then they went perfectly quiet. A flight of swans, white as snow, wheeled over the field and swooped low over the bleachers. They were so close you could see the feathers spread wide in the tips of their wings when they passed over the bench. And it was so quiet you could hear their wings beat against the air, like snow hissing on still water. They glided single file to where Annie was standing all alone in deep center field, and as they went by, she tossed the jerseys up in the air one at a time. As each jersey flew up into the air, a swan would duck his head and fly clean into the jersey, just like a kid tunneling into a turtleneck sweater. Then and there the Swenson boys turned back into their own rightful shapes. And you know, those jerseys didn't look half bad. All but the youngest brother's, Tommy's, whose jersey wasn't quite done. His right sleeve fluttered in the breeze where Annie had failed to complete the seam. In the sunlight the sleeve looked real white and it flapped about like a wing almost.

But the umpires agreed that if the Albert Lea team didn't object, he could play, and the Albert Lea team said sure, it was better than no game at all. Even so they couldn't get started yet 'cause Annie was running in from center field to home plate and kissing Coach and reminding him that Edward ought to choke up on the bat and thinking out loud about who to invite to the wedding. But things sorted themselves out somehow. Annie coached first base and Coach was behind third. They did pretty well even though they spent most of eight and a half innings just smirking at each other across the diamond. Tommy pitched. And though he never had much more than a fair fastball before turning into a swan, that day he had amazing stuff, a scroogie, a curve and a really brutal sidearm forkball. He struck out the side four times—maybe it was that flapping sleeve that did it but probably it was the forkball. His brothers didn't have their usual strength at the plate but their fielding was good as ever. Springfield came out on top four to three. Coach and Annie got married a month later, reception and dance at the VFW. It was quite a time. Yes, indeed. By then Coach had an idea Annie might not be so quiet and domestic as he'd thought, but he didn't seem inclined to complain.

Eight of the Swenson boys settled down in Springfield just like the Swensons had always done, playing slow-pitch softball in the summer, talking hot-stove league in the winter. But Tommy couldn't seem to stay in one place. Every year, come October, he'd be wanting to head south. He started in the semi-pros when he was seventeen. When he was nineteen, he got a tryout with the Cardinals and spent some time with their minor league clubs before he broke into the majors with that sidearm forkball. He had himself a few good seasons, too. You maybe heard of him. His teammates called him Swanny but I'll bet they don't know why.

Troll Bridge

Neil Gaiman

Neil Gaiman, born in 1960, is the author of the graphic novels Violent Cases *and the award-winning* Sandman *series (including the brilliant issue about a serial killer convention based on science fiction/fantasy conventions) and is coauthor of the very funny novel* Good Omens. *He is working on a very scary book for children. "Troll Bridge" is one of his rare short stories.*

"The Three Billy Goats Gruff" was one of my favorite fairy tales as a child. In this version there's only one "billy goat," and while it seems to be about escaping a troll, the story actually speaks of lost chances.

Troll Bridge

THEY PULLED UP MOST OF THE RAILWAY TRACKS IN THE early sixties, when I was three or four. They slashed the train services to ribbons. This meant that there was nowhere to go but London, and the little town where I lived became the end of the line.

My earliest reliable memory: eighteen months old, my mother away in the hospital having my sister, and my grandmother walking with me down to a bridge and lifting me up to watch the train below, panting and steaming like a black iron dragon.

Over the next few years they lost the last of the steam trains, and with them went the network of railways that joined village to village, town to town. I didn't know that the trains were going. By the time I was seven they were a thing of the past.

We lived in an old house on the outskirts of the town.

The fields opposite were empty and fallow. I used to climb the fence and lie in the shade of a small bulrush patch and read; or if I were feeling more adventurous I'd explore the grounds of the empty manor beyond the fields. It had a weed-clogged ornamental pond, with a low wooden bridge over it. I never saw any groundsmen or caretakers in my forays through the gardens and woods, and I never attempted to enter the manor. That would have been courting disaster, and, besides, it was a matter of faith for me that all empty old houses were haunted.

It is not that I was credulous, simply that I believed in all things dark and dangerous. It was part of my young creed that the night was full of ghosts and witches, hungry and flapping and dressed completely in black.

The converse held reassuringly true: daylight was safe. Daylight was always safe.

A ritual: on the last day of the summer term, walking home from school, I would remove my shoes and socks and, carrying them in my hands, walk down the stony, flinty lane on pink and tender feet. During the summer holiday I would only put shoes on under duress. I would revel in my freedom from footwear until the school term began once more in September.

When I was seven I discovered the path through the wood. It was summer, hot and bright, and I wandered a long way from home that day.

I was exploring. I went past the manor, its windows boarded up and blind, across the grounds, and through some unfamilar woods. I scrambled down a steep bank and found myself on a shady path that was new to me and overgrown with trees; the light that penetrated the leaves was stained green and gold, and I thought I was in fairyland.

A stream trickled down the side of the path, teeming with tiny, transparent shrimps. I picked them up and watched them jerk and spin on my fingertips. Then I put them back.

I wandered down the path. It was perfectly straight, and overgrown with short grass. From time to time I would find these really terrific rocks: bubbly, melted things, brown and purple and black. If you held them up to the light you could see every color of the rainbow. I was convinced that they had to be extremely valuable, and stuffed my pockets with them.

I walked and walked down the quiet golden-green corridor, and saw nobody.

I wasn't hungry or thirsty. I just wondered where the path was going. It traveled in a straight line, and was perfectly flat. The path never changed, but the countryside around it did. At first I was walking along the bottom of a ravine, grassy banks climbing steeply on each side of me. Later the path was above everything, and as I walked I could look down at the treetops below me, and the roofs of occasional distant houses. My path was always flat and straight, and I walked along it through valleys and plateaus, valleys and plateaus. And eventually, in one of the valleys, I came to the bridge.

It was built of clean red brick, a huge curving arch over the path. At the side of the bridge were stone steps cut into the embankment and at the top of the steps, a little wooden gate.

I was surprised to see any token of the existence of humanity on my path, which I was by now certain was a natural formation, like a volcano. And, with a sense more of curiosity than anything else (I had, after all, walked hundreds of miles, or so I was convinced, and might be *anywhere*), I climbed the stone steps and went through the gate.

I was nowhere.

The top of the bridge was paved with mud. On each side of it was a meadow. The meadow on my side was a wheat field; the other was just grass. There were caked imprints of huge tractor wheels in the dried mud. I walked across the bridge to be sure: no trip-trap, my bare feet were soundless.

Nothing for miles; just fields and wheat and trees.

I picked a stalk of wheat, and pulled out the sweet grains, peeling them between my fingers, chewing them meditatively.

I realized then that I was getting hungry, and went back down the stairs to the abandoned railway track. It was time to go home. I was not lost; all I needed to do was follow my path home once more.

There was a troll waiting for me, under the bridge.

"I'm a troll," he said. Then he paused and added, more or less as an afterthought, "Fol rol de ol rol."

He was huge: his head brushed the top of the brick arch. He was more or less translucent: I could see the bricks and trees behind him, dimmed but not lost. He was all my nightmares given flesh. He had huge, strong teeth, and rending claws, and strong, hairy hands. His hair was long, like one of my sister's little plastic gonks, and his eyes bulged. He was naked, and his penis hung from the bush of gonk hair between his legs.

"I heard you, Jack," he whispered, in a voice like the wind. "I heard you trip-trapping over my bridge. And now I'm going to eat your life."

I was only seven, but it was daylight, and I do not remember being scared. It is good for children to find themselves facing the elements of a fairy tale—they are well-equipped to deal with these.

"Don't eat me," I said to the troll. I was wearing a striped brown T-shirt and brown corduroy trousers. My hair also was brown, and I was missing a front tooth. I was learning to whistle between my teeth, but wasn't there yet.

"I'm going to eat your life, Jack," said the troll.

I stared the troll in the face. "My big sister is going to be coming down the path soon," I lied, "and she's far tastier than me. Eat her instead."

The troll sniffed the air, and smiled. "You're all alone," he said. "There's nothing else on the path. Nothing at all." Then he leaned down and ran his fingers over me: it felt like butterflies were brushing my face—like the touch of a blind person. Then he snuffled his fingers and shook his huge head. "You don't have a big sister. You've only a younger sister, and she's at her friend's today."

"Can you tell all that from smell?" I asked, amazed.

"Trolls can smell the rainbows, trolls can smell the stars," it whispered, sadly. "Trolls can smell the dreams you dreamed before you were ever born. Come close to me and I'll eat your life."

"I've got precious stones in my pocket," I told the troll. "Take them, not me. Look." I showed him the lava jewel rocks I had found earlier.

"Clinker," said the troll. "The discarded refuse of steam trains. Of no value to me."

He opened his mouth wide. Sharp teeth. Breath that smelled of leaf mould and the underneaths of things. "Eat. Now."

He became more and more solid to me, more and more real; and the world outside became flatter, began to fade.

"Wait." I dug my feet into the damp earth beneath the bridge, wiggled my toes, held on tightly to the real world. I stared into his big eyes. "You don't want to eat my life. Not yet. I—I'm only seven. I haven't *lived* at all yet. There are books I haven't read yet. I've never been on an aeroplane. I can't whistle yet—not really. Why don't you let me go? When I'm older and bigger and more of a meal, I'll come back to you."

The troll stared at me with eyes like headlamps.

Then it nodded.

"When you come back, then," it said. And it smiled.

I turned around and walked back down the silent, straight path where the railway lines had once been.

After a while I began to run.

I pounded down the track in the green light, puffing and blowing, until I felt a stabbing ache beneath my rib-cage, the pain of a stitch, and, clutching my side, I stumbled home.

The fields started to go, as I grew older. One by one, row by row, houses sprang up with roads named after wildflowers and respectable authors. Our home—an aging, tattered victorian house—was sold, and torn down; new houses covered the garden.

They built houses everywhere.

I once got lost in the new housing estate which covered two meadows I had once known every inch of. I didn't mind too much that the fields were going, though. The old manor house was bought by a multinational, and the grounds became more houses.

It was eight years before I returned to the old railway line, and when I did, I was not alone.

I was fifteen; I'd changed schools twice in that time. Her name was Louise, and she was my first love.

I loved her gray eyes, and her fine, light brown hair, and her gawky way of walking (like a fawn just learning to walk which sounds really dumb, for which I apologize). I saw her chewing gum, when I was thirteen, and I fell for her like a suicide from a bridge.

The main trouble with being in love with Louise was that we were best friends, and we were both going out with other people.

I'd never told her I loved her, or even that I fancied her. We were buddies.

I'd been at her house that evening: we sat in her room and played *Rattus Norvegicus*, the first Stranglers LP. It was the beginning of punk, and everything seemed so exciting: the possibilities, in music as in everything else, were endless. Eventually it was time for me to go home, and she decided to accompany me. We held hands, innocently, just pals, and we strolled the ten-minute walk to my house.

The moon was bright, and the world was visible and colorless, and the night was warm.

We got to my house. Saw the lights inside, and stood in the driveway, and talked about the band I was starting. We didn't go in.

Then it was decided that I'd walk *her* home. So we walked back to her house.

She told me about the battles she was having with her younger sister, who was stealing her makeup and perfume. Louise suspected that her sister was having sex with boys. Louise was a virgin. We both were.

We stood in the road outside her house, under the sodium yellow streetlight, and we stared at each other's black lips and pale yellow faces.

We grinned at each other.

Then we just walked, picking quiet roads and empty

paths. In one of the new housing estates a path led us into the woodland, and we followed it.

The path was straight and dark; but the lights of distant houses shone like stars on the ground, and the moon gave us enough light to see. Once we were scared, when something snuffled and snorted in front of us. We pressed close, saw it was a badger, laughed and hugged and kept on walking.

We talked quiet nonsense about what we dreamed and wanted and thought.

And all the time I wanted to kiss her and feel her breasts, and maybe put my hand between her legs.

Finally I saw my chance. There was an old brick bridge over the path, and we stopped beneath it. I pressed up against her. Her mouth opened against mine.

Then she went cold and stiff, and stopped moving.

"Hello," said the troll.

I let go of Louise. It was dark beneath the bridge, but the shape of the troll filled the darkness.

"I froze her," said the troll, "so we can talk. Now: I'm going to eat your life."

My heart pounded, and I could feel myself trembling.

"No."

"You said you'd come back to me. And you have. Did you learn to whistle?"

"Yes."

"That's good. I never could whistle." It sniffed, and nodded. "I am pleased. You have grown in life and experience. More to eat. More for me."

I grabbed Louise, a taut zombie, and pushed her forward. "Don't take me. I don't want to die. Take *her*. I bet she's much tastier than me. And she's two months older than I am. Why don't you take her?"

The troll was silent.

It sniffed Louise from toe to head, snuffling at her feet and crotch and breasts and hair.

Then it looked at me.

"She's an innocent," it said. "You're not. I don't want her. I want you."

I walked to the opening of the bridge and stared up at the stars in the night.

"But there's so much I've never done," I said, partly to myself. "I mean, I've never . . . Well, I've never had sex. And I've never been to America. I haven't . . ." I paused. "I haven't *done* anything. Not yet."

The troll said nothing.

"I could come back to you. When I'm older."

The troll said nothing.

"I *will* come back. Honest I will."

"Come back to me?" said Louise. "Why? Where are you going?"

I turned around. The troll had gone, and the girl I had thought I loved was standing in the shadows beneath the bridge.

"We're going home," I told her. "Come on."

We walked back, and never said anything.

She went out with the drummer in the punk band I started and, much later, married someone else. We met once, on a train, after she was married, and she asked me if I remembered that night.

I said I did.

"I really liked you, that night, Jack," she told me. "I thought you were going to kiss me. I thought you were going to ask me out. I would have said yes. If you had."

"But I didn't."

"No," she said. "You didn't." Her hair was cut very short. It didn't suit her.

I never saw her again. The trim woman with the taut smile was not the girl I had loved, and talking to her made me feel uncomfortable.

I moved to London, and then, many years later, I moved back again, but the town I returned to was not the town I remembered: there were no fields, no farms, no little flint lanes; and I moved away as soon as I could, to a tiny village, ten miles down the road.

I moved with my family—I was married by now, with a toddler—into an old house that had once, many years before, been a railway station. The tracks had been dug up, and the old couple who lived opposite us used it to grow vegetables.

I was getting older. One day I found a gray hair; on another, I heard a recording of myself talking, and I realized I sounded just like my father.

I was working in London, doing A & R for one of the major record companies. I was commuting into London by train most days, coming back some evenings.

I had to keep a small flat in London; it's hard to commute when the bands you're checking out don't even stagger onto the stage until midnight. It also meant that it was fairly easy to get laid, if I wanted to, which I did.

I thought that Eleanora—that was my wife's name; I should have mentioned that before, I suppose—didn't know about the other women; but I got back from a two-week jaunt to New York one winter's day, and when I arrived at the house it was empty and cold.

She had left a letter, not a note. Fifteen pages, neatly typed, and every word of it was true. Including the PS, which read: *You really don't love me. And you never did.*

I put on a heavy coat, and I left the house and just walked, stunned and slightly numb.

There was no snow on the ground, but there was a hard frost, and the leaves crunched under my feet as I walked. The trees were skeletal black against the harsh gray winter sky.

I walked down the side of the road. Cars passed me, traveling to and from London. Once I tripped on a branch, half hidden in a heap of brown leaves, ripping my trousers, cutting my leg.

I reached the next village. There was a river at right angles to the road and a path I'd never seen before beside it, and I walked down the path and stared at the river, partly frozen. It gurgled and plashed and sang.

The path led off through fields; it was straight and grassy.

I found a rock, half buried, on one side of the path. I picked it up, brushed off the mud. It was a melted lump of purplish stuff, with a strange rainbow sheen to it. I put it into the pocket of my coat and held it in my hand as I walked, its presence warm and reassuring.

The river meandered across the fields, and I walked on in silence.

I had walked for an hour before I saw houses—new and small and square—on the embankment above me.

And then I saw the bridge, and I knew where I was: I was on the old railway path, and I'd been coming down it from the other direction.

There were graffiti painted on the side of the bridge: *Fuck* and *Barry Loves Susan* and the omnipresent *NF* of the National Front.

I stood beneath the bridge, in the red brick arch, stood among the ice cream wrappers, and the crisp-packets and the single, sad, used condom, and watched my breath steam in the cold afternoon air.

The blood had dried into my trousers.

Cars passed over the bridge above me; I could hear a radio playing loudly in one of them.

"Hello?" I said, quietly, feeling embarrassed, feeling foolish. "Hello?"

There was no answer. The wind rustled the crisp packets and the leaves.

"I came back. I said I would. And I did. Hello?"

Silence.

I began to cry then, stupidly, silently, sobbing under the bridge.

A hand touched my face, and I looked up.

"I didn't think you'd come back," said the troll.

He was my height now, but otherwise unchanged. His long gonk hair was unkempt and had leaves in it, and his eyes were wide and lonely.

I shrugged, then wiped my face with the sleeve of my coat. "I came back."

Three kids passed above us on the bridge, shouting and running.

"I'm a troll," whispered the troll, in a small, scared voice. "Fol rol de ol rol."

He was trembling.

I held out my hand, and took his huge, clawed paw in mine. I smiled at him. "It's okay," I told him. "Honestly. It's okay."

The troll nodded.

He pushed me to the ground, onto the leaves and the wrappers and the condom, and lowered himself on top of me. Then he raised his head, and opened his mouth, and ate my life with his strong sharp teeth.

* * *

When he was finished, the troll stood up and brushed himself down. He put his hand into the pocket of his coat, and pulled out a bubbly, burnt lump of clinker rock.

He held it out to me.

"This is yours," said the troll.

I looked at him: wearing my life comfortably, easily, as if he'd been wearing it for years. I took the clinker from his hand, and sniffed it. I could smell the train from which it had fallen, so long ago. I gripped it tightly in my hairy hand.

"Thank you," I said.

"Good luck," said the troll.

"Yeah. Well. You too."

The troll grinned with my face.

It turned its back on me and began to walk back the way I had come, toward the village, back to the empty house I had left that morning; and it whistled as it walked.

I've been here ever since. Hiding. Waiting. Part of the bridge.

I watch from the shadows as the people pass: walking their dogs, or talking, or doing the things that people do. Sometimes people pause beneath my bridge, to stand, or piss, or make love. And I watch them, but say nothing; and they never see me.

Fol rol de ol rol.

I'm just going to stay here, in the darkness under the arch. I can hear you all out there, trip-trapping, trip-trapping over my bridge.

Oh yes, I can hear you.

But I'm not coming out.

A Sound, Like Angels Singing

Leonard Rysdyk

Leonard Rysdyk is a 1990 Clarion West graduate. His teacher, Pat Murphy, urged him to submit this, his second story, for the anthology. Rysdyk's first story appeared in Aboriginal Science Fiction. *He has also completed a novel, and teaches English at Nassau Community College on Long Island.*

It is not apparent from either the title or early part of the story what fairy tale suggested "A Sound, Like Angels Singing," but its inspiration will become obvious by the tale's end. Readers will find this offering a bit more raw and brutal than most of the stories in Snow White, Blood Red.

A Sound, Like Angels Singing

"WE MIND OUR MEAT," SAID NAILS. "THAT'S enough for us." She licked the man's hand, then bit it.

"But you must have heard," said Tail, bending low to pull off a strip of the man's forearm muscle.

Lips grumbled, "I did. Woke me." He took a finger between his paws and meticulously gnawed the palps down to the bone. The fingernail fell off. Then he moved to the flesh on the second joint.

"Though your belly was full?" said Nails. Her tail swished through the filth of the alley where the body had been dumped. Flies landed on her food, but she kept on eating.

"Aye, and no cat near," said Lips. "Nor dog. Nor man." The air was sharp with the smell of death.

Snout stopped eating and looked up. Her soft, round face was damp with blood. "Sounded like angels to me," she said dreamily. She arched her back to keep her tender, swollen teats from dragging on the cobblestones.

"What do you know of angels?" said Nails with her mouth full. "Forget it. Mind your meat. Mind your littles."

"More like a dinner bell," said Tail. He sniffed for a second at his consort, Snout, then went back to eating. "It made me hungry."

"It was music," Snout insisted, "like on the feastdays."

Lips stood up on the man's forearm and looked down the alley as if he smelled a cat. "Can't forget it," he grumbled.

"Augh!" said Nails, and she lunged at him with her teeth. Lips shifted back on his hind legs and parried her with his claws. He raised up and showed his teeth. Nails relented, then crawled to the other side of the carcass and found a fresh place to bite.

"Foolish talk," she muttered. "I hope we've heard the last of it." Blood and saliva ran down her chin.

When they were full to bursting, the family went back to the den. Snout lay on her side and gave suck to her young: weak white things with toothless jaws. Lips chased Nails clumsily. Their feet scratched on the straw and potsherds, but she wouldn't let him mount; instead, she nicked him and he backed off and farted at her. She didn't retaliate. She was too weak from overeating. The nest settled in for the night. "Short teeth," said Nails. "Short teeth," her family answered and closed their eyes. With the warm, dark den pressing them on all sides, they settled to sleep.

At noon the sound came, high and bright like a hawk searching among the spires of the town. Lips' eyelids flickered and he got up. He took a step toward the opening of the den, but Nails ran in front and blocked his way.

"Where are you going?" she said.

"Going?" said Lips.

"You were leaving the nest. Where?"

"Don't know." He paused to think, but instead he heard. "The sound," he said.

"You need to rest," said Nails. "Lie still and get fat."

"The sound," Lips said. Nails bared her teeth.

Suddenly Snout was trying to climb over them, but Nails cuffed her. "What?" Snout said. "What'd I do?"

"The sound again," said Lips. "Hear it?"

"Forget it," said Nails.

"But it's so beautiful," Snout said.

"Can't sleep," said Lips. He tried to pass again, but Nails' claws were on his front feet. Their bodies clogged the opening.

"Hmmm, hmm!" said Tail sleepily from deep in his throat. He was pressing forward from the back of the den. His snout poked out over Snout's humped back.

"Mind your sleep," said Nails. "Mind your littles." She wouldn't let them out and she stood guard for a few minutes, pressing them back. Then as suddenly as it had started, the sound stopped.

The nest slept through the day and, at dusk, they went back into the alley between the half-timbered, whitewashed buildings where the dead man lay. Decay perfumed the air and the nest's eyes bulged when they saw, not just the man they had half devoured, but a girl-child thrown on top of him. They would eat until their teeth were worn to stubble.

"Thank God they killed the dogs," said Tail. His mouth watered.

The sound of the nest's jaws, snackering tooth on tooth, was as loud as the buzzing of the flies. Shadows darkened the alley.

"What dreams I had!" said Snout.

"After the sound started," Tail said, then stopped suddenly. His eyes bulged and he caught his breath. His chest heaved and the mucus spattered in his wet nose until he spat out a piece of tendon. It bounced toward the corner where the roaches crawled. He coughed once, then buried his jaws again in the man's calf. "My stomach growled until it stopped," he said.

"You are idiots for that sound," said Nails. "I slept. Until you fools startled me, I slept and grew fat. I will again tonight."

"The sound," said Lips, wriggling his hindquarters uncomfortably. "Disturbing."

"Sleep and grow fat," said Nails. "Tomorrow there may be no scavenge."

The nest ate diligently, climbing over the corpses and finding soft places to gnaw, but as the last ray of red light left the alley in darkness the sound began again: a lilting that might have been the wind, only more beautiful, more evocative—a west wind in winter promising a thaw.

"There it is," said Snout. "Oh!"

"Cats and traps!" said Nails. She hissed. "Mind your meat!"

Snout dropped the bone she was gnawing and waved her tail, her eyes lifted to the red sky above the alley.

"Snout!" said Nails and dropped her scavenge too. She looked at the others. "Tail!" she said. "Lips!" None of them heard her; none of them ate. Snout took a step, then paused, her nose in the air. The others took a step or two each, hesitating. Then they gave in and began to trot.

Nails outran them to the end of the alley. She lunged at them and slashed with her teeth.

"What are you doing? This is a trick I say: cheese in a trap. Will you run to your deaths?"

"This sound is so—exciting," said Tail.

Snout said, "So sweet, so beautiful."

"Hear what it's saying, Nails? Can't you?" said Lips. "Fresh meat. Warm, dry dens."

"Bah," said Nails.

"Nights without cats," said Tail. "Sleep without fleas."

"Heaven," said Snout, "and the sound of angels singing."

"It's a trap and a trick," said Nails. "You know men—men and their tricks!"

They looked past Nails; they did not answer. They pressed her back, out of the alley.

"Look!" said Lips.

The street was a stream of hair and tails.

With a rush of excitement, the nest plunged in and Nails was swept along like a twig in a millrace. Bodies pressed around her; claws stepped on her tail. She fell; she floated to the top. She was carried on.

The sound was everywhere now but it was strongest up ahead and it was moving forward, leading them.

Nails tried to stop but the others drew her forward. She jumped and dodged, tried to work her way to the back. She called for her family but they didn't answer.

The stream flowed through the town gates now, like rain into a sewer, water through a sluice. They were outside the walls and Nails could smell the sweet grass along the lane. She tried to reach it, but was pulled on. They pulled her, her own kind: big, small, black, brown, male and female. Tiny white nestlings, barely able to walk, barely able to see. Nails felt a softness of flesh under her paws: nestlings trampled underfoot. The adults ran on, losing themselves to the sound. Lost already.

"Snout! Tail! A trap! Can't you see?" Nails called, but she knew they had no ear for her voice, could hear only the sound and whatever it was saying. "Lips! A trap! Lips!"

The ground was sloping up now and Nails was almost at the back of the pack. She heard the others call out, "Cheese!" or "Flesh!" or "Heaven!" but she smelled none of those things. Squeals rose from the stream. One leaped over another to be first into the promised land.

First into the trap, Nails thought. She fought the pressure, was carried forth and fought more. A figure stood beside the path, the pack roiling at his feet. He smelled of spices and played a pipe. His purple hose clung to legs as thin as gnawed bones. At his feet, the pack disappeared like water over a dam. They leapt over the cliff.

Nails struggled fiercely now, biting and clawing those who pulled her on. Suddenly, she was free. She ran, turned her back on the cliff and the piper: she pointed her nose toward the town and ran. Out of breath when she reached the bend in the road, she stopped and turned. Her family was behind her, their littles trampled and crushed. The squeals of the pack stopped. The sound stopped. Silence.

Nails trotted along the road in the dark. The trip back to town seemed to take longer than the trip to the mountain. Maybe because the magic was gone. Maybe because she traveled alone.

Fat, sad and tired, Nails slowed and stopped again on the road under the stars, a black thing in a black place. Maybe she had been wrong, she thought. Maybe the sound she didn't understand really *had* been the voice of angels, as Snout said it was. It didn't seem to her that heaven—whatever that was—had been just over the cliff, but all the others seemed to think so. What was in the sound that made them so sure?

Nails wished she hadn't bit Lips the last time he tried to mount her. She wished she had waited longer to wean Snout. She wished she could be with them, even if they hadn't found heaven. She turned back toward the cliff, hesitated and took a step.

Footsteps crunched on the gravel and the air bore the scent of a man coming her way. She turned again and trotted toward the town.

When she reached Hamelin, the gates were wide open, even though it was night. Torches flared from the walls and people shouted. Nails plunged into the grass, found a chink in the town wall and pushed through. She was walking in an alley when she heard a sound. Not the thin, keening of the pipe this time, but the clash of the church bells. Was it matins already? Or some song, perhaps the town's anthem? She had depended on the others to tell her such things.

Sounds were all one dull din to Nails: one tone, one register. Notes were as indistinguishable to her as the grinding together of stones or the rumblings of her belly.

The others had loved music, but for Nails, it never held any enchantment.

Puss

Esther M. Friesner

"Puss-in-Boots" is a well-known tale penned by the sixteenth-century French fairy tale master Charles Perrault. Esther Friesner has taken the story of the wily cat and the master he serves, and turned it effectively into a dark, chilling adult fairy tale. (For another interesting variation on the tale, see Angela Garter's "Puss in Boots" from her collection The Bloody Chamber.*)*

Friesner is one of three American writers of fantasy to emerge from the same dormitory at Yale University (the other two being Delia Sherman and Paula Volsky). She is a prolific storyteller with a long list of novels to her credit that cross the spectrum from breezily satiric to dark and disturbing fantasy, including the humorous Unicorn U. *and* Yesterday We Saw Mermaids.

Puss

THE BOOTS WERE ONLY THE BEGINNING. I STILL FEEL his hands on me, hard fingers driving deep into my ribs, jamming the heavy, clumsy sheaths of scarlet leather onto my hind legs while I squalled and spat until he cuffed me silent.

"Now walk!" he bawled, drunk with the bit of wine his own coin had bought. "Stand tall, you worthless animal! I'll make my fortune with you yet. There's fools enough in this wretched world who'll pay good money to see a trained cat."

Where had he ever gotten them, the boots? I never doubted that the world was as he painted it: cruel, cold as a dry tit, full of soulless shells like him who'd do anything to hear two coins chink-chink together in their fat, hairless palms. Surely that was how he had found the man to make them.

Oh, how they hurt me! No cat was ever born who'd willingly ask for such a crippling. He had me under the forelegs and swung my body forward—first one side, then the other—in imitation of human strides.

"Walk, damn you! The old fool said as you were special—pox take him. Must be something more to it than a gaffer's babblings, or it's all up for me. *Walk!*" His sour breath was full of curses for me and his father; his brothers, too, snug in their more comfortable patrimonies of mill and farm. They knew nothing and cared less that the youngest of the three now spent his night in a stable, kneeling in piles of horse-fouled straw, torturing a cat.

I could not walk—not like that—and he was too great a fool to bide and seek my true talents. So it seemed I should be free, soon or late. All it wanted was the taste of blood.

I let myself hang limp in his hands, deadweight. He groaned. I could see the self-pity bubbling up in his eyes behind the fat, ready tears of a drunkard. "Worthless." He held me off the floor so the boots with their heavy soles and heels pulled my hind legs down. The pain raced clear up my spine, a white fire in my brain.

"Worthless!" This time it was a shout, and a shaking to go with it. My eyes clouded with the red haze. Rage filled my mouth, called up the ghosts of my true teeth—not these paltry stubbins good for reaping only mice and rats. Oh, the hunger!

"Damn the old man." Now he was sniveling. I got another shake for his father's imagined sin. "All those years a-dying, and Bill and Tom crowding 'round the bed, simpering like daub-brained girls." And another shake yet for my poor, spinning head. "Cunning bastards. One to keep deathwatch, one to stiff-arm me off, keep me far from the old turtle so's it'd look as if I didn't care was no one there to shut his eyes for him after. Well, it worked, blast them all to hell for it! Mill and farm gone, and nothing for me but *this!*"

And he swung me back and flung me hard against the stable wall.

The boots were my death. I could not twist in midair and take the fall as I should, not with them weighing me down. I felt my ribs shatter as I hit the rough-hewn boards, my spine come unstrung with a single snap against a jutting beam. My limbs crumpled under me when I slipped down into the straw, all skewed. Warm, salty blood welled over my tongue. I let my mouth hang open and the thin, red flow trickled out, dampening the golden dust that overlay the straw. Soon, through the death of this small, much-punished husk, the Change would come and work its power. Soon I would be free.

But the pain was too fierce. The fury in my veins wailed impatiently for my lost wings, for the clean, knife-bright freedom of the air. Peace alone commands the Change, and I was too much dominated by wrath, trapped in a skin once glossy and sleek under a loving hand's care. Now drab and dirty, matted with filth, it would be a relief to shed it once the compact was fulfilled.

It was very hard, the dying, and long. He did his part to hurry it on, standing over me, driving a sprung-toed shoe into my belly. Air tore out of my lungs, scraped my throat with agony as a shallower breath forced its way back in. These mortal bodies cling to life too strongly.

"Stupid cat. Hell have you." I heard him stagger out

of the stable, still cursing. Clouds fell across my eyes. Alone, finally left in peace, I sought the hidden power of the blood. Now the Change must come, in solitude, with the old sea's taste fresh and metal-tangy on my tongue.

Change. The clouds darkened; only the savor of blood remained, the copper bloom at the heart and core of being.

Change. Scent and touch followed sight and sound into oblivion. I felt my self tearing free from the blood-woven web of the world. As my soul struggled, I sensed without seeing that the filthy stable had faded away around me. Laved by the shapetide, my dying shell lay upon the strand that lies between time and time.

Child? She came as I knew she must come, as she comes for all of us when the Change is imminent. Some of my folk say she was the first to find the way to the shore where the shapetide runs. Some call her goddess, all name her Mother. Her voice was a tender hand upon me, dulling my failing body's pain. I felt the layers of fur and flesh peeling away like the falling petals of a rose.

I am here, I answered in the only true speech. With more than eyes I saw her. She loomed above me, her great yellow eyes warming me. Their fire seared all else away, even the bones of evil memories. My spirit sprang from my broken chest, taking wing against the wind.

Child, you must return. Keen as a hatchet blow, cold as a plummet into an ice-crusted river, that sharp saying. My battered soul snapped back into its aching vessel and my sightless eyes stared wide. *What? But the compact—*

Is unfulfilled. I heard the sorrow in her words. *The debt is unpaid. You owe—*

I owe nothing! My spirit-self leaped up anew, still molded by my latest shape, and hissed and spat defiance against her who may never be defied. *What debt have I ever owed that wasn't paid in full through my own blood?* I gestured with a phantom paw at my fallen form, at the blackening trail now sluggishly oozing from a gaping, ashen mouth. *You see his handiwork, O Mother. Can you call all accounts anything but paid? I owe him nothing but death.*

And that, I swear, was the first I ever thought about that sweet possibility.

Her sigh was summer's own breath. *The debt was never owed to the son, but to the father. It lies over you yet, as heavy as the earth now lying over him.*

And I knew what she said was true, for there are no lies in the true speech.

I will heal you, she said, *and you will remember your debt.*

No! No! I did not seek memories, did not want them, would break my heart over them if she forced them on me. But her hand was upon me, her wings over me, and the great, scaley shelter of her body coiled around me. We are nothing in her shadow. I felt bone grind in healing dance against bone, and as her breath penetrated fur and flesh I was compelled to see.

Remembered firelight flickered amid the shadows in my eyes. A young man knelt among old pillars. Few from his village knew that such a ruin stood so near the plowland, fewer still would speak of it at all. But to come there—! And by night. And knowing enough half-truths of us to come bringing blood.

He knelt before the great altar in the wild place and

made his plea in the tongue so few recalled. We hid among the toothed and jagged pillars, harkening, curious, intrigued to hear our own words stumble out into the midnight air from the lips of a mortal man. Eyes aglow we watched and listened, hungering to drink deep if only he would make the smallest misstep, the flimsiest missaying to give himself into our power.

Not until then, though. We are a well-ruled people.

Wizard? my sister asked, nose wrinkling with greed.

I do not think so, I replied.

He must be, she maintained, mantling her wings against the autumn chill. Blue stars danced in her eyes. *None other would have the skill or courage to find us.*

Oh, I think he has courage enough. I licked a finger, still red from the sweet blood of his offering. It was too long dead to be more than a stomach-stay. He had not seen us dip hand and paw and wingtip into the pooled crimson in the brown earthenware bowl before him. We choose who may see us, and how, as reward or punishment. It was only goat's blood, but it was good enough. *See? He trembles.*

And you call that courage? A hero does not tremble, my sister said with scorn.

A hero does not have brains enough to know when to be afraid. The truly brave man knows, but goes on despite his fear. My ears twitched. He spoke our language well. Wisdom as well as courage, then. *I think that this time, I will be the one,* I said, and I did not stand on further saying, but chose my shape and stepped out of the shadows to make him mine.

I let the wings linger only long enough for him to see them and know that it was no common cat who had walked into his firelight's weak circle to save him. He gave a hoarse, glad cry, as one who has gambled away his soul but reaped a prize worth the loss, and fell full-length upon the tiles.

The compact was made. It was made in the old way, the true way, with a taste of better blood than a slaughtered goat's. Not Change blood, though; not blood spiced by death's proximity. The blood I took bubbled up from veins still taut with life, good for binding my life to his will, nothing more.

From that time forward, we knew each other, and what each might ask of each. So long as he lived, his thoughts were naked to me. So long as he laid one charge upon me that remained unfulfilled, I was in his thrall. His wants were desperate, but modest: a little land, a mill, the means to aid his parents in their old age. The homely shape I chose would never betray my nature or our pact.

By wisdom and by art I gained his humble prizes, and for my pay had love and gratitude and, better than blood, the rich feast of his mind. For my folk, immortal so long as our bodies are not entirely destroyed, the death-seasoned thoughts and feelings of humankind are dainty fare. He gave me no blows, seldom a harsh word from his lips all the days of our bonded life, and only a look of bewilderment and pain when my skills could not call his young wife's breath and blood back into her body after that third birth.

He is all I have left of her, I heard him say to the midwife as he gazed down upon the infant in its cradle. It tore at me to see him so desolate. I vowed then to make this last child of his a gift past common value, for the father's sweet sake. That night, when the older boys had been taken to his sister's house and his wife lay shrouded on the hearthside floor and the babe wailed in its cradle, for love of him I broke the laws that bound me . . .

Who are you? He startled me, making me spring back from the cradle before I could take up the child. He stood in the doorway between common room and bed-chamber, eyes red from too little sleep and too much weeping. The only weapon in the house was an old, rusty dagger of his father's, but he had found it.

Don't you know me? I was a fool to ask. In my new shape, lawless, a Change made boldly by a blood-drop softly stolen from her corpse—Oh, bitter!—how could he hope to know me?

He held a rushlight high in the hand that did not clasp the dagger. *Who are you, girl?* he repeated. The blade lowered slowly. *What are you doing here, at this hour, with neither cloak nor dress to clothe your nakedness? And why do you hover near my child?*

I have come for his welfare, I said, creeping subtly nearer to the sleeping babe once more. I laid my hand on the cradle's lovingly carved wooden canopy. *I have come to bring him blessing.*

He did not cross himself. Not once since that night when he sought us in the wild place did I ever see him make the pale god's sign. *I know you, then.* His voice shook like a candleflame. *You are one of the Old Folk, spirit. Say, by whatever honors your word, if your blessing be blessing true.* For he had heard the old tales, and knew how the Old Folk delight in a double-deal, and for the precious sake of his son's life he was afraid.

Dread not, I told him. *I am not one of the Folk you fear. They were infant shades when my people held this earth. We are the first begotten children of the old sea whose salt still seasons every living creature's blood, the children of Change, shapeshifters, the shapetide's masters. And O, my master, you do know me.*

He stared. Well he might stare! For I was dark and sleek and beautiful and I wore the shadows with more gallant grace than a princess in all her satins. Because the blood I had stolen was cold, so cold, the Change was incomplete—a dusky down clung like velvet to my body, and as I crouched by the cradle I could hear the whisper of my tail flicking back and forth across the floorboards.

I could hear too how his tongue scraped over dry lips as he looked at me. He threw the rushlight in among the banked embers and they flared. The dagger fell to the floor at his feet and he folded to his knees beside me as if he would pray.

Wild prayer, sweet prayer, prayer to serve a power older and darker than the pale god's teachings! Hands knotted in my hair, lips ardent at my throat, at the glowing mounds of my breasts, a ferocious, half-starved suckling made me shudder to the roots of my wombs. The flagstone floor pressed hard against my back until I could bear the chill of it no more and threw him down in my place so that I might spring on top of him as if he were my meat—a mock hunt, a feigned kill, a true feasting. White claws still curved from my fingertips, and I used them to slash away his flimsy muslin shirt. My mouth burned against his chest, the small and dainty bud of a nipple teasing thrills of anticipated joy from my rough tongue. I let one fang graze over it slowly, drawing out the moment, the full exaltation of our senses. He moaned in pain that was no pain when my small, sharp, cunning teeth nipped his flesh the instant before the fangs sank deep and the bright blood spilled into my mouth.

Coupled so, I needed no other coupling, but he did, and his need was my master. He wrestled me to the floor again and burned his way inside me while the last shimmering red drops fell in a sweet rain over my cheeks, my eyes. My whole body shook with the force of his thrusts, my tail curled up to lace his legs, and my claws raked him without breaking the skin, my little jest. Then he shuddered, gasped his name for me, and fell away.

A bad fall that! An evil fall! For as he rolled from me, blind chance let his arm loll back to drop across the still, shrouded, cold clay that shared our hard bed on the farmhouse floor. He turned his head and saw that in our tumblings we had pulled aside a span of shroud, leaving her face unveiled. Oh, cold! Winter's own miserly heart laid bare and bony over lips he had once devoured as madly as mine. I felt revulsion clutch talons around his heart, with shame to make it burn.

White as ash, her face, but ashes hold the phantoms of fires. The ghostly eternal flames that are the pale god's dogs rose up from the corpse. My master thought he had already pawned his soul, but what is pawned may some day be redeemed. This crime said he had sealed it irrevocably for the burning.

In guilt, he sought to deny all blame; in fear, he sought to weld blame to another.

Monster! he cried, scrambling from me. *What have you made me do?* His eyes darted from the white face of his dead wife to the red of his living babe, and he stretched out his arms to either one as if they were pinioning nails to be driven through his helpless hands. *Go! Get out of my sight! Mercy of heaven, what have you done to me?*

Then he saw the dagger. It leaped to his hand—not to kill me, no, not even then—and darted for his throat;

he would drown the hellflames in blood. My shriek and spring were faster, my own hand quick to strike the blade away. It spun from his fingers, and dropped into the cradle.

Yowl, little one! So newly born, so newly blooded. I snatched the babe from the cradle in fear, then saw our luck: only a scratched cheek. I touched the wound, blood dewing my fingertips.

He grabbed the baby from me. *Dark beast, you will not have him, too!*

I pressed my fingers to my lips with the pain his hard words gave me, my fingers still moist with the infant's blood. How could I resist and still be what I am? My tongue darted out to taste . . .

And he saw whose blood it was I'd sampled. Under the weight of ignorance all his world crashed around him. He sank down, hugging the infant tight against his chest until I thought him like to smother it. *Lost! The gift of blood makes you their creature! Oh, my son, my son!* His moan was wild enough to tear open the burning paps of the stars.

I crept near. He was tiptoe on the edge of madness, my poor master. A whisper of wrong saying and he would topple in, taking the babe with him. *Hush, you grieve too deeply*. I gave him comfort. *To bind, the blood must be a willing gift. He is as free as any newborn child, I swear.*

He dared to lift his eyes from the babe, his face haggard. *By what can you swear?* His voice was the rattle of dry bones in armor.

By the gift I meant to give him, I replied, taking breath. *I will suckle him. He will be my son, too, and from me gain the blood-blessed power of unending life. For the love I bear you, Master—*

For love, you would turn my son into . . . He did not finish. The frenzy was draining from him, reason returning. All that he said was, *No.*

I bowed my head. What bound us now went beyond the laws of blood. He turned from me, to tuck his son back into the cradle. Every flicker of the firelight that fell upon his bared and bloodied chest sent an ache of longing through me. *You will not—you will not banish me for this?* I begged.

What a thought! Still turned from me, he rocked the child. *After all you have done for me, for my parents . . .* He sighed. *But I do wish you would return to the shape you had before. It is less . . . disturbing for me.*

Because it was his will and not mine, I could slip back into cat-form without a second blood-theft from the corpse: a Change command is not a Change desired. Later, by the fireside, he took me into his lap and said, *You are my finest treasure, Puss; my dearest love shall have you. From this day forward, you are his. Guard him, make his fortune, set him high.*

It could not be. By all our laws, I had but one master. He would not see that. Love blinded one eye, Death the other. *One wish, and I will ask no more.* He scratched behind my ears and tickled the fur under my chin. *For love of me, breed him to princes.* He made no further request of me until the day he died.

Breed him to princes.

You see, Child? Her voice tugged me gently back into the present. *When you stole that poor dead woman's blood for your master's sake, you bound yourself to him beyond the grave. Though he is dead, his wish survives and fetters you. You chose it so. Satisfy it and be free.*

My broken prison still entrapped me, but I managed to open and shut my eyes once, slowly, so that she might understand my submission. Fingers of sweet healing stroked my fur. Bone knit to bone, raveled skeins of bloodthreads mended. I licked my whiskers, wildly seeking the precious taste of blood, and rasped my tongue over nothing. The strand where the shapetide ran melted away beneath me. The stable walls shook with the anguish of my howls.

Hush, she counseled. *Bear this, fulfill the final compact, and your freedom will follow.* Her wings were moonbright, soothing my waking eyes. The stable walls could not hope to hold them. Timbers splintered and collapsed outward into the frosty night. She stopped to sweep me up against her breast and carried me off into the woodland.

She left me standing by a stream, black water dappled with the silver of shattered stars. The boots still clamped my feet tightly, but her parting gift was the Change that let me walk upright in them, in the teeth of the pain.

My nose sifted the air for scent. Rime hung on every indrawn breath; I breathed diamonds. And then *his* smell—a stink to rake me raw. He was near, he must be. She never would have brought me this far else.

Can you name the look to put on his wide, coarse face when he saw me coming toward him by moonlight, the little heels of my scarlet boots crunching deep and surefooted into the snow? Astonishment is a milky name to put to such an expression, and it turned wholly to vapor in the blast of hot shock when I opened my mouth and greeted him in human speech.

The satin sash, the velvet cape, the little felt cocked hat with its fluttery plume, he fetched them all at my bidding. I never asked how he got them. Thievery had a hand in it, I am sure, and bullying where thievery was too blunt a measure. He obeyed me utterly, in awe, and his reward was my promise: *I will breed you to princes.*

So my task began.

There is always a king fool enough to dismiss wisdom in the name of novelty; he was not too hard to find. To see a cat walk in boots, and talk, and then to hear that it comes bringing you gifts of game—well! There's a hard lure to resist. He was fat faced and ruddy, that old king, his jowls marbled like fine beef. The white wig on his head was tipsy from the hasty hand he'd used to put it on, showing the mottled patches of bulge-veined scalp beneath the hairdresser's masterpiece. At that first interview he wore no crown.

The second time I came calling, he corrected the oversight. I was a wonder, but after the initial thrill of seeing a creature so unique, he must have noticed that his court was paying just as much attention to me, and not enough to him. Therefore, pomp. I and my sack of grouse and pheasant must wait outside the grand throne room while trumpets sounded and pigeon-chested heralds bawled, "The emissary of the Marquis of Carrabas!"

The first time, he greeted me in a mere antechamber, but this was the crystal-hung jewel of all the rooms in his palace. Everywhere I looked, my eyes met spotless white, or gleaming gilt, or the brilliant, blind sheen of mirrors. The courtiers stood in stiff rows of starched lace and embossed brocade, lips quivering like pinned butterflies behind the fluttering shields of fan and handkerchief and glove. Splendid as a winter's dawn, the king upon his massive, golden throne. Lost, or deliberately put aside, the childlike expression of avid wonder he'd worn when first he laid eyes on me. His wig was on straight, too.

"You may approach us," he intoned, stretching forth his scepter. It was so knobbed and crusted with gems that it looked like a tree-branch warted over with strange, sparkling fungi. Tiny red-heeled shoes with golden buckles squeezed his feet. I could have smiled. *Hail, fellow sufferer! Greeting, my brother in torment! Let us put aside sham, Your Majesty, and find a place apart where we can kick off these painful bindings and be what we truly are.*

I knew better than that, though, and the obeisance I made before the throne was every aspiring courtier's model of perfection. Loosening the hempen ties of the gunnysack, I brought forth each succulent bird one by one, praising it on points and plumage, noting well the plumpness of breast and thigh until I'd robbed the old man of all his plastered-over dignity and had him slavering, eyes aglow with nurtured gluttony.

He recovered himself enough to thank me and my master, the Marquis, for our kind attentions. The more rhapsodic his praise, the surer I knew that words were all we'd have from him in recompense. That was all right: what he would not give freely, I had means to take, in time. Besides, my plans had cause to thank his words, for had he not spent so much time enamored of his own tongue, I might never have beheld the princess.

She came late to the high-ceiled audience chamber, entering without excuse or ceremony. Tall and proud, she was a creature lacking shame or fear. The courtiers parted before her, wheat stalks bending away from the reaper's hook. Planked in panels of heavily embroidered white satin, sleeves dripping gold lace, diamonds frosting her dark hair, she cut through the room like the hungry black fang of the plow.

Breed him to princes.

Yes, and such a one as this. I met her eyes and liked what I saw. We were kin. She was born to be a devourer of men. It would serve him right.

Courts are great places for gossip. I made it my business to glean some before I left. The king commanded his cooks to offer me refreshment, which all of us took in a salon where the walls were hung with rose taffetta, and serving maids goggled to watch a cat drink wine. I lingered as long as I might, lapping glass after glass and cocking a pointed ear to catch any crumb of knowledge the courtiers might let fall. I departed the castle with an empty gunnysack and a brain crammed full of information.

It would please king and daughter to go out driving next day, by the river road. It was cold the morning I brought my old master's son to the riverbank, the ice and snow gone, but their specters still lying over land and water. I do not think any human mind could fathom the wicked glee of my heart when I told him to strip naked and jump in.

Mistake nothing: I would not have him die. His death would never bring my freedom. Oh, but it was a rare pleasure to see him stare at me, disbelieving, and be brought up short by recollection of my fine promises, and obey. I destroyed the rustic smock and hose while he floundered in the chill water, cursing. I had hardly done it when the rattle of coaches from the road summoned me to the next part of my plan.

"Help! Help, ho!" My paws flailed the air; I brandished my plumed hat to make the coachmen see so small a creature as a cat before the horses trampled me. "Robbers, thieves, rascals and hounds! They have despoiled my good master, the Marquis of Carrabas!"

The coaches reined up sharply, the beef-faced king shouting orders that were obeyed instants before they fully left his lips. Lackeys scuttled down the frozen bank to haul my old master's son from the water. Horseblankets wrapped him in their stable smell, stinging my eyes with remembrance of all I owed him. He was bundled into the king's own coach, and I scrambled after.

He was not so stupid as I feared. He kept his mouth shut, scenting fortune. The king marked him for a modest man, but I felt a tug at my spirit and read contempt in the princess' green eyes. Together we were whirled back to the castle, and while the king decked out my old master's son in cloth-of-gold and satin, I paced before the fire.

"Puss." My name, a hiss. Green eyes behind the heavy draperies, and a white hand beckoning me into the shadows. My whiskers twitched. Her scent was all jasmine and gillyflower. There was a small door, a passage suitable to servant's use, or assassin's. This lavishly appointed chamber granted to my lord, the Marquis of Carrabas, was one reserved for those of whom the king still cherished doubts.

I followed her, vanishing as cats are wont to vanish. There were no lights in the narrow passageway, a lack which troubled neither her nor me. Fresh air stirred the small fur of my face and we were in a deserted hall. From there three twists and a roughcut flight of stairs brought us into the princess' own chamber.

No white here, nor frail yellow gold, nor any of the pallid waterwashed colors most prescribed for princesses. Bed and floor and walls were draped and spread and hung with rich stuffs colored like a dragon's hoard, like the spoils of a long-dead city. My scarlet boots clicked over little, winking tiles like those I had known of old, among the tumbled pillars of my home. A fireplace of black marble grinned, glibly hideous with gargoyles. On the abandoned needlework frame I saw the icy, critical stare of the pale god's mother.

"Come to the window, Puss," the princess said. There was but one. It was narrow and dingy-paned, a poor view for a royal lady. Her eyebrows, feathery as a moth's arched high with bitter amusement. I leaned against the slanty sill and gazed across the green lands to a vast forest fencing the horizon.

"There, to the east," she directed. "One turret is all you can make out from here, beyond the trees; a turret like a thorn. A thorn in my father's side greater than the one my mother lodged in his heart when I was all the heir her body could bear him."

I saw it then, a tower sere and brown. The setting sun's last light was swallowed up at a gulp by the hungry stones. I dropped from the window, landing on my booted feet. "Whose castle is it, Highness?"

"Who knows?" Her laughter fell around my ears like chips of stone. "It lies over one of the finest trade routes in these lands, that much I know, and guards the freest, shortest passage to the sea. Much good that does our people. It has been decades since any man of our kingdom was fool enough to try herding his goods over that road."

"None come back?" I did not need to question when I saw the answer in her face.

"None whole," she replied, her little pink mouth a hard line. "Once, when I was out riding the meadows as a child, I saw another horse come galloping toward me. He was very beautiful, a roan, and riderless. But from the silver saddle on his back there hung a heavy sack, and when I leaned forward to grab his bridle, it fell into the grass. He bucked and plunged away from me, heels kicking out to shatter my poor pony's hind leg. As we fell, he raced away. My pony limped and screamed, bobbing and lurching back to the stables where one of my father's men cut her throat for mercy. I was left behind."

"And the sack," I said.

"Oh, yes. The sack." A pin whose tip is black with poisoned gum can leave a scratch behind much like her smile. "Would you like to know what was in the sack, Puss?"

I did not need that knowledge. "Their heads?" My black-slit eyes held hers. "Or if they were men who died, then—"

She shrieked with what was almost mirth. "Really, Puss! I expected more discretion of such a fine courtier. To speak of such things before a virgin." She pressed her hands against the granite sill until the knuckles bulged and whitened. "All the messengers my father ever sent there vanished. Even knowing what my father knew, all of them carried pretty vellum scrolls offering the castle's unknown lord my hand and body in exchange for free trade and safe conduct. When you arrived, I hoped you had come to tell us that it is the lair of your dear master, the Marquis of Carrabas."

I cocked my head. "Why?"

"Because if my life is a mere trader's token, to be sold to that castle's lord, I would like to purchase it back myself. I have the price." She left the window to kneel before a small painted chest at the foot of her bed. The olivewood casket she lifted from it might have housed the grisly relics of a saint. The black-blade dagger it did contain was exquisite, a tangle of inlaid silver lying like cobwebs over the amber handle. Having dazzled my eyes with its spare loveliness, she replaced it in its casket, dropping a single fold of plain linen over the blade like a shroud.

"I see my wedding gift must wait," she said.

That night, while my old master's son ate and drank at the king's own table, I found occasion to draw aside His Majesty's prime minister and issue formal invitation to the castle of my lord the Marquis of Carrabas on the morrow. His look went from perplexity to cold cowardice when he heard exactly where I would have him bring his sovereign.

I raised a paw to staunch his babblings. "My lord the Marquis of Carrabas is well aware of all atrocities committed against your people. I tell you, Lord, they are a gall on his heart, not the work of his hands at all. What can a younger brother do, when title and power are held by a madman? I do not like to recall how many times he and I were dragged to the brink of death at his elder brother's insane fancy. My kind can only offer so much protection to our charges, you know."

"Yes, yes, to be sure," the prime minister huffed and fumbled. "That is, I have heard the stories—Three wishes, isn't it? Or is it the baptismal gift I am thinking of? Oh dear, so many tales . . . Do you fairies all subscribe to the same protocols?"

A cat's eyes hide humor wonderfully well. "Your pardon, but I am not at liberty to say."

"Doubtless, of course." He coughed into his fist. "Then I may assume the former lord is . . . dead?"

"He will not trouble us more. Only bring His Majesty and his honest daughter to my lord's castle tomorrow noon, and you shall see for yourself how truly things have changed within the realm of my lord the Marquis of Carrabas."

That night, I crept up by arrow slit and ivy and unplastered crack between stone and stone into the princess' chamber and stole the dagger from its olivewood coffin. I had no sword, you see, and my old master's son would never let awe of me make that great a fool of him. He still remembered all he'd done to me. Put a blade in my paw, he? Oh, certainly! But I must have a sword.

The stableboy drowsed, and the horse was wild enough to recognize my lordship and come silently. I leaped onto his bare rump, straddled his neck, hooked claws through his mane, and turned him down the right road.

All that night we galloped through plowland and woodland until in the hours before dawn we came into plowland again. How simple, to terrorize the peasants as they went stoop-shouldered to their chores! They had never seen my like, and a gambol of my dagger before their faces was enough to convince them that worse than their current master's wrath awaited them if they disobeyed me.

"Carr-Carrabas?" The old man stumbled over the alien name. "We are to say that these lands belong to the Marquis of Carr—Cabra—?" He rubbed his gnarled hands up and down the handle of his mattock as he forced the words into memory.

His wife screwed her leathery, toothless face into a grimace that could have been anger or fear or even—miracle!—defiance. "Creature, if our true lord hears of this, he will kill us."

"*If*, old woman," I said. "But the dead hear nothing."

Her muddy eyes, the whites yellowed as old parchment, slid sideways toward the turret. She never looked in that direction willingly. "He is not dead."

"Much changes, Mother." I flipped the dagger from paw to paw. What I lacked in the dexterity of human fingers, I made up for in adaptive skills gathered through many centuries and many skins. Thumbs or no thumbs, my grip was sure. "You never thought to see his death, did you? Well, neither did you think to see a being like myself, yet here I am! Get used to wonders."

She shook her head. "I will not believe in anything unless I see it with these eyes. Until I see him dead, my lord lives, and while he lives, I know the power of his rage. I know nothing about you, Cat. For all I know, you are my lord himself, come in one of his many shapes to test our loyalty."

"What? Could it be—?" Her words struck ice into the old man's heart. He dropped his mattock and clutched his throat with both hands as he fell to his knees beside my steed. "Mercy, my lord!" he shrilled, hunched into a rocking ball of terror nearly under my horse's hooves. "I knew it was you—in truth, I did! And if you would have your slave tell these strangers that these lands belong to the Marquis of Carrabas, shall I disobey your command? Oh, have mercy!" He grabbed for my boots, making the horse shy.

"Enough!" I spat. "I bring you a new master, know it! The old, bad days are done. A lighter hand will lie over your lives if you are loyal to him. Easier tribute, more left behind to fill your own bellies, an end to fear, all these for the ones wise enough to stand for my lord the Marquis of Carrabas. But as for those too foolish to see the good of this exchange of masters, the exile's road, the landless man's death."

The old man was past confusion now. I could almost hear the flapping of a thousand wings inside his hollow skull. The old woman, though, had hard-soled feet planted deep and certain in the earth. She would not yield.

"Trickster!" she screeched. "Get gone and leave us to our work! We will have no new masters!" She banged my mount a hard blow on the rump with the handle of her hoe. The horse belled and reared. I clung madly to the mane, but kept my seat and never lost the hold on my dagger.

"I say you will!" My mouth stretched wide in a hiss of fury. A jab of my claws turned the stallion and sent him barreling down upon her. She shrieked as the hooves struck her to the dirt. I wrenched the beast's mane, making him wheel and trample her again and again, until her blood ran brown as the muck where her old man still groveled.

At last she was dead enough to satisfy even her own doubts. I urged my mount on, leaving her mate to crawl timorously toward her body, as if afraid he lacked the right to claim even that. From the next hilltop's rise I called back to him, "Remember! These are the lands of—"

And between sob and sob over the mangled corpse I heard him choke out the name, "—the Marquis of Carrabas!"

The other peasants I encountered were more tractable. Shepherdesses and cowherds and goose girls will say anything without wasting too much thought over it. That was good. It freed my mind to think over something the old woman had said before:

For all I know, you are my lord himself, come in one of his many shapes to test our loyalty.

How many shapes? The shape of a roan stallion, to bring a young princess a ghoulish gift? The shape of a cat in boots and courtly finery, to trick his peasant bondsmen? The shape of something fit to kill such a cat, too? It was not a thought to bring me comfort.

The castle lay open, drawbridge down over a moat clotted almost solid with silt and tousled weeds. The keep itself was full of the cold, sour-salty smell of rancid blood. My boots sounded echoes from the great hall's floor of lapis lazuli and snowy marble slabs, the echoes flying up to roost among the nests of golden owls who perched on the painted rafters. Torches burned red on the walls, and there was an underthread of bitter incense burning, too feeble to erase the ingrained reek of death. I licked my lips with hunger and went on.

He lolled upon the throne in ogre's guise, so warted and tusked and walleyed that his hideousness reduced itself to caricature. A yearling calf bawled and struggled in his hairy fist, liquid brown eyes brimming with mortal terror. I dreamed I scented its mother's milk still wetting the mottled pink-and-black muzzle. A wrench of the ogre's free hand tore head from neck. He let the gouting blood gush over his purple gums as if he were a harvest hand draining a noonday wineskin.

Then he was a man, Change effected in an eyeblink. "Greetings, Cousin." He jumped from the sword-scarred throne and sauntered toward me, trim and elegant in blue satin and steel. His narrow waist, his ample chest, his long and supple legs and arms were all crisscrossed with glimmering chain. He carried its weight light as spring, and the galley slave's collar and manacles were jeweled to show he wore them only in submission to himself.

He bowed, black boots pointing elegantly. I doffed

my hat and made a poor imitation of his polished gesture. He laughed. "Why do we stand on ceremony, Cousin? It has been too long since one of my own kindred came calling. Will you take some refreshment?" He waved at the drained body of the calf. "There is plenty more where that came from, and enough for all."

Outlaw. Renegade. Lost. We have them among our number, as do mortals. They break the laws of blood and binding, pilfer Change and cheapen it past redemption by boldly taking what must be willingly offered. For this, in time, they forfeit the rebirth that is our right. Masters of many skins, slaves of a single life that even a clever mortal may someday steal away, they can be truly killed. Therefore they live with fear. Therefore they slay as many mortals as they can. They are the ones who have earned us all the name of monster. We are brought up to condemn them out of hand. We know how close we ourselves tread to the paths of darkness they have chosen.

And yet this mortal mask of his with its evil, exciting beauty made me burn.

I drank the blood he offered because it was offered. Hat and sash and silly boots lay cast aside, the dagger clattered to the floor. I watched his eyes grow wide and warm as I bloomed unclothed into the princess' guise. "You are an artist, little Cousin," he said, the sharp planes of his face crinkling with a badly mimed boy's mischief.

"This?" My hands cupped the weight of the princess' brown-tipped breasts. "No artistry here; it is not original."

"No?" He sounded disappointed. "I had hoped—"

"So few of us create. Surely you know that much,

even shut away here?" I went on. "We are all apes and magpies."

A shadow of storm fell across his face. "That is not so." The question my eyes sent him gained the further answer, "I own shapes that never were made in this papery-dull world."

It seemed to matter to him. I knew I could not take him in open combat—not with Change his good, obedient hound and me locked in this body. Still, the sword aside, there are venoms. You have only to know into which cup you must drop the fatal dose.

"I should like to see that," I said.

In a room small and dark, lit by a single brazier's light, he showed me. I sat cross-legged on a silk rug that tickled my thighs and I had a low table with a glass bubble of wine at my elbow. He stood across the cupped coals from me, playing the showman.

"Scales," he said, and raised a gold goblet to his lips. At once his lower limbs fused, blue satin ending in a muscular coil of serpent's body which itself ended oddly in a peacock's full-fanned tail.

I nodded, impressed, but careful not to let it show. He saw only polite acknowledgment in my eyes and lost his smile. There was another small table, twin to mine, on his side of the fire. It held besides the empty goblet two rock crystal bowls awash in red. "Claws," he muttered, and drank one of them dry.

The beast he became had a human face, a lion's forequarters, and the hindparts of a dragon. Emerald horns curled from its head, and its talons were all keen obsidian. "Oh," I said. "How charming."

An enraged roar burst from the monster's throat, then broke into unintelligible rumblings. He lapped the second crystal bowl empty and was his man-shape again. "You do not find these forms original enough for your taste, Cousin?"

I let my laughter walk the wire between indifference and scorn. "You have lived too long alone," I replied. "The mortals have crammed their scribblings and daubings with a host of patchwork creatures like these."

"I suppose you could do better."

I shrugged. "We may never know." I indicated the empty vessels.

"Is that all?" Hands on hips, he grinned. "Then a bargain, Cousin. One more attempt for me to impress you out of hand, and if that fails then I shall take you to my storeroom and give you the means to match or master me at Change. Will you?"

I pretended detachment. "Try."

"Wings," he announced, and ducked behind an ill-hung tapestry. He emerged still man-form, but with the broad, black wings of a bat springing from between the chains lashing his back. A smile showed the sweet, sharp teeth he'd borrowed to complete the shape, white fangs between which a snake's tongue darted wickedly.

But oh, the greater magic of his eyes.

His eyes were blood afire, the lure of Change's ancient, eternal promise. I could not see that and be still and still be what I am. I stood and came toward him, as a bird must stumble near and nearer to the viper's yellow eye. His wings oared the air, folded themselves around me. I felt their leathery skin embrace my nakedness, wrapping me in lightless, inescapable captivity. And I did not desire the light; I desired only the dark, and the blood, and him.

His forked tongue licked a painful line of yearning along the taut line of my jaw, then traced a cool, teasing arabesque over my throat. The heat of his breath seared away the dew his pretty tongue left behind, and the power of its hard, dry flame offered up every part of me for the burning.

"Do you give it willingly?" he whispered. "Do you give it willingly, the blood?"

I could not speak. I could only nod my head and let it droop to one side like a dying flower. I heard him chuckle, and felt the stab of fangs in my own flesh, the short, strong suction, and the ecstacy that lifted me past any I had ever known; then the release as he let me go. I heard my voice cry out, begging him not to leave me yet, to come back, to take more, more, all that I had in fee for that unholy consummation. My fingers clawed his wings, only to feel them melt away into smoke and laughter.

"You see?" Through blurred eyes I looked up to see him back to his unaltered man-form, mocking me. I lay crumpled at his feet, hands clinging to his boots, face pressed against his thigh so hard that the chains branded my cheek.

I gathered my wits and let go my hold. Some quality of my former shape remained to let me regain my feet with a feline grace and sureness I did not really feel. I made an effort to brush the dust from my skin the way a cat uses washing to ignore the world. "I admit I am impressed," I said, subduing my voice so it should not quaver. "Only—" I forced a yawn "—only it is such a shame that . . ."

"That what?" Suddenly he lost mastery of the joke.

"Oh, nothing. Silly. It was flawless, your last shape, I think; a sophisticated exercise. I found it pleasant, playing your mortal victim's part. Did I do it well? You can be proud enough of it without—"

"*What* is a shame?" He roared well even out of lion's form.

"That so small a Change takes so much blood to manage," I answered. "There, that's all."

He grabbed my wrist and dragged me under the tapestry. The stair concealed there led, as I suspected, to the storeroom he had mentioned. The chamber had eight sides and was windowless. I thought we must be in the turret that the princess could see from her quarters, and wondered whether she was gazing this way even now, before the royal coaches departed to bring my lord the Marquis of Carrabas home.

Beeswax candles tried to sweeten the air. A thick oak board set on trestles was the only piece of furniture. The woman on the table was whiter than the shell of my old master's wife. A serviceable kitchen knife with a blade curved like the dying moon lay on her breast, below the slit in her throat. Whimperings and hoarse prayers in many voices came from the curtained alcoves all around us. Behind one dusty velvet hanging I heard a child wailing for its dam.

Not for long. He snatched up the knife and darted behind the drape. The wailing rose to a scream, died to a gurgle. Two full cups were in his hands when he came back.

"Would you call this measure much blood, Cousin?" he asked, his eyes grim. View halloo, the artist challenged!

I took the cup he gave me and considered it long enough to irritate him more. "It is scant enough."

"Now let it be you who names the Change we must effect on so little substance, and the prize shall go to the one who best meets it," he said.

"Prize?" I blinked. "We did not speak of prizes. What can I give you, who are already lord of this grand estate?"

He pinched my chin so hard I gasped. The savor of my own blood was a disturbing ghost on his breath. "If you win, Cousin, you may name your own prize; and if I win, I know enough to take what I want."

He let me go, and I stepped back, trying not to let him see me shake. "You shall have it," I promised, raising the cup to him in pledge. "Now, let me see the full range of your art. Great monsters, great beasts, fiends too immense for these human cattle to comprehend, those are all very well and good. You are a peerless architect for monuments. But do you have also the jeweler's subtle touch? Can you work your creations in the perfection of miniature?" Here I lowered my eyes modestly. "My sisters claim that when I slip skins and Change myself into a small, smoke-gray fieldmouse, no one can approach the refinement I bring to that form."

His brow furrowed. "That is all your challenge? A mouse?"

"I know it does not sound like much of a Change to someone like yourself, but it is harder than it sounds. With monsters, fear distracts your audience; they overlook details, miss flaws. And it is my specialty. I warn you, I will be a very exacting critic; see that you are the same! But if you feel uncomfortable trying something new—"

"Drink!" he shouted, and clinked his cup so hard against mine I feared he'd spill them both. Fortune had it otherwise. We drank; he Changed first, as I knew he must. That was all I needed. I pounced.

He was delicious.

The storeroom captives I freed knew right away it was a miracle when a cat in boots and sash and cape and high-plumed hat came to their rescue. They were more than happy to throw all their strength into clearing away the worst of the "ogre's" souvenirs and scrubbing down much of the castle. Liveries were found, shaken out, the best ones darned here and there and put on. Instead of being turned into supper, they rejoiced to be transformed into the loyal servitors of the Marquis of Carrabas, ready to receive their lord and his regal guests. And if His Majesty the king found their manners to be a little rough and their garb a little shabby, he ascribed it to the lax standards of the previous reign.

They were wed next week, my old master's son and the stone-eyed princess. Her father never asked her opinion of the match, but neither did he question why his son-in-law turned over all the treaty papers and marriage documents to me for reading and written imprimatur.

The boots would not let me curl up to sleep outside the marriage-chamber door. I stood instead, ears pricked, and heard it all. She would not have him, he would have her. The bonds were sealed, he said, making her his by right. Away from king and court, he did not hesitate to use the harshest language of his simple upbringing. She answered in kind, but her haughty words were slapped from her mouth at once, and then again, and a third time for the joy of it. She used a name to him then that changed open slaps to knuckled pummeling. She was choking on sobs when he had her. The pain he gave her crashed over me with such intensity that I scarcely felt it when my last bond to my old master broke and I was free.

Breed him to princes. Well, I had done that. I could go. But I waited by the door instead until his grunts and her groans alike ended. I waited in the silence that came. I waited until the door itself inched back on its hinges and she crept into the hall.

"A fine bargain you made me, Puss," she said when she saw me, making me taste her bile. There were red blotches under her eyes that would blacken, and a spill of red from the middle of her lower lip. Her lace-edged lawn gown too was patched with blood, the coin of my bought liberty. Seeing what he had made of her, I knew I had gained a freedom I would never enjoy, until . . . unless . . .

In speechless apology I offered up the dagger I had stolen. She shook her head, refusing it. "A raw girl's fancies. I was a fool. That sliver can't kill him. The blade's too short for any mortal wound."

"You might slit his throat," I suggested.

"His neck is like a bull's. I haven't the power of a butcher's arm, and if I cannot end it with the first blow, he will wake, take the blade from me, and then—then—" Her legs folded beneath her. She knelt on the stones, wringing her hands. "My father has his trade agreement, my husband has his castle and my dowry. I am no use to either, any more. Do you know what he said to me? *Except for the money you bring me, princesses and peasant girls fuck the same!* If I attempt his life, the law is with him if he kills me. Even if it means I must live with him, I do not want to die. I hate myself for being such a coward, but—Puss, oh Puss, what shall I do?"

I knew what I must do. While one is captive, none are free, and freedom's price has always been the same. My grip was firm on the silver-webbed amber handle. The pain was not so much. I showed her a brave face, and to her spirit's credit she did not shrink away in loathing or dismay when she saw me stand before her with the dagger driven deep into my breast. With the last of my blood-choked breath I told her to pull out the blade, and also how she might repay the gift I freely offered her now. As she raised my draining body to her lips, she also pressed my mouth against the pulsing vessel she had opened for me just beneath her ear.

So now we lie here, she and I, feeling the gentle warmth of Change steal over us. (Our Mother has approved and welcomed her; all is well.) She will cling to her original shape, I think, until confidence in her new life grows. So did we all, at first. She will still look like the princess she was born, though with those few small, elegant refinements I have suggested to her. As for me, my choice is made. Call it his memorial. If I could have let him live and still obtained my freedom, he might have me wrapped in those fiery black wings yet.

My own wings form, unfurl, stretch across the moonstreaked floor. Hers extend in turn to brush the dagged edge of mine in greeting. We smile at one another.

I never knew you were male, Puss.

You will learn, love, that such nice distinctions as ever male or female are for mortals. Ah, but what small fangs you have! Next time, perhaps you will be bolder.

You will see, Puss, that they are good enough for what I have in mind. She guides me back through the closed bedroom door and shows me she is bold enough after all.

And when the servants find him in the morning, will they first gasp at the bloodless body of their one-week's master, or question what has become of his wife?

Or will they only stare at what we tore from him in trophy and in trade for one tiny, wrinkled, scarlet boot?

The Glass Casket

Jack Dann

Jack Dann is the author or editor of over thirty books, including the novels Junction, Starhiker, *and* The Man Who Melted. *His short stories have appeared in* Omni, Playboy, Penthouse, *and most of the leading science fiction magazines and anthologies. His latest works include* High Steel, *a novel coauthored with Jack C. Haldeman II, and the historical novel about Leonardo da Vinci,* The Path of Remembrance *(Doubleday/Bantam).*

"The Glass Casket" is an adaptation of "The Glass Coffin," a fairy tale by the Brothers Grimm. Dann says of the story:

"When I first read the tale, I could not help but imagine it set in Renaissance Italy, for the Renaissance was a time when magic was as legitimate a pursuit as philosophy, theology, science, or art. A time of great brutality and sensitivity, eroticism and religion, and brilliant painting and poetry.

"So I set this story in the time of Leonardo da Vinci, Niccolo Machiavelli, and the poet, philosopher, and magus Pico della Mirandola. An aura of magic and mysticism surrounded Pico della Mirandola, who spent his short but brilliant life searching the cabbalah and other occult sciences for the meaning of truth and love and beauty. I have questioned what the handsome, larger-than-life Pico della Mirandola would do if he found the object of his desire. Indeed, what would any of us do?"

The Glass Casket

I lived in a great palace as I wished,
Now I am lodged in this little coffin,

My room was adorned with fine tapestry,
Now my grave is enveloped by cobwebs.
—FRANCOIS VILLON, ballad

IT WAS DURING A DARK TIME OF MURDER AND CONspiracy and war that the astrologer and physician Pico della Mirandola, a direct descendant of the Emperor Constantine, began to hear the whispery voices of the forest.

He heard them in the great cathedral on Easter Day when Giuliano de Medici was murdered by henchmen of the pope. He heard them when he exorcised Sandro Botticelli, who had become so obsessed with the frail and beautiful Simonetta Vespucci that he fell into a deadly melancholy.

And he heard them when he attended Simonetta's funeral.

He heard them constantly. He heard them as the whispering of trees, of shadows and spirits and forest creatures; the whispering of darkness. But he also discerned a human voice, a woman's voice. The genius who had unlocked the secrets of the Cabbalah and had written the brilliant *Platonick Discourse upon Love* was himself dying of a sickness of the soul.

And so it was that his patron, Lorenzo the Magnificent, gave him permission to leave the protection of the city.

All of Florence was under interdict from the pope, who had conspired to assassinate Lorenzo and extend the Papal States. When that failed, he excommunicated every Florentine citizen; his soldiers pillaged the countryside, raping and murdering and setting entire villages afire.

It was during that lawless and dangerous time that Pico della Mirandola left his beloved city. He wore a white, wool gown and a crown of laurel: the traditional garb of the physician. Peasants bowed to him as he passed. He was certainly a comely boy, actually extraordinary looking. He had very pale skin, penetrating gray eyes, white even teeth, a large, muscular frame, and reddish-blond hair. He was sweating in the heat.

He was a man possessed.

The whispers gave him direction; and after journeying for two days, they began to clarify and he could hear the woman's voice, could make out her words. She was calling to him, as the sirens had called to Odysseus. He felt he was being touched by fire, by love itself, just as he was at the moment of his birth when a circular flame had appeared above the bedstead.

Now he understood that those birthing flames were not for him alone; they were a portent joining him to another.

On the third day, at dusk, he came to a village deep in the dark mountains of Tuscany. It was no more than a ruin of a chateau surrounded by a few poor houses, which all had steep, thatched roofs. A curving street, empty but for a few pigs, led down to a church and a cemetery.

The smeary gray sky suddenly, as if by a fiat of the immortals, turned purple as a bruise and then black, merely a set piece for the eternal stars and the full moon. This place was damp and hot, as if bordering on Hell itself, for here, in these mountains, the bowels of the earth released its effluvium, the white curls of steam called *soffioni*. And nearby was the forest, a high wall as black as the sky. The trees were like stone, and as massive and implacable as the outer curtain of a fortress.

The sweat evaporating on his skin chilled him, and he could smell his own fear. The cold darkness of leaf and bole seemed to reach out to him, enveloping him where he stood, as if he were already in the forest.

But the darkness was inside him, a phantasm that was growing like a cancer. Every rustling leaf whispered his name, and he had all he could do to quell his overwhelming desire to enter the forest. He would not obey the sweet, small voice that called him; nor would he succumb to the presence of the forest, the whispering of darkness, the penetrating darkness, clammy and close and sentient. He knew he was being watched; hundreds of feral red eyes gazed at him, a hundred dark, poisonous spirits waiting to inhabit him.

And he knew that he could not remain outside, exposed to the forest. Certainly not at night. It would be too dangerous, even with his prepared medicines. He needed a hearth and food and human company.

He knocked on the great doors of the chateau and on the rough-hewn doors of every cottage, but no one would answer; although surely there were people inside, for light glowed through the vellum-covered windows. Even the church was locked. Dogs barked and snarled, as if they were creatures of the forest.

But on the edge of the town closest to the woods, a grimy-looking white-haired man wearing a tattered coat made out of brightly colored patches of cloth opened his cottage door to Pico. The man was toothless and looked to be eighty.

"What do you want?" he asked, slurring his words. One side of his face was paralyzed and looked waxen, like old, polished leather.

"I was overtaken by the night, and I would like to stay in your cottage. Just until morning."

"Go somewhere else," said the old man. "I don't need the likes of you. There's enough sorcery here."

"You mean the woods?" Pico asked.

"And I don't wish to stand here and talk with you." He began to close the door, but Pico held it open. He was surprised at the strength of the old man, who suddenly let go of the door and returned to his dinner of boiled meat and bread. He sat before the hearth, which took up almost an entire wall; a fire was crackling, sending flickering shadows into the corners.

"How can you stand it so warm?" Pico asked.

The old man shrugged. "There's food enough. Take

what you want, and you can sleep in the bed in the corner."

But hungry as he was, Pico went to the bed and fell asleep immediately. He dreamed that he was deep inside the forest, listening to the gentle whisperings of root and bark and leaf, listening to ghosts and spirits shimmering through the smoky yellow shafts of light that pierced the mantle of leaves. Indeed, the forest itself seemed to be made of smoke, and greens and browns of infinite variations melded one into another. Here was peace, security, wholeness. Found so simply in the forest. He saw the woman, who had been calling him; she resolved out of the mossy dampness, out of the haze and mist, and she radiated heat. She was fire itself, yet her skin was pale and he imagined it to be cool. Her dark hair was thick and long and braided in the style of the women of Florence. She smiled at him, but she was tentative, embarrassed, as if unsure he would accept her. She was naked, her shoulders freckled, her breasts small. And he yearned for her.

But then a shadow seemed to cover him; and as if waking from one dream and falling into another, he saw the old man leaning over him. The old man wore a pure white gown like his own. Pico tried to pull away, but the old man held him down as if he were a child. And he reached into Pico's chest with his outstretched hand and grasped his heart. He would squeeze it until it burst.

Pico gasped, choking, as one often does in sleep and A scream jolted him awake.

He recognized the voice; it was hers.

Disoriented, he looked around the room for the old man. But the house was empty, the fire dead, and a dim light, almost a twilight, suffused the room. There was a commotion outside, though. A great crashing and thundering.

Pico sensed something wrong with the room, something unreal, as if the geometry of line and angle were not quite right; there was another loud crash, and he rushed outside.

And found himself standing in a clearing in the forest.

Still enveloped in a dream.

Before him a huge black bull and a red stag were charging at each other. He could smell blood and their musty, animal reek. Then they struck each other with such a force that the entire forest could not swallow the sound. The ground trembled. The bull slashed at the stag with its horns, goring it; and as the stag fell back, shaking its great head, its branching antlers cut the bull like sabers.

The beasts circled each other, each one bleeding; and then the stag, which was larger than any horse Pico had ever seen, charged the bull with such fury that part of its antlers broke upon impact. But a spear of the antler was buried in the bull's flesh. The bull shook its head once, groaned, and sank to the ground; and as it did, its form began to change.

Into the form of a man.

The old man who had opened his door to Pico.

Yet the stag kept thrusting with its antlers until the old man's gown was wet with blood. Then it turned its attention to Pico, who was watching with astonishment. As he turned to run, the stag cornered him against the great bole of a tree. Its huge antlers were like daggers, but Pico finally understood that the great beast would not hurt him, but wished him to climb upon its broad back.

And so did Pico ride through the shadowy, moonlit woods, grasping the stag's neck as branches whipped past like arrows.

Although he could smell the stag's blood and gamey stink, he could not awaken. He was trapped in someone else's dream; and the forest which had swallowed him, although deep and dark and implacable, was absolutely silent.

The boundary of the phantasmic forest was a rocky cliff, but Pico could make out the outlines of a grand castle, a fortress that seemed to be cut in relief out of the rock. There the protruding shape of a tower, there crenellations and battlements, there the high segments dotted with arrow loops, which were probably small caves in the rock face. But this was no natural formation, for there were windows fitted with shutters and grills . . . all transformed into stone.

The stag halted and Pico climbed to the ground. The creature knocked its antlers against the cliff, and with a groaning and deep reverberation, a door began to open in the stone. It had hardly shown a crack when an explosion threw Pico backward. Fire belched from the crack and smoke poured out, as if from the very bowels of the earth. Pico lost sight of the stag, yet he could see the fiery opening into the cliff.

"Enter without fear, Pico della Mirandola," called the voice that was now familiar. "No harm will be done to you."

Pico thought to run, for he conjectured that since the forest had stopped whispering to him, he might be able to escape it, to leave this phantasm and return to the world of substance. But he could not leave yet, not when the pure voice he had followed was still calling him. He gathered his courage and intoned the *expurgatio a sordibus*, an incantation to purge the filthy vapors and influences that might contaminate his pneuma—that might have already poisoned the life-spirit flowing along with his blood like a mist through his veins.

And he stepped through the door.

He found himself in a huge, high-ceilinged hall. Walls, floor, and ceiling were constructed of blocks of polished stone. There were glyphs engraved in some of the stones, but Pico could not read them: they were not Greek or Latin or Hebrew letters. He crossed the hall several times, wondering what he was supposed to find here, then paused in the center of the room. He determined that there was nothing here for him, when the stone beneath his feet began to sink.

It carried him straight down into darkness. A chill wind whipped around him, numbing his face and hands; and Pico prayed, for he thought he was falling into Hell itself.

Then blackness turned to gray and, with a vertiginous shift in motion, he found himself standing in a room duplicating the great hall that could only be miles above him now. A dim roseate light permeated the room; it seemed to have no source of its own, but radiated equally from every object.

This room, unlike the one above, was filled with objects, all made of glass; their outlines were difficult to discern in the wan, magical light. There seemed to be bottles and vases everywhere: in niches cut into the walls; on tables made of the same flawless cut glass, which seemed to float in the air; and even on the polished stones of the floor. All of the vessels contained a turquoise-colored vapor; and although Pico's curiosity was piqued, he did not decant any of them: their vapors might well be poisonous. There were also glass chests, some so transparent that they were difficult to see when looked upon directly.

One such chest caught Pico's attention. It was set against the wall across the room. He detected it only by its ghostly outline: the mere hint of an object. When he bent over it and peered inside, he could see an entire village in miniature: a fortified castle and a town protected by a wall with battlemented walks. The tiny thatch-roofed houses were built close together along the narrow, rectangular streets, for most of the land within the walls was used for grazing and planting. There tiny trees, and there, movement. Could it be cattle? But Pico's fascination was suddenly interrupted by an explosion.

Something on the far end of the room had caught fire. It was burning furiously; the flames, as if feeding on pitch, spread quickly.

Pico stepped backward as a wave of heat rushed over him.

And he heard her voice once again.

"I am here, Pico della Mirandola. The fire is illusion. You can pass through it."

"But I can feel its heat," Pico heard himself say. Deep inside the flames, he could see the outline of what looked to be a glass casket.

When she did not reply, he gathered his courage and passed through the fire. The flames became vague, visible only from the corner of the eye, as were so many of the objects in the room.

He looked down at the casket. It contained a pale-skinned, dark-haired, naked woman.

The woman who had called to him.

The woman who had appeared to him in a dream.

Even as she appeared to sleep, he could hear her speak.

"Please help me," called the voice. "If you push back the bolt of the coffin, you can slide the top away."

And as Pico followed her instructions, she suddenly awakened and clutched her throat, as if she were wrestling with unseen hands trying to choke her. Her eyes were open wide, terrified.

"Hurry." The voice was but a whisper in his mind. He slid the glass top away from the coffin with such force that it fell to the ground and shattered. It was only when the top was lifted, and the spell broken, that she stopped choking and took a deep breath.

Pico helped her out of the casket and carried her across the room. She sat on the floor, the small of her back against the wall, her arms around her knees. Then she looked at him and a quick smile passed across her face. "Yes, you are the one in my dreams."

He kneeled beside her, enthralled, as if the magic of her presence was stronger than any he had encountered in the forest. "I've fallen in love in a dream," he whispered.

"As have I," she said. "But this is real, as you shall see." She leaned forward to kiss him, and Pico could not resist desire and destiny. But she suddenly pulled away from him, as if shocked at her own behavior; only then did she try to cover her breasts. She looked around the room, rose, slid past him, and walked around until she found a small crystal table upon which rested thin blue vials. She decanted one, and then another, and another. Objects appeared in the room: books and benches and tapestries; chests and closets; tables dressed with linen; a chessboard; paintings; and all manner of instruments:

psalteries, hurdy-gurdies, and a harp. And she, too, was transformed. She was now dressed in a crimson gamurra with a brocade of gold flowers and sleeves of pearls. A turquoise cape was wrapped around her shoulders. Surely, the clothes of a queen. The hall itself was darker, smaller, and more in focus now. The smoky, luminescent magic was evaporating. The phantasmic fire had disappeared. The glass vessels could be clearly seen, although their contents were still clouded by vapors.

She walked around the room, investigating, until she found the glass chest that contained the castle and town, and then returned to him and took his hand. "We must not remain here. Let me show you my castle, my town. It is in there." She looked toward the chest.

"I have seen it," Pico said. But you must tell me how—"

"Help me gather up the glass vessels and the chest. I will explain everything to you."

"At least tell me your name."

"Ginevra."

Ginevra . . .

They placed the glass chest and other vessels on the large stone that had carried Pico down from the upper reaches of this place. And as soon as they had done so, the stone rose, carrying both of them and everything they had gathered into the upper hall, which now looked exactly like the room they had just left: the same tapestries, tables, linens, paintings, and displayed instruments. They crossed the room to the doorway, which led to open air.

But the surrounding countryside was vague, unreal, and Pico could not make out whether he was seeing forest or mountains or meadow; it was a world cloaked in vapor. Or rather a world unformed, unfinished.

"Now, Pico della Mirandola, you shall see your new country and home as it really is," Ginevra said; and after they had carried everything outside, she opened the top of the chest. As the vapors were released, the town in the chest came into being as vague, ghostly shapes below them. Slowly, thatched roof cottages, streets, stalls, and shops came into focus, became real. The countryside resolved into hills and meadows and furrowed fields, and the purple shadows of mountains appeared in the distance. And the stone cliff behind Pico and Ginevra returned to its original form: a castle.

As Pico and Ginevra decanted the vessels, the sounds of talking and laughing could be heard in the distance. People could be seen in the streets and fields. Time was once again in effect, as if there had been no interruption. The church bell rang midday. The sky was pellucid; the gauzy clouds seemed stationary. Pico felt the warmth of the sun on his face, and he watched the woman beside him, feeling the shock of love that only comes to the young.

"Now I will tell you my story," Ginevra said, after the last vessel was decanted. She took his hand and showed him her private gardens, which flanked the castle, gardens where statues of Hercules and Hera and Diana stood among ancient cypresses and clipped hedges like the shades of a forgotten pantheon. "An old man who was traveling to Milan asked us for a night's lodging. As there is not an inn for miles hereabouts, my brother and I took him in as a guest."

"And your parents?" Pico asked.

"They have been dead for two years, may God bless their souls," Ginevra said. "Plague."

Pico nodded. The scourge had touched everyone.

"The old man said that he was the personal physician and theurgist to Giovanni de' Bicci, who rules your own Florence. And indeed he performed such miraculous entertainments that we held a feast in his honor for the entire town. If you stuck a pin through a word in the Bible and but told him the word and how many pages the pin had pierced, he could tell you the corresponding word. He performed various magics and transformations . . . he even made the soul of our priest as visible as the moon, which is what it resembled. My brother was very impressed with him."

"Ginevra, did you not think it strange that he claimed to be physician to Giovanni de' Bicci? Giovanni has been dead for fifty years."

She looked perplexed. "That's impossible."

"What year is this, then?" Pico asked.

"Why, it's 1400 . . . Pico?"

He shook his head and indicated that she should continue her story. If he was caught in her dream, then it could well be 1400. But if *he* were the dreamer, then it was 1479.

She hesitated, then went on. "The night before he was to leave, I had gone to bed early and left him to my brother. I had no sooner fallen asleep when I was awakened by the most beautiful music. I cannot describe it, but I started to call my chambermaid to find out what it was. I could not speak, and I felt that I must be dreaming, having a nightmare, when I saw my door open. My door is always locked. Nevertheless, it opened, and the theurgist approached me. He said that the music was for me, that he had willed me to hear it to awaken me. Then he offered me his heart."

"But he was an old man," Pico said.

"Yes," Ginevra said, "the very same old man who tried to squeeze the life out of your heart in his cottage by the woods." She smiled exultantly. "But he failed to keep you from me."

She led Pico through the postern gatehouse and back into the damp coolness of the castle proper.

"He came to me later that night in the guise of a young man. In fact, he looked like you. But I could see him as he really was, and I told him to get out. I wanted none of his magicks. That enraged him, and he bound me with a spell. I tried to call out to my brother, who was in the castle, but the old man had taken my voice. I was paralyzed . . . and could only gaze at him while he took me on the bed." She shuddered, then recovered herself and said, "You saw my brother as the stag who killed the theurgist. He brought you here to me."

"I saw a bull transformed into the old man," Pico said. "But how—?"

"When I awoke, I rushed to find my brother to tell him what had happened," Ginevra continued; as she was of noble birth, she was unused to being interrupted. "But his servant said he had gone hunting with the old man. I was frantic, I knew something was wrong. I rode with my servant toward the forest, but one of the horses stumbled and broke his leg. I continued alone, and found the old man leading a beautiful stag by a rope, which was tied tightly around its neck. I asked him the whereabouts of my brother. I asked him how he came upon the stag, but he only laughed. Then he mumbled something I could not make out, and I felt myself falling from my horse, falling ever so slowly, and when I regained consciousness, I was imprisoned in the glass casket, as you found me. He had reduced my castle and shire to the size of toys and transformed people and objects into vapor. If I would only agree to be his, he would decant the bottles and return everything to the way it was.

"He could read my thoughts; and when he saw how I hated him, he said he would leave me in the casket until my hatred turned to love. I fell into a deep sleep, and in my sleep I called for help. I saw you in my dream, and you were wrapped in fire. I called to you through nightmares, for I felt a thousand evil spirits sapping my soul."

"Why did you see me and not another?" Pico asked.

Ginevra shrugged nervously, then said, "My element, my *fortuna*, is fire. Perhaps it was fire that brought us together. When I was born, my family saw pale fire flicker around me. They said it was an omen. When I saw you wrapped in fire, I, thought it was an omen. So I called to you."

"I, too, was born in fire," Pico said.

"I could feel myself gaining strength as I focused on you," Ginevra said. "I could see what you saw. I was privy to your eyes and thoughts."

"Then you know what I am thinking now?" Pico asked.

"I know only what *I* am thinking," Ginevra said, squeezing his hand. They had climbed narrow stairs and were looking down from a recess in the tower wall into a small chapel. The stained glass seemed to be overflowing with light; and the light, a tangible rainbow, fell across the wide, stone window frame.

Ginevra knelt and prayed, and then led Pico to her chamber, the same room where the Milanese magician had raped her, where now she was to find love and rapture upon her down-stuffed pillows and mattress.

But even in his ecstasy, Pico della Mirandola once

again heard a voice whispering to him . . . commanding him to return to his own time.

The days passed quickly, growing shorter toward fall; and Pico was, indeed, in love with Ginevra. Time did not quench his desire for her, for her company, only modulated it. He was free, content, and happy, yet his thoughts were of Florence. If Ginevra and this place were all part of a dream, it was one of such detail and substance and beauty that he could be content to continue dreaming.

The voice that called to him, that chastised and reminded him, was his own. Ginevra's dream of love, as beautiful as it was, could not contain him. He was homesick for his own time, his own people, his own world. The true path of his destiny was with Lorenzo de Medici. It was a loveless destiny, but it was destiny nevertheless.

Yet he ignored it for as long as he could.

Finally the time came to tell Ginevra that must return home. To his own time. To the dream he had once imagined as reality. He promised to return, and she seemed to understand.

"But how will you find your way back to me?" Ginevra had asked.

"I will listen for your voice. . . ."

The leaves had changed color and some of the trees were already bare when he left her and her retinue standing by the edge of the forest . . . the forest that surrounded her town and castle. The woods were quiet, quiet as the moment before a fire, after the birds and animals have left. Only the scrunch of his feet on leaf and twig could be heard.

And when he reached the end of the forest, he came upon the Tuscan village. The place where the phantasm began. There stood the chateau, the curving street, the stone church. But the cottages had all been burned and the villagers slaughtered. The cottages were still smoking.

Here was the work of the soldiers of the Holy See.

Pico walked through the village to see if anyone had been left alive, but even the children had been put to the lance. Soldiers of the pope or the Medici . . . the result was always the same. He came to the cottage where the theurgist had tried to kill him in his sleep. It, too, was smoking rubble.

And as he stood near the forest, he listened. Listened for Ginevra's voice. But there was nothing . . . nothing but silence.

Thus did Pico della Mirandola glimpse the emptiness of destiny in the silent ashes of this nameless village. For he was now deaf to Ginevra's soft voice, which was calling to him even now, promising him love and contentment and salvation.

Knives

Jane Yolen

Jane Yolen is one of America's leading writers of modern fairy tales, published for both children and adults in numerous picture books and collections such as Tales of Wonder, Dreamweaver, The Girl Who Cried Flowers, The Faery Flag, *and* Neptune Rising. *She has also published an important book of essays about fairy tales and children's literature titled* Touch Magic, *and is the editor of the Pantheon Folktale Library's* Favorite Folktales from Around the World. *Yolen lives in western Massachusetts.*

The following is a dark, unsentimental, and thoroughly adult look at the story of Cinderella.

Knives

Love can be as sharp
as the point of a knife,
as piercing as a sliver of glass.
My sisters did not know this.
They thought love was an old slipper:
pull it on and it fits.
They did not know this secret of the world:
the wrong word can kill.
It cost them their lives.

Princes understand the world,
they know the nuance of the tongue,
they are bred up in it.
A shoe is not a shoe:
it implies miles, it suggests length,
it measures and makes solid.

It wears and is worn.
Where there is one shoe, there must be a match.
Otherwise the kingdom limps along.

Glass is not glass
in the language of love:
it implies sight, it suggests depth,
it mirrors and makes real,
it is sought and is seen.
What is made of glass reflects the gazer.
A queen must be made of glass.

I spoke to the prince in that secret tongue,
the diplomacy of courting,
he using shoes, I using glass,
and all my sisters saw was a slipper,
too long at the heel,
too short at the toe.
What else could they use but a knife?
What else could he see but the declaration of war?

Princes understand the world,
they know the nuance of the tongue,
they are bred up in it.
In war as in life they take no prisoners
And they always marry the other shoe.

The Snow Queen

Patricia A. McKillip

Patricia A. McKillip lives in New York's Catskill Mountains. She is an award-winning writer of poetic, distinctive fantasy novels for both children and adults, including the ground-breaking Forgotten Beasts of Eld, *the sensual* Stepping from the Shadows, *and her most recent novel,* The Sorceress and the Cygnet. *Forthcoming is the sequel,* The Cygnot and The Firebird.

In Hans Christian Andersen's famous children's tale, the Snow Queen freezes young Kay's heart and steals him away to her palace of ice. McKillip's Neva is as cold and sharp as ice; she is the kind of Snow Queen any of us might encounter. This is an exquisite adult fairy tale, complex, sensual, and subtle.

The Snow Queen

Kay

THEY STOOD TOGETHER WITHOUT TOUCHING, WATCHing the snow fall. The sudden storm prolonging winter had surprised the city; little moved in the broad streets below them. Ancient filigreed lamps left from another century threw patterned wheels of light into the darkness, illumining the deep white silence crusting the world. Gerda, not hearing the silence, spoke.

"They look like white rose petals endlessly falling."

Kay said nothing. He glanced at his watch, then at the mirror across the room. The torchières gilded them: a lovely couple, the mirror said. In the gentle light Gerda's sunny hair looked like polished bronze; his own, shades paler, seemed almost white. Some trick of shadow flattened Gerda's face, erased its familiar hollows. Her petal-filled eyes were summer blue. His own face, with sharp bones at cheek and jaw, dark eyes beneath pale brows, looked, he thought, wild and austere: a monk's face, a wizard's face. He searched for some subtlety in Gerda's, but it would not yield to shadow. She wore a short black dress; on her it seemed incongruous, like black in a flower.

He commented finally, "Every time you speak, flowers fall from your mouth."

She looked at him, startled. Her face regained contours; they were graceful but uncomplex. She said, "What do you mean?" Was he complaining? Was he fanciful? She blinked, trying to see what he meant.

"You talk so much of flowers," he explained patiently. "Do you want a garden? Should we move to the country?"

"No," she said, horrified, then amended: "Only if— Do you want to? If we were in the country, there would be nothing to do but watch the snow fall. There would be no reason to wear this dress. Or these shoes. But do you want—"

"No," he said shortly. His eyes moved away from her; he jangled coins in his pocket. She folded her arms. The dress had short puffed sleeves, like a little girl's dress. Her arms looked chilled, but she made no move away from the cold, white scene beyond the glass. After a moment he mused, "There's a word I've been trying all day to think of. A word in a puzzle. Four letters, the clue is: the first word schoolboys conjugate."

"Schoolboys what?"

"Conjugate. Most likely Latin."

"I don't know any Latin," she said absently.

"I studied some . . . but I can't remember the first word I was taught. How could anyone remember?"

"Did you feed the angelfish?"

"This morning."

"They eat each other if they're not fed."

"Not angelfish."

"Fish do."

"Not all fish are cannibals."

"How do you know not angelfish in particular? We never let them go hungry; how do we really know?"

He glanced at her, surprised. Her hands tightened on her arms; she looked worried again. By fish? he wondered. Or was it a school of fish swimming through deep, busy waters? He touched her arm; it felt cold as marble. She smiled quickly; she loved being touched. The school of fish darted away; the deep waters were empty.

"What word," he wondered, "would you learn first in a language? What word would people need first? Or have needed, in the beginning of the world? Fire, maybe. Food, most likely. Or the name of a weapon?"

"Love," she said, gazing at the snow, and he shook his head impatiently.

"No, no—cold is more imperative than love; hunger overwhelms it. If I were naked in the snow down there, cold would override everything; my first thought would be to warm myself before I died. Even if I saw you walking naked toward me, life would take precedence over love."

"Then cold," she said. Her profile was like marble, flawless, unblinking. "Four letters, the first word in the world."

He wanted suddenly to feel her smooth marble cheek under his lips, kiss it into life. He said instead, "I can't remember the Latin word for cold." She looked at him, smiling again, as if she had felt his impulse in the air between them. His thoughts veered off-balance, tugged toward her fine, flushed skin and delicate bones, something nameless, blind and hungry in him reaching toward another nameless thing. She said,

"There's the cab."

It was a horse-drawn sleigh; the snow was too deep for ordinary means. Had she been smiling, he wondered, because she had seen the cab? He kissed her anyway, lightly on the cheek, before she turned to get her coat, thinking how long he had known her and how little he knew her and how little he knew of how much or little there was in her to know.

Gerda

They arrived at Selene's party fashionably late. She had a vast flat with an old-fashioned ballroom. Half the city was crushed into it, despite the snow. Prisms of ice dazzled in the chandeliers; not even the hundred candles in them could melt their glittering, frozen jewels. On long tables, swans carved of ice held hothouse berries, caviar, sherbet between their wings. A business acquaintance attached himself to Kay; Gerda, drifting toward champagne, was found by Selene.

"Gerda!" She kissed air enthusiastically around Gerda's face. "How are you, angel? Such a dress. So innocent. How do you get away with it?"

"With what?"

"And such a sense of humor. Have you met Maurice? Gerda, Maurice Crow."

"Call me Bob," said Maurice Crow to Gerda, as Selene flung her fruity voice into the throng and hurried after it.

"Why?"

Maurice Crow chuckled. "Good question." He had a kindly smile, Gerda thought; it gentled his thin, aging, beaky face. "If you were named Maurice, wouldn't you rather be called Bob?"

"I don't think so," Gerda said doubtfully. "I think I would rather be called my name."

"That's because you're beautiful. A beautiful woman makes any name beautiful."

"I don't like my name. It sounds like something to hold stockings up with. Or a five-letter word from a Biblical phrase." She glanced around the room for Kay. He stood in a ring of brightly dressed women; he had just made them laugh. She sighed without realizing it. "And I'm not really beautiful. This is just a disguise."

Maurice Crow peered at her more closely out of his black, shiny eyes. He offered her his arm; after a moment she figured out what to do with it. "You need a glass of champagne." He patted her hand gently. "Come with me."

"You see, I hate parties."

"Ah."

"And Kay loves them."

"And you," he said, threading a sure path among satin and silk and clouds of tulle, "love Kay."

"I have always loved Kay."

"And now you feel he might stop loving you? So you come here to please him."

"How quickly you understand things. But I'm not sure if he is pleased that I came. We used to know each other so well. Now I feel stupid around him, and slow, and plain, even when he tells me I'm not. It used to be different between us."

"When?"

She shrugged. "Before. Before the city began taking little pieces of him away from me. He used to bring me wildflowers he had picked in the park. Now he gives me blood-red roses once a year. Some days his eyes never see me, not even in bed. I see contracts in his eyes, and the names of restaurants, expensive shoes, train schedules. A train schedule is more interesting to him than I am."

"To become interesting, you must be interested."

"In Kay? Or in trains?"

"If," he said, "you can no longer tell the difference, perhaps it is Kay who has grown uninteresting."

"Oh, no," she said quickly. "Never to me." She had flushed. With the quick, warm color in her face and the light spilling from the icy prisms onto her hair, into her eyes, she caused Maurice Crow to hold her glass too long under the champagne fountain. "He is beautiful and brilliant, and we have loved each other since we were children. But it seems that, having grown up, we no longer recognize one another." She took the overflowing glass from Maurice Crow's hand and drained it. Liquid from the dripping glass fell beneath her chaste neckline, rolled down her breast like icy tears. "We are both in disguise."

The Snow Queen

Neva entered late. She wore white satin that clung to her body like white clings to the calla lily. White peacock feathers sparkling with faux diamonds trailed down her long ivory hair. Her eyes were black as the night sky between the winter constellations. They swept the room, picked out a face here: Gerda's—How sweet, Neva thought, to have kept that expression, like one's first kiss treasured in tissue paper—and there: Kay's. Her eyes were wide, very still. The young man with her said something witty. She did not hear. He tried again, his eyes growing anxious. She watched Kay tell another story; the women around him—doves, warblers, a couple of trumpeting swans—laughed again. He laughed with them, reluctant but irresistibly amused by himself. He lifted champagne to his lips; light leaped from the cut crystal. His pale hair shone like the silk of Neva's dress; his lips were shaped cleanly as the swan's wing. She waited, perfectly still. Lowering his glass, the amused smile tugging again at his lips, he saw her standing in the archway across the room.

To his eye she was alone; the importunate young lapdog beside her did not exist. So his look told her, as she drew at it with the immense and immeasurable pull of a wayward planet wandering too close to someone's cold, bright, inconstant moon. The instant he would have moved, she did, crossing the room to join him before his brilliant, fluttering circle could scatter. Like him, she preferred an audience. She waited in her outer orbit, composed, mysterious, while he told another story. This one had a woman in it—Gerda—and something about angels or fish.

"And then," he said, "we had an argument about the first word in the world."

"Coffee," guessed one woman, and he smiled appreciatively.

"No," suggested another.

"It was for a crossword puzzle. The first word you learn to conjugate in Latin."

"But we always speak French in bed," a woman murmured. "My husband and I."

Kay's eyes slid to Neva. Her expression remained changeless; she offered no word. He said lightly, "No, no, *ma chère,* one conjugates a verb; one has conjugal relations with one's spouse. Or not, as the case may be."

"Do people still?" someone wondered. "How boring."

"To conjugate," Neva said suddenly in her dark, languid voice, "means to inflect a verb in an orderly fashion through all its tenses. As in: *amo, amas, amat.* I love, you love—"

"But that's it!" Kay cried. "The answer to the puzzle. How could I have forgotten?"

"Love?" someone said perplexedly. Neva touched her brow delicately.

"I cannot," she said, "remember the Latin word for dance."

"You do it so well," Kay said a moment later, as they glided onto the floor. So polished it was that the flames from the chandeliers seemed frozen underfoot, as if they danced on stars. "And no one studies Latin anymore."

"I never tire of learning," Neva said. Her gloved hand lay lightly on his shoulder, close to his neck. Even in winter his skin looked warm, burnished by tropical skies, endless sun. She wanted to cover that warmth with her body, draw it into her own white-marble skin. Her eyes flicked constantly around the room over his shoulder, studying women's faces. "Who is Gerda?" she asked, then knew her: the tall, beautiful childlike woman who watched Kay with a hopeless, forlorn expression, as if she had already lost him.

"She is my wife," Kay said, with a studied balance of lightness and indifference in his voice. Neva lifted her hand off his shoulder, settled it again closer to his skin.

"Ah."

"We have known each other all our lives."

"She loves you still."

"How do you know?" he said, surprised. She guided him into a half-turn, so that for a moment he faced his abandoned Gerda, with her sad eyes and downturned mouth, standing in her naive black dress, her champagne tilted and nearly spilling, with only a cadaverous, beaky man trying to get her attention. Neva turned him again; he looked at her, blinking, as if he had been lightly, unexpectedly struck. She shifted her hand, crooked her fingers around his bare neck.

"She is very beautiful."

"Yes."

"It is her air of childlike innocence that is so appealing."

"And so exasperating," he exclaimed suddenly, as if, like the Apostle, he had been illumined by lightning and stunned with truth.

"Innocence can be," Neva said.

"Gerda knows so little of life. We have lived for years in this city and still she seems so helpless. Scattered. She doesn't know what she wants from life; she wouldn't know how to take it if she did."

"Some women never learn."

"You have. You are so elegant, so sophisticated. So sure." He paused; she saw the word trembling on his lips. She held his gaze, pulled him deeper, deeper into her winter darkness. "But," he breathed, "you must have men telling you this all the time."

"Only if I want them to. And there are not many I choose to listen to."

"You are so beautiful," he said wildly, as if the word had been tormented out of him.

She smiled, slid her other hand up his arm to link her fingers behind his neck. She whispered, "And so are you."

The Thief

Briony watched Gerda walk blindly through the falling snow. It caught on her lashes, melted in the hot, wet tears on her cheeks. Her long coat swung carelessly open to the bitter cold, revealing pearls, gold, a hidden pocket in the lining in which Briony envisioned cash, cards, earrings taken off and forgotten. She gave little thought to Gerda's tears: some party, some man, it was a familiar tale.

She shadowed Gerda, walking silently on the fresh-crushed snow of her footprints, which was futile, she realized, since they were nothing more than a wedge of toe and a rapier stab of stiletto heel. Still, in her tumultuous state of mind, the woman probably would not have noticed a traveling circus behind her.

She slid, shadow-like, to Gerda's side.

"Spare change?"

Gerda glanced at her; her eyes flooded again; she shook her head helplessly. "I have nothing."

Briony's knife snicked open, flashing silver in a rectangle of window light. "You have a triple strand of pearls, a sapphire dinner ring, a gold wedding ring, a pair of earrings either diamond or cubic zirconium, on, I would guess, fourteen karat posts."

"I never got my ears pierced," Gerda said wearily. Briony missed a step, caught up with her.

"Everyone has pierced ears!"

"Diamond, and twenty-two karat gold." She pulled at them, and at her rings. "They were all gifts from

Kay. You might as well have them. Take my coat, too." She shrugged it off, let it fall. "That was also a gift." She tugged the pearls at her throat; they scattered like luminous, tiny moons around her in the snow. "Oh, sorry."

"What are you doing?" Briony breathed. The woman, wearing nothing more than a short and rather silly dress, turned to the icy darkness beyond the window-light. She had actually taken a step into it when Briony caught her arm. She was cold as an iron statue in winter. "Stop!" Briony hauled her coat out of the snow. "Put this back on. You'll freeze!"

"I don't care. Why should you?"

"Nobody is worth freezing for."

"Kay is."

"Is he?" She flung the coat over Gerda's shoulders, pulled it closed. "God, woman, what Neanderthal age are you from?"

"I love him."

"So?"

"He doesn't love me."

"So?"

"If he doesn't love me, I don't want to live."

Briony stared at her, speechless, having learned from various friends *in extremis* that there was no arguing with such crazed and muddled thinking. Look, she might have said, whirling the woman around to shock her. See that snowdrift beside the wall? Earlier tonight that was an old woman who could have used your coat. Or: Men have notoriously bad taste, why should you let one decide whether you live or die? Piss on him and go find someone else. Or: Love is an obsolete emotion, ranking in usefulness somewhere between earwigs and toe mold.

She lied instead. She said, "I felt like that once."

She caught a flicker of life in the still, remote eyes. "Did you? Did you want to die?"

"Why don't we go for hot chocolate and I'll tell you about it?"

They sat at the counter of an all-night diner, sipping hot chocolate liberally laced with brandy from Briony's flask. Briony had short, dark, curly hair and sparkling sapphire eyes. She wore lace stockings under several skirts, an antique vest of peacock feathers over a shirt of simulated snakeskin, thigh-high boots, and a dark, hooded cape with many hidden pockets. The waitress behind the counter watched her with a sardonic eye and snapped her gum as she poured Briony's chocolate. Drawn to Gerda's beauty and tragic pallor, she kept refilling Gerda's cup. So did Briony. Briony, improvising wildly, invented a rich, beautiful, upper-class young man whose rejection of her plunged her into despair.

"He loved me," she said, "for the longest night the world has ever known. Then he dumped me like soggy cereal. I was just another pretty face and recycled bod to him. Three days after he offered me marriage, children, cars as big as luxury liners, trips to the family graveyard in Europe, he couldn't even remember my name. Susie, he called me. Hello, Susie, how are you, what can I do for you? I was so miserable I wanted to eat mothballs. I wanted to lie on the sidewalk and sunburn myself to death. The worms wouldn't have touched me, I thought. Not even they could be interested."

"What did you do?" Gerda asked. Briony, reveling in despair, lost her thread of invention. The waitress refilled Gerda's cup.

"I knew a guy like that," the waitress said. "I danced on his car in spiked heels. Then I slashed his tires. Then I found out it wasn't his car."

"What did I do?" Briony said. "What did I do?" She paused dramatically. The waitress had stopped chewing her gum, waiting for an answer. "Well—I mean, of course I did what I had to. What else could I do, but what women like me do when men drop-kick their hearts out of the field. Women like me. Of course women like you are different."

"What did you do?" Gerda asked again. Her eyes were wide and very dark; the brandy had flushed her cheeks. Drops of melted snow glittered like jewels in her disheveled hair. Briony gazed at her, musing.

"With money, you'd think you'd have more choices, wouldn't you? But money or love never taught you how to live. You don't know how to take care of yourself. So if Kay doesn't love you, you have to wander into the snow and freeze. But women like me, and Brenda here—"

"Jennifer," the waitress muttered.

"Jennifer, here, we're so used to fending for ourselves every day that it gets to be a habit. You're not used to fending, so you don't have the habit. So what you have to do is start pretending you have something to live for."

Gerda's eyes filled; a tear dropped into her chocolate. "I haven't."

"Of course you haven't, that's what I've been saying. That's why you have to pretend—"

"Why? It's easier just to walk back out into the snow."

"But if you keep pretending and pretending, one day you'll stumble onto something you care enough to live for, and if you turn yourself into an icicle now because of Kay, you won't be able to change your mind later. The only thing you're seeing in the entire world is Kay. Kay is in both your eyes, Kay is your mind. Which means you're only really seeing one tiny flyspeck of the world, one little puzzle piece. You have to learn to see around Kay. It's like staring at one star all the time and never seeing the moon or planets or constellations—"

"I don't know how to pretend," Gerda said softly. "Kay has always been the sky."

Jennifer swiped her cloth at a crumb, looking thoughtful. "What she says," she pointed out, tossing her head at Briony, "you only have to do it one day at a time. Always just today. That's all any of us do."

Gerda took a swallow of chocolate. Jennifer poured her more; Briony added brandy.

"After all," Briony said, "you could have told me to piss off and mind my own business. But you didn't. You put your coat back on and followed me here. So there must have been something—your next breath, a star you glimpsed—you care enough about."

"That's true," Gerda said, surprised. "But I don't remember what."

"Just keep pretending you remember."

Kay

Kay sat at breakfast with Neva, eating clouds and sunlight. Actually, it was hot biscuits and honey that dripped down his hand. Neva, discoursing on the likelihood of life on other planets, leaned across the table now and then, and slipped her tongue between his fingers to catch the honey. Her face and her white negligee, a lacy tumble of roses, would slide like light past his groping fingers; she would be back in her chair, talking, before he could put his biscuit down.

"The likelihood of life on other planets is very, very great," she said. She had a crumb of Kay's breakfast on her cheek. He reached across the table to brush it away; she caught his forefinger in her mouth and sucked at it until he started to melt off the chair onto his knees. She loosed his finger then and asked, "Have you read Piquelle on the subject?"

"What?"

"Piquelle," she said patiently, "on the subject of life on other planets."

He swallowed. "No."

"Have another biscuit, darling. No, don't move, I'll get it."

"It's no—"

"No, I insist you stay where you are. Don't move." She took his plate and stood up. He could see the outline of her pale, slender body under the lace. "Did you say something, Kay?"

"I groaned."

"There are billions of galaxies. And in each galaxy, billions of stars, each of which might well have its courtiers orbiting it." She reached into the dainty cloth in which the biscuits were wrapped. Through the window above the sideboard, snow fell endlessly; her hothouse daffodils shone like artificial light among the bone china, the crystal butter dish, the honey pot, the napkins patterned with an exotic flock of startled birds trying to escape beyond the hems. Kay caught a fold of her negligee between his teeth as she put his biscuit down. She laughed indulgently, pushed against his face and let him trace the circle of her navel through the lace with his tongue. Then she glided out of reach, sat back in her chair.

"Think of it!"

"I am."

"Billions of stars, billions of galaxies! And life around each star, eating, conversing, dreaming, perhaps indulging in startling alien sexual practices—Allow me, darling." She thrust her finger deep into the honey, brought it out trailing a fine strand of gold that beaded into drops on the dark wood. As her finger rolled across his broken biscuit, she bent her head, licked delicately at the trail of honey on the table. Kay, trying to catch her finger in his mouth, knocked over his coffee. It splashed onto her hand.

"Oh, my darling," he exclaimed, horrified. "Did I burn you? Let me see!"

"It's nothing," she said cooly, retrieving her hand and wiping it on her napkin. "I do not burn easily. Where were we?"

"Your finger was in my biscuit," he said huskily.

"The point he makes, of course, is that with so many potential suns and an incredibly vast number of systems perhaps orbiting them, the chances are not remote for life—perhaps sophisticated, intelligent, technologically advanced—life, in essence, as we know it, circling one of those distant stars. Imagine!" she exclaimed, rapt, absently pulling apart a daffodil and dropping pieces of its golden horn down her negligee. The petal pieces seemed to Kay to burn here and there on her body beneath a frail web of white. "On some planet circling some distant, unnamed star, Kay and Neva are seated in a snowbound city, breakfasting and discussing the possibility of life on other planets. Is that not strange and marvelous?"

He cleared his throat. "Do you think you might like me to remove some of those petals for you?"

"What petals?"

"The one, perhaps, caught between your breasts."

She smiled. "Of course, my darling." As he leaped precipitously to his feet, scattering silverware, she added, "Oh, darling, hand me the newspaper."

"I beg your pardon?"

"I always do the crossword puzzle after breakfast. Don't you? I like to time myself. Eighteen minutes and thirty-two seconds was my fastest. What was yours?"

She pulled the paper out of his limp hand, and watched, smiling faintly, as he flung himself groaning in despair across the table. His face lay in her biscuit crumbs; the spilled honey began to undulate slowly out of its pot toward his mouth; coffee spread darkly across the wood from beneath his belly. Neva leaned over his prone body, delicately sipped coffee. Then she opened her mouth against his ear and breathed a hot, moist sigh throughout his bones.

"You have broken my coffee pot," she murmured. "You must kneel at my feet while I work this puzzle. You will speculate, as I work, on the strange and wonderful sexual practices of aliens on various planets."

He slid off the table onto his knees in front of her. She propped the folded paper on his head. "Nine fifty-seven and fourteen seconds exactly. Begin, my darling."

"On the planet Debula, where people communicate not by voice but by a complex written arrangement whereby words are linked in seemingly arbitrary fashion by a similar letter in each word, and whose lawyers make vast sums of money interpreting and arguing over the meanings of the linked words, the men, being quite short, are fixated peculiarly on kneecaps. When faced with a pair, they are seized with indescribable longing and behave in frenzied fashion, first uncovering them and gazing raptly at them, then consuming whatever daffodil petal happens to be adhering to them, then moistening them all over in hope of eventually coaxing them apart . . ."

"What is a four letter synonym for the title of a novel by the Russian author Dostoyevsky?"

"Idiot," he sighed against her knees.

"Ah. Fool. Thank you, my darling. Forgive me if I am somewhat inattentive, but your voice, like the falling snow, is wonderfully calming. I could listen to it all day. I know that, as you roam from planet to planet, you will come across some strange practice that will be irresistible to me, and I will begin to listen to you." She crossed her legs abruptly, banging his nose with her knee. "Please continue with your tale, my darling. You may be as leisurely and detailed as you like. We have all winter."

Gerda

Gerda heaved a fifty-pound sack of potting soil off the stack beside the greenhouse door and dropped it on her workbench. She slit it open with the sharp end of a trowel and began to scoop soil into three-inch pots sitting on a tray. The phone rang in the shop; she heard Briony say,

"Four dozen roses? Two dozen each of Peach Belle and Firebird, billed to Selene Pray? You would like them delivered this afternoon?"

Gerda began dropping pansy seeds into the pots. Beyond the tinted greenhouse walls it was still snowing:

a long winter, they said, the longest on record. Gerda's greenhouse—half a dozen long glass rooms, each temperature controlled for varied environments, lying side by side and connected by glass archways—stood on the roof of one of the highest buildings in the city. Gerda could see across the ghostly white city to the frozen ports where great freighters were locked in the ice. She had sold nearly all of her jewelry to have the nursery built and stocked in such a merciless season, but, once open, her business was brisk. People yearned for color and perfume, for there seemed no color in the world but white and no scent but the pure, blanched, icy air. It was rumored that the climatic change had begun, and the glaciers were beginning to move down from the north. Eventually, they would be seen pushing blindly through the streets, encasing the city in a cocoon of solid ice for a millennium or two. Some people, in anticipation of the future, were making arrangements to have themselves frozen. Others simply ordered flowers to replicate the truant season.

"I'm taking a delivery," Briony said in the doorway. "Jennifer isn't back yet from hers." She had cut her hair and dyed it white. It sprang wildly from her head in petals of various lengths, reminding Gerda of a chrysanthemum. Jennifer loved driving the truck and delivering flowers, but Briony pined in captivity. She compensated for it by wearing rich antique velvets and tapestries and collecting different kinds of switchblades. Gerda had persuaded her to work until spring; by then, she thought, Briony might be coaxed through another season. Meanwhile, spring dallied; Briony drooped.

"All right," Gerda said. "I'll listen for the phone. Look, Briony, the lavender seedlings are coming up."

"Of course they're coming up," Briony said. "Everything you touch grows. If you dropped violets from the rooftop, they would take root in the snow. If you planted a shoe, it would grow into a shoe-tree."

"I want you to sell something for me."

Briony brightened. She kept her old business acquaintances by means of Gerda's jewels, reassuring them that she had only temporarily abandoned crime to help a friend.

"What?"

"A sapphire necklace. I want more stock; I want to grow orchids. Stop by the flat. The necklace is in the safe beneath the still life. Do you know anyone who sells paintings?"

"I'll find someone."

"Good," she said briskly, but she avoided Briony's sharp eyes, for the dismantling of her great love was confined, as yet, only to odds and ends of property. The structure itself was inviolate. She turned away, began to water seedlings. The front bell jangled. She said, "I'll see to it. You wrap the roses."

The man entering the shop made her heart stop. It was Kay. It was not Kay. It might have been Kay once: tall, fair, with the same sweet smile, the same extravagance of spirit.

"I want," he said, "every flower in the shop."

Gerda touched hair out of her eyes, leaving a streak of potting soil on her brow. She smiled suddenly, at a memory, and the stranger's eyes, vague with his own thoughts, saw beneath the potting soil and widened.

"I know," Gerda said. "You are in love."

"I thought I was," he said confusedly.

"You want all the flowers in the world."

"Yes."

He was oddly silent, then; Gerda asked, "Do you want me to help you choose which?"

"I have just chosen." He stepped forward. His eyes were lighter than Kay's, a warm gold-brown. He laughed at himself, still gazing at her. "I mean yes. Of course. You choose. I want to take a woman to dinner tonight, and I want to give her the most beautiful flower in the world and ask her to marry me. What is your favorite flower?"

"Perhaps," Gerda suggested, "you might start with her favorite color, if you are unsure of her favorite flower."

"Well. Right now it appears to be denim."

"Denim. Blue?"

"It's hardly passionate, is it? Neither is the color of potting soil."

"I beg—"

"Gold. The occasion begs for gold."

"Yellow roses?"

"Do you like roses?"

"Of course."

"But yellow for a proposal?"

"Perhaps a winey red. Or a brilliant streaked orange."

"But what is your favorite flower?"

"Fuchsias," Gerda said, smiling. "You can hardly present her with a potted plant."

"And your favorite color?"

"Black."

"Then," he said, "I want a black fuchsia."

Gerda was silent. The stranger stepped close to her, touched her hand. She was on the other side of the counter suddenly, hearing herself babble.

"I carry no black fuchsias. I'm a married woman, I have a husband—"

"Where is your wedding ring?"

"At home. Under my pillow. I sleep with it."

"Instead of your husband?" he said, so shrewdly her breath caught. He smiled. "Have dinner with me."

"But you love someone else!"

"I stopped, the moment I saw you. I had a fever, the fever passed. Your eyes are so clear, like a spring day. Your lips. There must be a rose the color of your lips. Take me and your lips to the roses, let me match them."

"I can't," she said breathlessly. "I love my husband."

"Loving one's spouse is quite old-fashioned. When was the last time he brought you a rose? Or touched your hand, like this? Or your lips. Like. This." He drew back, looked into her eyes again. "What is your name?"

She swallowed. "Why do you look so much like Kay? It's unfair."

"But I'm so much nicer."

"Are you?"

"Much," he said, and slid his hand around her head to spring the clip on the pin that held her hair so that it tumbled down around her face. He drew her close, repeated the word against her lips. "Much."

"Much," she breathed, and they passed the word back and forth a little.

"I'm off," Briony said, coming through the shop with her arms full of roses. Gerda, jumping, caught a glimpse of her blue, merry eyes before the door slammed. She gathered her hair in her hands, clipped it back.

"No. No, no, no. I'm married to Kay."

"I'll come for you at eight."

"No."

"Oh, and may I take you to a party after dinner?"

"No."

"You might as well get used to me."

"No."

He kissed her. "At eight, then." At the door, he turned. "By the way, do you have a name?"

"No."

"I thought not. My name is Foxx. Two x's. I'll pick you up here, since I'm sure you don't have a home, either." He blew her a kiss. "Au revoir, my last love."

"I won't be here."

"Of course not. Do you like sapphires?"

"I hate them."

"I thought so. They'll have to do until you are free to receive diamonds for your wedding."

"I am married to Kay."

"Sapphires, fuchsias, and denim. You see how much I know about you already. Chocolate?"

"No!"

"Champagne?"

"Go away!"

He smiled his light, brilliant smile. "After tonight, Kay will be only a dream, the way winter snow is a pale dream in spring. Tomorrow, the glaciers will recede, and the hard buds will appear on the trees. Tomorrow, we will smell the earth again, and the roiling, briny sea will crack the ice and the great ships will set sail to foreign countries and so shall you and I, my last love, set sail to distant and marvelous ports of call whose names we will never quite be able to pronounce, though we will remember them vividly all of our lives."

"No," she whispered.
"At eight. I shall bring you a black fuchsia."

Spring

"Dear Gerda," Selene said. "Darling Foxx. How wonderful of you to come to my party. How original you look, Gerda. You must help me plan my great swan song, the final definitive party ending all seasons. As the ice closes around us and traps us for history like butterflies in amber, the violinists will be lifting their bows, the guests swirling in the arms of their lovers, rebuffed spouses lifting their champagne glasses—it will be a splendid moment in time sealed and unchanged until the anthropologists come and chip us out of the ice. Do you suppose their excavations will be accompanied by the faint pop of champagne bubbles escaping the ice? Ah! There is Pilar O'Malley with her ninth husband. Darling Pilar is looking tired. It must be so exhausting hunting fortunes."

"Tomorrow," said Foxx.

"No," said Gerda. She was wearing her short black dress in hope that Foxx would be discouraged by its primness. Her only jewels were a pair of large blue very faux pearls that Briony had pinched from Woolworth's.

"You came with me tonight. You will come with me tomorrow. You will flee this frozen city, your flower pots, your patched denim—" He guided her toward the champagne, which poured like a waterfall through a cascade of Gerda's roses. "And your defunct marriage, which has about as much life to it as a house empty of everything but memory." He had been speaking so all evening, through champagne and quail, chocolates and port, endlessly patient, endlessly assured. The black silk fuchsia, a sapphire ring, a pair of satin heels, gloves with diamond cuffs were scattered in the back of his sleigh. Gerda, wearied and confused with too many words, too much champagne, felt as if the world were growing unfamiliar around her. There was no winter in Foxx's words, no Kay, no flower shop. The world was becoming a place of exotic, sunlit ports where she must go as a stranger, and as another stranger's wife. What of Briony, whom she had coaxed out of the streets? What of her lavender seedlings? Who would water her pansies? Who would order potting soil? She saw herself suddenly, standing among Selene's rich, glittering guests and worrying about potting soil. She laughed. The world and winter returned; the inventions of the insubstantial stranger Foxx turned into dreams and air, and she laughed again, knowing that the potting soil would be there tomorrow and the ports would not.

Across the room, Kay saw her laugh.

For a moment he did not recognize her: he had never seen her laugh like that. Then he thought, Gerda. The man beside her had taught her how to laugh.

"My darling," Neva said to him. "Will you get me champagne?" She did not wait for him to reply, but turned her back to him and continued her discussion with a beautiful and eager young man about the eternal truths in alchemy. Kay had no energy even for a disillusioned smile; he might have been made of ice for all the expression his face held. His heart, he felt, had withered into something so tiny that when the anthropologists came to excavate Selene's final party, his shrunken heart would be held a miracle of science, perhaps a foreshadowing of the physical advancement of future *homo*.

He stood beside Gerda to fill the champagne glasses, but he did not look at her or greet her. Not even she could reach him, as far as he had gone into the cold, empty wastes of winter's heart. Gerda, feeling a chill brush her, as of a ghost's presence, turned. For a moment, she did not recognize Kay. She saw only a man grown so pale and weary she thought he must have lost the one thing in the world he had ever loved.

Then she knew what he had lost. She whispered, "Kay."

He looked at her. Her eyes were the color of the summer skies none of them would see again: blue and full of light. He said, "Hello, Gerda. You look well."

"You look so sad." She put her hand to her breast, a gesture he remembered. "You aren't happy."

He shrugged slightly. "We make our lives." His champagne glasses were full, but he lingered a moment in the warmth of her eyes. "You look happy. You look beautiful. Do I know that dress? Is it new?"

She smiled. "No." Foxx was beside her suddenly, his hand on her elbow.

"Gerda?"

"It's old," Gerda said, holding Kay's eyes. "I no longer have much use for such clothes. I sold all the jewels you gave me to open a nursery. I grew all the roses you see here, and those tulips and the peonies."

"A nursery? In midwinter? What a brilliant and challenging idea. That explains the dirt under your thumbnail."

"Kay, my darling," said Neva's deep, languid voice behind them, "you forgot my champagne. Ah. It is little Gerda in her sweet frock."

"Yes," Kay said. "She has grown beautiful."

"Have I?"

"Gerda and I," Foxx said, "are leaving the city tomorrow. Perhaps that explains her unusual beauty."

"You are going away with Foxx?" Kay said, recognizing him. "What a peculiar thing to do. You'll fare better with your peonies."

"Congratulations, my sweets, I'm sure you'll both be so happy. Kay, there is someone I want you to—"

"Why are you going with Foxx?" Kay persisted. "He scatters hearts behind him like other people scatter bad checks."

"Don't be bitter, Kay," Foxx said genially. "We all find our last loves, as you have. Gerda, there is someone—"

"Tomorrow," Gerda said calmly, "I am going to make nine arrangements: two funerals, a birthday, three weddings, two hospital and one anniversary. I am also going to find an orchid supplier and do the monthly accounts."

"You're not going with Foxx."

"Of course she is," Foxx said. Gerda took her eyes briefly from Kay to look at him.

"I prefer my plants," she said simply.

An odd sound cut through the noise of the party, as if in the distance something immense had groaned and cracked in two. Kay turned suddenly, pushed the champagne glasses into Neva's hands.

"May I come—" His voice trembled so badly he stopped, began again. "May I come to your shop tomorrow and buy a flower?"

She worked a strand of hair loose from behind her ear and twirled it around one finger, another gesture he remembered. "Perhaps," she said cooly. He saw the tears in her eyes, like the sheen on melting, sunlit ice. He did not know if they were tears of love or pain;

perhaps, he thought, he might never know, for she had walked through light and shadow while he had encased himself in ice. "What flower?"

"I read once there is a language of flowers. Given by people to one another, they turn into words like love, anger, forgiveness. I will have to study the language to know what flower I need to ask for."

"Perhaps," she said tremulously, "you should try looking someplace other than language for what you want."

He was silent, looking into her eyes. The icy air outside cracked again, a lightning-whip of sound that split through the entire city. Around them, people held one another and laughed, even those perhaps somewhat disappointed that life had lost the imminence of danger, and that the world would continue its ancient, predictable ways. Neva handed the mute and grumpy Foxx one of the champagne glasses she held. She drained the other and, smiling her faint, private smile, passed on in search of colder climes.

Breadcrumbs and Stones

Lisa Goldstein

Lisa Goldstein is a Bay Area writer who won the American Book Award for her fantasy novel The Red Magician. *She is also the author of* The Dream Years, Tourists, *and other works that seamlessly blend the real with the fantastic.*

"Breadcrumbs and Stones" is a powerful, moving story about the metaphorical language of fairy tales and their meaning for one particular family. It takes the symbols to be found in the German tale of Hansel and Gretel and examines them anew.

Breadcrumbs and Stones

My sister and I grew up on fabulous stories. Night after night we would listen, spellbound, as my mother talked of kings and queens, of quests through magical lands, of mythical beasts and fantastic treasure and powerful wizards. As I got older I realized that these were not the tales my friends and classmates were hearing: my mother was making them up, piecing them together from a dozen different places.

She seemed like a queen herself, tall and pale, a woman made of ivory. When I was a child I was sure she was the most beautiful person I knew. Yet she changed when she went outside the house, when she had to deal with grocers and policemen and bank tellers. Her store of words dried up and she spoke only in short, formal phrases. Her accent, nearly nonexistent at home, grew worse. But she never lost her grace or became awkward. It seemed instead as if she changed like one of the heroes of her stories, turned from a living woman into a statue.

I rarely thought about my childhood. But now, as we waited at the hospital, my father, my sister and I, all these things went through my mind. My mother's condition was the same, the nurse had told us: she was sleeping peacefully. There was no reason for us to stay.

We stayed, I guess, because we couldn't think of anywhere else to go. "They've got her in a room with a terminal patient, a woman who's had three operations so far," my father said. He was angry and on edge; every few minutes he would stand and pace to the soda machine. "What kind of atmosphere is that for her?"

My sister Sarah and I said nothing. Was our mother a terminal patient, too? We knew only that she had been in and out of the hospital, and that her illness had been diagnosed at least a year before my father told us about it. There were so many things we did not say in our family; we had grown used to mystery.

Finally Sarah stood up. "There's nothing we can do here." she said. "I'm going home."

"I'll go with you," I said quickly.

Sarah lived in a one-room apartment in the Berkeley hills. She had a couch that turned into a bed and a wall of bookshelves and stereo equipment, and very little else. She made us some tea on a hot plate and we sat on the couch and sipped it, saying nothing.

"Do you think she's been happy, Lynne?" Sarah asked finally.

"What do you mean?"

"Well, if she's—I don't think she's got much longer.

Do you think it was all worth it? Did she have a good life? Did we treat her all right?"

"I don't know. No, I do know. She always tried to be cheerful for us, but there was something—something she kept hidden. I don't know what it was." We had been talking about her in the past tense, I noticed, and I resolved to stop.

"Was it us?"

"I don't think so." I thought of our father, an American soldier she had met after the war. Did she ever regret marrying such an ordinary man? "Maybe it was—maybe it's Dad. She felt she made a bad marriage."

"Maybe it was something about the war," Sarah said.

We had asked, of course, what had happened to her in the war. She had been born in Germany, but her parents had managed to place her with a Christian family and get her forged papers saying she was not Jewish. She looked like what the Nazis had considered Aryan, tall and blond, so the deception had not been difficult. She had worked in a glass-blowing factory, making vacuum tubes. Her parents had been sent to a concentration camp and had died there; we had never known our grandparents.

"Maybe," I said.

"Do you ever think—I sometimes wonder if I could have survived something like that. When I was twelve I thought, This is the age my mother was when she went to live with the foster family. And at sixteen I thought, This is when she started at the factory . . ."

"No," I said, surprised. She had never told me any of this.

"And what happened to our grandparents. I think about that all the time, that something terrible is going to happen. That's why I don't have any furniture, because at the back of my mind—at the back of my mind I always think, What if I have to flee?"

"To flee?" Perhaps it was the unusual word that made me want to laugh, and that, I knew, would have been unforgivable.

"She hardly told us anything. I used to imagine—the most horrible things."

"You shouldn't think of things like that. She had it better than most."

"But why didn't she tell us about it? Everything I know about her life I heard from Dad."

"Because—Because she had to be secretive in order to survive, and she never got over it," I said. I had never spoken about any of this before, had not known I knew it. "Once when I was a kid, and we were in some crowded place—I think it was an airport—I tried to get her attention. I kept calling, 'Mom. Mom,' and she wouldn't look at me. And finally I said, 'Hey, Margaret Jacobi,' and she turned around so fast . . . I thought she was going to hit me. She said, 'Don't ever mention my name in a public place.' "

"I know. And she would never fill out the census. She hid it away that one time, remember, and a man came to the door . . ."

"And she wouldn't talk to him. He kept threatening her with all these terrible things—"

"And then Dad came home, thank God, and he answered it."

"I thought they were going to take her away to jail, at least."

I was laughing now, a little nervously, hoping I could make Sarah forget her terrible thoughts. But then she said, "Why do these things happen?"

"What things?"

"You know. Cancer, and concentration camps."

But I had no idea. Why did she have to ask such uncomfortable questions? The best I could do was change the subject and hope she would forget about it.

The next week my father called and told me that my mother had asked for me. I hurried to the hospital and met him and Sarah at her bedside. But by the time I got there her eyes were closed; she seemed to be asleep.

"They had to give her a shot—she was in a lot of pain," my father said. "They told me she was getting better." He seemed barely able to contain his anger at the doctors who had given him hope. I could see that he needed to hold someone responsible, and I understood; I felt the same way myself.

My mother stirred and said something. "Shhh," I said to my father.

"Did you feed the dog?" my mother asked softly.

We hadn't had a dog in years. "Did you—" she said again, her voice growing louder.

"It's okay, Mom," I said. "Don't worry."

"Good," she said. "Sit down. I'll tell you a story if you like, but you'll have to be quiet."

We said nothing. Her eyes opened but did not focus on any of us. "The princess came to the dark fortress," she said. Her accent was very strong, the "th" sound almost a "d." "It was locked, and she didn't have the key. Did I tell you this story before?"

She had told us so many over the years that I couldn't remember. "No, Mom," I said softly.

"I'll tell you another one," she said. "They went to the woods." She stopped, as if uncertain how to go on.

"Who did?" I said.

"The children," she said. "Their parents took them to the woods and left them there. Their father was a poor woodcutter, and he didn't have enough to feed them."

To my amazement I realized that she was telling the story of Hansel and Gretel. She had never, as I said, told us conventional fairy tales; I think she considered the Grimms too German, and she avoided all things German after the war.

"The woodcutter's wife had convinced him to leave the children in the woods. But the children had brought along stones, and they dropped them as they walked. The woodcutter told his children that he and his wife would go on a little ways and cut wood, and they left the children there. The children went to sleep, and when they awoke it was dark. But they followed the stones back, and so they came home safely."

I hadn't ever heard this part. The way I knew it Hansel and Gretel had dropped breadcrumbs. But all fairy tales were hazy to me; I had trouble, for example, remembering which was Snow White and which was Sleeping Beauty.

"The woodcutter was pleased to see his children, because he had felt bad about leaving them in the woods. But his wife, the children's stepmother, soon began to complain about not having enough food in the house. Once again she tried to convince her husband to take the children to the woods. And after a while he agreed, in order to have peace in the house.

"The children overheard their parents talking, as they had done the last time, and they went to gather stones again. But this time the door to the back was locked."

She closed her eyes. I thought she had fallen asleep and I felt relieved: her story had made me uncomfortable. "The door was locked," my mother said quietly, one last time.

When I think of that summer I see my sister and me in her apartment in the hills, sitting on her couch and sipping tea. She was an elementary school teacher on summer vacation, and I had taken a leave of absence from my job to be available to my mother. By unspoken agreement we started going to her place whenever we left the hospital. We were trying to understand something, but since we weren't sure what it was, since our parents had chosen to reveal only parts of the mystery at a time, we had long, circular conversations without ever getting anywhere. It was the closest we had been since childhood.

"What happened to Hansel and Gretel?" I asked Sarah. "The children drop breadcrumbs instead of stones the next time, and the birds eat the breadcrumbs so they can't find their way back, and then—"

"Then they meet the witch," Sarah said. "I've read it to the kids at school hundreds of times."

"And the witch tries to—to cook them—"

"To cook Hansel. Oh my God, Lynne, she was talking about the ovens. The ovens in the camps."

"Oh, come on. She'd never even seen them."

"No, but her parents had. She must have been trying to imagine it."

"That's too easy. It was the children who were threatened with the oven in the story, not the parents. And just because you try to imagine it doesn't mean everyone else does."

"I used to think they looked like those ovens in the pizza parlor. Remember? They took us there a lot when we were kids. Long rows of shelves, black and hot. I wondered what it would be like to have to get into one."

I thought of the four of us, sitting in a darkened, noisy pizza parlor, laughing at something one of us had just said. And all the while my little sister Sarah had been watching the ovens, imagining herself burning.

"Don't tell me you never thought of it," she said.

"No, not really."

"You're kidding. It happened. We have to face the fact that it happened."

"Yeah, but we don't have to dwell on it."

"How can you ignore—"

"Okay, I'll tell you what I think. If I had survived something like that, the camps, or having been in hiding, I would be grateful. I would think each day was a miracle, really. It would be a miracle to be alive."

"And what about the people who died? The survivors feel guilty just for being alive."

"How do you know?"

"I have books about it. Do you want to see what the ovens looked like?" She stood and headed toward her bookshelves, and I saw, alarmed, that she had a whole shelf of books on the concentration camps.

"No, I don't."

She stopped but did not sit back down. "What must that be like, not to have a home?"

"She does have a home. It's here with us."

"You know what I mean. A whole generation was wiped out, a whole community. All their traditions and stories and memories and customs."

"She has stories—"

"But she made them all up. She doesn't even have stories of her own—she forgot all the ones her parents told her."

"Come on—those were great stories. Don't you remember?"

"That's not the point. She'd lost everything. Dad was always having to tell her about Jewish holidays and customs. She'd forgotten it all."

"She remembered Hansel and Gretel," I said, and for once Sarah had no answer.

A few days later my father called to tell me that my mother was better. She would stay in the hospital for more tests, but he thought that she would be going home soon. I was surprised at the news; at the back of my mind I had been certain she would never return. Perhaps I had absorbed some of Sarah's pessimism.

The day she came home I invited the family over for dinner. My place was larger than Sarah's, with a dining table and dishes and silverware that matched. Still, when I looked around the apartment to make sure everything was ready, I realized I had pared down my life as much as my sister had. I had no close friends at the software company where I worked, I had never dated any man for longer than six months, and I had not lived with anyone since moving away from my family. I never discussed politics or gave my opinion on current events. In Berkeley, California, perhaps the most political city in the United States, I had never put a bumper sticker on my car, or worn a campaign button, or come out for one candidate over another. These things were no one's business but my own.

I had even, I saw now, started to drift away from Sarah. My sister's words came back to me, but they weren't very funny this time: What if I have to flee?

My parents had dressed up for dinner, as if they were going to a party. My mother wore an outfit I remembered, a violet-gray suit, a gray silk blouse and a scarf of violet gauze, but it was far too large on her. Her skin was the gray-white color of ashes, and her blue veins stood out sharply on her neck and the insides of her wrists. I had seen her in the hospital and was not shocked at the changes; instead, I felt pity, and a kind of squeamish horror at what she was going through.

I don't remember much of that dinner, really, just that my mother ate little, and that we all made nervous conversation to avoid the one thing uppermost in our minds. And that my mother said she wanted to hike through Muir Woods, a favorite spot of hers. Sarah and I quickly volunteered to take her, both of us treating her request as the last wish of a dying woman. As, for all we knew, it was.

It was sunny the day I drove my sister and mother across the San Rafael Bridge to Marin County and up into Mount Tamalpais. The road wound up past the dry, bleached grass of the mountainside. Then, as we went higher, this began to give way to old shaded groves of eucalyptus and redwood. Light shot through the branches and scattered across the car.

We parked at the entrance to Muir Woods. It was a weekday and so the place was not too crowded, though the tourists had come out in force. We went past the information booth and the cafeteria, feeling a little smug. We did not need information because we knew the best places to hike, and we had packed a lunch.

There is a well-worn circular trail through the woods that brings you back to the parking lot, and there are paths that branch off from this trail, taking you away from the crowds. We chose one of these paths and began to hike through the trees. Squares and lozenges of light fell over us. The ground was patterned in the green and brown and gold of damp leaves and twigs and moss. We could hear a brook somewhere beneath us, but as we climbed higher up the mountain the sound faded and we heard only the birds, calling to one another.

After a while my mother began to lag behind, and Sarah and I stopped, pretending we were tired. We sat on a rock and took out the sandwiches. When I gave my mother hers I brushed against her hand; her skin was as cold as glass. We ate in silence for a while.

"There's no good way to say this, I suppose," my mother said. Sarah and I stopped eating and looked up, watchful as deer. "You children had an uncle. My brother."

Whatever revelation we were expecting, it was not this one. "You would have liked him, I think," my mother said. "He loved children—he would have spoiled you both rotten. His name was Johann."

Uncle Johann, I thought. It sounded as distant as a character in a novel. "What happened to him?" Sarah asked.

"We were both adopted by a Christian family," my mother said, and I saw that for once she would not need prompting to tell this story, that she had probably rehearsed it over and over in her mind. "You remember, the one I told you about. And then when we were old enough we began to work in the factory, making the vacuum tubes. Once I dropped some of the liquid glass on my foot—molten glass, is that the right word? I still have the scar there." She pointed to her right foot. The scar, which I had never noticed, was hidden by the hiking shoe.

"Everyone laughed, I suppose because I was new at

the work, and so clumsy. But Johann came to my side immediately and put towels soaked in cold water on the burn."

She did not look at either of us as she spoke. It was as if she was compelled to tell the story to its end, without stopping. Yet her voice was level and calm, and I could not help but think that she might as well be telling us one of her fabulous stories.

"Johann was a little hotheaded, I think. At home he would talk about sabotage, about making vacuum tubes that didn't work or even about blowing up the factory, though I don't know where he would have gotten the dynamite. He talked about his connections in the Underground. We were together nearly all the time, in the factory and at home, and I knew that he had no connections. But I could not help worrying about him—the Germans were taking younger and younger men into the army as the war began to turn against them, and I knew that soon it would be Johann's turn.

"Near the end of the war, as more and more young men were drafted, the Germans brought in prisoners from the labor camps to work in the factory. We knew that these prisoners were probably Jews, and it made Johann angry to see how they were treated—they had to work longer hours than we did and had less to eat at the midday break. He wanted to do something for them, to contact them in some way.

"We got into horrible arguments about it. You must understand that we hardly ever talked to our fellow workers for fear of giving ourselves away, and so the only company we had was each other. We had become like two prisoners who had shared the same cell for far too long—for a time we could not say anything without giving offense.

"I told him I thought these prisoners were better off than the ones in the camps, because by this time we had begun to hear terrible rumors about what went on in those places. I said that he could do nothing for them, that he would only raise their hopes if he went to talk to them, and that he would be putting himself in danger for nothing. And I pointed out that they didn't speak German anyway—they seemed to be mostly Hungarians and Poles.

"As I said, we couldn't speak to each other without causing pain. He called me a coward. He said—oh, it was horrible—he said that I had lived among the Germans for so long that I had begun to think like one, that I believed myself superior to these people. And—and he said more, too, of a similar nature."

I noticed that my mother had said it was horrible, but that her expression and her tone still did not change. And that she did not stop telling her story but continued on as calmly as though she were reading it from a book. Her fingers picked at the sandwich, dropping pieces of it on the ground.

"So I didn't speak to him for a week. I had only my foster parents to speak to, and I—well, I was an adolescent, with an adolescent's certain, impatient opinions about the world, and I had started to hate my adopted family. They were Germans, weren't they? And so at least partly responsible for this war and the dreadful things that were happening. I had heard the remarks my fellow workers made about the Jews at the factory, and I thought my foster parents must feel the same way. So what if they had saved my life, and my brother's life? Perhaps I hated them for that, too, for their courage and generosity.

"Was Johann right? I don't know. We might have

been able to help these people, but I can't think how. Perhaps if everyone who felt the way my brother did had done something—I don't know.

"We used to walk each other home when our shift ended, but now I started going home by myself. I couldn't bring myself to speak to anyone. I felt that I was alone, that no one understood me. The war might not have existed, I was so deeply buried within myself.

"There was a young man at the factory, a German, who began to watch me as I worked, who always seemed to be next to me when I turned around. I thought he was a spy, that he knew my secret. You children, oh, you've lived such a pampered life—you have no idea what we went through. We had to suspect everyone, everyone. Then one of the women who worked near me said, 'I think Franz is in love with you.'

"Of course I hated him—I don't have to tell you that. He was a German. It's strange, isn't it? We had such strong feelings about each other, and we had never spoken a word together.

"When he saw that Johann and I had stopped walking home together he started to wait for me at the end of my shift. I tried everything I could to avoid him, but some days it just wasn't possible. I was terrified that he would make some remark about the Jews working in the factory, and that I would not be able to contain myself and somehow give myself away. After a week of this I was desperate to make up with Johann again, to have everything the way it had been before. I hadn't forgotten what he had said to me, but I had convinced myself that it didn't matter. Well, you've been adolescents too—you know how quickly you can change your feelings about something.

"I managed to avoid Franz, and I waited outside the factory when my shift ended. But Johann didn't come out. Soon all my fellow workers had gone home, and the new shift had started, and I still didn't see Johann. I went back inside.

"Did I ever tell you what the factory looked like? It looked like hell. Whenever people say anything about hell I always nod, because I know what they're talking about. The place was huge, with low ceilings and almost no light to work by, just the yellow flames of the gas jets. It was hot in winter and like a furnace in summer, with everyone's jet on all the time. We dipped into the big vats of liquid glass and blew our tubes, and that was all we did, eight and nine hours a day. We were allowed to sit down only at the midday meal.

"At first I couldn't find Johann at all. Then I saw that he was walking over to the part of the factory where the Jews worked, and that when the guard looked away he passed a note to one of the prisoners. The other man read it and then turned on his jet of fire and burned it. And neither of them had looked at the other.

"Johann grinned when he saw me and said, 'It's all taken care of.' I wondered what he meant, but I was so glad he was talking to me again that I didn't really care. And maybe he had been right; maybe he could do something for these people.

"When we left the factory I saw that I hadn't gotten rid of Franz after all—he was waiting for me at the door to the factory, and he was smiling, as if he knew something. Had he seen Johann? But I felt something of my brother's confidence, and I put Franz out of my mind until the next day.

"Franz sat next to me during the midday break. 'What is your brother doing?' he asked.

" 'What do you mean?' I said. I am a very poor liar; I had always dreaded the thought of someone, anyone, asking me questions.

" 'I saw him the other day talking to the Jews,' Franz said. To this day I cannot stand to hear a German say the word 'Jew'—'*Jude,*' they say, in that horrible accent."

She did not seem to realize that that "horrible accent" was her own as well. I said nothing.

"What was wrong with Johann? Franz asked. He leaned closer to me and raised his voice at the same time. I was desperate to ask him to speak quietly but I could say nothing, or his suspicions would fall on me. Was Johann a Jew-lover? Some kind of spy?

"I felt battered by his questions. He became more offensive. Why did I never leave my brother's side? Was I in love with him? Was I a Jew-lover as well? If I knew something about my brother's activities I had better go to the authorities and tell them, hadn't I?

"Then he said something I have thought about every day of my life. 'I might just go to the authorities with what I know,' he said.

" 'What do you mean?' I said. 'Don't be stupid. He hasn't done anything.'

" 'Good,' Franz said. 'You'll stop me, won't you?'

"It's obvious to me today that he wanted to—to blackmail me. That he wanted me to walk home with him, or he would report Johann. And probably he wanted more as well, wanted sex, though I tried not to think of that at the time. I was young, and very sheltered, and even the thought of having to speak to him made me shudder with disgust. So I convinced myself that that could not be what he meant, and that he had no proof against Johann. And, for all I knew, Johann had not done anything. So I avoided Franz, and a week passed, and I began to relax.

"Only once in all that time did Franz try to contact me. He walked by me and gave me a note, and I burned it without reading it. I thought that that would tell him I wanted nothing more to do with him, and that he would leave us alone.

"But the next day when we came to work the prisoner who had gotten Johann's note was gone. Johann noticed it first, and I felt him become stiff with fear beside me, terrified to go to his place in the factory. 'What?' I said. 'What is it?'

" 'You don't know anything about anything,' Johann said. 'Don't worry, I'll tell them that.'

" 'What's happened?' I said, but at that moment three men in the uniform of the Gestapo came into the factory, and Johann began to run.

"One man guarded the door, so the only place Johann could go was up the stairs. There were several floors above us—I think they were offices—but we were not allowed to go off the first floor and so I had never seen them. Johann must have run as far as he could go, until he was trapped, and then they brought him back down—" She was crying now, but her expression still had not changed. She wiped at her eye with her hand. "I saw him on a Red Cross list after the war. He had died in Auschwitz."

Sarah and I said nothing. We were not a family used to confidences, to strong emotion. I wondered how my mother could have kept this story from us for so many years, and what I could possibly say to her. And I remembered Sarah's question—"Do you think she was happy?"—and I thought that nothing could be more irrelevant to her life.

"Does Dad know?" Sarah asked finally.

"I think so," my mother said.

You *think* so? I thought, horrified. How had she told him? With hints and misdirection, just as she had always answered our questions, until finally he suspected the worst? But my mother had become silent. We would get no more stories today. For the first time, I thought she looked very old.

We began to walk back. Had Gretel, I wondered, come back to the forest with her daughter? Many years later, when she was an old woman and tired of secrets, had she taken her daughter by the hand and followed the old path? What could she have said to her?

"This is where our parents left us, in that clearing by the brook. And here's where we saw the cottage. Look there—the trees have come and claimed it. And this is where the oven was, this place where all the leaves seem burnt and dry. We saw these things when we were young, too young, I guess, and all we knew was terror. But there were miracles too, and we survived. And look—here is the path that you can take yourself."

It seemed to me that all my life my mother had given me the wrong story, her made-up tales instead of Hansel and Gretel, had given me breadcrumbs instead of stones. That she had done this on purpose, told me the gaudiest, most wonder-filled lies she knew, so that I would not ask for anything more and stumble on her secret. It was too late now—I would have to find my own way back. But the path did not look at all familiar.

Recommended Reading

Fiction and Poetry

Katie Crackernuts, by Katherine Briggs
A charming short novel retelling the Katie Crackernuts tale, by one of the world's foremost folklore authorities.
Beginning with O, by Olga Broumas
Broumas' poetry makes use of many fairy tale motifs in this collection.
The Sun, the Moon and the Stars, by Steven Brust
A contemporary novel mixing ruminations on art and creation with a lively Hungarian fairy tale.
Possession, by A. S. Byatt
A Booker Prize winning novel that makes wonderful use of the Fairy Melusine legend.
Sleeping in Flame, by Jonathan Carroll
Excellent, quirky dark fantasy using the Rumplestiltskin tale.
The Bloody Chamber, by Angela Carter
A stunning collection of dark, sensual fairy tale retellings.
The Sleeping Beauty, by Hayden Carruth
A poetry sequence using the Sleeping Beauty legend.

Beyond the Looking Glass, edited by Jonathan Cott
A collection of Victorian fairy tale prose and poetry.
The Nightingale, by Kara Dalkey
An evocative Oriental historical novel based on the Hans Christian Andersen story.
Provencal Tales, by Michael de Larrabeiti
Rich, subtle, adult fairy tales based on French legends.
Jack the Giant-Killer and *Drink Down the Moon,* by Charles de Lint
Wonderful urban fantasy novels bringing "Jack" and magic to the streets of modern Canada.
Tam Lin, by Pamela Dean
A lyrical novel setting the old Scottish fairy story (and folk ballad) Tam Lin among theater majors on a midwestern college campus.
The King's Indian, by John Gardner
A collection of peculiar and entertaining stories using fairy tale motifs.
Blood Pressure, by Sandra M. Gilbert
A number of the poems in this powerful collection make use of fairy tale motifs.
The Seventh Swan, by Nicholas Stuart Gray
An engaging Scottish novel that starts off where the "Seven Swans" fairy tale ends.
Fire and Hemlock, by Diana Wynne Jones
A beautifully written, haunting novel that brings the Thomas the Rhymer and Tam Lin tales into modern-day England.
Thomas the Rhymer, by Ellen Kushner
A sensuous and musical rendition of this old Scottish story and folk ballad.

Red as Blood, Or Tales from the Sisters Grimmer, by Tanith Lee

A striking and versatile collection of adult fairy tale retellings.

Beauty, by Robin McKinley

Masterfully written, gentle and magical, this novel retells the story of Beauty and the Beast.

The Door in the Hedge, by Robin McKinley

The Twelve Dancing Princesses and The Frog Prince retold in McKinley's gorgeous, clear prose, along with two original tales.

Disenchantments, edited by Wolfgang Mieder

An excellent compilation of adult fairy tale poetry.

Kindergarten, by Peter Rushford

A contemporary British story beautifully wrapped around the Hansel and Gretel tale, highly recommended.

Transformations, by Anne Sexton

Sexton's brilliant collection of modern fairy tale poetry.

Trail of Stones, by Gwenn Strauss

Evocative fairy tale poems, beautifully illustrated by Anthony Browne.

Swan's Wing, by Ursula Synge

A lovely, magical fantasy novel using the Seven Swans fairy tale.

Beauty, by Sheri S. Tepper

Dark fantasy incorporating several fairy tales from an original and iconoclastic writer.

The Coachman Rat, by David Henry Wilson

Excellent dark fantasy retelling the story of Cinderella from the coachman's point of view.

Snow White and Rose Red, by Patricia C. Wrede
A charming Elizabethan historical novel retelling this romantic Grimm's fairy tale.
Briar Rose, by Jane Yolen
An unforgettable short novel setting the Briar Rose/Sleeping Beauty story against the background of World War II.
Don't Bet on the Prince, edited by Jack Zipes
A collection of contemporary feminist fairy tales compiled by a leading fairy tale scholar, containing prose and poetry by Angela Carter, Joanna Russ, Jane Yolen, Tanith Lee, Margaret Atwood, Olga Broumas and others.

Modern-day fairy tale creators

The Faber Book of Modern Fairy Tales, edited by Sara and Stephen Corrin
Gudgekin the Thistle Girl and Other Tales, by John Gardner
Mainly by Moonlight, by Nicholas Stuart Gray
Collected Stories, by Richard Kennedy
Heart of Wood, by William Kotzwinkle
Fairy Tales, by Alison Uttley
Tales of Wonder, by Jane Yolen

Non-fiction

The Power of Myth, by Joseph Campbell
The Erotic World of Faery, by Maureen Duffy
"Womenfolk and Fairy Tales," by Susan Cooper
Essay in The New York Times Book Review, April 13, 1975

Beauty and the Beast: Visions and Revisions of an Old Tale, by Betsy Hearne
Once Upon a Time, collected essays by Alison Lurie
What the Bee Knows, collected essays by P. L. Travers
Problems of the Feminine in Fairy Tales, by Marie-Louise von Franz
Collected lectures originally presented at the C. G. Jung Institute
Touch Magic, collected essays by Jane Yolen
Fantasists on Fantasy, edited by Robert H. Boyer and Kenneth J. Zahorski
Includes Tolkien's "On Fairy Stories," G. K. Chesterton's "Fairy Tales," and other essays.

Fairy tale source collections

Old Wives' Fairy Tale Book, edited by Angela Carter
The Tales of Charles Perrault, translated by Angela Carter
Italian Folktales, translated by Italo Calvino
The Complete Hans Christian Andersen, edited by Lily Owens
The Maid of the North: Feminist Folk Tales from Around the World, edited by Ethel Johnston Phelps
Favorite Folk Tales from Around the World, edited by Jane Yolen
The Complete Brothers Grimm, edited by Jack Zipes
(For volumes of fairy tales from individual countries—Russian fairy tales, French, African, Japanese, etc.—see the excellent Pantheon Books Fairy Tale and Folklore Library.)

Terri Windling

Terri Windling is a four-time winner of the World Fantasy Award for her editorial work. She was for a number of years the Fantasy Editor at Ace Books in New York, where she introduced many new writers, including Charles de Lint, Steven Brust, Emma Bull, and Sheri S. Tepper, to the field. She created the Adult Fairy Tales series of novels (Tor Books), cocreated the Faerielands series (Bantam), and has edited or coedited twelve anthologies prior to this one. Currently, she lives in Tucson, Arizona, and Devon, England, where she is a visual artist, often incorporating fairy tale text and imagery into prints, paintings, and collages. Her work has been shown at the Boston Museum of Fine Arts and around the country.

Ellen Datlow has been Fiction Editor of Omni *Magazine since 1981. She has earned a reputation for encouraging and developing the short fiction of writers such as William Gibson, Pat Cadigan, Tom Maddox, Dan Simmons, K. W. Jeter, and Terry Bisson, and for publishing Clive Barker, Stephen King, William Burroughs, Jonathan Carroll, and Joyce Carol Oates in* Omni. *She and Terri Windling coedit the World Fantasy Award-winning anthology series,* The Year's Best Fantasy and Horror *(St Martin's), and she is the sole editor of* Blood Is Not Enough *(Berkley),* Alien Sex *(Roc), and* A Whisper of Blood *(Berkley). She is working on an erotic horror anthology.*